S.J. Dea... ... 1... le o...
of Wales. ... ... burning principalities he ma... ...d to
study theoretical physics at Cambridge, get a job at BAE, marry
and have two children. He now lives in Essex.

Praise for S.J. Deas:

'A page-turning novel, unpredictable and suspenseful, haunted by
intriguing twists and turns . . . The characters are vividly portrayed,
three-dimensional and convincing' *Historical Novels Review*

'A deliciously atmospheric read . . . This wintering army,
oppressively non-moving, trapped by snow and ice, contains more
than enough drama and action to fill a whole series of books' *For
Winter Nights*

'Deas writes at a furious pace . . . It is his wonderful descriptions
and his creation of a powerfully charged atmosphere that really
capture the reader' *We Love This Book*

'I take my hat off to the author for his ability and desire to portray
all of this horror and dirt . . . Highly recommended' *Parmenion
Books*

'Vivid and atmospheric . . . A very enjoyable and refreshing read
that gave you a new understanding of the time and the New
Model army and how it was anything but united' *Reality's A Bore*

'Deas has delivered an intriguing, drama-laden, heart-thumping
crime thriller with historical accuracy and authenticity' *Storm in the
Stacks*

'Exciting, authentic and totally absorbing. A brilliant must read'
Linda's Boo...

By S.J. Deas and available from Headline

The Royalist
The Protector

S.J. DEAS

the Protector

headline

First published in Great Britain 2015 by
HEADLINE PUBLISHING GROUP

First published in Great Britain in paperback in 2016 by
HEADLINE PUBLISHING GROUP

1

Cataloguing in Publication Data is available from the British Library

ISBN 978 1 4722 1702 8

Typeset in Aldine 401 by Avon DataSet Ltd,
Bidford-on-Avon, Warwickshire

Printed and bound in Great Britain by Clays Ltd, St Ives plc

Headlin   e and
recyclabl   naged
forests an   cturing
processes   lations

London EC4Y 0DZ

www.headline.co.uk
www.hachette.co.uk

For poets and lovers and dancers, and for everyone who wonders why the devil gets the best lines.

'What if the breath that kindled those grim fires,
Awaked, should blow them into sevenfold rage,
And plunge us in the flames; or from above
Should intermitted vengeance arm again
His red right hand to plague us?'

John Milton, *Paradise Lost*

I had foot-slogged my way for six months across half the country and back again. I had found nothing except a numbness, and the stale dregs of straw-strewn taverns in the villages I passed. Uxbridge, this one, I think.

'I'd wager she got bored and run off with some other fellow.'

Six louts sat around a table together. I did not see which of them said it. They were watching me, listening to me foul drunk on watery beer, wine-slurred and moon-faced, waxing loud of my missing Caro, ranting and railing at the smoky air and the vicissitudes of a fickle and heartless fate. I had barely noticed their presence in the tavern until that lucid moment. I saw them now. They were laughing.

She wouldn't do that. Not my Caro.

They looked back at me as I turned, and their laughing fell off their faces. Among all the things I am, I am a large man and a soldier, and have been so for too many years. I have killed men, and I have seen men die. As I took a step towards them they rose from their table and bunched together, ready to stare me down.

'What did you say?' I could tell from their eyes and their exchange of glances which of them had spoken.

'I said I'd wager your wife tired of your talk and has run off with some other fellow, you sot.' He stood across their table from me – given courage, perhaps, by the knowledge I would have to pass through his friends to reach him. I did not feel so inclined. I raised my foot and smashed a kick into that table, slamming it into him. He howled, as did I, a roar of such fury and despair that I could not imagine it was my own. I would have jumped after him and pulled him out and beaten him half to death, I think, but instead I staggered and fell, unbalanced by drink as I was. I floundered to find my feet and a boot connected with my ribs, and then another. I barely felt them. I stumbled against the wall, almost fell into the fireplace, and lurched a drunkard's punch at the nearest of the men who now set upon me. Another and another. I lashed with my feet. I try, now, not to imagine what a sight I made, flailing limbs, the mournful snarls and howls of a pitiful fury. Perhaps I gravely injured a stool or two before they had me. The air filled with shouts, a thick cloying smoke of them. The men seized me between them. They carried me out to the street and held me up, and beat me and beat me again. Blow after blow. I felt them in the distance. I saw the fists fly at my face, knuckles clenched, bloody and raw from the blows before. I remember most clearly of all the moment before my eyes closed. The spittle-flecked, twisted faces. The fist like a knuckle of ham.

It was not the last. I felt a handful more, like the shake of distant drumbeats through the air, but I was no longer among them. I had taken myself to another place and another time. I was in my house. My empty home, and where once had been laughter and smiles and movement, now was cold, still air. The table stood bare, and I sat alone.

The pans were neatly hung in the kitchen, the blankets folded in the closet. There were clothes in the dresser. Old dresses my Caro had once worn. In the room where our son John had slept, I found shirts and smocks I had never seen before. They were years old, but already for a boy taller than the lad I remembered. He would be starting to grow traces of his first beard now. He would be almost a man, old enough to pick up a pike or a musket. Old enough to fight. In a corner beside my daughter's bed I found an old cloth doll. Discarded. The girl I remembered had loved that doll. She'd taken it everywhere, but it was a child's toy, and she would be sixteen years now, and all childish things long forgotten.

Six years since I had left them for the King's banner. Outside, snow lay heavy on the ground, but no one had lit a fire in these hearths for months. I ran my hand through the dust by the fireplace where we had once sat, and my fingers came back thick with it. I wrapped myself in blankets and lay on the bed that my Caro and I had once shared. I shivered myself to sleep, and in the morning I left again and did not come back.

In the place and time from which I had come, in the summer evening outside an Uxbridge tavern, the men beating me had gone. There were others looming over me now, faces in soldiers' coats; and then I slipped between them to the past once more, and they were Cromwell and Thomas Fairfax. They would force the King to terms before the year was out, they said, but I no longer cared. My home had abandoned me. My family had waited as long as they could, but I had not come back in time. I had tried to tell myself, in all the days that followed, that I would find them again. That they would be alive. They had left our home with a quiet determination, with no sign of haste or fear, and my Caro was strong and wilful. One way or another she would survive. I told myself she had found some haven where she and Charlotte would be safe from marauding soldiers, where my son would find good honest work and never wear a soldier's coat as I had done; but it was a fragile hope, and somewhere I had lost it.

Did I throw it away? Did I simply misplace it? Did it quietly slip into the dark one night as I slept? I couldn't say, for at first I didn't notice it was even gone.

CHAPTER 1

I opened my eyes and strained to see. There was no window in the cell where I found myself, but somewhere there was candlelight, and it was enough to show that I was alone. I heard the heavy tread of boots on stone coming closer. My head pounded. I was not, I will confess, at my best. I tried to recall how I had come to be in this place, and found I could not entirely be sure.

The boots stopped at the door to my cell. I heard voices outside.

'He's a surly bastard. Are you sure you want him?' I thought I had perhaps heard that voice last night.

'Not greatly, but I have my orders.'

The second voice I knew better, though it was one I had not heard for nigh on six months. A deep, syrupy baritone, almost musical. A voice I had once imagined belonged to a thespian or a minstrel or to some courtly fool too cowardly ever to fight, but I had long since learned the error of that impression. It was a voice I had not wanted ever to hear again. Henry Warbeck. Cromwell's man.

The air around me stank. I could not imagine a more noisome reek. Animal filth, rank and foul.

A bar lifted on the other side of the door. Reluctant iron

hinges squealed open. Two men stood in silhouette against the light outside, one making way for the other.

'Hello, Falkland,' said the syrupy voice. 'Dear Lord but you smell rotten.'

'Warbeck,' I croaked. 'Am I in hell, then, and the devil has sent you?' I tried to rise and found my legs too unsteady. The dim world of the cell around me seemed to swim and shimmer. I managed as far as hands and knees and then had to stop. I feared I might vomit. It was a shameful thing for Warbeck to see me like this.

'Grief, Falkland. Do you even know where you are?'

'Uxbridge, I think.'

Warbeck hissed his disgust. He turned to the guard who had opened the door. 'Get him out of here.'

The guard hesitated, torn perhaps between the authority in Warbeck's voice and some sense of other duty – or so I thought until I saw Warbeck reach to the purse on his belt; I understood then that the hesitation was simply an invitation. I heard a jangle of coin. I staggered to my feet. I would not, I told myself, have some jailer drag me out of here. I would walk on my own.

The guard came in. He took my arm. I flinched, ready at once to shake him off, but I sensed an unexpected gentleness in his hand, and so I let him steady me. I have been in more than one jail in my time, and I have never come to expect kindness. The soldiers who supervise Cromwell's prisons are taught to view their charges with scorn, that their prisoners are somehow lesser men and less godly, though in truth they are simply less lucky.

'Mister Falkland, is it? Come on then, Mister Falkland.' The guard helped me to the door. Warbeck uttered a grunt of disdain and turned away ahead of us.

'You need a bath, Falkland,' he said.

I had imagined myself, until now, to be in some prison built to cage men, but as I walked through the door I saw this was not the case. Four more low stone rooms opened onto either side of this dingy corridor. On one side the doors were closed, but on the other they were open. The first room was empty, save for a covering of muck and straw, but in the next lay a sow, suckling a litter of pigs. They could not have been more than a few days old.

'Yours?' I asked the guard, whom I began to suspect was no guard at all.

'Aye.' He sounded proud, as I suppose any man would be to have such a treasure.

Warbeck opened the door at the end of the corridor. Brilliant light flooded in, far too bright. I squeezed my eyes shut and cringed, feeling my way blindly as the guard helped me on. I knew when we crossed the threshold. The sunlight was bright and warm. A glorious English summer's day in this year of Our Lord sixteen forty-six.

We left the pig-farmer's sty, and my 'guard' was, I think, more than happy to see the back of us. Warbeck had come on horseback. He had brought a second mare, and I am ashamed to say that my first dismal efforts to mount the animal were comical at best, I who was once a cavalryman under Prince Rupert himself. When Warbeck had finished pouring scorn with his eyes and I had finally settled myself in the saddle, he led us to the centre of Uxbridge, to a tavern of some size. He walked me in through a back door – I was at least able to dismount without sprawling across the stables – and took me upstairs to a room, and, shortly, to a bath.

I suppose I might have considered myself fortunate he didn't simply hurl me into the nearest pond or brook. I have done the same and worse with drunks in my time.

I sank into the lukewarm water. I was still intoxicated, yet I was no longer so far gone as to feel no shame. I had made a fool of myself the night before, and I had paid for it in bruises and a bloody lip. I was lucky it had not been worse. Warbeck might ask me, as indeed might any man, what had brought me to Uxbridge. He might ask me why I had drunk myself stupid and then entered into a fight with a man I'd not laid eyes on until an hour before, a man too well equipped with friends.

I cupped my hands and lifted the water to my face. It was already murky. I stared as best I could at my own reflection, trying to understand what nature of man looked back. Hollow, haunted eyes. Straggly hair, half of it grey around the sides of my head. Not much on top. The beginnings of an unkempt beard, untouched for nigh on two weeks now.

Behind me, the door opened. I recognised the tread of Warbeck's boots from my pigsty prison.

'Are you sober yet, Falkland?'

'What do you want, Warbeck?' He'd pulled me from a prison cell before, a darker one than today. Back then it was Newgate, where I'd been due to hang, just another royalist soldier to be rid of, but Warbeck had taken me away. He'd stuffed me in a carriage with a sack over my head, all the way to Parliament, and now here he was again.

'Cromwell wants you.'

That was all that had saved me from Newgate. Cromwell had heard of me. I had had a use.

'I have more pressing things,' I said now.

'You can tell him that yourself, Falkland. Once you're fit to meet him.'

'I have a family to find. Tell him to go to hell.' I heard the emptiness of my words, and perhaps Warbeck heard it too, for he didn't reply at first. I sank a little deeper into the tepid water and closed my eyes. I heard him breathing, slow and steady and, when I listened closely, with a slight rasp. Warbeck wasn't entirely well. I couldn't put my finger on what it was, but he'd been this way since we'd first met. I'd had a hood over my head at the time, and the rotten reek of his breath lingered in my memory.

I heard him open his mouth. The wet smack of his lips. I knew what would come next. Threats. Something to remind me of how little he cared for someone who had once fought for the King. But he surprised me.

'Your family weren't waiting for you when you reached your home in Launcells, then?' he asked.

'It's a truth I've learned in the long years of this war,' I said, 'that a man should never have hopes, for nothing so crushes him as the dashing of them.'

Warbeck waited a heartbeat or two. I heard his breathing change. 'If that's your answer, Falkland, I'll be very happy to take any money you might have to pay for your incarceration last night. Otherwise you can go back where I found you. It's a nice enough sty for a pig, I suppose. There might be a magistrate from St Albans come by in a couple of weeks, but I dare say they won't wait that long. Another couple of days and they'll kick you onto the streets penniless and ragged and covered in filth. Is that what you want?'

I had taken a beating. I hurt. I was missing my purse. I had nothing. In truth, I'd had very little to begin with. I hoped I'd given the rest of them a bruise or two to remember me by. I feared I had not.

'Get yourself dressed, Falkland,' Warbeck said, after another moment of silence.

'How did you find me?' I asked.

I heard him hawk up a gob of phlegm and spit it to the floor. 'It wasn't hard. I've known whole companies of militia stumble more quietly through the kingdom than you do. A blind deaf mute on a lame mule might track you down.'

He left, his boots tapping across the floor. I sat in the filthy bath, drifting through the torture of the last months, my futile wanderings from one failure to the next, and it was only when the water was cold enough to make me shiver that I was able to pull myself away. I scrubbed myself clean, though the dirt clung to me with the tenacity of despair. I dressed, and immediately I stank again. My clothes were filthy too. When I stumbled out, Warbeck was waiting with a pitcher of milk and a hunk of stale bread. I drank the milk and felt my stomach churn, sour and unwelcoming. The bread was as hard as wood. I should have saved the milk to soften it, but Warbeck was in no mood for further delay. He grimaced at my sorry state and hurried me outside. A fresh pain stabbed between my eyes, while I screwed up my face against the brightness of the sun. It was as well that I had once been a cavalryman and knew my way to mounting a horse almost in my sleep. At least this time I didn't fall. Warbeck led us on, and my mare did as all horses will do if not otherwise steered, and men too: it followed. I dozed as the sun rose through the morning, slumped on the animal's back and grateful for Warbeck's silence, my mare vexing him now and then when she stopped to snatch a mouthful of whatever passing vegetation caught her fancy. I did nothing to hurry her along. I barely noticed the lanes and villages through which we passed.

By the middle of the day my head had begun to clear. I chewed at that piece of bread a while, and gradually became aware that we had not reached the fringes of London as I had imagined, but were in fact deep in the countryside with hills all around us. I drew alongside Warbeck.

'Where are we going?' I asked him.

Warbeck gave me a look as if mildly surprised to find me still alive. 'To Cromwell, Falkland. Was that not clear?' He turned his head away. I supposed he meant to lapse into silence; then a smirk crooked his lip. 'Do you know how things have changed since the winter, Falkland? Or has it all passed you by?'

I knew a little, but will admit I had not paid much heed to the affairs of King and Parliament these last few months. I had a notion that the war was coming to some end, although whether in victory for one side or the other, or simply the petering out of a country steeped in exhaustion, I had little idea. It wasn't my war any more. I'm not sure it ever was.

'The King has come to terms.' Warbeck couldn't resist a little smugness. 'You know this could all have ended eighteen months ago? At the tavern where we took your stink and tried to wash it off.' He sniffed and wrinkled his nose. 'Without much joy, it seems. The King sent the Duke of Richmond there to negotiate a peace. The arguments lasted almost a month, I believe, but the King asked too much. He'll rue that. He should have given more when he had the chance. Now he has nothing.' Warbeck spat, and there was a vicious glee to his words. Perhaps he thought to rile me for all the years I'd fought for the royal standard, but he should have known me better. I was only glad to have an end to it.

'Is the King back in London?' I asked.

Warbeck let out a little sigh and shook his head. 'The King is in Newcastle. He surrendered to the Scots a month ago, and now cosies up to them while making new demands. Parliament has yet to agree the terms of his return.'

'So men still fight?'

'Fight? Hardly. Prince Rupert holds Oxford. His surrender is a formality. Fairfax and Cromwell have the city under siege.'

Thomas Fairfax. Black Tom, as I had known him. 'He still commands the New Model Army then?' I had wondered, after the events of the winter, whether Cromwell would tolerate him.

'That he does. There are no other armies left for the King, Falkland. Hopton surrendered back in March and there have been no battles in the field since then. Exeter fell in April, Newark in May. It's done. Over. Your king has lost.' My king. Always *my* king; but I found I could muster no energy to argue.

Cromwell was camped outside Oxford then, was he? That explained why we weren't riding for London.

'If it's all done and finished, Warbeck, why bother with me? What do you want?' I could think of nothing I wanted from him in return, nothing from Cromwell, nothing from any of them. Not one of them could give back these last futile years.

'Seeing you as I found you, I wonder very much the same,' sniffed Warbeck. 'Perhaps Cromwell will take a look at you and realise he has made a mistake this time.'

I no longer had a penny to my name. What little I owned, I had lost in that Uxbridge brawl. I could not, I realised, remember the face of the man who felled me.

'You may find him in a good mood, though,' Warbeck chuckled on. 'His daughter Bridget is about to marry Henry Ireton.'

The name was familiar. 'Edgehill?' I asked, but that wasn't it. Some other battle, and it took another moment before the name sank deep enough. Ireton had been at Naseby, when Cromwell and Fairfax and the New Model had given the King his most bloody defeat. Prince Rupert had charged Parliament's left wing and completely broken it. I remembered that charge. I had been a part of it. Ireton had been there, and we had captured him for a time, although the crazed uncertainty of that day made me view everything I remembered through a fog of doubt.

'Naseby,' I muttered.

'He was with Cromwell at Gainsborough in 'forty-three, too,' mused Warbeck. 'And at the siege of Bristol last September.' He bared his teeth in what was perhaps meant as a smile. 'You might even get to see him, if that pleases you.'

I could not say that it did.

We rode on through fields and lanes. Warbeck lapsed into silence again, and I found I had nothing to say and no questions to ask. These last six months, since that bleak, lonely Christmas in Launcells, I had searched for where my Caro might have taken our children. I had looked in all the places I could think where she might have sought refuge, and I had found not one trace of her. Towns and cities ravaged by war and siege, *those* I had found aplenty, but nothing more. Slowly my searching had turned into something else. It was as though my life before I marched with the King to Yorkshire, years ago now, had ceased to exist, or had been an illusion, some trick planted in my memories that had never truly been real. I was, I realised, as lost as they.

CHAPTER 2

I was not best pleased, on the morning that followed, to find myself again amid the encampment of the New Model Army. We rode through its outer sentries and perimeter before midday, yet I was already hungry after our early start. This was no monstrous city of tents as I had experienced once before, but more resembled the camps I had come to know while fighting for the King; spread out as it was, the sheer size of the New Model was not so apparent. Fairfax's army of Parliament was no doubt scattered in a multitude of commands and companies about Oxford, barring escape to the last of the King's ministers. Farms and barns had been commandeered, and I saw clusters of tents here and there. In the distance, towards the city, I saw a single narrow column of smoke. There was no sound of gunfire, no far-off crack and pop of muskets, no smell of burned powder in the air. Soldiers basked in the sun in their shirtsleeves; others cleaned their muskets or sharpened their knives, or whittled at wooden figures and played idle games of stones and dice. There was no urgency to their manner. If this was a battle, it was an uncommonly peaceful one.

We passed through one camp to another and the next,

pausing a while as Warbeck dispatched a messenger ahead of us. I had a sense we were traversing the north of Oxford. We carried on this way for several miles, moving from camp to camp, each one never quite out of sight from the next. It was a strangeness, as we did, to see every soldier in the same Venice Red. Under the King I had grown accustomed to many different companies assembled all in their own colours, each matched to the Lord who commanded them. Parliament had been the same way until early in '45, when they'd created the terror of the New Model and endeavoured to make everyone the same; but even come the winter of that year Fairfax had struggled to realise his ambition. Now it seemed that he had succeeded. Everywhere we went each man looked like every other, until I had no notion of the size of this army save that it seemed endless.

We came in the early afternoon into an area of open parkland. There were a greater number of tents and soldiers here than I had seen in the other camps. Warbeck moved through them and drew us to a halt before an old manor house that wore signs of recent battle. Cannon shot had savaged its walls, and one of its small towers was burned out. Warbeck dismounted and beckoned me to do the same. We started towards the house, but we had barely taken a step when we were startled by a soldier running from the tents, waving his hands and urgently calling on us to halt.

'Sirs! Sirs! I beg you, keep away!'

I regarded the man. He seemed very earnest in his fear and, I thought, more concerned for our safety than for his own. I looked the manor over. It did not strike me as being on the point of collapse.

''Tis a most wicked spirit inside!' the man exclaimed.

'Fie on your spirits!' snarled Warbeck. 'Where's Cromwell?'

'The gatehouse, sirs.' The soldier beckoned; Warbeck and I led our horses in his wake to a much smaller house, little more than a pair of rooms one atop the other with a few tiny windows.

'Cromwell billets here now, does he?' Warbeck shrugged. It would have been unthinkable in the King's army for the King to occupy so mean a residence, or for any of the Lords and Princes who served under his command to do so; but then this was the way of Parliament's New Model, where Lords would serve commoners, and peasants command Princes. As a man who had once been the son of a lowly tenant farmer, I saw little in it one way or another, but I had served many Lords who saw a very great deal.

Warbeck banged on the door and entered without waiting to be summoned. For my part I found myself distracted by an unexpected verse etched into the gatehouse stone.

> Much suspected by me,
> Nothing proved can be,
> Quoth Elizabeth prisoner.

I had no notion what to make of it, but it struck me nonetheless, and I was staring at it when Warbeck returned through the door, glowering with tight-clenched fury.

'Falkland! Would you tarry so to attend your king?'

I did not remind him that Cromwell was no king, nor did he consider himself remotely as such; I did not say it, but it was in my mind as I hastened to follow.

My first sight of Oliver Cromwell had perhaps been at Edgehill or Naseby, or some battle in between where we had both happened upon the same field, but I would not have recognised him there. My first sight of his face had been in Westminster, in a vast and gloomy space that had made him seem small. Here he was again, in a very different setting, four stone walls pressed around us, yet once again he sat behind a desk between an ink pot and a pile of parchment on one side, and a bible on the other. He was dressed as I remembered him, in a black gown and a wide collar of stark white, though here he struck me more a soldier than I remembered, and reminded me less of a scarecrow. I had seen him at other times, dressed for battle, and quite a sight that had made; but here he carried more the air of a scholar, or even perhaps some medieval alchemist. His nose and chin both remained as large as ever, and his hair still hung unkempt around his shoulders.

'Falkland.' He was sitting on a farmer's stool and staring at the piece of parchment in front of him with a fierce and studious concentration. He didn't look up, but his voice was exactly as I remembered it, with a nasal quality as if spoken from the back of his throat. 'I will be with you shortly.'

I saw a hat on a peg behind me, and a soldier's coat.

Abruptly, Cromwell put his parchment down. He tapped the pile as if warning it that it was not forgotten, and that it should not misbehave while his attention was elsewhere. His eyes fixed on my own. 'You stopped to read the words on the wall outside, Falkland?' He cocked his head and then smirked as I began to stutter an answer. 'Oh don't look so surprised. Everyone does. Queen Bess wrote them when her sister Bloody Mary kept her a prisoner here.' His glare transferred to Warbeck. 'Do you know why all my soldiers are sleeping in tents in the fields and not inside Woodstock

Manor? Because they have declared it haunted.' His eyes flicked between us. 'Perhaps that's a mystery for you, Falkland. What ghost haunts that manor? A very human one, I greatly suspect. Shall I employ you to exorcise it?'

'Employ a minister,' I suggested.

'What denomination do you recommend?'

'Perhaps you should ask that of your ghost.'

Our eyes met and we stared one another down a few moments before Cromwell again tapped a finger to his pile of parchment. 'This is the end, Falkland. The King has written his permission to the governors of all his garrisons to surrender. It is only a matter of days now.' Even he, it seemed, couldn't resist a little sense of triumph.

'You see, Falkland,' needled Warbeck.

'Congratulations on your victory, sir.' I offered Cromwell a mocking salute. 'I can tell you from the very depths of my heart, I am grateful without reservation for an end to this war. I long since lost any care for who might wear the crown of victory. Did you bring me here to crow of your triumph? If so then you can consider it done, and I will be gone.' I made no move, though. Cromwell, corvine as he could appear, was not a man given to crowing.

'I need you to find someone who has gone missing.' The look he gave me was pinched and sour. I waited for more, but Cromwell was not forthcoming. I felt my lips press together. A cold fury shivered my whole being.

'You will find others more suited to such a task, I assure you.' I was shaking.

'Is the name John Milton familiar to you?' Cromwell, if he had noticed it at all, paid no heed to my discomfort.

'It is not,' I said.

'I pulled you from Newgate last year, Falkland, because I believed you were a man of conscience. You showed that to be true. You were a King's man once, and then you were mine, but I do not believe you have much loyalty to either, and hold a great deal more to simple, honest truth. Do those words strike you as fair?'

I nodded. My loyalty to anything other than William Falkland and his wife and children had long withered to nothing. I felt suddenly tired to my bones. 'Whatever it is that you want me to do, I'm quite sure you can find someone better suited to do it.'

'But *I* am not, Falkland. John Milton is a polemicist, a pamphleteer, a wordsmith of the highest order. In this war, he has spoken stridently for Parliament. His words carry weight and influence. Some weeks back his sister Anne disappeared. It's quite apparent she has been taken. Abducted. It is assumed in London that—'

'Have there been any demands? A ransom?' I will admit a pleasure in interrupting this occasional scarecrow who would soon, by all appearances, be the master of England.

'No, Falkland, there have not.'

'Then she was probably robbed, raped and murdered.'

I had silenced, for a moment, even Cromwell.

'It is what happens in war,' I said, without much gentleness. 'I am sorry to say it, but you are a soldier too and so you know the truth. For my own part I have seen it too many times. War does not breed men to gentleness.'

For a long time Cromwell looked at me and I found I couldn't read him at all, couldn't tell whether he regarded me with pity or with anger; and I realised, as I returned his gaze, that I had spoken as much to myself as to him. I had been speaking of my Caro, of my John and my Charlotte. The walls between which I stood shimmered from a sudden tear. I looked away. I could no longer meet Cromwell's eye.

He allowed the moment to pass, and quietly resumed. 'It is assumed in London, and widely and loudly spoken by Milton himself, that Anne has been taken by supporters of the King who are determined to silence him. True or otherwise as that may be . . .' He shook his head. 'Look around you, Falkland. This war is finished. The King is finished. He is brought to terms and no force in Heaven or Earth can change what must be. But I would have an end to it sooner rather than later. I do not need a man of any cloth or colour firing the blood of either Roundhead or Cavalier, not until this is done. Another week, Falkland, or perhaps a month, and Oxford will capitulate. That is the last of the King's armies of any note, but there will remain recalcitrant strongholds. I couldn't even tell you how many, up and down the country. A quiet surrender and an end to recrimination is preferable to a bloody storming of each. The King is in Newcastle with the Scots. I cannot stop the wolves in London from baying for his blood, but I would ask them to bay quietly, at least, for they already know I will not let them have it. It is a delicate time.'

He rose and went to stand at a window, basking in the sunlight from outside as if it might wash away the grey that always seemed to shroud him. He had his back to me now, but that didn't stop him. 'I require a man of conscience again, Falkland. I require someone who can move among the supporters of both King and Parliament with equal ease. I require someone who is competent. Above all I require a man who will not be bought, who places his own integrity above petty politics, who has no axe to grind of his own. I require a man I can trust, and that is you, Falkland.'

Perhaps he meant to flatter me with such words, but I barely felt it. I had already decided I would not help them again.

'I would appreciate a quick resolution.' Cromwell hesitated, then moved from the window and returned to his stool. 'If it's royalists, then bring me their names as discreetly as you can. If it's not, then you may bring me their heads if you prefer. You may go.' He had already returned his attentions to his parchments.

'No,' I said.

I wasn't sure that Cromwell even heard me. Certainly he showed no sign of having done so; and when he looked up a moment later, I think his surprise was that I was still there. That I had been dismissed and yet remained standing before him.

'No,' I said again. 'Find someone else.'

Warbeck growled behind me. A soldier, doubtless he was not used to men rejecting an order from his master, but Cromwell I knew to be cut from a different cloth. As a member of Parliament he would be more accustomed to those around him being disagreeable. He watched me for a while, and then let out a long sigh.

'Your family, is it? I did hear you were still looking for them.' He shook his head, not waiting for an answer. 'You believe them to still be alive?'

'I must,' I told him. I could not, even in my darkest moments, contemplate otherwise. The notion was incomprehensible, even if I had lost all hope that I would ever find them.

'Indeed, how could you not?' He raised an eyebrow. 'I'm sorry to hear it, Falkland.' He leaned forward. 'Nevertheless there—'

'No.' For the second time I interrupted him, and this time Oliver Cromwell did not take it so mildly. He jumped to his feet and banged his fist against his desk, and for a moment we eyed one another like two bullocks in a field, sizing each other up. I did not flinch. Perhaps he found me more disagreeable than I had supposed. Or perhaps he objected to my interrupting him – certainly I would not have escaped painful and violent censure for such behaviour towards the King. *Was* that what Cromwell saw himself to be now? I had thought not, but men can change. This victory in Oxford would bring unprecedented power to Parliament, and thus to its leaders.

Slowly, Cromwell resumed his seat. 'Falkland, when we met after Warbeck saved you from the noose in Newgate, I was signing letters to the mothers and fathers of the men who died at Naseby and Abingdon and Bristol. Do you remember?'

I did. It had struck me as uncommonly odd at the time to see a commander of a great army concern himself with such a detail. Certainly the King would have left trifles of condolence to his commanders – but then Cromwell was, I had come to understand, a man of details.

He was waiting for me to speak, as if that memory might jog something into motion, as if I would come to some great revelation without having to have it held up in words before me. When no such epiphany came, he gave a little shake of his head.

'I know who my soldiers are. I know who fights in my

companies and regiments. I know their names. I know their homes. I send letters to their families. Falkland, your son—'

'My son?' My fists clenched at my sides. I took a step towards Cromwell. I felt Warbeck tense behind me. 'What do you know of my son?' Caro would have kept him to the house if she could, but would he have escaped her and run away to war? To join Hopton's glorious sweep of Devon in '43? Would he have been taken and conscripted into one of the militias as so many young lads were? I'd seen boys younger than my John in Crediton in the winter, defeated royalist bands swept up and devoured. It wasn't unconscionable that my son had become a part of this monster New Model. He could have been in that camp not a hundred yards from me, and I would not have known.

Cromwell fixed me with a steady eye. 'Nothing, Falkland. But there are men and even women to whom I have given the duty of keeping such records.' He glanced at Warbeck as he said this, and I had the sense of a secret exchange between them. 'I will have them help you. John Falkland, is it? If he has become a part of the New Model then likely as not they will find him. Even if someone has heard of him . . . And *if* I find him . . .'

He did not need to say any more. If they were to find my son, they would like as not find my Caro, for John would know to where she had fled, and his sister too.

Cromwell returned to his papers. 'Milton's sister was married to Thomas Agar. He disappeared at the start of the fighting, some years ago. There were two sons by her first marriage and a daughter by Thomas. Find out what became of Anne Agar, Falkland, and I will see what can be done. I am, as I think you will agree, not without resource.'

I was being dismissed once more, and this time I had no retort. I backed away and turned. Warbeck held the door as I blundered out into the sunlight. I did not quite know what I had done or to what I had agreed, save that I had searched for six months for my children and I had not found them, that in my heart I had quietly given up all hope, and that Cromwell now, of all people, had offered me a new crumb of it; and though I thought I knew better, I also knew that I could have only one answer, as he must have anticipated from the very start.

Warbeck leaned in to me. He was shorter than I and had to crane his neck to hiss into my ear.

'You understand your choice, Falkland? You have the resources of Parliament if you help us. Or I can take you back where I found you.'

CHAPTER 3

We left shortly after. Lord Fairfax was on his way to Woodstock Manor, and while there were few things upon which Warbeck and I might share a view, 'Black Tom' Fairfax was one of them, for in Crediton we had both given him reason to regard us as other than friends. We rode the way we had come, through the scattered camps around the north of Oxford and then east towards London. We stopped at the same coaching inn as before. There seemed to be a change in the air. The day was glorious summer, a sweet warm breeze, butterflies and birdsong. The fields around Oxford, even here where the fighting lingered, were green. Cattle grazed in their pastures. I saw orchards of apple and pear trees, fields of wheat and barley and, I think, corn and the vines of hops. The country was ready to feed itself, and the landscape no longer bore the scars and marks of war. There were no deserter soldiers prowling the roads, bandits and footpads and highwaymen. It was absurd, perhaps, to think such things – the country was surely the same England I had known these last few months, wounded and often hostile – yet in that afternoon of travelling through the shire of Oxford, I found a little peace within myself.

We eased our weary bones from the backs of our horses

and sat ourselves down inside the inn to a welcome cup of ale and a slab of what I suspected was the same stale bread we had eaten in Uxbridge – although I will admit that after a long day with a hungry belly I was not inclined much to care. Warbeck, while I ate my fill, studied his fingernails, then unbuckled his boots and eased free his feet. I ached, and I had still not quite shaken myself free from the aftermath of Uxbridge, and so as we finished our meal I thanked Warbeck for his hospitality and declined the offer of a place by the hearth and a cup of wine. I took myself to my bed. I tried to close my eyes and will myself to my dreams – a soldier learns to sleep when there is sleep to be had – but for once they eluded me. I found myself staring at the rafters above, seeing my Caro as I had seen her last, waving farewell both to me and to her father. She had worn a cheery smile, but I knew she must fret, watching her men ride to war. Our children had not come, unable to bear seeing me go. I wondered, as I lay in that inn, what had gone through their heads. I closed my eyes and thought of the scent of Caro's hair when she stood close to me, of the feel of it between my fingers when she pressed against my chest. I am not ashamed to admit that I wept a little, staring up at those rafters. Cromwell, damn the eyes of that man, had given me a sliver of light, and yet I could not shake the memory that he had done this once before, and that it had come to naught.

We rode into London on the next afternoon, an early start and a long ride that left us both weary. I shuddered a little as we passed down the Tyburn Road from the gallows on the corner towards Newgate. The road was a busy one, loud with raucous conversation and the tuneless singing of carters, and of drovers herding animals into London for slaughter, but Warbeck turned south and left the crowd before we reached Newgate itself and its bedevilled prison. I thought at first that he meant to lead me to Parliament, but instead we rode through fields past Charing Cross and St Martin's church. I was, I will admit, surprised and a little heartened to see that Charing Cross still stood. I had seen so many towns with their market crosses torn down by Puritans in the name of their peculiar version of God.

A little way past St Martin's Lane, Warbeck turned into an estate of houses of recent construction. He reined in his horse outside a tavern on the west side of Rose Street, the Bucket of Blood, but then paused. We could both clearly hear, not at all far away, the hubbub of some crowd out on the streets towards the river. I thought perhaps it might be a riot or some other gathering of the mob, but the shouts that rose above the general noise weren't cries of anger and protest, but of joy and excitement. Ignoring Warbeck, I kicked my mare into motion once more and pushed on towards the sound. I did not know this part of London – indeed, I knew very little of the city – but it was clear that we were among men of influence and wealth. The very houses themselves spoke of it with their size and many windows.

I turned left at the end of Rose Street, following my ears. Very soon I passed a church and its yard, surrounded by yet more houses, and entered onto the outer edge of some great open space – a market square perhaps, but larger than any I had seen before – around which were arched colonnades. On the south side were a number of sheds and stalls selling fruits and vegetables. Two Puritan ladies in severe – yet I fancied expensive – dresses hurried past me as I entered. In the middle part of the square a stage had been set, and a masque was being played out, complete with scenery. I had never seen such a thing done out in the open like this, yet I could hear barely a word of the players' speech over the din of the crowd. Around the edges, musicians and dancers vied with the masque to court the favour of the onlookers at the fringe. I supposed there must have been more than two hundred persons congregated around the square, though the press of the crowd was light save at its heart before the stage. The clothes of the watchers spoke of prosperous men.

A carriage crossed the far side of the square in front of two of Cromwell's cavalrymen. I could not make out the arms on the side.

'The King took offence to the condition of Long Acre and the houses that surrounded it,' Warbeck sneered as he drew alongside me and caught my look. 'He granted the Earl of Bedford a licence to build a piazza in an Italianate style.' If words could burn, those last from Warbeck would have set a torch to every house around us.

'What are they celebrating?' I asked. I had lost track of the days again and wondered if there was some festival I had forgotten.

'What do you think, Falkland? Victory. They're celebrating the King's defeat. The city's been making merry ever since he fled Oxford for Newcastle.'

I turned away. The fighting had never come to London, though I knew of several London regiments who had marched to battle. The people here had never known the bite of siege, but they had felt the stranglehold of war nevertheless. The last winter had been long and bitter. The

Thames had frozen in November and not thawed for four months. Without Newcastle coal to burn in their fires, many had simply frozen; although the air, at least, had been clearer. I suppose I understood their joy, a simple relief that it was all over, but I could not share it.

'Is it a trick, Warbeck? Will Cromwell keep his bargain?' We led our horses back to the Bucket of Blood.

'You heard, Falkland. He made you no promise.'

'But—'

'He kept his last one, didn't he?' Warbeck shook his head, full of pity for me and my faithlessness. 'We'll take a little rest and sustenance,' he said, 'and get you some clothes that don't smell like you slept in a pigsty. Then I'll take you to the Milton house. It'll be late by the time we get there, but the sooner the introductions are made, the better. When we come back, we'll talk about your own business. I dare say you won't let it be forgotten for an instant unless I promise otherwise. After tonight I'll be leaving you to get on with finding Anne Agar while I attend to matters of my own.'

We stabled our horses, although Warbeck instructed the stable hands to do no more than loosen their saddles and not to feed them much, as we would soon be leaving again. 'If you have any desire to continue as I found you, the Bucket of Blood provides ample opportunity for both drunkenness and brawls,' he told me. 'There are bare-knuckle fights arranged here more nights than not.' Inside the tavern Warbeck sent a lad scurrying to find clothes that might fit me, then sat me down with a cup of weak ale.

'I dare say I should tell you a little of John Milton before you meet him, since he's what this is really about, and I suppose his name might mean nothing to someone who has spent little if any time in London these last few years. Milton is a strident voice for Parliament's cause. He speaks with ardour and passion about many things, and Cromwell is not shy over showing his favour. He is resented by some, and loathed by many who took to the King's standard. His opinions are uncompromising. He is not quite with Lilburne's Levellers and their notions of freeborn rights, who would see kings abolished entirely, but I imagine he was happy enough when Parliament bowed to a petition for Lilburne's release.'

'So he has enemies,' I said. 'But then what man who speaks with a public voice does not? Do they have names?'

'They surely do, but Milton will give you more than enough.'

'What about Anne herself? Or the rest of the family?'

'There's the father,' Warbeck said at last. 'The elder John Milton. He's not well, Falkland, and you'd do best to leave him alone. He was a scrivener and a very successful one. Anne was his oldest child. She had two surviving sons by her first husband, Edward Phillips. They are John and Edward. John's the oldest. You'll meet him and ask him a question or two, I dare say. He led the search for his mother when she went. She has a daughter too, younger. There is little more to say of any of them.'

'And what there is I'll hear from their own mouths.' I knew that Warbeck would colour every word and phrase to mean whatever suited him. To know the truth of any man's story, one must hear it from his own mouth, in words of his own choosing. Warbeck, for example. How he spoke of Anne. *Had* two sons. *Was* his oldest child. 'You think what I said to Cromwell is right, don't you? You think she's dead.'

Warbeck made as if to protest, but we were interrupted by the arrival of a deliciously aromatic venison stew. We had not eaten since breaking our fast that morning, and I took my time over it, thick nubs of first-of-the-season carrot and onion with large chunks of juicy flesh, all served with a thick, meaty broth in a hollowed loaf of bread. It was a meal fit for a lord, I thought. There would no doubt be bowls of pottage for lesser men. I watched Warbeck chew on a piece of venison.

'I'd imagined you more the sort to eat as the servants do,' I said.

Warbeck made a face and shook his head. 'I do not believe that one man should own another, but I see no reason they must eat the same.'

'Why does John Milton imagine his sister disappearing is not her own matter, born of her own affairs?'

'You wouldn't ask if you'd met him.' Warbeck snorted. 'But don't you want to hear that from his own tongue?'

'I do. And I will. But humour me. Do you think he's right?'

'Edward Phillips died when Anne's sons were both young. She married Thomas Agar later that same year. I'm told that Thomas and Edward were great friends when Edward was alive. Phillips was Deputy Clerk of the Crown in the Chancery Office. When he died, Agar took his position. Agar took up arms for the King in 'forty-two and hasn't been seen since. Edgehill did for him, it seems. I see no enemies in Anne Agar's affairs, and her boys are too young to have made any of substance. John Milton, on the other hand, makes enemies like rats make fleas. So yes, I do.'

I could imagine any number of motives for the abduction of a family member of a prominent Parliamentarian, particularly at such a time, and all of them in the vein Cromwell had already described: to attack and threaten an enemy of the King. It vexed me. I will admit that I hoped for something more obscure. Something to do with Anne herself and not her brother, so I might prove Cromwell and his suspicions wrong. In that regard I had nurtured a hope as we rode together that I might unravel something to do with her husband; but missing through four years of war was not a promising beginning.

Warbeck was watching me. 'Three things, Falkland,' he said. 'Three reasons for an abduction. For money, for influence or for revenge.' He shook his head. 'Three weeks and no demand for ransom. So it's not money.'

'What about Anne herself?'

'What about her?'

'You were investigating her vanishing, were you not, until Cromwell sent you to find me so that I might do it instead?' It was a guess. A shrewd one, perhaps, for I knew Warbeck to be a trusted intelligencer for Parliament's cause. Warbeck's hesitation told me I was right.

'There's nothing to know,' he said after a moment.

'But her husband declared for the King.'

'What of it?'

'Did that not vex her brother, this strident voice for Parliament?'

Warbeck laughed now, and I saw I was showing my ignorance. 'Milton and Thomas Agar were firm friends, by all accounts, and his folly for the King changed nothing.'

'And Anne herself? Does she side with Cromwell and Fairfax? Or is she dutiful to her husband even though he is gone?'

'I have no idea, Falkland. Find her and ask her yourself.'

I was at the end of my patience. 'How do you know she hasn't simply found her missing husband and run away to be with him? How do you know she's been taken against her will at all when no one has demanded anything for her release?'

There had to be some evidence, I thought, something Warbeck had not shared, and I saw at once that I had again struck a chord. I found I had struck a chord in myself too – but, as fortune would have it, the boy sent to find clothes for me returned as Warbeck and I regarded one another. I did not like to ask from where these clothes had come, but at least they didn't smell of filth and pigs. I withdrew to the stables, stripped and dressed again in baggy black breeches that hung loose to my knees, a plain shirt and a short, unstiffened jacket, black as well. I had seen men dressed this way out in the Covent Garden piazza, although most also wore a large lace collar which I, apparently, would not. Warbeck's boy had also found me a short black cloak and a narrow-brimmed conical hat. Were it not for the battered tan soldier's boots I wore and the mud-coloured leggings beneath, I would have looked quite unremarkable, a poor gentleman farmer perhaps, who could not afford a collar. As it was, with my boots, I imagined I must look like some yellow-footed crow.

I was done when Warbeck came to join me. He readied our horses, and we rode eastward to Fleet Street, where the air took on a quite distinct tang of inks and of Dutch paper. As with the Tyburn Road, we quickly found ourselves pressed on all sides by the bustling traffic of commerce, and I will admit I was quite struck by it. I had visited London only twice before, and had hardly seen much of the city throughout my sojourn in Newgate. The other time had been with Caro's father to pledge our arms to the King against the Scots, and I did not remember such a lively place. In my memory I saw quiet streets, a scattering of carriages and horsemen. Here men ran back and forth with energy and numbers I had not seen since I had been a cavalryman with Prince Rupert, drilling ourselves on the eve of fateful Naseby; but instead of pikes and muskets, the men here scurried with long, heavy rolls of paper over their shoulders, or else hurried, backs bent under bound bundles of pamphlets and polemics, their fingers stained dark with ink. It seemed that hardly a house here remained untouched by the flourishing growth of the presses which infested this part of London.

'It is a convenience to us to be so close by,' Warbeck said. 'As often as not, Milton will pass this way as he goes about his business. He has plenty of friends on Fleet Street.'

'And enemies?'

'Those too, I dare say.' Warbeck chuckled at some joke he made for himself and chose not to share, and turned us north from the throng before we crossed the Fleet bridge. We followed the old city walls to Newgate. I shuddered as we passed through the gate itself and its new prison to one side.

'Old memories, Falkland?' Warbeck goaded. 'Milton's house is beyond, a little past the Alders Gate.' He reined in his horse and stopped for a moment, and I wondered if it was deliberate to do so right outside the prison arch. 'Falkland, you try to ask it but you never quite do: I have no reason to imagine Anne Agar taken by royalists save that

Milton himself is adamant. But I have no reason to imagine her taken by any other, and this is not Basing House or Scarborough, and there are no royalist looters roaming the streets for rape and robbery and murder, as you so indelicately put it. But I will say this: Anne did not disappear of her own free will. She was taken, and there is a witness to it, and John Milton is quite certain that those responsible are the King's sympathisers.'

'Then I will find them and talk to them.' I took a deep breath. In Warbeck's mind it seemed that the case was already half solved. All that remained was to determine the royalists who had taken Anne and hold them to account. I vowed then that I would not make such a mistake as to think of Anne merely as 'Milton's sister' or 'Thomas Agar's wife'. Perhaps Milton and Cromwell and Warbeck all had it right and she was a pawn in some dispute, but I saw no reason to assume this to be true. Why not a matter of the heart? Perhaps Anne Agar was simply weary of waiting for a husband surely dead, and had taken matters into her own hands. Perhaps she had found another?

I found myself oddly disliking the thought and told myself I should not think it, and then saw I was a fool, for though I knew nothing of this Anne Agar, I did know that she was not my Caro, and I should not think of her as though she was.

'How far away are they?' I asked.

By way of an answer Warbeck set his horse to walk again along Newgate Street. The stench of that cursed prison seemed to follow as we left. The breeze, perhaps, or memories – I wasn't sure. The streets narrowed and grew quieter. Timber houses were arrayed along them; with their dark, tar-covered beams stark against white lime-washed walls, they reminded me of the narrow cobbled streets of York. Although the houses seemed large compared to the cottages I had grown used to in Launcells, they were pressed together, some separated by tiny, dark alleys, others so close that even a child could not have squeezed between them; and they overhung the street with their upper storeys, casting those below into gloom and shadow. Their windows were tiny, of leaded glass, and several of the houses were of sufficient age that the great beams supporting them had warped and bent, here and there giving entire streets a sense of teetering rather like a band of drunken soldiers leaning upon one another. Now and then, through the alleys between the houses, I glimpsed open stretches of muddy ground. Dried dirt rose in puffs as we passed. It was not a rich part of the city built of fresh quarried stone, not like the houses of Covent Garden close behind the Bucket of Blood, nor ever would be. It was a place of craftsmen and tradesmen. It surprised me. I had expected at the very least a small manor house for any 'strident voice of Parliament'.

'His wife's family are from Oxford,' Warbeck said at last. 'The Powells.' I wondered for a moment if that was why Cromwell had sent Warbeck to find me, that I might enter a city of royalists under Parliament's siege, a man who had once fought for the King but was now Cromwell's intelligencer. I dare say Warbeck would have relished such an irony.

Perhaps he saw the roll of my eyes. He laughed aloud.

'Oh don't fret, Falkland. When the King fled Oxford, he wasn't the only one. The Powells shelter under John Milton's roof now.'

In sight of the old Roman Londinium walls, half their stone long since stolen, Warbeck stopped outside a house like any other, if perhaps a little larger. It was one of several that backed onto a small piece of common ground on which roamed chickens and geese. I thought I saw at least one pig.

Warbeck hammered on the door. The man who opened it was slender and short. There was something oddly shy and girlishly fragile about his features, which stood in stark contrast to his pale, watery eyes as hard as diamonds. Both his hands were scarred, one from what I took to be a powder burn, the other traced with the fine, jagged white lines that were often marks of old knife fights. Here was a man who was a soldier. I stood taken aback, for I took him to be Milton himself and found I had imagined someone quite different; however, after an awkward moment of silence, he introduced himself to me instead as Peter Fowles, an acquaintance and friend of the family. He seemed acquainted with Warbeck too, and did not ask our business; rather he immediately led us inside through a narrow and windowless hall towards the heart of the house. This we traversed, and passed before the stair and out the back into a small yard set against the common ground. A man stood feeding his chickens there. He turned to face us as we came outside.

'John Milton.' Warbeck tucked his hands behind his back and gave a little bow as though presenting a new recruit to a senior officer. 'This is William Falkland.'

CHAPTER 4

The first impression of a man, I find, is often telling. It is rarely entirely right, but it is also rarely entirely wrong. I did not like John Milton, and John Milton did not like me, and I cannot begin to describe exactly why. In appearance he was an ordinary enough man, not greatly tall or short. He was dressed as I was, in black, except he wore black shoes and leggings into which he had tucked his breeches, and he had a lace collar around his neck. His hair was long and lustrous and fell in waves well past his shoulders, which other men might, perhaps, have envied. He was neither slight nor stocky, but had the plain, simple build of a man who has not spent his life working the fields, either farming them or marching them with a pike across his shoulder. His nose was long and slender and very slightly crooked, but what held my gaze was the curling disdain at the very corner of his mouth, and the tired contempt he seemed to cherish in his eyes.

He looked at me, assessing me as I had done to him. His eyes drooped and remained fixed on my boots.

'*This* is Cromwell's new intelligencer? This gangly, yellow-footed scarecrow, some barrel-chested lout stuck upon with broom-handles for limbs?' Milton finally released my boots from his gaze and settled for staring at Warbeck instead. I, it seemed, had now ceased to exist. 'I am well aware of the deceptive perils of appearance, but Henry, did you drag him from a ditch?'

'From a sty, as it happens.' Warbeck raised an eyebrow and eased a little more syrup into his voice. 'Parliament's army is camped around Oxford, John. The King is in Newcastle plotting with the Scots. These are precarious times, and we have few men to spare. Master Falkland has served us well in the past. He has a knack for directness I thought you might appreciate.'

The two squared up to one another, eye to eye, and I will admit that I took some pleasure in seeing Warbeck so discomforted as Milton stared him down. For a few seconds neither said another word, until I became quite convinced they would stare at one another the entire day, without any intent to withdraw.

'I apologise, sir, for my appearance,' I said. 'I am fresh from the road.' I could not see whether I had made any mark with my words so I turned to the other man, this Fowles who had let us in. 'What say you, sir, to this disappearance?'

I supposed Fowles would tell me no more than Warbeck had done in the Bucket of Blood, but I did not expect the startled look I received. Fowles opened his mouth to reply, but got no further before I felt a tug on my arm, and now John Milton was almost dragging me inside, past the stairs leading to the upper rooms, and into a small study at the back of the house that I immediately understood to be where he worked. The window looking across the patch of common ground was large and let in a good light; the air was musty and dry, and with a smell of ink that took me back to the rather more rancid atmosphere of Fleet Street. Books were piled high, and papers too, covering every spare inch of space. Printed pamphlets, mostly, among a scatter of hand-written pages. Milton ushered me inside. It seemed not to trouble him at all to manhandle me so, though I was clearly larger and stronger and might easily have resisted. Here was a man, I thought, very much accustomed to mastery of those around him. He pushed me at a hard-backed chair to sit me down, but I kept to my feet and refused. He stepped back then, and shot me a disagreeable look. As Warbeck followed us in, Milton withdrew behind his desk and its barricade of pamphlets. He sat.

'Falkland. William Falkland.' He spat my name to the floor with such careful precision that I could easily imagine him grinding it under his heel. 'So you're Cromwell's royalist turncoat, are you?'

My fingers curled into fists. I did not much care about his scorn, one way or the other, although I wondered what I could possibly have done to have earned so much of it. But I was, I came to understand in that moment, spoiling for a fight. Not with any particular man, nor over any particular grievance save the grievances I carried against God for what He had done to this country and to my family. If it was combat Milton sought, I would gladly give it. 'I was not aware that the departure of the King from London had been accompanied by the departure of courtesy,' I snapped.

'Falkland!' Warbeck's tone carried a warning, one I found I had no particular desire to heed; but Milton took this as opportunity to direct his ire elsewhere. He turned on Warbeck.

'You had led me to expect some prancing royalist in my house, Henry. Hard enough when it's royalists who have

taken my poor dear sister, when their villainous ilk threaten
everything I have come to cherish in my heart.' His eyes
narrowed and flicked back to me. 'They ooze among us,
Henry, sidling sideways to pick our pockets of both decency
and coin while our eyes are awed by their fatuous puff of
pomp and ceremony. Still, I was prepared to tolerate some
silky, perfumed milk-skin if that man might move easily
among my enemies. This?' He stared at me. 'This man gives
every appearance of a common soldier, Henry, and while I
cannot object to a simple man of simple ways, I cannot see
how this helps our cause. This man will enter the confidence
of a duke or an earl? I do not think so.'

'William Falkland agreed to serve as Cromwell's agent
some months . . .' began Warbeck. His voice had that oily
quality I'd come to recognise in him when he was seeking to
flatter. There would, I decided, be none of that.

'I am no one's man,' I said abruptly. 'I serve neither the
King nor Parliament, John Milton, and I find no slight in
being called a common soldier, for that is what I am.'

'Nor was one meant, Master Falkland. Not in *that*, at
least.' The look he gave me was peculiarly intense.

'You have royalists in your house already,' I said. 'Your
wife's family. Your sister's family.' I looked at him closely.
'Your sister herself, even?' Yes. I caught a flash of anger and
guilt. Perhaps Anne was simply ambivalent, but she certainly
didn't share his vitriol. 'The war, it seems, is done. Hurrah, I
say, for an end to fighting. But I am lackey neither to the
King nor to Cromwell. We have a bargain, my aid for his,
that is all.'

For one long moment, John Milton sat motionless, as if
considering my speech. After that moment his shoulders

slumped. He let out a little sigh, and all the anger seemed to blow out of him. He sank into his chair, deflating like a punctured bladder. 'William Falkland.' He shook his head. 'I have heard your name. Thomas Fairfax has an opinion of you, sir.'

I braced myself. I didn't doubt that I had made an impression on Black Tom after my visit to his camp in Crediton. 'We have crossed paths,' I said.

'Falkland, my sister has been taken, but the attack is against *me*.' Apparently I was not to hear the nature of Black Tom's opinion, then, merely that he had one. 'I do not mean to flatter myself when I say this, though I dare say it must sound that way to you. Anne has no secrets. She has no enemies. She has no money. Knowing this, why else would anyone take her?'

'Yet you have received no demands, sir.'

Milton shook his head. 'They will wait. When the King offers his terms he will ask for what is simply outrageous. Parliament will refuse them, and *that* is when the demand will come. They will call on me to write a palimpsest decrying the greed of Parliament, howling at their unreasonable denial of our now mild and meek King Charles who, contrite in his defeat, has learned invaluable truths and will now reign good and wise as King of England and Scotland, a veritable saint, no less, and why not reconcile ourselves with Rome while we're at it? I will not do it!'

Warbeck, I saw, was nodding. I tried to imagine whether this Milton truly carried such influence; then I saw that it hardly mattered. What mattered was that the men who had taken his sister thought it so.

'It is hard,' I said, 'to conceive that anyone would imagine such a possibility of undermining your resolve. I do not know you, sir, but I hear you are fierce in Parliament's cause. Surely those in London whose sympathies lie with the King would know you better?'

This seemed somewhat to confuse him. I suspect he sensed a slight, but could not find it in my words. 'Your meaning?'

'I am simply wondering, sir, who it is who might know you and yet imagine that a ploy such as you describe could possibly work.'

Milton shook that aside as though a mere nothing. 'Desperate fools will clutch at anything, and you would be tested to catalogue a bigger collection of desperate fools than the King's sycophants who yet lurk in the City of London.' He looked sideways at me and then at Warbeck. 'You think he can walk through the King's supporters here and simply ask them? They are lords. *He* looks like a peasant. You might as well have sent an ass.' He fixed me with another glare. 'They hate me and fear me, William Falkland, and be assured that I revel in every bile-drenched syllable of their attack. They are fumbling oafs, and their words are as sharp as a dullard's club.'

'Your wife's family—' I got no further.

'Ha! The Powells?' I swear that had we been in a tavern he would have hawked up a mouthful of phlegm and spat it into the fire – if it had not already emerged aflame from between his lips, that is. He glanced at Warbeck. 'Did you tell him, Henry?'

Warbeck shook his head. Milton's eyes glowered like hot coals.

'My worst enemies live under my own roof, Falkland. Mary and I were married in 'forty-two before the fighting started. When it did, she ran back to her family. They were royalists then and are royalists now. What behaviour, I ask you, is that of a wife, to defy her husband so?' He shook his head. 'But she was young, very young. The change was too much for her. It was a childish thing, to run back to her home, that is all, and I have long since forgiven her. Yet the Powells!' Dark thunderclouds furrowed his brow. 'What should a gentleman do when his daughter absconds from her willing marriage? Why, he should scold her and return her! Yet three long years they kept her and did their utmost to turn me away!' He let out a snarl and then fixed me with a look. 'Not that that is of any matter to you, Falkland. But they will not help you find Anne. Oh, I dare say they will offer all manner of words and platitudes and wringing of hands, but the bald fact of the matter is that they have no friends here any more. The King's supporters in London will no more speak to them than they will speak to you. They are, you see, paupers in all but name. They have nothing. In their defence, I will say only this: I am now quite convinced they are not part of the conspiracy that took her. They are too stupid for that.'

'Were they more friendly with Anne?' I asked.

'What do you mean?'

The lurking fury across Milton's brow warned me to choose my words with care, to tread with a light step. 'I mean that, while you yourself have a clear grievance, your sister was married to someone who took to the King's banner, not to Parliament. And I take it from your answer before that Anne took no great offence to this. So I wonder if the Powells, who also supported the King, might—'

Milton waved the notion away. 'Anne was loyal to both her husbands, but she knew better than to interfere. She was not friendly with the Powells. They were as civil as is required from those forced to live under a single roof, that was all.' He grimaced. 'This would not have happened if Thomas was here.'

'Thomas Agar? Her husband?'

'No, Falkland. Thomas Becket! Saint Thomas Aquinas! Clearly I mean her husband, who chose the wrong side for reasons built on fallacies and delusions of such potency they were beyond even *my* wit to undermine. But a good man, nonetheless. I would have been happy to shelter him under my roof. He would have found her, too. He would not have let go until he did.'

A familiar sentiment, I found. 'What happened to Thomas Agar?'

'He went north to fight for the King and he never came back, that's what. What else?'

'There were no letters?'

Milton shook his head. 'He was never one for such.'

'I heard he was lost at Edgehill.'

'It is a supposition, but we have no news of him since.'

I shifted uncomfortably from one foot to the other. Now that Milton's initial fury had subsided, it was clear to me that he thought very highly of his sister, and that the bond between them was strong. It had hurt him to lose her, and so it did not please me to go where next I knew I must. I sat down, at last, in the chair to which he had pushed me, and pulled myself a little closer.

'Cromwell told me your sister was taken. Everyone I have spoken to has said the same. I am sorry, but I must ask: is it not possible that she was the victim of a different crime, darker and yet sadly far more mundane in these times?'

'You mean robbed and murdered?' Milton looked as though I'd struck him. He rose from his chair and glared at me from across the room. 'That's what it is, isn't it? Was she robbed and murdered and her body tossed into the Thames or the Fleet or the Ty?' He came back to the desk and stood, leaning over me. 'Is that what you mean, William Falkland? You're asking me if my sister isn't more likely dead?'

'Yes. That is exactly what I am asking.' I didn't move, nor flinch nor back away. Milton had spent the war in London. I had spent six years as a soldier. I did not think, if it came to blows, that I would be much troubled. But still, his anguish spoke to me. I had faced the same thought every day, every morning: my son, my daughter, my Caro.

He looked me hard in the eye. 'No,' he said. 'John and Master Fowles found someone who saw it happen.' He pushed himself away.

'John?'

'John Phillips,' said Warbeck quietly. I had quite forgotten he was even there. Milton had a way of filling a room with himself, leaving no space for any others. 'Anne's eldest by her first husband, Falkland.'

'Then I'd like to speak to him.' I glanced at Warbeck. 'Is this the witness you told me of?'

Milton's voice filled with derision. 'A witness indeed! Some whore from Borough Market who watched my sister bundled into a carriage like a Venetian carpet and did nothing about it! Would have kept her silence too, no doubt, if Peter hadn't loosened her tongue with a sixpence.'

I stood up. 'I would like to speak with John, and with Peter Fowles, and with this witness, and with the Powells too if I may. Are they here?'

I caught, for a moment, an expression of disbelief from Milton, as if he couldn't understand why I should make such a bewildering request. He looked to Warbeck, who remained silent, then finally spoke with a weary disdain of such exaggerated artifice that it seemed he set himself to make the very air weep at the burden of my presence. 'Why not, Master Falkland? Why not indeed? I shall assemble my entire household for you to ply with your questions, if that is what is required for you to pass through my doors and begin your rooting around among whatever scraps the King's supporters in London may deign to offer.' He stormed out of the room, leaving Warbeck and me alone.

'He is known for his words,' said Warbeck quietly, 'not for his patience.' He cocked an eye my way. 'Too much for you, Falkland?'

I didn't answer. Instead I took one of the pamphlets from the desk, chosen simply because it was the easiest to reach. I started to read the cover.

POEMS
of
Mr. John Milton
BOTH
ENGLISH and LATIN
Compos'd at feveral times

Beside the title was an engraved picture of someone who might have been Milton, but if that was the intention then I could imagine the poet's ire at being presented in such a way, moon-faced and out of proportion. Beneath was an inscription in what I took to be Greek. I had never learned to read any language but English and a little Latin. Perhaps

my own John or Charlotte might have understood it – I had
no doubt that Caro would have had a tutor for them.

I opened the pamphlet and browsed the words inside.

And though the shady gloom
Had given day her room,
The Sun himself withheld his wonted speed
And hid his head for shame,
As his inferior flame
The new enlightened world no more should need:
He saw a greater sun appear
Than his bright throne, or burning axle-tree could bear

I stared at the words, perplexed. I had thought Milton to
be a polemicist, a pamphleteer, that his 'poems' would be
nothing but satire lampooning whoever had caught his ire.
But here were words of eloquent beauty, an ode to the birth
of Christ, it seemed.

I put the pamphlet down as Milton returned. Two young
men followed in his wake, the second one barely more than
a boy. I took them to be John and Edward, Anne's sons. Last
of all came the man who had met us at the door, Fowles.
The boys stood awkward and flighty as Milton sat himself
down. There was no glimmer of recognition, but I saw in
their faces something very different from that which I had
seen in Milton himself. Anguish tempered with hope. I felt I
understood them at once.

I rose to introduce myself.

'John and Edward Phillips? I am William Falkland.'

'You're come to find the monsters who seized our
mother?' asked the younger, Edward.

'I—'

'Of course he is,' snapped Milton, 'but don't get your hopes roused, lad. Cromwell, whom we have clearly offended in some manner, has sent us a sop to the King's supporters while the King cowers among the Scots.' He glared at me again, while the boys settled themselves against the door, huddled together. The older regarded me coldly, while the younger mostly kept his eyes fixed to the floor. When Milton wasn't looking, I saw he threw me the occasional furtive glance.

'Here!' Milton barked. He leaned back in his chair and spread his arms wide, a grand gesture of theatre I imagined he might use when addressing Parliament. 'The day wears on. I am hungry and with much to do, and you will learn nothing you have not already been told, but let's be on with it. Shall I rouse my father from his bed for you, Falkland? Would you see a sick old man stagger and wheeze for your amusement?'

'Does he have anything pertinent to say?' I snapped. 'If he does then it's perfectly agreeable to me to sit where he lies and listen to his words.' I looked squarely at John Phillips. 'You went looking for your mother when she didn't come home. What happened?'

'She left for Borough Market,' said Milton before the lad could answer. 'She goes there often. There was nothing unusual or untoward about it except that she did not return.' His words were brisk and clipped, hurrying to an end with almost indecent haste. I looked at the Phillips boys. The older said nothing. The younger, when my eyes wouldn't let him go, gave a slight nod.

'When did you know something was amiss?' I asked them.

Milton rolled his eyes. 'When she didn't come back! Do you suppose we waited a day? A week? Do you imagine my sister some vagrant parted from her mind who takes to wandering the streets of London for endless hours? Anne is a vigorous woman. She is not one to waste time. When she was not back by the middle of the afternoon, it was quite clear that something was amiss. *Quite* clear.'

'Mistress Mary was very worried,' said the younger lad. Milton shot him a livid glance.

'Who organised the search?' I asked.

'I did,' said Fowles. He moved to stand close beside Milton. His voice was soft and soothing. 'John wasn't here. Younger John' – here he glanced to John Phillips – 'was beside himself. She'd been gone for hours, you see, Falkland, and it wasn't like her. Young John said he wanted to go and look for her. He asked me for help, and so of course I did what anyone would do.'

'You went to Borough Market?'

'We did. She'd gone there to buy ribbon.'

'What was her mind?' Again I looked to the two lads who were her sons.

'What do you mean?' demanded Milton.

'I am asking as to her mood. Did she appear troubled on the day before she disappeared?'

I swear Milton almost raised his fists to me. 'She did not *disappear*, Falkland! She was taken! Now that you have roused my entire household from their business, you might find it of some value to attend to what they have to say! My sister was, if anything, unusually invigorated. She had been for days, ever since we heard the news of the King's flight from Oxford. It was patently clear from that very moment that his defeat was utter and total, that the war would soon be over, and that Parliament's victory was complete. The news gave her renewed energy.' He hesitated for a moment, and his words lost their agitation. 'I suppose she thought she might see Thomas back. Or at least hear what became of him.'

'Young John and I went to the market,' said Fowles, quietly. He, at least, seemed of even temper. 'We asked at the stalls where she would have gone. It seemed she had arrived and gone about her common business. There was no suggestion of anything amiss. I . . .' He took a breath and looked away for a moment. 'I feared for the worst, Master Falkland, and so I gave a few coins to some of the men who dwell in the market, and who saw Anne often enough to recognise her face. We searched the alleys all the way to the river shore. It was a relief when we did not find her.'

I could see the older son, John, straining forward. He had something he wished to say but yet dared not speak. I met his eye.

'There was a witness,' I said.

He nodded, but again Milton spoke in his stead. 'I already told you, Falkland! The whore who saw my sister taken by two men and stuffed into a carriage as a cook might stuff a pheasant!'

'You are certain of her story?' I tried to ignore Milton.

'Of course he is!'

'Did she describe the men?'

John Phillips shook his head. Milton clenched his fists. 'Men who wore black much as you do, Master Falkland, and with beards and hats, a description that might encompass half of London for all the use of it.' He snarled. 'One might have thought that a whore would have more of an eye for such things.'

'One might indeed.' I found we were in agreement. I rose. 'Gentlemen, I am sorry to have taken so much of your time. I will need to speak to this woman for myself.'

'Then take your leave, Falkland, and be about it.' Milton glanced to the window and the fading summer afternoon. 'A fine time of day for finding whores, I would say.'

I had had, I decided, enough of John Milton. I have long considered patience to be one of my virtues, my temper slow and hard to rouse, but I will admit that in Milton I had found a man who might best me. With the two of us alone I might have ascribed his caustic tongue to grief and worry; but with Anne's sons present he had grown more abrasive still, oblivious, it seemed to me, of their own hurt.

'I will need her name,' I said. 'And where to find her.'

'I'll show you to her.' Warbeck rose to stand beside me. 'Gentlemen, we bid you good night.' He rose and moved to the study door, and the two Phillips boys almost tripped over one another in their haste to make way for our departure. I took one last look around the room. Milton stared after me. John and Edward Phillips had already dismissed me and were whispering to one another. The strangest look of all came from Fowles, with his fragile face and his scarred soldier's hands. He watched me all the way out. There was no hostility or hope in that gaze, but I sensed from those cold eyes a watchfulness that I was at a loss to explain.

Warbeck strode along the hall, arrowing for the door, his long, fast steps betraying his agitation. I, however, felt eyes on me. I paused, and when I looked behind I saw a young lady, many years Milton's junior, and with such a round belly that I knew she was both pregnant and with not long to go. She stood on the last step of the stair, motionless. Beside her was a young girl, about ten years old, the same age as my Charlotte had been when I had left to go to war. She stared at me with wide, sad eyes. Anne's daughter, I was sure. A few steps further up sat an older man, head bowed, and a woman of similar age at his side. They struck me as timid folk. All except the girl gawped back at me as though they were thieves caught red-handed. Eavesdroppers.

'You must be Mary.' I looked at the young woman. The way her eyes wouldn't let go of me set me thinking that perhaps there was something she wished for me to know. I took another step, and then called back to the study. 'Master Milton, did your sister have friends about the city? People upon whom she might have called on her way to the market? Or on her return?'

Milton came quickly to the door, but not before the older Powells cast me a nervous glance, while Mary caught my eye with the glimmer of a smirk. All three, I thought, had things they wished to say, yet Milton had not bade them, and so they held their silence.

'My sister,' snapped Milton, ushering me away once more, 'has friends throughout London thanks to the work that both she and her husband have done. Had she called upon one, they would have told me. She did not.'

I doffed my hat and took my leave. I would return, I thought, to the subject of Anne Agar's friends and what Mary Milton might know that her husband did not. Clearly there was something, but I would not get to it while Anne's brother was standing before us.

CHAPTER 5

'You may as well take me back to Uxbridge where you found me.' I did not bother to wait until we rounded the corner of the street before I stopped and turned on Warbeck. 'This will not do.'

Warbeck's look was one of scorn and pity. 'Did he rub your fur the wrong way, Falkland? Did he not tickle you under your chin and tug your ears and pat you on the head? Were you expecting some fawning gratitude for the application of your time? When I found you, you were stinking drunk and rolling in pig shit. I am of the same mind, to take you back and return to Cromwell, and tell him you were a waste of his time.'

'Do so then, for this is a waste of mine. And of yours, and anyone else who involves themselves. John Milton claims that some mysterious club of the King's supporters took his sister to spite him. I will say, Warbeck, having met such men, that the notion had seemed unlikely to me. Now it is a different matter. I cannot say whether royalists are responsible or not, but it strikes me quite forcefully that any decent man who has ever met John Milton, whether for King or for Parliament or the Pope himself, must surely bear him some grudge. Your gentle friend has made it entirely clear that he places little value in my assistance. I believe, now, that the list of suspects may be narrowed to anyone in Christendom who has met him.' I turned to go, although I will admit that I did not entirely know to where. It occurred to me, too, that the horse I rode belonged to Warbeck.

'Falkland!'

Yes, I was indeed speaking in haste, but there seemed little purpose in pursuing any further conversation with John Milton. I stopped my horse and took a few deep breaths to calm myself.

'Falkland, John Milton is known far and wide for the barbs that line his tongue. There is not one man among his friends who has not felt the lash of it. He cares deeply for his sister, and his sister has been taken from him. He is . . . affected by it.'

'You all keep telling me the war is all but done. Perhaps Anne received news, at last, of her husband. Perhaps it is as simple as that.'

'You forget that she was seen being taken.'

I was indeed forgetting. It was true, too, that Milton's manner had changed when he spoke of Anne's missing husband. Royalist or not, there had been a warmth there.

'If she had received news do you not think she would have shared it? You imagine her someone who would abandon her sons without word, for weeks on end? Yes, they are almost grown men, but there is a daughter too, by Thomas, a good few years younger than the Phillips lads.'

'I know. I saw her as we left.' The look in her face. Loss and fear and a flicker of hope. Try as I might, I could not stop that look from tugging at me. She was so young.

'You cast her as a mother who would abandon a daughter

too young to have come into her own?' Warbeck shook his head. 'You need to talk to the whore, Falkland. Her name is Jane Hardwick. She lives on Clink Street across the river.'

He was doubtless right. Milton had slipped under my skin, that was all. I found myself caught. Yes, there was the Borough Market whore who claimed to have seen Anne being taken, but whores will say anything for a sixpence. It was more, though. The atmosphere in the house was wrong. I could almost feel Anne's presence through her absence. I had never met the woman, and indeed had heard little about her, but I found myself picturing her every bit as forceful as Milton himself, yet in a very different way. Beneath his bluster, had I seen a desperation? And her sons, too. She was their anchor, then? What kept them at peace with one another?

I cursed softly and glared at Warbeck. 'Isn't this where you tell me that if I don't do as Cromwell bids then I shall never see my wife and children again? That all the resources of mighty Parliament to search this land from top to bottom in my name shall now be denied?'

Warbeck shook his head. 'I don't need to tell you that, Falkland. You already know it perfectly well.'

And there was the trap that Cromwell had laid me, daring me to cast aside the scant hope he had given. I sought a pithy retort, but the moment was stolen from me by the sight of the old man I had seen on the steps behind Mary Milton, now hurrying on to the street in our wake. He cast his eyes back and forth, saw us, and fair ran to catch us before we could ride away. He spared no glance for Warbeck but came directly to me, so close to my horse, and with such a look of desperation in his eye, that I feared he would clutch at my leg like some distraught widow.

'Master Falkland! Master Falkland! Thank the Lord I caught you before you left.'

'Master Powell?' I guessed. 'You are Mary's father?' I watched him closely, waiting to see what he would say.

'Master Falkland, you are a King's man. Is it so?'

'I would not call myself that now, but I fought in the King's armies until I was taken after Naseby.' In my heart I was no other man's man at all, but in this England now one must have one's allegiances. 'I was imprisoned in Newgate. I am employed, now and then, by Cromwell, in exchange for my freedom.' It was the truth, as blunt and bald as I could make it. Milton surely already knew.

'Master Falkland, I beg you to help us. We were for the King too. Master Milton blames us for . . .' he glanced at Warbeck, and then looked back at me as if asking if I understood his meaning. I thought I did, but saw no reason to say so.

'For?' I would have him say it, so I might watch his eyes as he did.

'Master Falkland, when Master Milton came to stay with us after his touring of Europe, he was most taken with our Mary, and she with him. He knew so many things and he was always good with words . . . Well, sir, you've seen how it is, but he can praise and flatter with the same passion as he might damn a man. He is like he is now because he fears for Anne . . . but I lose myself. Master Milton and my Mary were swiftly wed, but it was a very different life in his house to that in ours as he wooed her. You've seen how he can be. She was a foolish girl. She ran away.'

'Milton said as much.'

'He thinks we kept her from him, but that's not how it was. She came to us as the war started. We were in Oxford. There were armies roaming the country, the roads awash with rapacious men, sir, and she was so young! What, I ask you, was a good father to do?'

I had been with those armies. I could think of only a handful of times they had roamed the roads from Oxford to London, but nonetheless more than none.

'He blames you?' I asked.

'Yes!'

'You certainly did not do all you could to return her.'

'She was a child, Master Falkland!'

'Old enough that you were happy for her to marry.' I shrugged. 'But that is by the by. They appear reconciled to one another now, so all is well, is it not?'

'Indeed, sir.' Powell's fawning was beginning to grate against my nerves. I do not take kindly to scornful men, but I found Milton's disdain irked me less than this whining flattery. 'The King fled Oxford—'

'And you fled too. Tell me, Master Powell, when did Mary return to London?'

'Last year.' While the monster of the New Model roamed southern England. Naseby, Abingdon, Winchester, Basing House. Yet Mary Powell had travelled to London and never mind the danger. I found in myself a little unwanted sympathy for Milton's ire.

'So with the King gone and Oxford surrounded by the armies of Parliament, you came to London and begged John Milton to shelter you, though you had kept him from his wife for three years?'

'I . . . Sir, she begged us to keep her!'

A little of both, I thought, but none of this had any bearing on Anne. A notion came to me: 'Were Mary and Anne friends?'

'Yes!' Powell sounded grateful, as though a weight had been lifted from him. 'Yes, sir, they were. After Mary came back to London, Anne was like an older sister. They were the closest confidantes, Master Falkland. They shared everything. It was Anne who convinced Mary to return. She was the one . . . Sir, she keeps his temper in check. Now that she is gone, I fear . . . Master Falkland, it is no secret that Milton took us in as a kindness to Mary, nor that he did so because Anne asked it of him. He despises us and has done so ever since the King took to the field. Now Anne has gone, he is all that lies between us and destitution. If anything happens to her . . . If it is true that the supporters of the King . . . Sir, he will disown us!'

'So Anne is missing and now you think of your own plight?' I wondered what he thought I might do to aid them. Discover that Anne had, in fact, not been taken by supporters of the King, I supposed, a notion I continued to find unlikely. I told him so. It seemed to Powell to be a great relief. He took a step, at last, away from my horse.

'Please sir! You've seen how he can be, but it's missing Anne that makes him so. We've all been ill-at-ease since the house-breaker came. Please find her, sir. For all of us.'

'House-breaker?'

'Oh indeed, sir. It was months ago now, but it unsettles him still. A rival polemicist came to steal the words he had been preparing on the New Model.'

'The man was caught?'

'No, sir.'

I frowned and looked to Warbeck, but he only shrugged. I turned back to Powell. 'There are names, though. People Milton suspects?'

Powell nodded. 'Will you find Anne for him, sir?' he asked. At that I scoffed.

'John Milton is arrogant, cocksure and entirely dislikeable. I will certainly not be finding Anne for *him*.' At such words Powell swelled up with glee and, perhaps, a little pride. 'You may do me a service, sir,' I said, 'and learn the names of Milton's pamphleteer rivals. I am in the Bucket of Blood in Covent Garden. Since it seems unlikely to me that Milton will grant me leave to speak with his wife, you might take the opportunity to convey anything she may wish to say.'

I watched him go, thinking a little less unkindly of him. It is a terrible thing to be in a war at all, but an even more terrible thing to be on the wrong side of it come the end.

'If I am to remain, I will be finding Anne Agar for herself,' I said very quietly.

'Pardon?' Warbeck had sidled up on my blind side, as he was wont to do. I think he has a natural instinct for it.

I shook my head and kicked on my horse. We walked together side by side back towards Newgate. Twilight was upon us and the crowds were thinning, and yet even now the city seemed charged with an energy. 'This whore from Borough Market,' I said, as we passed under the Newgate itself. 'Is she a prison whore?' Clink prison was every bit as infamous as Newgate, if not more so. I had no doubt there would be plenty of royalist men locked up in those cells. Perhaps that was where Milton found his notion of a conspiracy of the King's loyal subjects against him.

'Exactly that. Go to her tomorrow, Falkland. She'll be

working now. Better to find a time when she's not looking for money.'

I looked to the sky. Indeed she would. The sun had not quite set, but these June days were long.

'I need to speak to Milton's wife.' All three of them had been hiding secrets on John Milton's stair, I was sure of it. The older Powells had given me theirs, perhaps, but I had no faith that they would come to find me in Covent Garden with word from Mary. That left Mary herself, and Peter Fowles. I would, if I was not mistaken, get more gossip from Mary than from any number of taverns and inns where the King's supporters might be found. The difficulty would be in speaking with her alone.

We rode back across the Fleet and laboured through the crowds of Fleet Street, seemingly undiminished by the onset of twilight; hustle and bustle and noise and the air still charged with the scent of ink. By the time we stabled our horses in the Bucket of Blood, the sun had set. Warbeck summoned a bowl of pottage for each of us and found a quiet spot close to the door. The Bucket of Blood was lively that night, and well attended. Outside on the streets groups of raucous men passed back and forth, shouting their slogans at one another. A space had been cleared on the tavern floor and a thick layer of straw laid down.

'There's going to be a fight, is there?' I had seen this arrangement many times, the straw laid down to soak up the blood – arranged fights were as common as the pox in the army camps I had attended, particularly in winter when there were no battles to be fought. Soldiers grew easily bored.

Warbeck shrugged. 'The tavern earned its name, Falkland.'

'Milton guards her too closely,' I muttered, thinking still of Mary. 'I will need you to separate them.' But Warbeck was already shaking his head.

'I've done my duty here and have business of my own.'

Our pottage arrived, brought to us by a scrawny boy no more than twelve years old who looked as though he needed sustenance far more than either Warbeck or I. From the far end of the tavern where the straw had been laid, a ragged cheer rose. The first of the fighters, it seemed, had arrived.

'I will not argue that Milton does not have enemies,' I said. I had to lean in to Warbeck now to be heard over the roars of a man who styled himself 'Bloody Tom'. I took this to be the tavern's local champion, as he began at once to call on anyone to challenge him. A mixture of cheers and boos followed as a first foolish victim stepped forward. 'But when a man has enemies, they tend to act against the man, not to abduct his sister.'

Warbeck shook his head. 'You don't understand, Falkland. But how could you? You need to have lived in London these last few years to know the power that man wields. Parliament fawns on him for the strength of his words. When his wife ran back to her family, he issued his Divorce Tracts. I suppose a man like you would not have heard of them, but in London they are infamous even now. There were several in Parliament who thought them far too excitable. The fools asked for them to be withdrawn and Milton censured. His response was to publish another tract, on the imperative freedom of the presses. He speaks strongly in favour of the freedom of every man to express their view without interference by either King or Parliament. He has many powerful friends, and equally many who very much dislike him. But when he speaks, he sways minds. I can think of few better candidates for the King's supporters to try to bring to their cause. He will not speak for the King himself – I doubt any force in Heaven or Earth could drive him to that – but his silence might suffice. You have seen how the to and fro goes around Oxford, negotiating the terms of the city's surrender. Imagine how it will be with the King. Of course, it will not be a surrender, merely a debate on the powers that Parliament will permit him and those it will keep to itself. One way or another, those terms will shape England for a hundred years and more. They are important, Falkland, and Milton has the power to sway them.'

I tried to believe him, to imagine that a man like Milton, living in his house like an impoverished schoolmaster, might have within him such potency. I suppose I had no reason to think otherwise, but I struggled most of all simply to find any reason to care. Such matters seemed so remote from the life I had led in Cornwall, content as it had been, and to which I longed to return. Perhaps Warbeck was right and we would all be touched in some way by whatever accord was finally reached – indeed, if we were not then what had been the point of it all? For what had we all been fighting? Yet I could not feel it anywhere in my heart. A woman whose husband had gone to war and never returned; a woman taken from her family with a daughter and two anxious sons left behind, those were things I could grasp.

A gasp and then a round of laughter broke from the crowd, yelling at one fighter or another to get to his feet. I will admit the shouts and catcalls set my blood flowing. I had never joined in such fights, for I thought them a business for fools and had no wish for any broken fingers or other bones, nor to lose my teeth. Parliament's pikes, sabres and muskets tried hard enough in that regard. But I had joined the crowds now and then, and even wagered on the outcome in those early years when the enemy had been the treacherous Scots. Now I scraped my bowl clean and got to my feet, but only in time to hear a snarl, a wet smack and a crash, and a collective sucking of breath through teeth. By the time I had pushed far enough through the throng to see for myself, the first challenger was being dragged by his feet out of harm's way. His face was a bloody mess. At least he wasn't dead. I had known it happen sometimes.

The champion fighter, Bloody Tom, raised a fist in victory. He had bandages across his knuckles and they were heavily stained with blood – whether his or from the poor unfortunate on the floor, I could not tell.

'Three shillings!' cried another man, narrow and wiry and with a nose like a hawk, who danced about behind Bloody Tom as though inflicted by the madness of St Vitus. 'He may not be pretty any more, but that's a lad with three shillings in his pocket come morning. Three shillings. Six if you take Bloody Tom to the floor. Who else would have a try?'

'What if we win?' cried a voice from the crowd.

'Then you'll be our new champion,' cried the dancing man. 'And earn yourself a shilling every night.'

I was surprised. I had expected these fights to be for pennies, as they had been among the soldiers. Covent Garden, it seemed, offered rich pickings.

A soldier stepped forward in the Venice red of the New Model. 'I'll take your shillings, friend.'

The chatter of the crowd fell away as every eye turned to

look at him. I am not a small man myself, but this soldier was a giant, as broad as he was tall, a far cry from the poor sop who'd first been thrown to this Bloody Tom's fists. The quiet remained until the dancing man – who had fallen momentarily still – hopped again from foot to foot and nodded his head and beckoned the soldier forward. The noise surged as men shouted their bets to one another, far more than for the first challenger. The soldier stripped off his coat and his shirt. He was young, I thought, hardly a man at all, and yet he was enormous.

'He's a big fellow,' said the man in the crowd next to me. 'I'd say he's going to give our Tom a run.'

'If I was a man to offer a wager, I'd still put my money on your Tom,' I answered. There is only so far that strength and size can take a man in a fist fight. A certain ruthlessness is needed that can only come from experience. A willingness to do whatever is needed to bring the other man down. Soldiers in battle learn this or they die, but the young soldier here, I thought, had not seen enough of the world.

'Your two shillings to my one. I say Parliament's man floors our Tom.'

I shook my head. 'I would take that wager if I had a shilling, but I do not.'

The soldier had wrapped strips of cloth around his knuckles in the manner of a man who had fought this way before. The crowd quietened. Bloody Tom paced and punched his fists together with the restless hunger of a wild animal in a cage. There was no calling of the fight to begin – the dancing man simply withdrew, and the two fighters ran at one another. Each grabbed the other and began trying to wrestle their opponent over. I fancied the soldier might have been the stronger, but Bloody Tom had his tricks. He stamped and bit and gouged until the soldier broke his hold.

I turned and forced my way back to our table. Warbeck had not left his seat. 'Seen enough, Falkland?' he asked.

'I'll talk to your Miss Hardwick of Clink Street. After that, I don't see what's to be done. Find another intelligencer, one with whom Milton can converse as a civilised man.'

'I'm not convinced such exists,' Warbeck spat. 'But you'll do what Cromwell asks of you like any other man. That's my last duty tonight, to remind you why.'

I tried to draw him on what he meant, but at that moment came a roar from the crowd and a crash as someone hit the straw hard. From the boos that followed I took that to mean the fight was finished. Warbeck waved at the boy for another cup of ale for each of us.

'Fancy your chances, Falkland?' His lip curled, but I could not be sure whether it was from disdain for me or for the entertainment itself. I drank down my cup, thinking I might turn for my bed. There seemed little reason to stay; but as I rose, Warbeck beckoned me to wait. A moment later the soldier I had seen at the fight came and sat beside us. He was limping, and the right side of his face was puffy and purple from at least one savage blow and perhaps more.

'Falkland, this is Daniel Waterhouse,' Warbeck said. 'You lost, then, did you, Waterhouse?'

The big man grunted.

'Go and tell her he's here. Bring her down.'

Waterhouse had barely sunk into his chair, and he rose again with some reluctance. I cocked my head at Warbeck. *Her*? And who was here? Did he mean me? But Warbeck only turned and looked over his shoulder, ignoring me until we both saw the big soldier Waterhouse ploughing his return through the crowds of the tavern. He did indeed have a woman beside him, but not the whore of Clink Street as I had begun to imagine. I did not recognise her at first, but when at last I saw who it was, I jumped to my feet, spilling my cup in my surprise.

'Miss Cain?'

CHAPTER 6

I had met Kate Cain in Crediton as her lodger while I investigated strange deaths in Cromwell's New Model Army. I suppose it was inevitable that she had become embroiled in my unravelling of what had transpired there, but I had always felt a guilt in that, come the end, her life had been put in danger perhaps as much as my own. I had heard that Cromwell had taken her under his wing in some way, or at least had looked out for her to the extent of finding her a means of supporting herself. And yes, I had thought about her now and then as I searched the land for my beloved Caro. Not once, though, had it entered my mind that she might still be in London; if I had considered her at all, I supposed she must have returned home after the winter lifted, after Black Tom's army had moved on. Yet here she was. I confess that I stared at her longer than was gentlemanly.

'Kate!' I said wonderingly, at a loss for anything more. Already I sensed Warbeck's lip begin to curl.

'Falkland.' If there was anything to be said in my defence, it was that Miss Cain appeared every bit as surprised as I at our reunion. Her night-black hair had grown long since I had last seen her, and her clothes, though simple, were no longer tattered and threadbare. Her eyes I remembered, green and sparkling. She had a glow to her. London life had filled her out a little, added a roundness to the hollow cheeks I remembered. In Crediton we had all been starving.

'You look well,' I blurted, before I at last remembered my manners. I bowed and put out my hand. 'A pleasure once more, Miss Cain.'

Kate returned a dainty curtsey and gave me her hand. I touched my lips to the back of it as though I was some nobleman. I fancy the curl of Warbeck's smirk must have reached all the way to his nose, but I didn't look and nor did I care. Here was a reason, if there was no other, to be in London . . .

It was like an icicle dropped beneath my shirt. Warbeck, in his deviousness, had brought her here with precisely that thought in mind. I let Kate's hand fall and withdrew to my chair. My thoughts tumbled in confusion, defying all effort to marshal them.

'You knew, I think, we had found some employment for Miss Cain?' The look Warbeck gave me was sly. He had baited his hook and I had swallowed it whole, and both of us knew it. He beckoned for another cup of beer. 'Miss Cain is working in the Inns of Court.' He told me some story of how Cromwell and Fairfax were compiling a great ledger of soldiers drafted into the New Model, of who they were and their commanders, and the companies they had fought with and from where they had come. I confess I did not give his words my full attention. I was too busy staring at Miss Cain. I think perhaps I stared too long, for she turned a little red, while Warbeck's words stumbled to silence. He looked at me askance. 'Is something wrong, Falkland?'

I must have been looking at her as though I was seeing some sort of ghost. In truth I felt that I was.

Kate looked away. 'It is good, Master Falkland, to see you well,' she said.

'I thought you could not read,' I blurted. 'How can you keep a ledger for Cromwell's army?'

There were kinder things I might have said. Many. But my mind remained in such disarray that I spoke the first thought that came to me. Kate seemed to shrink into herself.

'I could read a little before,' she said shyly. 'I have learned more. Master Warbeck has been helping me.'

I found I did not much like this revelation. I fixed Warbeck with a hard eye, and then wondered at the force of my own vexation. Warbeck merely shrugged. 'Not in person,' he said. 'We have found, however, that Miss Cain has an eye and a memory for names.'

'It's because of you,' said Kate. She smiled at me then, a quiet twitch of her lip that nevertheless warmed me beyond reason. I think I had not seen anyone gift me a smile since Kate and I had last parted, not one. 'There are so many who have lost their families. Mothers who have lost their sons, sons who have lost their fathers. You told me your story, and I thought of you after I left Crediton.'

'I supposed you would go back.'

'I meant to.' She shook her head. 'But while I waited in London for the winter to pass there were so many others who had left their homes, uprooted by this army or that, who had not heard from their soldier sons for years. Or men who had fought as you did, and then returned home to find their families gone, fled with no word as to where. I asked Master Warbeck if there wasn't something to be done. And so it is.' She reached across the table and touched my hand. 'Did you find them, Falkland?'

The question took me unawares. I found myself blinking back tears. I shook my head.

'I did not,' I said.

Warbeck coughed. 'Parliament is concerned,' he said, 'now the war is all but done, to return the country to good order. It is a task suited to Heracles himself and will not be finished in any haste, but it must be done. Miss Cain has begun it. Cromwell is eager to keep proper records. He would acknowledge all the men who have died fighting for Parliament's cause.' His voice turned dry. 'Whether the King and his court will act similarly only the King can say.'

He emptied his cup and turned his eye to Waterhouse, the soldier whose presence, despite his size, I had hardly even noted. Waterhouse nodded and jumped to his feet.

'Good luck with both your searches, Falkland. I will send word now and then to inquire after your progress.'

Warbeck turned and left without another word. Waterhouse followed him away, and Kate and I were left alone. Behind us, the crowd gathered for the fights cheered as another bout began. I had to lean towards Kate to hear her over their baying.

'What does he mean?' she asked.

'A woman has disappeared from her home. Warbeck has me searching for her.'

Across the table I had to shout to make myself heard. I shifted my seat so that we sat next to one another, close enough that I could smell her, a scent far sweeter than Warbeck's rotten breath.

'I am sorry,' I said.

'For what?'

'For what I said. That you couldn't read.'

She laughed, and I wished I could have lived with that

laugh beside me for days. 'I've not become a lawyer or a writer of palimpsests, Falkland. But well enough for this.'

'Then I am pleased for you.' I felt a terrible pulling inside me, a longing I could not quite place. For all things lost, for my Caro and my son John and my Charlotte, but bigger even than all of them together. A crude, foolish wish that this cursed war had never happened. I had felt it before – I dare say every soldier who ever left a wife behind has felt much the same at times – but here and now it was stronger than I could ever remember it. 'Are you happy, Kate?' I asked. I watched her closely.

'I am . . . content, Falkland. I do not go hungry. I do not want for shelter. I would . . . I miss my home a little. But I see that what Warbeck has asked me to do will make a difference. You know my father was pressed? At least this way I know that he still lives. I know that my home awaits me in Crediton now the army has gone. It is a comfort.' She took my hand.

The tavern boy stopped for a moment beside us and silently filled my cup. I had not asked for more and fumbled for my purse, forgetting for a moment that I had none; but he shook his head.

'From the gentleman who dined with you, sir,' he said. 'He said to keep your cup full for as long as you like.'

He left. I looked back at Kate. Her eyes were shining with . . . I could not say. Pride, perhaps, and perhaps happiness, and perhaps some sadness too. 'I'm sorry they weren't waiting for you, William,' she said.

She squeezed my hand tight, and I felt as if a stream inside me, long frozen, was swelling with spring rain. I had not told anyone of my search, for I had not had anyone to call a friend. I drew my hand away and drained my cup, seeking the courage to face again the last six months. I had thought that war was a wasteland, a desert empty of joy and meaning, but nothing in all my years of fighting had felt as desolate as the months since I had laid down my sabre.

'When Cromwell let me go, I went from Crediton to Launcells. I returned in time for Christmas. I was afraid I might be so changed that my children wouldn't recognise me, that I would be a stranger to them. What if my Caro thought me long dead? What if she had mourned me and buried me . . . ?' I had to stop. It was too hard bringing these memories to the surface. I had buried them in the months of searching that came after.

'Falkland?' Kate's fingers remained wrapped around my own. A simple touch of sympathy, of a pain known and shared, but I drew away nonetheless. Her kindness over-whelmed me. A tenderness more and I would weep, and a grown man with a grown son should never weep. I do not say I haven't seen it, after bloody battle, but here in a London tavern, half taken with drink? No.

'They were gone,' I said. 'I had thought of so many things, come with so many fears, but I had not once imagined that they simply would not be there. I still wonder which play of the endless to and fro of armies was finally enough for her.'

'Did they not leave word?'

I shook my head. 'When I asked after them I was told she had left for Bristol. There was a sense to that. The King had held Bristol since early in the war. Caroline's father had had friends there.'

I closed my eyes and drained another cup. I could feel the beer in my blood, in my head. The journey to Bristol had not been kind. That winter of '45 had been bitter. The roads were choked with snow. Cromwell had sent me from Crediton with a horse, an old mare, but she was thin and weak, and the cold and my haste between them had killed her, and me a cavalryman who should have known better. I had come upon Bristol close to exhaustion.

My thoughts were swimming. 'They had been and gone. Two years ago now. Caro had come looking for me. They had thought I was in Yorkshire.' I had indeed been in Yorkshire under Prince Rupert's command, but the King had summoned him south again rather than finish the taking of the north.

Kate took my hand once more. This time I did not resist.

'The winter was terrible. Food was scarce. Prince Rupert had surrendered Bristol to Parliament some months before . . .'

I had to stop again. I hated myself for those lost months, wondering, as always, what might have passed had I left Bristol and carried on my search at once. I had been too weak, simply that. The Gilroys, friends of Caro's father, had fed me and nursed me back to my strength, and I knew, in the plain, straightforward way of a soldier, that I would have died crossing the country in the dead of winter, but I hated myself nevertheless.

The tavern boy came past again with another cup for me.

'I left Bristol on the back of a cart in the spring. It seemed that they had been seen by everyone and no one. So many people had come and gone, fleeing this army or that in all the pointless back and forth.'

The Bucket of Blood seemed to slide before my eyes. I stared at Kate, filled with a terrible longing. I had spent so many months alone.

'In Nottingham I chanced upon the remains of a company of soldiers of which I had once been a part. They had thought me dead. I had taken a musket ball in the leg two years before, and the wound had turned bad, and it is rare to recover from such injury. One told me of a woman who had come asking after me in the winter of 'forty-four. She had brought with her a young man and a pretty girl close to being a woman. They had told her what they knew – that my company had returned to Oxford, and me with it. They had told her they thought I was likely dead.'

I staggered to my feet. The drink was taking me. I would soon collapse as no man should permit himself, awash with regrets and memories that seared me no matter how I cherished them. It was all I could do not to simply close my eyes and take the sweet oblivion offered before me.

Kate took my arm to steady me. Grateful, I leaned on her. The warmth and the smell of her befuddled me. I staggered towards the steps.

'And then?' she asked, as she helped me up the stairs.

'I was in Oxford for the whole of that winter. The King's surgeons saved my leg and maggots ate away the rot. I survived. Somehow I always do. They did not come.' I could not face why. My Caro had been searching for me even though she feared me dead, and yet she had not arrived. Something had happened to them. In my heart I knew it, and I could no longer stop the tears. As I reached the top of the stairs I tried to push Kate away so she would not see them. I staggered from her, and lost my feet and crashed into a wall. I slumped against the thin plaster. In that moment it seemed that everything about me, everything I had ever touched, was ruin.

'Go away, Kate,' I whispered, my voice hoarse, but she did not. She stood over me and hauled at me and dragged me to my feet. My arms were around her and her closeness again overwhelmed me. I cupped her face and ran my fingers through her hair. The length of it fascinated me. It had been short before.

'Let's get you to bed, Falkland.'

I stared at her. I think, had she met my eye, I might have kissed her and then regretted it deeply; and perhaps Kate sensed the same, for she looked quickly away. Together we staggered to the room Warbeck had paid for.

'Coat, Falkland.' She unravelled it from me. I closed my eyes, trying to not think of her as she pressed against me and thus thought of her all the more. I hated myself, and yet I could not help it. As soon as she was done, I fell to the mattress. My head swirled, full of thoughts of Kate and Caro and despair and the longing. I felt her at my feet, pulling at my boots, still stained with pig filth from that sty in Uxbridge. She spoke some words, but I was too lost in my own torment to hear them.

'Stay.' I could not stop the plea. It shames me, even now, that I should have asked such a thing, but it was not born of some base carnal lust. I couldn't stand to be alone, that was all.

If she answered then I didn't hear it. I sank into a pit of darkness punctured by the screams of dying men. Edgehill. Naseby. They all blurred into one. I thought, as I vanished into that hole, that I felt a hand upon my head, stroking at my hair the way my Caro used to do, but I could not rightly say if it was Kate or whether I simply imagined it.

CHAPTER 7

I awoke far too early on the following morn, still drunk and with my head spinning like a top. For a moment I imagined myself back in Uxbridge, that the last few days had been nothing more than a dream. In Uxbridge, too, I had drunk myself to stupidity, driven by despair.

I floundered for the chamber pot and emptied my stomach into it. Beside the bed, a cup of weak ale sat waiting for me. I drank half and was promptly sick again. I saw my boots by the door, placed neatly side by side. My coat was folded on the floor.

'Kate?'

I was alone.

I was parched, too. I drank the rest of that cup of watery beer and emptied my bladder. Thus relieved I lay back and fell asleep once more.

The sun was high when I rose again. The day seemed already half done, and I had in mind that I would speak to the prison whore in Clink Street. I fumbled to remember her name. In my mind I had laid other plans, too. I groped for them. Milton's wife, Mary. I had wanted to speak with her. I could not remember why.

My head throbbed, though perhaps not as badly as I

deserved. I forced myself into my boots and stumbled down the stairs in search of something to eat. By the looks of the Bucket of Blood, I had not been alone in my excesses of the evening. A boy was sweeping up the straw from where the fights were held. Old stains of blood marked the floor beneath. There were perhaps half a dozen bodies still littering the commons, men sleeping off the night before, snoring where they had fallen. The Bucket of Blood that morning seemed a strange parody of the battlefields I had seen.

'There's not enough blood,' I muttered to myself. Nor severed limbs, nor wails and screams of the crippled and the dying.

'Falkland? William?'

I jumped and turned sharply, and then winced as my head regretted such vigorous action. Kate sat at the same table she and I had occupied the night before. She had an empty bowl in front of her. A second bowl sat waiting for me; it was salty and greasy, and whatever warmth it had once had was long fled. With eager gratitude I set upon it nevertheless, and devoured it with shameless greed.

'I am . . . sorry,' I said to her when I was done. I imagined, ashamed, that I had behaved poorly the night before, although wrapped in my own aftermath as I was, I could not be entirely sure. But her smile said enough. She did not reach to take my hand this morning, yet there was a warmth in her face. A sadness too, I thought.

'There is nothing to forgive,' she said.

'I fear I wept.' I knew it. *That* I had not forgotten.

'I have seen more men weep in my few months in London than in all my years in Devon.' Kate met my eyes for a moment. 'Many through sadness, but not all. I saw an old man who wept with joy when his son came home. A son he had not seen for three years and thought was dead.'

'And that is what Warbeck has you do?' I resolved there and then that I would not, in future, drink to excess when Miss Cain was near.

'It is.'

I could see no harm, yet I turned the notion over in my mind nevertheless. I could just about conceive of Cromwell asking that such a thing be done simply for the good of it, but I could not imagine Warbeck having any part if it did not serve his own purpose.

'Did you stay here all night?' I asked.

'No, Falkland. I could not. I might have curled up beside you and listened to you snore and saved myself a walk across the city, but it would be remembered. People would talk. Besides, it's not so far to the Inns of Court.' In that, at least, I knew she was right. Warbeck and I had passed them on the way to see John Milton.

'I'm glad.'

For a moment I thought the look she gave me to be strange, as though I had said something to hurt her. In truth I was glad simply because my memories of the previous night showed I could not trust myself to act as I should. I had been drunk, and that I could avoid, but it troubled me nonetheless.

'This is no place for a lady,' I said.

'I've seen worse.' Her smile returned. 'Besides, I make no claim to be a lady, Falkland. In London I can pretend to be whatever I like, but you know better. I am a farmer's daughter.'

'You're a farmer's daughter and I was a farmer's son, and you will find no better people in this country.' We laughed at that, and I finished my bowl of broth and called for a loaf of bread. It seemed Warbeck was paying for my accommodations and my sustenance, and I saw no reason not to make the most of it.

'Master Warbeck thinks you will abandon your task. Will you?'

'The woman I'm looking for, her name is Anne.' I looked away. 'I have to go to see someone who claims to have seen her taken, a prison whore.' I did not much believe in this story Milton had told. It seemed unlikely – more probable that the whore had seen something else entirely, or had made up her tale from new cloth on hearing there was a reward. I had seen that often enough. 'If I knew a way to do so, I would speak to Mary Milton without her husband's shadow looming between us. I think of all of them she perhaps knew Anne the best. I do not favour the notion that men still loyal to the King took Anne so they could threaten John Milton. It flatters him, but where is Anne herself in such a scheme?' I shook my head. Milton struck me as a peacock. Among the King's men, people like him strutted loud and brightly coloured, filled with orders and contempt in equal measure for anyone they imagined a lesser man. Milton wore no bright cloth, but he made up for his colours in words.

Cromwell would have me believe that his hopes for peace, and indeed the very fate of the nation, might hang on Anne's return. I found that I had little but scorn for such dramatic ideas. An arcane royalist plot to silence a single man seemed doubtful. The plight of Anne's sons, however, was another matter.

'Falkland.' Miss Cain leaned towards me a little. 'I will do what I can for you, whatever you choose.'

I wished I had some way to thank her. I would have embraced her for that kindness, done so as a friend and nothing more. 'Thank you,' I said.

'I have a notion,' she returned, 'that I may be able to help you with Lady Milton.'

I straightened. 'How?'

'Meet me at the Inns of Court when you're done with your prison whore and I'll show you.' She rose to leave; when I asked her to explain herself, she smiled coyly and told me I would have to wait and see, but that she had a plan. I will admit that, as I watched her go, I was intrigued enough that I almost followed. But I did not; I had other matters to attend to, or so I thought.

I filled my pockets with more bread and a little cheese and whispered a silent thanks to Warbeck's unknowing generosity. I walked away from the Bucket of Blood to the throng of Fleet Street and its plethora of printing presses. It remained as I had seen it with Warbeck: men hurried to and fro with great rolls of paper, with bundles of printed tracts and palimpsests, Dutch corantos, and even, now and then, newsbooks. I passed a small cart laden with bottles of ink and overheard a vigorous debate as to the price of it. Through the chaos I walked briskly, easing the stiffness from my legs and clearing the clouds from my head with fresh summer air – though in truth the air was already sharp with the smells of ink and paper, while the nearby stink of the Thames bloomed across the city in the rising heat.

I reached the London Bridge, always a constant bustle, filled along either side with its tiny shops and kiosks, with men and women selling everything from cabbages to cages of rats to bootlaces. Crossing it I felt as though I had traversed the border into some foreign land. I looked about me and saw at once that the southern part of the city was a poorer place. The King's palace and Parliament were on the northern bank of the Thames; following them were the great churches and the other palaces and grand houses of the lords of England. The courts of law and all the instruments of government had grown up around them, and wealth and grandeur around those in turn. The south had none of this. What the southern shore had was the Clink, the oldest prison in England.

Clink Street, where Warbeck had said I would find Miss Jane Hardwick, ran from the gates of the prison eastward along the shore of the Thames before turning south into Borough Market, where Anne had gone searching for ribbon. The market itself was a tousled bustle of jostling crowds, a din of hawkers, and rife, I imagined, with pickpockets. In my fragile state it reminded me more than anything of the clash and press of two blocks of pikemen coming together on a battlefield, and I was glad to force myself free of it. I found Clink Street easily enough, not far from the bridge; it was instantly clear that the houses around the prison were home to desperation and poverty and little else. They were falling down, or else had never properly been assembled, were tiny and leaning askew, propping one another up along narrow, dirt-covered streets. A few children played in the open, throwing sticks and handfuls of filth at one another, and at the mangy dogs snuffling through the refuse. An occasional shambling drunk staggered by, already oblivious to the world despite the hour. I passed a body lying by the side of the road, covered in mud, and could not tell whether the fellow was alive or dead; yet as I bent to inspect him, he jumped up and grabbed my hand and started to throttle me, filling the air with foul-breathed curses. He took me for a thief, I think, come to rob him, although of what I could not imagine. I threw him off easily enough, and he lurched away.

The commotion brought a few of the whores to their windows and, when they saw in their midst a stranger of some sort who might have coin in his purse, quickly drew them out to the street to crowd around me. I told them I was looking for Jane Hardwick, but it soon became clear that I would have nothing from these women without payment. I had no money, and so I gave them the cheese and bread I had taken from the Bucket of Blood to share among themselves, and offered myself to their tender guidance.

'I can take you to Miss Jane,' offered one, shrewder than the rest; and I, in my foolish naivety, allowed her to lead me away into some alley where she stopped and pressed herself against me. 'Call me Jane if you like, sir,' she said, and reached inside my coat. When I pushed her aside she cursed and swore, shrieking volleys of invective loud enough to rouse the dead from their nearby catacombs. I beat a hasty retreat, seeing I would get nothing more from these desperate women without an offer of coin. I had accomplished nothing, and so resolved instead to make my way to the Inns of Court and the far more welcome company of Miss Cain, when I heard another woman calling out to me.

'Here about that gentlewoman who was taken, is you, sir?'

A woman wearing nothing but a filthy shift stood in a

doorway at the foot of a narrow flight of steps. As I started towards her she hurried out, pulling the shift tight around herself, dancing her bare feet across the muck-strewn street. Her hands and arms were stained with dirt, and her hair was an unruly thatch. The left side of her face was swollen around an ugly bruise beneath her eye, a sad hazard of her profession. I knew soldiers who beat their whores now and then, and I had never understood it; but then I had never been one to seek solace and escape among the camp followers of the King's army.

She stopped in front of me.

'Miss Hardwick?' She seemed so small and frail. I immediately felt a pity for her. 'You know why I'm here?' I asked.

'Course.' She sniffed hard and then picked at her nose. 'I already told them others what I saw. I saw that woman you're looking for. Anne, isn't that her name? That's what the other men said, anyway. Saw her walking on towards the Clink. A carriage pulled up, right beside her, it did. Two men got out. She started away from them, quick like she was afraid. They grabbed her and took her off. That's what I saw.'

I looked past her to the house from which she had emerged. It struck me as odd that she would come out into the street to talk to me. She must have been sitting in her window looking out, and heard me asking after her. A stroke of fortune, indeed.

'The men from this carriage. You saw them?'

She tilted her head at me and stuck out her jaw, a gesture half triumph and half defiance. 'I did. One of them I saw clear. He wore plain clothes, much like those you wear yourself, and nothing to make him in any way distinct. But I knew his face. Long and narrow with hollow cheeks. He has a beard, black but streaked with a little grey. It came to a point and it was as long as his nose. He has an old scar that runs across his cheek too. His _left_ cheek,' she added, clearly pleased with herself. 'I seen him before. He goes about with that horror of a man John Ogle, locked up in Clink by the grace of God and Parliament for the safety of us all.' Miss Hardwick leaned back. She folded her arms and cocked her head. 'There it is. That's what I saw. Got a shilling for me, have you?'

'Not yet.' The name Ogle was familiar. A Lord Ogle had been one of the King's commanders. I had billeted with his company near Winchester briefly in '43 under Hopton. Yet something here felt awry. I could not shake the sense that Miss Hardwick had been both waiting for me and expecting me, but how could that possibly be so? 'The carriage. Where did it come from? The prison?'

She shook her head.

'What did it do after they took Anne?'

She shrugged. 'Just tore off quick.'

'Which way?'

'Down the street.' She looked at me as though I was mad. 'Where else? There's nothing but the Clink the other way.'

'Did the carriage have any arms drawn on the side? On its doors?'

She shrugged again. 'I saw what I saw, and that's all. Can I have my shilling now?'

'What did the men say? How did you know the woman was Anne?'

'I seen her in the market now and then, at the ribbon-seller's stall.' She hesitated. 'And I heard one of the men call her name.'

'Did you hear anything else?'

'No.' Such was her impatience to be away from me now that it had her almost dancing from foot to foot, strangely at odds with her initial desire that I should hear her story.

'How many men were there?'

'Two. They came and took her.'

'Two and a driver of the carriage, or did the driver come down to help his friend?'

She hesitated again. 'Two and the driver as well.'

'What did he look like? The driver?'

'Didn't see clear. Look, I told you what you want. Now I need to go. I don't work, I starve. It's not like it is for you rich folk. So give me my shilling.' She half lunged for the purse on my belt, though had she taken it she might have been sore disappointed at what it contained.

I caught her wrist, and her impatience and ire at my questions vanished at once, replaced by an animal fear.

'I don't have a shilling,' I said. 'Where were you when you saw all this?'

'Why you asking? I told you who did it. Now let me go!'

'Where were you?'

'Sitting at my window and watching the world pass by. Let me go or I scream!'

I let go of her, and she turned and fled. As she did I thought for a moment to run after her and corner her. Had I had money in my purse then I might have done so, and offered her a fat reward to spill a little truth for me, to tell me how she had known my purpose and why the eagerness to rush out and share with me what she had already told others; but as I had no shillings it would be left to me to beat it out of her with my fists, and I could not countenance that. Many men act as beasts, both on and off the field of battle, and we are none of us perfect, and all of us tested, and I had already failed such tests too often.

I turned my back on Clink Street, though I knew I must return, either with a full purse or with Warbeck and his threats. I forced my way again through the bustling crowds of Borough Market and London Bridge to the Earl of Lincoln's Inns, wondering if I would ever find Jane Hardwick again, or whether she would disappear, traceless. I did not much fancy the notion.

A fellow who knew his way about the Inns of Court gave me directions to Miss Cain's lodgings. I knocked on the door and was taken aback when a lady answered. I do not say that I did not recognise her, for I knew Kate as soon as I saw her face, but in all other ways she was much changed. She wore a dress of some fashion and a bonnet. The cloth was plain, but she had decorated it with ribbons in a way that I had seen was popular in London. I would not have mistaken her for a marchioness, but nor would I have taken her to be a farmer's daughter. My irritation at the women of Clink Street and at the clouds still lingering in my head from the night before were instantly forgotten.

'I am . . . speechless,' I said. I looked down at myself, still dressed in the same clothes Warbeck had given me the day before. I had slept in them. The plain truth was that I had no others.

'Take me with you to their house,' said Miss Cain, 'and tell me what questions you would have me ask. I will be a friend to this Mary Milton. I will console her. We will be ladies together . . .' She smirked.

'I need to speak with Milton's guest, Fowles. While I do, I would know if Anne had secrets she kept from her brother, but shared with his wife.' I looked her up and down. 'And you, Miss Cain, have been spending altogether too much time with the likes of Henry Warbeck. His guile has rubbed off on you.'

She drooped her eyes at me as we set off once more for Cripplegate, walking arm in arm, both of us a little stiff at our charade. 'You think I do not have guile of my own, Master Falkland?'

'All too much, I suspect.' I wished, fervently, that I possessed a change of clothes.

We returned to Cripplegate and the Milton house. I knocked on the door, and the younger of the two boys, Edward, answered. He appeared less than pleased to see me again, but he moved aside and allowed us entrance.

'I need to speak with your brother,' I said. 'And Master Fowles. Is he here?'

'I will call my uncle.'

'No need,' I said. I could already hear Milton and Fowles from the back of the house. Milton's voice was raised, berating Fowles for some slight, but he stopped abruptly as he heard me in the hall and came storming out, red-faced.

'You again? I thought we were done with you.'

'You'll be done with me when I have done as Cromwell has instructed,' I answered brusquely. 'I need to speak to Master Fowles.'

'Did you speak to the whore?'

'From Clink Street? Yes.' I faltered then, on the brink of telling him that I did not much like what I had heard, my

suspicions of her story, but that would not do. I fancied
Milton did not want to hear it, and if she had known I was
coming for her then she had surely heard it from someone
in this very house. 'I would like to know from those who
spoke to her what she said on the day Anne was taken.' I
moved aside to allow Kate to present herself. 'This is Miss
Cain. I hope you don't mind that I have brought a guest.'

'I can't imagine you gave my minding a moment's
thought before you brought her here, whoever she is.'
Milton bowed sharply to Kate. I half expected, from the look
he gave, for him to say something unforgivable. Indeed I'm
quite certain it crossed his mind, but at the last he thought
better of it. 'You come to us at an awkward time, Miss Cain.'
He ushered us – I could almost say pushed us – into the
front parlour, calling for his wife. Mary, when she attended
us, looked pained. She offered her hand.

'You are well, I hope,' I said to her.

'As well as any woman in her condition,' snapped Milton.
'Do try not to fatigue her. Fowles!' He strode away towards
the back of the house. 'Fowles! Cromwell's man has come to
take you away!'

'It's hard this far along,' Kate said to Mary. I looked at her
in some surprise, and she met my look with one of her own,
amused and little pitying, perhaps.

'I had not imagined you as midwife, Miss Cain,' I said.

She ignored me and went to Mary's side. 'Do you have a
name for the child?'

'John if a boy.' Mary glanced about as if looking for
Milton to return. She hesitated, then spoke again. 'Anne
for a girl.'

A quiet fell upon us. We sat all together in awkward

silence until Milton returned. Fowles followed after, and I have rarely seen a man with such a nervous look, like deer spooked and ready to run at the drop of a pin. The curse of living with John Milton, I supposed. Did he have nowhere else to stay?

Miss Cain took Mary by the hand. 'Let us leave these men to their talk. We shall speak of lighter things.' Mary nodded, and I thought her grateful for an excuse to leave, though Milton looked far from pleased.

'I have spoken to Miss Hardwick of Clink Street,' I said, my words quick and harsh before Milton could object to his wife's escape. 'Master Fowles, I will admit some qualms about what I have heard. I need to know if what she told you is the same as she told me.'

'*I* already told you,' snapped Milton. 'She saw Anne bundled into a carriage. If you do not have the wit now to look for the villains who took her, I cannot imagine what use you will be to my sister!'

'I have a name,' I said. 'Of someone who might have been a part of it.'

Silence filled the parlour. I will admit I savoured the moment of watching Milton struck dumb. I settled more comfortably into my chair. Mary and Miss Cain had made good their exit. I would take my time now, and allow Kate to ease her way into Mary Milton's confidence.

'A name?' whispered Milton. 'Who?' Despite my dislike of the man, I could not help but soften to the naked hope I saw on his face.

'I will come to that. But first I wish to apologise, sir. No doubt many matters of great concern weigh heavily on your shoulders, of which the disappearance of your sister is surely the greatest. I have not shown the tolerance that your burden deserves.' It pained me to fawn so. I took a deep breath and settled my eyes on Fowles.

'*Abduction*, Falkland,' Milton spat. 'My sister did not disappear like some fractious spirit. She was not wafted into the sky on a breeze like so much smoke. She was foully taken from the street and bundled screaming into a carriage!'

'Screaming?' I watched Fowles steadily and wished Milton could be quiet so the man might speak for himself. Fowles' demeanour suggested he very much wished to be elsewhere, and thus I was quite determined not to let him escape until I had found out what unsettled him so. 'Who was among the party who scoured Borough Market?'

Milton stamped his foot. 'We have already *told* you, Falkland! Fowles here and my nephew John went to look for her. When there was no trace, Fowles here raised a company of men to search.'

I cocked my head to Fowles.

'So it was,' he shrugged.

'And your party found no trace of Anne?'

'Only the whore.'

'Jane Hardwick of Clink Street.' I nodded. 'Who found her, exactly?'

Fowles shrugged again. 'One of the men. I don't know his name.'

'You didn't know these men?'

'No.' Fowles frowned. 'Why?'

'But one of them brought her to you. Did you pay them?'

'Tuppence each for their time. Sixpence if they found trace of her.'

I paused at this. 'And Miss Hardwick. Was she known to these men?'

Fowles hesitated. I could see him pondering the direction of my questioning. 'I . . . do not know one way or another.'

'Did you speak to her directly?'

'Of course they did,' snapped Milton. 'Do you take us for fools?'

'What did Hardwick say?'

'That she had seen my sister picked up like some sack of cabbages and bundled into the back of a carriage!' Milton jumped to his feet. 'We have *told* you this, Master Falkland! Do you not believe us? Have you not heard the same from the whore herself? Do you think us all a part of some conspiracy of deceit standing to hide my sister from my own self? Perhaps we have her tied in the cellar, is that what you wonder?'

'Did Miss Hardwick mention anyone by name, Master Fowles?'

He licked his lips as he considered this. 'No.'

'Who, Falkland?' Milton could barely keep himself in his chair. I drew a careful breath and let a little silence pass between us.

'Do you perhaps have something with which I might wet my throat? I find myself a little parched.' It passed more time for Kate.

Milton snapped and yelled. Edward Phillips came hurrying in, and as the door swung wide I caught another glimpse of Anne's daughter, lurking in the hallway with her wide, startled eyes. They had both been outside with their ears pressed to the wall, I fancied. I met Edward's eye, but he looked more scared than guilty.

Milton sent him away. After a minute Edward returned with a cup of watered wine for me and nothing for the others. I doubted Milton could have made his intention clearer to be swiftly rid of me, short of drawing a blade and running me through. I shook my head and met his eye.

'I have met more courteous greetings from Parliament's pikemen. Courageous, honest men, I don't doubt.'

Milton glowered and said nothing. I turned to Fowles.

'It was you, wasn't it?' I let the question linger in the air. I meant that it was him who had spoken to Miss Hardwick, but for a moment I caught a look on his face of absolute shock. I had seen it before, on the face of a man who stood beside me as a musket ball came from nowhere and struck him in the chest. We had, we thought, been alone. The musket had been a hundred yards from us, hidden in a wood. We flushed him out once we knew he was there and put an end to him, but I could never quite forget the look of surprise on the soldier's face beside me. White with shock and horror. He was dead before he fell off his horse. Fowles recovered himself quickly, but I would not forget what I had seen there.

'I mean that you were the one who spoke to the whore,' I said.

'Young John and I spoke with her together, sir.'

'What did she say?'

Milton jumped to his feet. 'That she saw—'

I had had enough. I rose to face him down and bellowed in his face. 'Sir, I do not ask what you *think* she said. I ask the gentlemen who spoke with her to relate, to *me*, the *exact* words spoken. I am quite certain, sir, that no mention was made of sacks and cabbages.'

He was a slight man, John Milton, and I have always been broad, yet he met me face to face and eye to eye. Had we each carried a sabre at our sides, I could not say for sure that one of us might not have drawn a blade, and a fine end to Cromwell's order that would have been. I would not, however, back down, for I could not see what offence I might possibly have given save that I had once fought for the King. Milton, it seemed, was equally determined. Perhaps we might have stood there for the entire rest of the day, staring one another down, had not Peter Fowles quietly spoken between us.

'Let it be, John. Cromwell has sent this man. Let him ask his questions. I will answer you, Falkland, as best I can. I found men and organised the search. I ordered that we would each cover different parts of the market and the streets surrounding it. Young John and I took the roads we thought mostly likely, leading back to the Bridge and across the river. I instructed the others to return to the centre of the market after a certain time. When we concluded our own search, several of the men I had promised to pay were waiting for us with this woman. They told us she had seen Anne. I asked her for her name and she gave it. Then I asked how she knew Anne, and she replied that her brother's wife's sister sells ribbon in the Borough Market, and that Anne Agar often frequented their stall. I asked her what she'd seen. She told me Anne had been walking on Clink Street towards the prison when a carriage had pulled up and two men had come out. They had accosted her, and one had spoken her name. She heard Anne cry out, and saw her take a few steps away as if about to run, but the two men took hold of her and grappled her into the carriage. The doors closed and they all hurried away at some speed.'

I watched Fowles closely as he spoke. Something about this story did not ring true. I was glad, then, that I had been to Clink Street that day.

'She thought she knew one of the men, that she had seen him about elsewhere,' he finished, 'but she could not place him at first nor give a name.'

'Perhaps you might help with that, Master Falkland,' snipped Milton.

'Clink Street is hardly on the way back to Cripplegate,' I said. 'It goes nowhere except from the market to the prison. Why would Anne be there?'

Fowles shrugged. 'I do not know.'

'Would she have any reason to visit the prison?' I turned to Milton, who bared his teeth.

'Perhaps, Falkland, some royalist bastards lured her with false stories of her poor husband Thomas, locked up inside?'

'With not a word to you before she disappeared?' I will admit to baiting Milton now, prolonging our discourse to give Miss Cain as much time with Mary as I could.

'Abducted, Falkland. Taken. *Kidnapped*. Removed against her will! When will you grasp this simple difference, man?'

'When I have seen or heard evidence to convince me,' I snapped back. 'If your sister said nothing at the time, then how do you know that Anne was *lured* there? Were there letters? Demands? Did she show them to you?'

'Why else would she go?' thundered Milton. 'What other possible reason can be conceived?'

'Falkland!' Fowles raised his voice for the first time. 'The whore gave a good description of one of the men she saw, the one she thought to have seen elsewhere. She said she knew his face. She said he had a long and narrow visage with hollow cheeks, and that his beard was black but streaked with a little grey. It came to a point and was as long as his nose, and he had an old scar that ran across his cheek.'

'Did she say which cheek?' I asked. This was, I thought, a curiously exact description, and remarkably similar to the one I had already heard.

'The left cheek. It took a little patience and, ah, encouragement, but though she did not know the man's name, she told us eventually that she had seen him before, several times, going in and out of the prison. She told us that she had herself been inside at times . . . This, sir, is when we determined that she was a prison whore.'

'But she didn't give you a name?'

'No.'

'She did to me,' I said. 'John Ogle.'

The name had meant nothing to me before, and it meant no more now, but it clearly meant a great deal to Milton. He positively flew out of his chair, and his hands clenched as if in desperate need of some throat to throttle. 'John Ogle? Cousin to Lord William Ogle? The man who held Winchester for the King for three years and refused all terms of surrender?' Milton's voice was murderous. 'Do you see now, Falkland? A King's man through and through, and one who will stop at nothing. *He* is behind this.'

My heart sank. I had indeed heard of Lord Ogle of Winchester, though only from a distance. I couldn't imagine that he would deign to speak to me beyond berating me for my cowardice in taking Cromwell's shilling. I would need to find this man with the scar on his face, then. Something in his description unsettled me, although I could not say what it was. A familiarity, perhaps? Had I met this man before in some soldier's camp? I did not think that I had, and yet . . .

'Fowles,' I said. 'This man with the scar. Do you have any notion who he is?'

Fowles shook his head.

'But you have not heard any word from this John Ogle? No threats, demands, no menaces, not even hints?'

'I dare say he bides his time,' snarled Milton, 'waiting for the King's terms to reach Parliament.' He came to stand before me again, but this time there was no confrontation in him. We were sudden allies, side by side, brothers about to enter battle together. It disconcerted me how violently the man's passions might shift. For a moment Milton closed his eyes as if offering a prayer. 'Falkland, dear Oliver has sent you. Find this man and I will give you every assistance at my disposal in questioning him. I will do what I can to ensure that this ogre of an Ogle will see you!'

'He is imprisoned in Clink, Milton. Consider him already found.' I turned to Fowles. 'I have seen Miss Hardwick's house. From the manner in which she related her tale, Anne must have had her back to her. And Anne is hardly an uncommon name. Did she tell you anything more of what was said?'

Fowles shook his head. 'She said only that they called her by her name. Anne Milton.'

I frowned, deep furrows creasing above my eyes. My head was beginning to hurt again, an unfortunate conse-uence of the previous evening.

'Master Milton, you told me your sister believes her husband is still alive. That she is searching for him.'

'She hopes, Falkland.'

'Then she still carries Thomas's name, does she not?' I could not make sense of it. Why would these men call her by her maiden name? It was almost as if they were drawing an arrow direct to Milton himself, as clear as could be. 'Fowles, who gave these men their sixpence? Did you? Because they had found you some manner of evidence?'

Fowles nodded. I wondered if perhaps the entire story was a fabrication, something made up for a sixpence, but it was too complete, too replete with detail to have been conjured there and then by a prison whore; yet something about it rang false. That very detail, precisely where it was needed; and I found myself then quite certain that Miss Hardwick had not told me all there was to know. She had made a story for John Phillips and Peter Fowles, and had trotted it out for me as well, almost the same words. What's more, she had all but sought me out to do so, only this time she had given me a name as well.

Someone had put her up to it.

'I thank you for your time.' I fixed Milton with a look. 'I will do what I can to find the man who took your sister. If you hear word from Ogle or any other, you know where to find me.' I rose and called out: 'Miss Cain!'

CHAPTER 8

Milton, I thought, could not have been more pleased to
see the back of me; yet we had gone but three steps
along the street when Miss Cain seized my arm and we
stopped. She pulled me away from any eyes that might watch
us from the windows and dragged me into one of the narrow
alleys that tunnelled between the houses.

'I need Warbeck,' I began. 'We need this woman from
Clink Street—'

'Never mind that.' Kate pulled me deeper into the gloom.
The adjoining rooftops touched over our heads, blocking
out the sky and sinking us into twilight. The street was
almost empty, and I did not see why, as Kate dragged me to
where no one would see us, we could not simply stroll our
way towards Newgate and talk as we walked.

'Anne has a secret,' Kate whispered. 'She hides it from
her brother and from her sons, but not from Mary.'

'What secret?'

'Mary doesn't know exactly, but Anne not long ago began
to make trips alone when Master Milton was out of the
house. Fleet Street, Mary says, for she returns with the smell
of the presses on her. And Falkland, if I wished to silence
John Milton with blackmail, I would certainly not take his

sister, I would take his wife, and I would not need to hold her against her will. I have learned more of John Milton in this last half-hour than I care to . . .'

For a moment I stopped hearing what Kate was saying. I will confess that I had, in part, begun to believe Milton's story of a conspiracy among the King's supporters to silence him, or at least that Anne had been taken against her will. The story of the whore of Clink Street, even if it was nothing more than a misdirection, offered almost no other explanation. And yet . . . if Milton *was* to be silenced, why his sister indeed? Why not his wife?

'Falkland!' Kate poked me.

'Sorry.'

'Mary and Anne spoke about men and suchlike more, I think, than Milton would like to hear. There are letters in Anne's room. Mary confessed to having seen them there. She will not say it, but I think Anne has a secret admirer!'

A secret admirer, an overbearing brother, a husband missing for four years now? Perhaps these letters would provide a quick and sudden end to the mystery. I could not, however, imagine Milton permitting me to see them. 'I fear I cannot simply ask for them. Does Milton know they exist?'

'No.' .

'Then I suppose we must tell him, and let him see for himself whatever it is they contain.'

Miss Cain shook her head with some force. 'No! Please, Falkland! Poor Mary lives in terror of his wrath. He will berate her horribly, both for prying into his sister's affairs and for not telling him sooner, I fear.'

'But if Anne has an admirer—'

'I left a ribbon behind.'

I rolled my eyes. Miss Cain drew me further along the alley to where it opened onto the patch of common ground behind the Milton house. Three other houses separated the end of our alley from Milton's back door. If he came out to his yard to feed his chickens, he would see us spying on him.

'I'm going to go back and ask if I might retrieve it,' whispered Miss Cain. 'When I do, I'll ask Mary if I might see the letters, or at least see into Anne's room . . .'

I shook my head. 'Milton won't allow it.'

'He won't know anything about it! Falkland, Mary doesn't show it in front of her husband, but Anne was dear to her, very dear. She weeps when there is no one to see. I'll tell her that it might help you to find her.' She pointed. 'Do you see the chicken shed?'

I did. It butted directly onto the back of the Milton house.

'Anne's room is above it. I'll ask Mary if I may take the letters and bring them to you. If she declines, I'll open the window to let in the air and then leave it ajar. When Mary and I leave, you can slip in and look at them yourself. None of them will ever know!'

I confess that I did not approve of this plan. I did not like the notion of slipping into John Milton's house like some common thief; but more, I did not like the notion of Miss Cain acting the part of an intelligencer. I saw how bright her eyes had become, how eager she was, but I had put her in harm's way once before, even though I had not meant to do so. I would not again. I shook my head.

'I shouldn't have brought you here, Kate.'

My words betrayed me with their lack of conviction.

'You must agree to my plan, William Falkland,' she tipped

her head in a most coquettish way. She was, I suddenly understood, toying with me. 'Otherwise I shall steal the letters myself.'

'Kate!'

'You told me you believed Anne to have secrets of her own, and that this notion of some plot by the King's supporters to silence Master Milton was a "phantom of his self-importance". I have found you a secret, Falkland. Do you not want it?'

I did not remember saying such a thing, but it did not surprise me to hear that I had. Now I had heard the testimony of Miss Hardwick I was no longer so certain that Milton was wrong, but I admit I still railed against it. It would have pleased me greatly to show his conspiracy to be a nonsense of his own imagining; and yet I still did not like the thought of forcing my way into another man's house. Cromwell had sent me to find answers in any way I could, but I had no doubt that a sufficiently strident complaint would see me returned to Newgate.

I laughed bitterly. Perhaps this time it would be the Clink.

'Well?' Miss Cain tapped her foot. I mulled over her proposal a while longer, hoping to conjure some better course of action, but found I could not. Nor would I entertain Miss Cain herself becoming a thief.

'Go, then,' I said, and felt a heaviness inside me. I went with her back through the alley as far as the street, and then left Kate to continue alone while I returned to the common ground. The geese I had seen on the previous day eyed me from across clumpy grass, but they were on the far side close to the old London wall and I was able to keep distant enough that they did not set upon me as a gaggle, full of hooting and honking to rouse everyone to their windows. The chicken shed, too, was largely empty, the birds roaming the grass. I climbed easily enough and sat there with my back against the wall of John Milton's house, one window to either side of me.

There I waited. With every heartbeat I found I liked this plan less. Were anyone to come out onto the grass and see me here, I would have more than a little difficulty explaining myself. It struck me as I paused there, tense as if ready for a battle, how Kate had changed since Crediton. I could not imagine the Miss Cain I had known in Devon becoming so bold. Not that she had lacked for strength when I had known her before, but she had had an army camped at her door and had been afraid. In London the war was far away. She had, it seemed, shed that fear.

Beside me, a few meagre feet from my head, a window rattled. I had become so lost in my wonderings that I almost let out a startled gasp. I heard Kate say 'It's so stuffy in here,' and it seemed as though she was right beside me. The window opened and her head came briefly through. She caught me a glance and then withdrew. 'I'm sure all will end well,' she said. I supposed she must be talking with Mary. 'Master Falkland was chosen by Cromwell himself, and not for the first time. He is a magnificent intelligencer. I cannot think of anyone better.'

My head grew, I think, a touch larger. I will admit to a little pride.

'The letters are gone.' The second voice was Mary. 'They were on the dresser.'

A pause. 'Does anything seem strange to you?' Kate again.

'I don't know what you mean. Come, we must go. John will be so angry if he finds us in here. Anne must have hidden them somewhere. I'm sorry.'

'Does . . . does anyone come in here now that Anne has disappeared?'

'No! John absolutely forbids it. Everything is to be kept exactly as she left it. Untouched. Please, let us go. There's nothing here.'

The window beside me drew almost but not quite closed. I thought I heard footsteps and then the loud shutting of a door. I waited a while longer, counted thirty heartbeats, and then shifted and slowly peered through the tiny panes. Anne Agar's room was empty. I opened the window again, slow and quiet, stepped over the sill and slipped inside.

A bed stood pressed between the two windows. Against the far wall was a dresser and a simple dark-stained wooden desk with drawers to either side, a mirror on top and a chair tidily before it. Next to the door was a wardrobe. The bed was neatly made. It was a simple room, a little dusty. Clearly no one had lived here for weeks.

I walked cautiously to the dresser, wary of creaking boards. A wooden box lay on top of it, open. It was empty, but I thought recently so. The corners inside were thick with old dust, but the middle was clean as though something had sat there until quite recently, though I couldn't say whether what had gone from the box had been taken before Anne had gone missing or after. I carefully opened each dresser drawer and groped inside. In one I found paper and quills and a pot of ink. In another neat bundles of ribbons, folded lace collars and scarves and kerchiefs. There was nothing hidden among them; I put them back as best I could. The dust on the desk had been disturbed, perhaps by Mary and Miss Cain or perhaps by some other. I couldn't tell.

One of the lace collars caught my eye. I had taken it from near the bottom. It was folded neatly enough, but it had been folded some other way before. There were creases set into it as though it had been sat that other way for many months. The current folds showed no creases at all.

I tiptoed to the bed and sank to my knees to peer underneath, hoping I might find a hidden box, but there was nothing; yet as I turned to rise something caught my eye under the dresser. I crawled across the floor and reached underneath to draw it out. It was a letter, half caught between the boards. It was strangely short, and seemed to have been written in a hurry.

Dear Lady Anne,

    Your letter was very welcome to me. Where I find myself, I believe Thomas was here not long before. I have word that Hopton's cavalry are close. Though I cannot be certain, I believe he is with them. The Lord fill our souls with thankfulness, that our mouths may fill with His Praises; and may He grant we never forget His goodness to us. These things strengthen our love for Him and our faith against more difficult times. Before Thomas and I face one another on the field of battle, I will endeavour on your behalf to send word to him. The lord bless you. I rest your most humble servant.

    Francis Lovelace

It was dated April 1643. Thomas Agar had disappeared from

the King's army late in 1642. Six months later and Anne had had someone looking for him? Yet all this had happened more than three years ago. I struggled to imagine how it mattered now.

I pocketed the letter and went to the wardrobe. The door creaked a little as I opened it. Inside were folded dresses and two thick cloaks. I ran my hands underneath them in case something lay hidden there, but found nothing. As quietly as I could manage, I crept to the window and eased back outside, closed it behind me and jumped down from the chicken shed. I felt oddly invigorated. Emboldened. Roused, perhaps, by the danger of discovery and the knowledge that I had made my escape unseen. In the alley where Miss Cain had first put forward her proposition, she was waiting for me.

'Did you find your ribbon?' I asked. Perhaps I sounded a little brusque, for she turned away from me.

'The letters were gone.' She sounded disheartened.

'No. Not all.' I brandished the one from under the dresser and gave it to her, forgetting for a moment that the Kate I remembered could not properly read; yet she took it from me, and screwed up her face and spoke the words aloud, slow and a little halting.

'Who is this Francis Lovelace?'

A broad smile spread across my face. 'I have not the first idea. But I'll wager Milton does.'

I walked briskly and banged on Milton's door. This time Milton himself answered. He stared at me in disbelief. 'Dear Heaven, man! Have you and your yellow blackbird boots now lost a ribbon too?'

I took a step closer to him, careful to keep my tone calm

and even, as though cooing to a newly broken mare who might easily spook and shy away. 'I understand, sir, that I was not welcome from the very moment you knew my purpose. But you must understand this: that I answer to Oliver Cromwell, not to you.' I did not like those words, even as I said them.

'You have no—'

I cut him off. 'Cromwell currently invests a siege upon Oxford. He is occupied. You have me, sir, and that is all. You tell me Anne had no secrets, yet you cannot tell me what purpose she might have had in visiting Clink Prison. What do you know of the letters your sister kept on her dresser?'

'What letters?'

'You do not know of them? Has anyone been into Anne's room since she disappear— since she was taken?'

'Certainly not.'

'Not even you?'

'Well . . . I . . .'

'I believe there to be a box of letters on her dresser. The box remains but the letters are gone. Who took them?' There was a cruelty, I will admit, to my questioning. I gave him no time to answer or to marshal his thoughts. I took some pleasure in John Milton's discomfort.

'What box?' he demanded.

'Who is Francis Lovelace, and why does he write to your sister?'

I had expected his bewilderment to continue, but instead he bellowed into the house. 'Fowles! John! Mary!' When he turned back, his face was twisted like a savage dog. He pushed me squarely in the chest, off from his doorstep and into the street. 'How dare you! Bad enough that Cromwell sends one of the King's own lickspittlers to be inquisitor among the very same King's supporters, oh yes, cosy as birds in a pie, but I can only wonder how he was not aware of the arrogance and insolence you carry, like all your fey cavalier kind. How dare you come to my door and suggest my sister – my sister who is married and has been searching for her husband ceaselessly for four long years – has carried on some manner of illicit correspondence? Do you mean now to suggest that she was gone to the Clink in search of some salacious tryst? Take your licentious slurs and be gone! I thank you for your information. I will see to the odious John Ogle myself. Good day to you.'

He turned as Peter Fowles came running to the door. 'Fowles, see this royalist turd away. Encourage him with as much force as you wish never again to darken this street with his libelling presence.' Milton turned his back. Not for the first time I found my hand twitching for the sabre I once carried.

'Sir!' I could not let him speak so. 'You go too far!'

'I?' He turned. For a moment the change in his face led me to think that he knew he had overstepped every bound of decency and was ready to make amends; but I could not have been more wrong. His voice dropped low and deadly. '*I* go too far? That woman you brought! She went into Anne's room, didn't she? That brazen wh—'

I did not let him finish, but seized him by the collar, one great hand wrapped around his neck. I strangled that word dead in his gullet. I would not have him say such a thing, not of Miss Cain.

'Be very careful, Master Milton, of what words you

choose to say. If you despise me because I was once a King's man, consider that I rode north with his army seven years ago to face the Scots. Consider that I have fought for my King for all this time, and have lost more than won, and that I am yet still alive, still here. I have had fair practice with sabre, pike and musket. Your sister is gone less than a month. I have not seen my family for four years, and I do not yet know what has become of them. I know that pain, John Milton, and I will find your sister if I can, and you may slur me all you wish as I do. But speak one word against Miss Cain and I will call you for it and have your head, and I will not care one whit if that must mean Newgate and Tyburn will follow.'

Fowles, I saw, looked distinctly uncomfortable, as though he knew he must do something but could not see what. If I had not guessed it before, I knew with certainty now that he had been a soldier from the way he held himself faced with violence to be had. He'd seen a fair share of the fighting, I thought.

I released my grip. 'Cast your aspersions elsewhere, John Milton, for it was I who went into Anne's room.'

Milton seemed to consider this for a moment. Then, without further word, he turned his back on me and returned to his house. Fowles and I were left alone in the street.

'There is no need,' I told him. 'I will escort myself away.'

'What's this about letters?' he asked.

'Milton will tell you, I have no doubt. I believe Anne Agar may once have had an admirer.' I watched him as I spoke. 'His name was Francis Lovelace. Is it familiar to you?'

Fowles considered this a moment, and then shook his head. 'No, sir, it is not.'

'Ah well. I'd hazard that it is to John Milton. The truth will out in the end. It always does.' I nodded. 'Good day, sir. I apologise for the disturbance.'

'Good day, Master Falkland.' Fowles nodded in return; but as he turned away I caught him.

'One more question, Master Fowles. I hear there was an intrusion into the Milton house some months ago. Is that so?'

Fowles nodded. 'Something to do with another writer of palimpsests, I believe.' He shrugged. 'I had not been in London long, and had barely made the Miltons' acquaintance at the time.' He turned away, marching quickly to Milton's door. I watched him go. He had sounded very certain that he knew no one called Francis Lovelace. He had looked me in the eye, firm and steady, and I was quite sure that he was lying.

CHAPTER 9

'Why would he lie?' Kate walked beside me with such a spring in her step one might have thought she had been made a princess. She was, in every way, like a cat who had stolen a feast of thick Cornish cream.

'I need to find who this Francis Lovelace was.' I needed to see Jane Hardwick again too, and, most of all, the scar-faced man she had seen, if he truly existed. Perhaps Warbeck might help me there. This John Ogle in Clink Prison would unlikely give me an audience, despite our once-common allegiances. Warbeck, I rather thought, would have ways and means of wrangling some cooperation.

'Who do you think took the letters?' Kate asked.

'Anne might have taken them herself.' I had to admit that it was possible. 'But I think someone searched Anne's room. Whether that was one of the same men Miss Hardwick saw in Clink Street, whether the search came before or after Anne was taken, these things I cannot tell.' I assumed, I realised, that the searcher was a man. Perhaps I was mistaken, but the poorly folded collar led me to believe it so. Someone had gone through all of Anne's belongings as I had done, looking for something, and they had not covered their tracks as well as perhaps they supposed. I do not say that women make for better thieves, but I do say that they are tidier and more practised in the folding of garments. In that regard, a woman would have covered her tracks with greater precision. I frowned most fiercely. 'I find I must wonder, Miss Cain, whether the previous intrusion upon the Milton house was indeed a rival polemicist, as Master Fowles implies.'

We walked past Newgate Prison yet again and out through the city gate. Miss Cain regarded it with a shiver of fascination.

'This is where they held you?' she asked.

'Not in the gate itself,' I replied. 'But in the new building on the south side.' I shuddered to remember those days. I had thought the world was done with me.

'What was it like?'

'Death,' I told her. For most of those I had known there, death it had been. I remembered the despair. It was a raw thing, torn open again these last few months as I sought my family to no avail. 'There were some, those who had money, who were able to buy themselves better accommodations. I could not say what it was like for them. My world in there was a filthy cell and a pot to piss in, shared with three other men who came and went as each was taken to the gallows. And leg irons.' I shivered to imagine the stink of the place, but found I could not remember it. It is strange how we become accustomed to what is around us, no matter how vile.

We walked together, and I felt the world subtly changed. Miss Cain had re-entered my life less than a day before, and already I did not feel the weight of my burdens so strongly. Warbeck had known, I suppose, that Milton would despise me for having fought for the King, and that he would rile me, and that I would rebel against what Cromwell wanted. It was already perfectly clear that Warbeck had put Miss Cain in my path as a means of keeping me set to my task. I wondered whether Kate was aware of her part in this; but I also found I did not much care.

'Warbeck is using you to keep me here.' I said it without reproach. I could not be angry with her, nor even with Warbeck, cold and cynical as he was. From a man such as him it was simply what I had come to expect. I was glad to see her again, that was all that mattered. I felt in her a sense of something worthwhile, something I had sorely lacked for too long.

We crossed the little bridge over the Fleet river and dived into the throng of Fleet Street. I did not remember there being so many printing presses when I had come this way with Caro's father. Or perhaps I simply hadn't understood them, what they were and what they were for, and the power they might wield. I knew better now. One of these, I supposed, printed Milton's own polemics. I wondered: did they vie for his custom?

'He told me you were coming to London,' she said after a time. 'He said I must look after you. That Cromwell had summoned you once again and you'd likely not be willing.'

'I was not,' I agreed.

'And now?'

'Warbeck would have me hope again. It is a fragile thing, but it exists. Can you find my family, Miss Cain, among your letters and records?'

She didn't answer at first. At least, then, she was honest. I would not have believed her if she had said that she could.

'Not if they're in Oxford,' she said at last. 'If your son

was joined to the New Model Army then perhaps, in time, I might uncover him.' She sounded doubtful even so.

'In time?'

'I do not think it likely, Falkland. I am sorry.'

'No matter. I did not think it likely either. What about this Francis Lovelace?'

She clasped my arm. 'Falkland, it's not like that. I don't remember seeing the name. If you could tell me what company he was with then perhaps there would be a chance. Without that . . . I would not know where to begin.'

I had thought as much. Warbeck's promises – no, *Cromwell's* promises – were worth nothing.

I stopped. Around us men and carts hurried back and forth. Everywhere I looked were bundles of printed paper, pamphlets, palimpsests, polemics, opinions, declarations, corantos. Strident voices cried them out. I had seen a printing press once before, tucked away like an unwanted secret, but here they were open for all to see. A score of them at least, perhaps even twice that number. For a moment I found myself drawn back to Milton's study with its piles of papers, but what I remembered most were his words of soaring poetry. They had touched me. They left me wondering what it would be like to see the man speak them aloud, what an orator he might be, the inspiration he perhaps brought to those who were not skewered by his prose. It was a shame. For all my dislike, it would have pleased me to hear him in full strident swing. To simply listen, instead of finding myself forced into a duel of verbal combat.

'Would you like to act the part of intelligencer again, Miss Cain?' I asked. Together we made our way along the street of presses, moving from one to the next, Miss Cain taking the left side and myself the right. The din was such that I had to shout to make myself heard over the cries and calls and the clacking racket of the machines. I tried to ask whether anyone had seen Anne Agar come to one of the presses, but my questions were barely heard. I asked of Milton instead, and was directed to the press that had printed his *Poems,* where a robust and energetic woman sat setting plates for her machine. It was a blessing to be where the noise was merely intrusive and not overbearing. I was barely through the door, however, when the woman swept upon me from where she sat, and took my hand and shook it. She sat me down.

'Ruth Raworth.' She smiled brightly. 'I haven't seen you before. You one of Moseley's?'

'I . . .' I barely had a chance to reply before she backed away and shook her head.

'No, you're not. I do apologise. Well now, then, what can I do for you, Master . . .'

'Falkland,' I told her. 'William Falkland.'

'And you have some words for me, Master Falkland?'

'I . . . No, I am inquiring as to whether you know John Milton's sister, Anne.'

'I certainly know *of* John Milton. But not of any Anne. Is there any reason I should?'

'No. She would be—'

I was interrupted as the door burst open. A young lad rushed inside with a roll of papers. He paid no heed to me at all, but thrust them into Miss Raworth's hands. 'Master Humphrey says two hundred for first light. What should I say?'

'Tell him I'll take a strap to him!'

The boy started to nod and leave.

'She would use her married name,' I said. 'Anne Agar.'

But for now, it seemed, I had become invisible. Miss Raworth took the papers and turned her back, spreading them out across the floor and beginning to rearrange them. The lad darted to the door, but without so much as turning to look at him Miss Raworth held up a hand. 'Wait, you.'

'Miss! I have three others to—'

'Wait!'

The boy paused in the door, dancing from foot to foot in his impatience. He glanced at me and grinned. 'Mister Milton's sister,' he said. 'I heard she went missing.' His grin turned to a leer. 'Or that perhaps she ran away.'

'Yes! Did you know—'

Raworth jumped up. She seized a bundle of pamphlets already fastened in twine and tossed them to the lad in the doorway. 'Here. You can take these back with you. And tell Moseley that if he wants two hundred copies at St Paul's for daybreak then he'd best send you back with what he already owes me.'

'Did you know Milton's sister?' I asked. The lad leaped from the doorway and dashed into the street. I ran after him. 'Do you . . .'

He was gone.

'And you, Miss Raworth?' I asked upon my return.

'Not that I know. Mind you, there's all sorts come and go, and not everyone uses their real name. Talk to Humphrey Moseley in his bookshop at Saint Paul's. He'll tell you everything you want to know about Milton, I dare say.'

'It's his sister I'm trying to find.'

'Don't know her.' The woman was back among her papers, seeing to their arrangement and now scanning each one closely. My presence seemed not to bother her – if I chose to stand and watch then that was my own peculiar business.

'Who was that boy?' I asked her.

'One of Moseley's. Don't know his name.' She paused and looked up for a moment. 'Sorry. Falkland, was it? I'm afraid I'm desperately busy. I don't think I can help you.'

'Milton's sister. Anne Agar. She used to come and see someone on Fleet Street. A printer, I think.'

'Never heard of her.'

I left Miss Raworth to her work and went back outside. Eventually I located Miss Cain among the throng and drew her aside, and found that her luck had been no better than mine. I told her, as I walked her away from Fleet Street, of the conversation I'd had. I would make a trip to Saint Paul's, I thought, to seek out this lad and question him.

We had reached the gates to the Earl of Lincoln's Inn. Beyond, across a great square, stood the chapel and hall, surrounded by residences for the lawyers and barristers, the benchers and readers. Somewhere here, I knew, was a library. It seemed an unlikely place for a farmer's daughter.

Miss Cain touched my arm. 'Come with me if you will. See it all for yourself. I have a room filled with letters and papers and manifests. Two pairs of eyes will serve better than one.'

She was thinking of my family again. I shook my head. I was tired and despondent and would be poor company. I had not entirely recovered from the previous evening and did not feel in the mood for poring over endless letters. And, too, I did not entirely trust my intentions. The night had taught me that much.

'It's late, and likely as not they're in Oxford,' I said, without great conviction. 'You will have no news of them until the terms of the city's surrender are agreed.' I wondered how much longer that would take. If Prince Rupert's surrender of Bristol was any gauge, then there would be several weeks of back and forth. I would do well to be there, though, on the day they opened to Parliament's army.

I withdrew and smiled as best I could. I watched her walk away across the yard, a half of me wishing I had not rejected her company for another few hours, for I found I very much did not want to be alone. My legs ached and my belly growled for something to fill it; but it was a deeper fatigue that ailed me. A tiredness of the soul.

I returned to the Bucket of Blood and asked for my supper. I had barely sat down when a silhouette caught my eye as it crossed the threshold. A man, slender and short but with a quick sharpness to his movements. I did not recognise him at first, not until he turned and I saw his face: none other than Peter Fowles. As soon as he caught my eye he came towards me with such great purpose that I half rose, anticipating hostility in his intent. He paused then, and held up his hands to show they were empty, and drew back his cloak to let me see that he came unarmed, though I could not be certain that he carried no daggers in his boots or tucked behind his back.

'I'm not here to fight with you, Falkland,' he said. 'But I did come to speak with you. May I join you?'

I returned to my seat, wary, and waved to one of the

tavern boys. Warbeck and Cromwell were paying for my suppers; they might as well pay for Fowles as well.

'You're very gracious,' Fowles said.

'Shall I hazard a guess?' I asked. 'Milton means to write to Cromwell, demanding another intelligencer. You are here to kindly ask me to withdraw. Did he send you or did you come of your own motivation? Understand, please, that I shall not take offence. Cromwell has asked this of me and I have agreed, but I am, I willingly admit, reluctant. I do not see him as my commander, nor any other man.' I watched carefully, searching for any reaction, but saw only puzzlement. He smiled, though I thought it forced.

'You're probably right about John, but I came to tell you about Francis Lovelace. But, Falkland, if I may ask, if what you say is true, why are you doing this at all?'

I sighed. From the very first I had not taken much of a liking to Fowles, but perhaps the fault for that lay more with Milton than with Fowles himself.

'I was offered something in return in a matter of my own concern.' That was the bones of it and I felt no inclination to say more. 'You told me quite certainly that the name Francis Lovelace was unknown to you.'

'I did. I couldn't speak openly in the street, and John would not entertain you in his house again. But I've come here directly to rectify my deception and give you the truth of the matter, at least as best I know it.' Fowles paused to gather his breath. 'Anne's husband Thomas disappeared in the early days of the war, most likely lost at Edgehill. Francis Lovelace was known to both Anne and John. When Anne learned that Francis would be travelling to the north to join with Lord Willoughby of Parham's company of militia in 'forty-three, she asked . . .' he shook his head. 'I'm sorry, Falkland. I get ahead of myself. Parham's militia was in Lincolnshire and planned to head north to join with Fairfax and take on the King's army in the north. If Thomas was still alive then there was a chance they would meet, though on opposite sides.'

I nodded. I remembered those days well, skirmishing to and fro, armies dancing back and forth. Edgehill had been a bloody nightmare from which both sides had staggered dazed. Perhaps the King had had the better of it, advancing south as far as Oxford, but Essex and Parliament's armies had never been truly broken, and the King had deemed them too strong to confront again directly. I had marched as I was told, with little notion of what transpired in the north after I left, but both Fairfax and Cromwell had been there in '43, that much I knew.

Fowles took a deep breath. 'Anne asked Francis to look for Thomas as best he could. It was a fool's errand. We were with Parliament. Thomas had fought for the King. I don't know how Francis thought he might be of service. I think he was infatuated. Or perhaps he merely wished to be the gallant gentleman. He was a common farmer like the rest of us, but London had given him airs, and he was always one to have his head turned by a lady, much to his own detriment in the end.'

'You knew him?' This much was obvious. Fowles chuckled.

'We were in the same company, Falkland. It was not a large one. I'm sure you know how it is. We all came to know one another, and Francis was quick to share his quest with all the rest of us. It's through Francis that I've become acquainted with the Milton house. Francis thought it some great adventure, some deed of knightly chivalry or some such nonsense. He thought we might help him.'

'Did you?'

Fowles laughed again. He paused as the tavern boy brought us each a trencher filled with a thick stew. 'How, Falkland? It all came to nothing. There was no means for Francis to find out whether Thomas Agar had been among the King's dead after Edgehill, or whether he was wounded or had survived. They were the enemy. I know he wrote letters to Anne. I dare say he spoke with great optimism, but there was never much chance he could succeed. Nor was he given one. He died in the summer of 'forty-three at Gainsborough. We were only gone a few months.' He took a moment and then drew closer. 'Falkland, it's all long in the past now. I don't doubt Francis meant to impress Anne, and I can't speak for his reasons, noble or otherwise. But I'm quite certain that Anne was merely in despair over the fate of her husband. There's no scandal to be found, and Francis is long dead. These letters are old and mean nothing.'

His concern seemed, to my mind, both profound and misplaced.

'I have no interest in scandal,' I told him. 'But I am curious: if this is all long in the past, why should the letters now go missing?'

Fowles shrugged. 'Perhaps Milton took them.'

I found the notion reasonable, but I did not believe in it. Yes, perhaps Milton had gone into his sister's rooms and yes, perhaps he had found the letters and read them; but then, if they were as innocent as Fowles suggested, why take them? From whom did he seek to hide them? Besides, I thought his surprise on the step of his house had been genuine enough, and I was quite sure that someone had searched Anne's room.

'I do not think so,' I told him. 'But perhaps you are right. They are certainly of far less interest than what Miss Hardwick has to say.'

Fowles nodded and sank into his chair, and I sensed a feeling of relief in his posture. As the tavern boy brought us each a cup of beer, I leaned forward. My next words were born of careful calculation. I watched him closely as I spoke them.

'Perhaps you might tell Milton, if he did indeed take those letters sent to his sister from Francis Lovelace, that his collection is not complete.'

I saw at once that I had hit the mark. Fowles froze, if only for an instant.

'There is something in those letters that matters to you?' I asked.

Fowles savoured a mouthful of his supper. He picked up his cup and held it between us like a shield as he composed himself.

'A little, I suppose,' he said at last. 'Francis Lovelace was a friend, though I didn't know him for all that long. It was a noble thing he set out to do. I wouldn't see him or his family, nor Anne, dragged into pointless tittle-tattle.'

I nodded as if content, though far from certain that Fowles was giving me the whole of the truth. 'Nor I.' I smiled as best I could, and regarded him steadily. I did not believe Fowles had come halfway across London to speak with me out of some sense of generosity. He had come because my discovery had disturbed him sufficiently to provoke him to action; and I found myself suddenly certain then: Fowles was here because of the letters, nothing more and nothing less. Because of something that was in them. It was *he* who had taken them, who had searched Anne's room; and surely then he knew something about whoever had taken Anne herself, whether he realised it or not. I did not see how or why, but it could not be coincidence, could it?

I waited until he finished his supper and then rose. 'I apologise,' I said, 'but I must retire early tonight. I will be visiting Clink Prison and John Ogle on the morrow, and I fear I will need all my strength for that. You may assure John Milton that I will call presently and return the last of Anne's letters once I am certain they have no relevance to her disappearance.'

We shook hands. His grip was tremulous and clammy. Somehow, he was afraid.

CHAPTER 10

I returned to my room and paced up and down a while, trying to divine why Fowles had felt so impelled to see me and tell me about Francis Lovelace. What was to gain when all he had achieved was to rouse my suspicions still further? He claimed to have come to rectify the lie he had told in front of Milton, and instead he had presented me with several more. That these letters between Anne Agar and Francis Lovelace were not evidence of some scandal I was prepared to believe, but that they were nothing? Quite the opposite, it seemed to me, at least to Peter Fowles.

It dawned on me at last why he might have sought me out: if my suspicion was correct and he had indeed been the one to steal Anne's letters then he had been looking for something in them and had not found it. He had come to me to press for information – to see if I had come upon whatever he was seeking by some other route. Like a fool I had told him that I, too, held one of Anne's letters. I had thought to taunt him and tease out his guilt – and so I had – but I had also given myself away. Yet I still did not see how letters from a dead man had led to Anne Agar being taken three years later.

Nor did the letter I held offer in its words any clue as to

its import. In the meantime I had reason to doubt Jane
Hardwick's story, an interview to be had with John Ogle,
and perhaps Anne's mysterious Fleet Street liaisons to
uncover; yet Fowles' interest was too much for mere
coincidence. He had been in the Milton house with John
and Edward Phillips when the abduction had happened, and
so could not have been a part of it, but what secret had those
letters held, and were *they* a part?

The hour grew late. From my room in the Bucket of
Blood I heard the ruckus downstairs rise and fall, the baying
of the crowd for tonight's fighters. I had left Miss Cain and
Fowles both, desperately needing to rest and to sleep, yet
now I felt more fully awake than I had since dawn. On
impulse I hurried down the stairs and out into the night
once more, wishing as I did that I carried a weapon. I walked
briskly, looking about me left and right as I came to Fleet
Street. The crowds had thinned, but the presses were still
hard at work, and errand boys still ran and wove back and
forth even at this late hour. I passed Lincoln's Inn and Grey's
Inn and then doubled back, scanning the faces of those
around me. I saw no one skulking in shadows. When I was
certain that I had not been followed, I returned to Lincoln's
Inn and Miss Cain's door. I banged heavily on it. I had, I
must confess, quite forgotten how long had passed since
sunset. When she did not answer at once, I banged again.

'Miss Cain! It's Falkland. I have need of your help.'

I heard a creak of wood. After a moment the door cracked
open and Miss Cain's head poked through. She looked
bleary-eyed. The room inside was dark. She was, I realised,
wearing only a nightdress. I took a step back and looked
away.

'Oh, my apologies! Please do forgive me. You were asleep.'

'I *was* asleep, William Falkland.'

'I should go. I'll return in the morning. Please, again, forgive me.'

'No, you can wait out there while I dress, and then you can tell me what on earth caused you to rush all the way over from Covent Garden at this hour.' She closed the door while outside I paced the corridor. When she opened it again, Miss Cain had covered herself in a plain black dress and bodice with a white collar. She turned away from me, opening the shutters of her room to let in the moon and then lighting a candle. I could not help but notice that, in her haste perhaps, she had not fully tightened the laces of her bodice, and that it hung a little loose.

'You told me you could not find this Francis Lovelace without knowing for what company he fought. I have that now. Peter Fowles fought for the same. They were both with Lord Willoughby of Parham in the summer of 'forty-three. With that, might you find them?'

'And this was what had you rushing from Covent Garden to my door in the middle of the night? Could it not have waited until morning?'

There was a strange tone in her voice I could not place. Of chastisement, richly deserved, but also of something else. Almost of disappointment. I did not understand it.

'No. Fowles came to see me after I left you. He told me that he and Lovelace had fought together, that Lovelace was searching for Anne's husband Thomas. He was correspond-ing with her as to his progress. This is what the letters were, or so he claims, but I am quite convinced there is something

more. I think it was Fowles who took them. I think he was
looking for something in them, and I don't think he found
it. Kate, I am quite certain that Peter Fowles knows more
than he would say . . .' I paused, allowing these revelations
to sink in. It occurred to me now – too late, of course – that
perhaps I was once again putting Miss Cain in peril's path by
invoking her aid.

She was staring at me, wide-eyed and aglow in the gloom.
I reached out and touched her arm. 'Kate. I need the names
of other men who might have known Francis Lovelace and
Peter Fowles, and which of them might currently be in
London. Can you help me?'

Miss Cain reached out to me. At first I thought she
intended to take my arm, or even to embrace me, but she
meant only to hand me the candle while she lit three more.
Illuminated this way, carrying one in each hand, she led me
out of her meagre quarters and along the narrow passages
through which I had already trod. We crossed the yard
behind the gate, passing through the moon-shadow of the
chapel to the library beyond; but Kate did not lead me
through its great wooden doors. Instead she took me further
on, around the back of it to a much plainer, ill-fitting
entrance that might as easily have been the door to some
pauper's house. A dark passage ran beyond, with tiny rooms
scattered to either side. Kate took me into the first. It was
fortunate that I am accustomed, tall as I am, to ducking as I
cross thresholds, for this doorway was particularly small, and
I had not only to duck my head but also to squeeze my
shoulders. The inside of the room was almost entirely
occupied by a table scattered with papers. Piles more lay
propped up against the wall. Kate set her candles down.

'This is where you work?' I asked. She nodded.

I looked about, disheartened. There were a great many letters piled high, it was true, enough that one might have been occupied with the reading of them for a full day or perhaps even two. But no more. The New Model Army's camp in Crediton, when I had seen it, must have numbered close to ten thousand men. I had heard Cromwell claim fifteen, and others suggest even more.

'This way, Falkland.' Perhaps Kate saw the disappointment on my brow, for she wasted no time in leading me to an adjacent room. Here were piled papers almost from floorboard to rafter and around every wall. There was a table, but it was entirely buried. The room was nigh on impossible to enter.

'*That* is where I work,' whispered Miss Cain. 'Now we sort through it all, looking for this militia of yours.'

I stared in horror. The task seemed insurmountable.

'Oh, take that sour look off your face, Falkland. You got me from my bed for this. Go and sit down in the other room and don't knock the candles. I'll bring you the first pile. What do you know about this Willoughby of Parham and where he campaigned?'

I told her as much as I could remember, that he had been in Lincolnshire at the start of the war, the commander of Parliament's forces there for a while. I knew from Fowles that his company had been at the battle of Gainsborough. In the King's army, we had come to know the commanders among our enemy. Willoughby had been under the Earl of Manchester, and had taken the surrender of Bolingbrooke Castle in the autumn of that year. In '44 I knew he was a part of the failed assault on Newark. After that I had not heard of him again. For all I knew, he was dead.

Kate frowned and complained that my clues were slender. She brought a pile of papers for me to work through, and then sat beside me with another. It was tedious work in the gloom, lit by only a few candle flames. I pored over letters and lists, notes of dispositions of companies and forces. There was a mine of information here, and if the King's supporters had ever heard of it, I was sure they would eye it with an eager envy. The names of many of the men who had fought for Parliament. Reprimands and commendations. Requisitions and lists of supplies.

I worked my way through my pile. When I reached the bottom of it, I saw that Kate was only halfway through her own; nevertheless, she stopped and brought me more. My eyes kept stealing glances of her as we worked. By the time I reached the bottom of my second pile our candles were burning low. My eyes were tired. To go through every piece of paper in that room, we would be here for weeks.

'Enough,' I said. 'We can start again in the morning.' I wondered if it might not be simpler to go and find Fowles and ask for the other names, although I feared I would not get an entirely honest answer.

Kate rubbed her eyes. 'I have found this much: Lord Willoughby of Parham remains, as best I can make out, alive and well. There is a complaint here from Cromwell himself regarding the conduct of his soldiers.' She slumped on her stool, despondent at our failure. I reached out and rested a hand on her shoulder. 'If you could find him, perhaps he would remember the names of his men.'

'I am proud of you, Miss Cain,' I said. 'You have made a home and a place for yourself here. I am glad of that. I know that it was in part my fault that you were forced to leave your home.'

'Do not blame yourself for that, Falkland.' She smiled. 'The New Model came and took our town from us all. Master Warbeck says this war will soon be done. When it is, I shall go home again.'

Perhaps she saw the pain in my eyes as she said that. She cupped my face in her hand.

'You *will* find them, William. You will.'

A part of me would have taken her in my arms there and held her tight. I rose and stepped back, before that part could speak too loudly.

'I should go,' I said. 'And you should go back to your bed. I'm sorry to have disturbed your sleep.'

Kate gathered the candles. She snuffed all but one.

'It's easier in the daylight,' she said. 'We will make better progress.'

I moved to the door. My feet seemed heavy and reluctant, the Bucket of Blood suddenly very far away.

'I have a blanket and a cloak,' Kate said. 'The nights are not as cold as those we both remember. You could bed down here if you wish. I'll bring you bread in the morning.'

'And be woken at dawn by some wandering bencher who will take me for a vagrant and kick me into the street?' I could not say I wasn't tempted, but I shook my head, and so we walked together side by side in the darkness, one tiny flame lighting our way. I had not planned it so, but I stayed at Kate's side back to her door. She opened it and took the candle, and then turned to face me, one of us on either side of the threshold. We looked at each another, the candle-flame between us. I felt a nervous energy loose inside me, of the sort I had felt when we were lined up for battle and Parliament's pikemen finally came into view.

'I . . .'

'Falkland . . .'

'Yes?'

'What?'

Another moment of silence. I took a small step away. It seemed the hardest step I had taken in a very long time.

'I must go,' I said. 'Good night, Miss Cain.'

'Good night, Falkland.' She smiled, and even then lingered a moment as if waiting perhaps for something more before she slowly shut the door. I stood there long enough to hear the latch go down.

It must have been past midnight by the time the night watchman opened the Lincoln's Inn gate for me, and I exited onto the street. The night was warm, balmy even, still full of the smell of London, sweet and yet sour, a gentle breeze bringing the stink of the Thames like a blanket over the ever-present waft of dung. I walked slowly this time, unable to cast away the image of Miss Cain standing in her doorway, her face lit by the candle she held between us. And yet now and then, as I blinked, her face seemed to change. She grew older and a little shorter. Her hair lightened and she was my Caro, and a great longing welled up inside me. Of a sudden I could think of nothing else but to be done with this wretched search. Oxford. I could not get it out of my head that my Caro was there.

I did not see the man who came up behind me, soft-footed as a fox in the night. Yet perhaps my soldier's instincts had not quite deserted me. At the very last I had a sense of something amiss. I started to turn, and so the blow that would have landed square on the back of my head caught me instead a glancing thunder across the ear. The pain deafened and staggered me. I reeled as the man came at me again. He carried some sort of club, but in the night I could see little more. I did not know him. I caught the second blow on my arms, raised to protect my face.

Another two men broke from the shadows, one to either side of me, each carrying a cosh of his own. I had no weapon, and three against one was no sort of fight I wished to make. I turned to run, and now there was a fourth man coming at me from ahead along Fleet Street. I heard – felt, almost – the others hard at my heels. I resolved to bull through this man who stood before me and simply knock him aside, but he was too shrewd for that. As we came together and I leaned my shoulder into him to batter him down, he ducked and grabbed at me. I staggered, unbalanced. I almost pushed him aside, but as he went down he wrapped one arm around my leg. I fell hard, smacking into the cobblestone. The impact dazed me for a moment but still I kicked out. My leg came free. I heard the man who'd caught me curse. I rose to my hands and knees, ready to run again, but the others were on me there before I could rise. A crushing boot stamped into my ribs, knocking me flat, and then another to the side, beating the wind out of me. I curled up as best I could, my arms wrapped around my head as they kicked at me and struck me with their clubs until I was all but senseless. One came at me with such enthusiasm that it fell to his friends to hold him back.

'Nathaniel!' Only then did he stop.

My eyes swam. They rolled me onto my back. A face loomed over me. I felt hands rummaging through my clothes. The man wore a long, dark coat; it looked to me like a soldier's coat. He had worn a hat when I first struck him, but now that was gone. His hair was well kept. He had thick, bristling brows, but what struck me most of all was that his beard was long and bushy in the manner of an old sailor, not well kept and trimmed to a point as was the fashion.

He found the pocket where I had tucked the letter stolen from under Anne Agar's dresser. He took it and drew away. I should have known it. I tried to move then, but the other men were quickly on me with their boots once more, stamping me down. I saw the man with the beard, in the moment before my senses finally deserted me, stoop to pick up his hat, and I saw that there was a ribbon in it. In the moonlight I could not tell the colour. Pale, that was all.

A boot struck the side of my head. A darkness fell upon me.

CHAPTER 11

I do not know how long I lay there, helpless. I remember I came to my senses enough to crawl away from the middle of that midnight street. I think I was able to stagger to my feet, but I cannot be certain. Perhaps I simply crawled across the stones. I found a dark corner, an alley or a doorway perhaps, a place shrouded in deepest shadow. I curled up there and allowed my consciousness to slip away. I did not dream as I huddled, but fell into a pit of utter blackness, an oblivion complete until the sky lightened and the sun began to rise and poke at my eyes to open.

I did not move, even after I was awake. For a time I simply could not. My ribs and back were battered, bruised and swollen. Every heaving breath was an effort and a pain. My head thundered. There was blood on my hands, dried hard but my own. When I dared to move at all, I found more on my face and on the side of my head where that first blow had landed. My hands, at least, had survived. They had not stamped them to the stones and broken my fingers. Perhaps I should have been grateful to them for that, but I was not.

I took my time. I have had my share of injury. On battlefields there are times when a man must run, no matter how grievously he hurts. But when the enemy is not upon him, a man must take his time to learn the extent of his condition. I have seen men run on broken legs and live because of it. I have seen men killed by such exertion when they might otherwise have lived. The blood on my face was old. There was plenty enough of it, but none fresh. I could breathe, though it hurt me to do so. Their blows had rained on my body and my legs were largely unhurt.

With great effort I lifted myself erect and stumbled back into Fleet Street. So early in the day, but there were already folk about their errands, boys and young women for the most part. I realised I had barely left the gates of Lincoln's Inn behind me before I had been set upon. They had been waiting for me then. I wondered who they were and how they knew.

A few steps told me I would not make it back to the Bucket of Blood. I staggered along instead the way I had come the night before, eternally grateful that the porters of Lincoln's Inn were early risers and had already unbarred the gates. Perhaps I seemed a most unusual sight to them, stumbling through their portal at such an early hour, battered and bloody-faced. I had half thought they might bar my entry, and I was surely in no state to offer any argument, yet they did not. Perhaps they remembered me from the day before and my visits to Miss Cain, or perhaps they were accustomed to members of their hostelry returning from all-night revelry considerably the worse for wear. In truth, I did not think much on it then.

They did not stop me but nor did they offer their aid. I lurched across the yard and fumbled my way up the steps to Miss Cain's room, and hammered once again on her door. It was not, I knew, the act of a gentleman – I should have done better returning to the rooms where we had worked through the night and awaited her arrival – but by then I was long past feeling that such things mattered. The bruises to my body had left me a cripple, but the pain in the side of my head, that first blow, burned ever harder, eating at my reason.

I hammered again. 'Kate! For the love of Parliament and King!'

'Falkland!' I heard her groan, and then movement. She came to the door. 'I am barely asleep . . .'

Her words died in her mouth when she saw me, and this time she did not tell me to wait outside. Her look of horror was terrible. I must have appeared as though I was dying.

'It's not as bad as it seems,' I told her, although I did not speak with great conviction. Miss Cain clearly did not believe me. She pulled the door wide and dragged me in and sat me on her bed.

'We need to summon a physician! At once!'

I tried to shake my head, but the pain was too much. 'It will all heal of its own nature,' I wheezed. I had seen my fill of surgeons and physicians. Surgeons, I will grant, are good men for the most part. They will do what needs to be done and make no complaint of it. Physicians, with their potions and poultices and leeches, I have no time for.

'You're bleeding, Falkland. Dear Heaven, what happened to you?'

I told her as best I could how I had been set upon. The burning along the side of my head had become unbearable, as harsh as the strike of a musket ball. I lay back.

'I will get a physician at once.' She crossed to the other side of the room. 'Avert your eyes, Falkland.'

There was no need. I could barely keep them open, much less turn my head. The distance from where I had slept the night to Miss Cain's door could not have been more than five minutes' walking for a man in his strength and at a brisk pace, yet it had all but drained me. The rush of blood through the swollen wound in the side of my head had done for me. I touched my hand to it and felt my fingers come back sticky. It had opened again.

'Spirits,' I murmured. 'Strong enough to catch alight. Please. If you can . . .' I barely had the strength to speak.

I did not catch Miss Cain's reply. Nor, indeed, did I catch very much at all for a time. My eyes closed, the room faded away, and I found myself washed up on some battlefield in the middle of the thrust and charge of it. Men howled all about, muskets fired, cannon roared, horses thundered and screamed. I had no idea where I was except that I was unhorsed, lying on the ground, not moving. Men I knew came for a moment to stand over me, men I remembered who had died on Edgehill; yet when they were gone and I found my feet a moment later, it seemed the battlefield was more akin to Naseby. I ran hither and yon, desperate to find my horse while musket fire surrounded me; and then I was alone, and all of Parliament's armies were on the charge towards me, and I could not run fast enough to outpace their horse. The first cavalryman caught up behind and cut me down . . .

I opened my eyes. All of a sudden we were not alone. Miss Cain was standing by the open door, though I had not seen her move and nor had I seen it open. A man stood behind her where no man had been but a moment before, a brute of a soldier so tall he could barely stand straight.

Another pushed past him and leaned over me. Warbeck; and I wondered if perhaps I was delirious and had conjured a new vision with which to torment myself, but then I smelled that rank breath of his. Warbeck touched at my ear. He might as well have stabbed a burning brand into the side of my face. I howled and pulled away and then howled again, beset by fresh pains.

'It's not deep,' he said. 'The ear is torn but it won't fall off unless the wound turns bad. Only God may decide that. The swelling beneath is more of a trouble. It will fade in time unless it kills him first.' He leaned in closer. 'Falkland? Do you know who I am? Can you hear me?' He did not wait for an answer but turned for a moment to Miss Cain. 'I suggest wrapping a piece of cloth around his ear so as not to risk it tearing again as it heals. You're a soldier, Falkland. You've had worse.' With these words he withdrew and addressed Kate once more. 'Did he tell you how it happened?'

I struggled to pull myself a little upright. The terrible burning was not as bad as I remembered. I must, I realised, have passed out again while Miss Cain had gone to fetch Warbeck, and that had been the reason for my visions of battlefields long past. The soldier in the door, now that I looked more closely, was no stranger. He had been in the Bucket of Blood that night with Warbeck. Waterhouse.

'They were after the letter,' I said thickly. As soon as I spoke, Miss Cain rushed to my side. She tried to force me to lie back, but I would not have it. 'Did you get the brandy?' I asked her.

'*I* brought the brandy,' snapped Warbeck. 'And if you want to drink yourself numb then I suggest cheap wine.' His look was pained. Miss Cain held up a bottle to my eyes.

'Here,' she said.

'You will need a strip of cloth to cover the wound,' I told her.

Miss Cain did not hesitate. She tore a strip from her nightdress.

'Now pour some of that brandy into a cup. Not too much.'

I watched as she did it. I was not looking forward at all keenly to what must come next, but I had seen it done enough times and I knew surgeons who swore by it as a means to keep a wound from going bad in the rare few times when such aqua vitae was to hand.

I looked to the soldier Waterhouse. 'You've got strength, lad. Come and hold me down.'

Waterhouse did not seem to entirely understand what I wanted from him, but he came to the bed as I had asked. I turned onto my side and begged him to lean his weight into me. When I was satisfied, I told Kate to have the bandage ready.

'But first you must tip your cup over the wound. Slowly. I will scream. Do not stop.'

Waterhouse was between us. I couldn't see her face but I sensed her hesitate.

'I'll do it,' said Warbeck. 'Are you ready, Falkland?'

I wished he would not. Warbeck, I thought, would take far too much pleasure in my agony.

And then it came. The first touch against my raw flesh felt as though Warbeck had touched the very sun itself to my head. I wish I could say that I lay still and gritted my teeth and took the pain in the manner of some stone-faced warrior, that I perhaps uttered some low, savage growl and no more, but it was not so. When the surgeons in Oxford took the musket ball from my leg, I had been as drunk as a dozen cardinals. Here I was not, and I had never felt such pain. I screamed, against all my own desire, and bucked and arched and twisted to wrest my head away from Warbeck's dripping. It took all of the soldier Waterhouse to hold me down.

I'm not sure that I noticed when it stopped. I felt hands lift my head and something wrap tight around me. A fresh pain that came with that. I tried to lash out, but Waterhouse kept me still until at last the burning began to recede. He held me a while longer until my twitching stopped, and then at last removed himself. I lay on the bed where he left me, wretched and dripping with my own exhaustion.

'I've seen men do better,' grunted Warbeck. 'And I've seen men do worse. Would you like to tell me how it is that I've left you alone for a mere day and already I have John Phillips banging at my door telling me how Milton is writing to Cromwell to demand you be locked up, or at the very least sent back to – in his words – whatever dungheap spawned you? And now this. Although I imagine it was not hard for you to exhaust Milton's patience. He has little enough for any man.'

I gathered what little strength remained to me. 'It was not John Milton who did this. Anne's room was searched and letters taken. I believe Peter Fowles to be responsible. I found one that had been missed. I let it be known to him that he had not taken them all. That was earlier the same evening. The men who attacked me, when they were done, they searched my pockets and took the letter I had recovered.

No one but he knew I had it.' I explained in detail what I thought I had learned and what Peter Fowles had told me. As I spoke, I found I could not accept that Anne's abduction was a random act by the King's supporters to silence John Milton. I do not believe in coincidence and happenstance. There was a connection to these letters, though I could not see it.

Warbeck regarded me with dubious eyes. 'Something from three years in the past, Falkland?' He shook his head. 'Cromwell sent you – against my advice, I will say – to find John Milton's sister, not to stir up some old tragedy long dead and buried.'

'I do not believe they are unrelated.'

Warbeck shook his head in disdain. He gestured sharply to the soldier Waterhouse. 'You need someone to look after you, Falkland. Waterhouse here can be your bodyguard. Go and find the men who took Anne. Have you spoken to the Clink Street woman?'

'I don't need your man following me about,' I snapped. Pride, perhaps, but I had been a soldier in the King's armies for six years before Cromwell's men finally took me down. I did not, I fancied, need some young man, barely blooded no matter how large he was, following me about like some oversized hound. Nor did I need Warbeck spying on me everywhere I went.

'As you like, Falkland.' Warbeck seemed not to care. 'Another good blow to that head of yours and you might not get up again. I'd have a care if I were you.' He bared his teeth and hissed between them as he loomed towards me. 'Milton is asking Cromwell to have you removed. May I remind you that the peace of this land may in part depend on finding Milton's sister? The man is like a keg of powder – useful but to be kept away from sparks. A very large keg of powder. So concentrate your mind and stop digging into the man's family.' He grunted something foul, shook his head and turned to go.

'Warbeck! Wait. I went to Miss Hardwick yesterday. She told me the same story you have already heard, but this time she gave a name. John Ogle, but . . .' I did not know quite how to put my suspicions into words. She had almost tried to rob me of a shilling for that name, yet she had run out into the street to give it to me. 'I have other questions, and I will need some money,' I said, before he could leave. 'I have nothing of my own.'

'I'm sure Cromwell will pay you for your time.'

'No. I need money now. I have doubts regarding Miss Hardwick. If I am to have this woman speak the truth, I will need to sweeten my questions. It seems I am also obliged to visit John Ogle in Clink Prison, and I will need to ease my passage into his presence. Though I don't imagine, if he has anything to do with this, that he will deign to speak with me at all.'

'I'll see that he does, Falkland. We'll go together. Tomorrow.' Warbeck took the purse from his belt and tossed it onto the bed. 'There. Don't come looking for any more.'

Warbeck and Waterhouse left. I lay back, and must have fallen instantly asleep a while, for when next I looked the sun was higher in the sky and the light through the windows much brighter. I felt a little more myself, though my head throbbed like a marching drum. I dragged my aches from Miss Cain's bed and looked at what I had done to the blanket. There were bloodstains, and it smelled of Warbeck's brandy. A gentlemanly gesture would have been to purchase a new one, but Warbeck's purse, I found, was mean.

I looked for Kate and found her in the room we had used in the night, poring over her papers. It warmed my heart how she smiled, how her face brightened to see me.

'I'm sorry to have brought such a disagreeable morning upon you,' I said. 'I must find you a new blanket.'

'I'm sure it will wash.'

'I should go. I should not trouble you with any more of this.'

Miss Cain rose and clasped my hand between her own. 'I've told you before, Falkland, they are not worth dying for.' She let go and took a piece of paper from her table. 'I found something on that militia company. It is a list sent to Parliament of the men fighting for Sir Willoughby of Parham after the battle of Gainsborough. There are close to two hundred names.' She shook her head. 'I don't think I can find which ones are still alive and which ones might be in London. But I will try, Falkland.'

I took the paper and perused it. A long list of names and the villages and counties from which they had come. I scanned it and found both Fowles and Lovelace. Lovelace was marked 'returned to the love and grace of God', as were a dozen others. He came, the paper said, from a village by the name of Rivenhall in Essex. I thanked Miss Cain for her help and her hospitality. I wished I could have shown my gratitude in some tangible way, but I had nothing more I could give her.

When I reached my room in the Bucket of Blood it was clear at once that someone had come in while I had been gone. They had made no attempt to hide their spoor, but had simply ransacked everything; still, I had so few belongings and kept them in such disarray that I might not have noticed had they not slit the mattress and pulled out half its wool and straw. I could not imagine what they thought I might hide in there; but they were, I supposed, the same men who had accosted me later in the night. I spoke briefly with the tavern boys who told me that several men had indeed come in looking for me – some of John Lilburne's Levellers, he thought. I supposed they had been searching for the missing letter, and I took some bleak amusement in imagining Peter Fowles' face when he finally saw what little I possessed.

I awoke late the next morning, and found myself oddly uncertain as to what I should do. Return to the Hardwick woman and lever the truth out of her about what she'd seen, that seemed the most obvious action, and then to John Ogle; but I felt very much as though the gaze of my enquiry was being directed. The rebellious part of my nature demanded I discard the whore of Clink Street and resume my search of Fleet Street for the secret of Anne's mysterious rendezvous, or else pursue the matter of Anne's letters – though how I might do so aside from simply confronting Fowles himself I could not see.

My head burned. The pain fuddled my thoughts. I felt a strong desire to ride, to clear my head, to get away from the city and its constant pressing throng. I could not, I decided, face the crowd and noise of Fleet Street today. I did not know how far it would be to journey to Rivenhall in Essex, but I will admit that the notion of a gentle canter along empty country roads with the summer breeze in my face appealed greatly more than the clamour and stink of London Bridge and Borough Market; yet wherever such thoughts might have led me, I was not to know. I descended the stairs, wobbling on my feet, to find Warbeck already waiting for me in commons. He gripped me by the arm and ushered me at once to the stables, no matter that I had not yet broken my fast. 'Falkland, Waterhouse has gone ahead. We have an interview with John Ogle this morning. I hope you're up to it.'

I grumbled something about the letters as Warbeck saddled my horse.

'Get Fowles out of your head, Falkland. Whatever he and Lovelace did it was years ago and not anything of our concern today.'

My head begged to disagree. I said as much.

'We have a witness, Falkland, who saw Milton's sister taken off the street and bundled into a carriage by a man known to associate with John Ogle, cousin to one of the King's most vigorous advocates. Fowles, whatever you may think of him, is not part of some royalist conspiracy. One way or another, Ogle will tell us where to find Anne, and then it will be done!' He had become energetic in this frenzy of words, and flecks of his spittle struck me as he spoke. I turned my head from the stink of his breath and nodded my acquiescence, although I wondered at the strength of Warbeck's vehemence. I had a notion we would need more than mere enthusiasm to unravel Anne Agar's fate.

Clink Street, when we reached it, was quiet at this time in the morning, though the bustle and hurly-burly of Borough Market was at its peak. A tinker sat at one end of it, shouting out his wares, most of them cheap candles made of tallow. Two women started towards us as they saw us come on our horses; then one pointed at me and they hurried away instead. They remembered my face. A carriage waited outside the gates of Clink Prison at the far end of the street. The arms on the side were not familiar, but that it had them at all spoke a great deal as to the importance of its passenger. I watched several men cluster around it, some of them prison guards, some of them armed militiamen who sat on the carriage roof. The carriage faced away, and I could not see who emerged from within. I watched as a scuffle broke out between the prison guards and the militiamen. It grew as far as pistols drawn before some authority I couldn't see called it to an end.

Warbeck stopped outside the lodgings of Miss Jane Hardwick. He bade me hold the horses and vanished inside, to be replaced shortly by the hulking Waterhouse.

'I'm to mind the animals, Master Falkland. You can go on in. I've done what needs to be done in the Clink. Ogle will attend on you and Master Warbeck when you're ready.'

I nodded. Waterhouse would surely do a better job of keeping thieves away from our horses than would I, with a bloodstained bandage around my head.

'How's the ear?' he asked.

'Still attached.' I couldn't think what else to say. Yes, indeed, it hurt a great deal if I wasn't careful, and often even if I was. 'For whatever reasons move such things, it has chosen to trouble me considerably today. I was once told by a surgeon that this was a sign of the healing setting in, but I did not believe it then and nor do I believe it now. Wounds are simply wilful and churlish that way.'

'I dare say you couldn't see it for yourself, Master Falkland, but it was an ugly one.'

'I was shot in the leg by a musket in 'forty-four. That was worse.'

'You seem a decent man.' Waterhouse frowned. 'Strange to think we might have traded shots across some field.'

'You carried a musket?' I had taken a man of his size to be a pikeman, surely.

'Both a musket and a pike, though not on the same day.' He laughed.

'As have I. And been a dragoon, and lastly a cavalryman.'

'Prince Rupert? Never like to face his horse.'

'We thought the same of Cromwell's Ironsides.' I took a moment to look this Waterhouse over. I had not given him much thought before. I had barely noticed him that evening when I had been reunited with Miss Cain. The circumstances of our second meeting had hardly been better. 'Do you have a family?'

He nodded. 'A farm near Sevenoaks in Kent. Two brothers and three sisters there.'

'A big one then.' I found myself smiling. 'One of your own?'

A huge grin split his face. It was odd, on such a bear of a man, to see him turn away, suddenly small and shy.

'I have a girl I'm sweet for, Master Falkland. I hope to marry her one day, but I have to make something of myself before I can ask for her.'

I smiled still, but I found my eyes had started to swim. My Caro had chosen me long before I knew it. Her father was lord of the manor and I was but a tenant farmer's boy. But still she had chosen me.

'Don't lose them, Waterhouse.' I turned away before he could see the glitter in my eye and climbed the steps into the lodging house. It was a rank and sordid place with the sour smell of too many people in too small a space. Every soldier's camp took on the same smell after a while; but soldiers moved on and left their stink behind them, while the hapless folk who lived in these hovels on Clink Street had no such luck. Hardwick's room was, I supposed, typical. Tiny, with barely enough space for a mattress and a wobbling, poorly made dresser. There was a chamber pot, half full and reeking. The only blanket was threadbare and stained. Her dress, bright and lurid at first glance, was little better. She had shoes, at least, but they had holes in them. It was the sort of squalor that only existed in a city. York had had places that were the same as this, and Bristol too, but I had not seen the like elsewhere. The bruise on her face had grown more colourful since we last met. I felt again a pity for her. A soldier is no stranger to whores and I had encountered plenty enough over the years, following the King's armies back and forth. They had none of them been as sorry as this one who sat before me.

She looked at me with disdain.

'So it's you again, is it, this intelligencer we're waiting for?' she spat. 'Got a shilling for me this time? Gave you your name, didn't I? Some of us got to work for a living.'

'On your back?' sneered Warbeck. 'You call that work? Only for the devil, whore.'

I held up a sixpence from Warbeck's purse. 'This man needs to hear it too. You saw Anne walking towards the prison. A carriage pulled up beside her. Two men got out. They grabbed her and took her off. You've seen one of them before. Long and narrow face with hollow cheeks, a beard streaked with a little grey and an old scar that ran across his cheek.' I tried to keep my eyes focussed on her. Every time I turned my head I was rewarded with a fresh wave of burning pain. 'His left cheek,' I added. 'And you've seen that man before. In Clink Prison with John Ogle.'

Miss Hardwick leaned back against the wall and folded her arms, though she never looked away from the sixpence between my fingers. 'There it is. That's what I saw. Is that it then? Do I get my shilling now?' She glanced to the door.

'Not yet.' The description she had given was, if I remembered rightly, exactly the one Fowles had related. Almost the very same words. 'The carriage. You didn't see where it came from. They took Anne and tore off down the street towards Borough Market. You knew it was Anne because you'd seen her often at the ribbon-seller's stall. And they called her name. Anne Milton.' I could see her starting to squirm. I had related her story as she'd told it, yet she was as scared as a Christmas goose.

'I done what you asked and told you what you want,' she said. 'Now I need to go. I don't work, I starve. It's not like it is for you rich folk.' She tried to move past me. I caught her wrist.

'What about the other man? Did you see him?'

'Had his back to me, didn't he? Why you asking all these questions again anyway? I told you who did it. Ogle. He's the one you want.'

'You were at your window when you saw all this?' Warbeck, I saw, had moved there and was looking out. I still had hold of Miss Hardwick's hand. I moved it up to my face. 'The scar on that man of John Ogle. Show me how it runs.' I let go of her.

Miss Hardwick poked me in the cheek and ran a line up

past the corner of my eye. As her finger came towards my ear I flinched away, already cringing inside at how it would burn if she as much as touched my injury.

'Warbeck,' I called. He turned. 'Miss Hardwick, would you show that to my friend?'

She repeated her gesture.

'Which cheek was that, Warbeck?'

'The right cheek, Falkland.' Warbeck's voice was bleak and gravelly. He understood, as I had suspected and now knew. I went to the window.

'Miss Hardwick,' I said. 'Please point to where the carriage stopped.' From the window, I thought, she could not possibly have seen and heard what she claimed.

'You have to go now.' There was a terror in her voice. I saw her poised to run.

'You said the carriage came up behind Anne as she was walking towards the prison. You said it tore away back towards the market. This road leads only from the market to the prison. There is nowhere else to go. Where did it turn around?'

'I . . .' Miss Hardwick stood for a moment, mouth agape. Then she bolted. I lunged after her. Warbeck bellowed from the window.

'Waterhouse!'

I almost caught her before she flew out of the front of the lodgings, but missed. It did not matter. Waterhouse stood there waiting. She ran straight into him, and he folded his arms around her and dragged her back up the stairs as easily as if she was a child. I had him sit her by the window.

'Where was the carriage?' I asked.

Sullenly she pointed down the street, a good way further along from the window where we sat.

'You could not have seen the men clearly from here,' I said. 'You could not have heard what they said.'

'I did see them, sir. I swear it.'

'What did you actually see?'

'What I said!'

Warbeck had a dagger in his hand. I didn't see how he came by it, but now he thrust it at Jane Hardwick's face and held it, point first, in front of her eyes, pushing it closer as she steadily recoiled until she could back away no further. 'There are worse places than this,' he hissed. 'Much worse.'

'Tell us the truth,' I said. 'And you will come to no harm. We will go, and nothing more will be said and done. But understand that we are servants of Parliament. If you obstruct us then there will be consequences.'

'You little liar.' Warbeck's lips drew back like an animal. 'Who put you up to this?'

I had my thoughts on that now, but I would let them come from the woman's mouth rather than my own.

'What did you actually see?' I asked again, as calmly as I could. I took her hand and gently turned Warbeck's shaking arm away. 'Did you see anything at all?'

'I saw Miss Anne, like I said.' Her voice was quite different now. Gone was the cocky, sneering disdain. Now she was tremulous and frightened. 'I was sitting at my window, sir. It was a quiet time of day. I saw Miss Anne. I did recognise her, sirs, from the market. My brother's wife's sister is the ribbon-seller, and Miss Anne goes there often. I watched her walk past like she was on her way up to the prison. It seemed strange, her being a lady of quality. A carriage came up behind her like I said. It stopped alongside and the door opened. A man came out. They talked a bit and then he and another man helped her in. They went off towards the prison and turned around and came back the other way and went off.'

'Did they force her?'

'I don't . . .' Her face wrinkled at the effort of remembering. 'Not as I saw, sirs.'

'Did you hear anything?'

She shook her head.

'Did they call her name?'

'I don't know, sir. They spoke for a moment, but I couldn't say what was said.'

'Lying whore!' hissed Warbeck.

I ignored him. 'And the men? Did you know them?'

A trembling took her. 'I said it all later that day, when they came looking and I was out on the streets. I said all that, all what I saw. Then the next morning the other man comes and bangs open the door without so much as a knock and . . .' She stared at Warbeck and the dagger he still held. 'He told me what it was I must have seen. About there being a struggle and that man what's Lord John Ogle's friend – and it's true, sir, I have seen him in Clink, both of them. And then later comes the same men as I told before, only this time it's just the two of them, and they ask the same things, and so I tell them what I've been told I has to say.' She shuddered. 'He was terrible, that man.'

'Who was terrible? The same man who came back later that day with John Phillips?' Fowles. At that moment I would have bet my horse that Fowles had been the one to come and threaten her. So this was where the story of a conspiracy among the King's supporters had been born.

'Oh no, sir. No, they were both gentlemen who came

asking after Anne and what I saw, sir, like yourselves. Kind, they were. But the other, the one who told me what I was to say, he was fearsome. I knew he would hurt me.' She was pleading now. 'You see it in their eyes, sir, sometimes. One look at that's enough to know. He was a killer, this one. And then he came back again, just two days ago. He told me someone else would be coming. You, sir. That's what he meant. And I was to look out for you and make sure I told the same story as before, and to make sure you knew it was Ogle's man what did it. He said you'd give me a shilling, and that he'd cripple me if I didn't do what he said.' She was sobbing now, tears rolling over the swollen skin of her cheek. I fancied the bruise there was from the same villain, a warning of what might come later.

'This man. What did he look like?'

'He had one of those ribbons in his hat, sir. Green. And a huge beard like he never trimmed it, like madmen do, and mad eyes too.'

Perhaps it was just as well I had no horse of my own to wager. The man she described wasn't Fowles at all. This was the man who'd beaten me to the stones of Fleet Street and taken the last of Anne Agar's letters.

I asked more questions until I was satisfied that I was hearing, at last, the truth. Anne had been walking towards the prison. A carriage had pulled up and she'd climbed inside. A man had helped her and she had not resisted. A man, therefore, that she knew. When I was done, I turned to leave.

'Her too,' snapped Warbeck.

'Sirs!' Miss Hardwick was suddenly clinging to my arm as if I would somehow protect her. 'Sir, you promised no harm!'

'I did.' I carefully plucked her fingers from my sleeve and gave her the coin I had offered. 'Leave her, Warbeck. She told the truth in the end.' I had little sympathy for the woman; I had, however, told her that she would not be harmed, and I would not stand by and do nothing while Warbeck made a liar of me.

'She tells the truth for a sixpence and lies for nothing at all,' sneered Warbeck. 'That says all I need to hear. I have a cell for her, and I'll throw away the key.' I tried to stand between them, then reeled away as Warbeck waved the dagger at me. 'You're so noble, aren't you, Falkland? Get out of my way!'

CHAPTER 12

Waterhouse stood behind me. Warbeck stood before me. I did not think he would stab me, but I was not entirely certain either way.

'What is she to you, Warbeck?' I took a step away and kept my hands in the open. I had no weapon of my own, but perhaps Warbeck was not to know. 'The women who follow camp say whatever they must to survive. All soldiers learn this, sooner or later.'

Warbeck's eyes flashed venom. 'Falkland, on this woman's word of what she saw, I have already placed spies around John Ogle. I have an intelligencer on his way to Oxford to watch his cousin while there are far greater matters of concern. Must I remind you again that the future state of England will be decided these next few months? And this whore thinks to meddle with such matters?'

I saw now what lay beneath Warbeck's fury. Not that Miss Hardwick had lied, but that he had believed those lies just as Milton had believed them. They had pointed him to a conspiracy among the King's supporters, and that was exactly what both Warbeck and Milton wished to believe. He had been duped and made into a fool, as much by his own desires as by anything else. If Anne Agar had gone willingly into that carriage then the conspiracy they both sought was a phantom of sand and vapour.

'It is not this woman whom you should punish,' I said, my voice as carefully calm as I could manage with a dagger still pointed at my chest. 'It is the man who told her what lies she must tell, and who made her so afraid that she told them.'

'Yes! Sirs, that's how—' Miss Hardwick did not finish her speech. Warbeck moved with a speed that surprised even Waterhouse, and struck her across the face with such force that she stumbled and fell back onto her sorry, squalid mattress. He then stood over her with a look on his face so dire that I thought he might murder her right before my eyes.

'Warbeck!' I raised my voice. 'I've seen the man who came to her. He was the one who took the letter from me. With a ribbon in his hat and a beard of unkempt chaos. He can only be the same. He's the one we want. Find him and this whole mystery unravels.'

Warbeck eyed me. I could see his thoughts. Beneath the brutality of his convictions, I knew Warbeck to be a man of fierce intelligence. He might be duped, as might any man, but he was no fool. He understood I was right.

'Come, then, Falkland.' He bared his teeth and hissed at me. 'Let us be at it.' He stepped away from Miss Hardwick, sheathed his dagger and pushed me towards the door; I thought for a moment that he had seen reason through his fury and meant to let Miss Hardwick go, but as we left he turned to Waterhouse. 'Take her back to Limehouse and let her rot. You can ride Falkland's horse.'

'Warbeck!' I stopped and turned on him.

'Do not cross me, Falkland.' He pushed me roughly on. 'I have no patience. The woman lied.'

'She was afraid!' I stopped him again, barring his path. 'She is no part of this.'

'You have no say!' Again he pushed at me. This time I stood my ground. I did not doubt that Waterhouse would barge me aside with ease, but Warbeck was a slight fellow. Quick and deadly as a stoat, but not enough of him to push a large man out of his path.

'Cromwell brought me here to solve this mystery because you could not.' I saw that now. The weeks of delay between Anne's disappearance and Warbeck dragging me from that pigsty in Uxbridge. His surly, churlish demeanour towards me. 'But I will need your help as much as you will need mine. Take the glory if it pleases you – I have no care for flattery nor for ambition – but let her go or I will turn my back. Your promises were always false. I have seen the task you have set before Miss Cain, the size of it. You will never help me find my family. Not through malice or lack of want, but simply because it is beyond you. You cannot. So you may keep Miss Hardwick or you may keep me, but you may not keep us both.'

I could not say, at that moment, why I stood my ground for this whore I barely knew, who had lied and cheated us, but I think now that it was not for her. I had told her she would be safe. Warbeck would make a liar of me. I could not stand for that, not from a man like him.

His fury was naked for a moment. He had always despised me. In Crediton, as we came to the end, I had thought that perhaps I had won him over. I saw now that I had not, nor would I ever, no matter what I did. I was forever tainted by the side I had chosen in this war, though I had tried to tell him before that I had not *chosen* anything, I had already been a soldier, loyal to my country and my king – one and the same, I had thought – when Parliament had raised its standards.

Waterhouse came out to the street behind Warbeck, grappling with Miss Hardwick. Warbeck spat at my feet.

'Let her go, Waterhouse,' he snarled. 'Leave her be.'

We returned in silence, the three of us, through the throng of Borough Market and the hubbub of London Bridge. We reached the cathedral of Saint Paul and set to part ways, Warbeck to his chambers in Gray's Inn, I in search of a bookshop. It took all of that time for Warbeck to muster the will to become civil again; but before he left he rounded on me, his voice a snarl through gritted teeth, its usual syrup gone.

'Falkland, the man who frightened that pitiful whore into spinning us his story. You're quite sure he is the same as attacked you in the street?'

I nodded. 'The ringleader.'

'He sounds very distinct.'

I had to agree.

'And you would recognise him again, if you saw him?'

Of that I had no doubt, unless he had seen fit to shear off his beard. There could not be many so unkempt in this London. 'But I have no notion of where to find him.'

'He wore a ribbon in his hat?'

'He did.'

'Of what colour?'

'It was night. Under the moon I could not tell. Pale rather than dark, that is all.'

'The whore said green.'

'Then we are looking for a man with a striking beard who wears a green ribbon in his hat?'

'We are looking for a Leveller, Falkland.'

The tavern boy from the Bucket of Blood had said something of the same sort about the men who had come looking for me that night. I told Warbeck.

'Falkland, I know these people. They meet in a tavern called the Whalebone now and then. That may be where we will find him. Come and dine with me two days from now,' he said shortly. 'My lodgings at twilight. If you do not find him some other way first, we will go to the Whalebone after we have eaten and look for your bearded madman. There will be a meeting of the Levellers then.'

He rode on towards the Fleet. I asked Waterhouse if he would return my mare to the Bucket of Blood, and then began to search the churchyard of Saint Paul's for the bookshop of Humphrey Moseley. I thought at first this might pose some difficulty, but the churchyard was home to several purveyors of books and manuscripts, and the very first person I asked was immediately able to direct me to his shop. I entered, and was set upon by the smells of paper and ink. I have never been much of one for letters, but I will admit a fondness for the scents that often attend them. I have twice visited a house boasting a library, the first time as a welcome guest, the second as a victorious invader with a carbine in my hand and a sabre at my hip. Both times I was struck by the peculiarly unique smell, and Moseley's bookshop was the same way.

A young lady sat behind a counter poring over some palimpsest. She glanced up as I came through the door. I looked over the manuscripts lining the shelves. There were many of what I supposed were plays, all authored by names unfamiliar. It struck me as odd to sell them, because even I, who had been fighting for the King up and down the north and west of the country, knew that Parliament had closed all the theatres of London and were hostile to such notions of frivolous fiction. Among names such as Henry Vaughan and Edmund Waller I found the same pamphlet of John Milton's poems as I had seen on his own desk. I could not resist the temptation to pick it up.

'Those are new,' said the woman. Her eyes followed me, quizzical.

'I've seen them elsewhere,' I said, and put them down. 'Though it seems strange to see these side by side.' I picked up Edmund Waller. 'This is the Waller who plotted against Parliament to turn London in favour of the King, is he not?'

'Sent to the tower for it.' The woman smiled. 'But they let him go after a few months and settled on banishment instead. I think he's in France now, but it might be Switzerland. My father published him last year.' She held out a hand. 'You're a new face. I'm Anne. Anne Moseley.'

I took her hand and shook it, though it seemed an odd gesture. 'William Falkland.'

Miss Moseley turned back to her counter and proffered another pamphlet. 'If you like Milton I might suggest Richard Crashaw's *Steps to the Temple*.'

'Forgive me,' I declined. 'I was hoping to speak with Humphrey Moseley concerning one of his errand boys.'

I sensed her withdraw a little. 'Has there been some trouble? Are you from one of the printers?'

'I am about the business of Parliament,' I said, and saw at

once how this put her further on her guard. 'In a matter of
assistance to John Milton,' I added. 'I am looking for a lad
who may have information. I saw him briefly last night at a
printer in Fleet Street. Raworth, I think her name was, but I
did not have the opportunity to question him, and I do not
know his name. Perhaps you can enlighten me?'

She frowned. 'If he had crooked teeth and a mop of
unruly ginger hair that looks more like a bird has nested
there, that would be John.'

'I would remember that, I think.'

'Harry, then.' She gave a look of apology. 'I'm sorry,
Master Falkland, but neither one of them is here at the
moment, and my father is about business of his own.'

'Perhaps you could ask young Harry to come by the
Bucket of Blood in Covent Garden and look for me there.
It's not so far from Fleet Street and I'll have a sixpence for
him. Tell him I have no quarrel. I am engaged by Parliament
to find John Milton's sister.'

I saw her face soften at once. 'I didn't know her,' she said.
'But we've all heard. Such terrible news. Taken by the King's
supporters, it's . . . it's terrible. To think that people we
thought of as friends could have done such a thing.'

She did not hide her sympathies, and it struck me as odd
that Milton would choose a royalist to be his publisher; but
then his sister's husband had gone to fight for the King and
Milton still spoke of him with affection. I had yet, I
understood, to pierce the surface of John Milton.

I bowed and thanked Miss Moseley for her help, and
returned to Covent Garden. I thought I might wander the
crowds of Fleet Street again and question every printer and
errand boy I could collar, looking for word of Anne, but by

the time I reached my room the burning at the side of my head had turned into a steady, throbbing thunder. I thought, then, to lay myself down to rest a while instead, but I found my mind in turmoil. Thoughts of Anne Agar and Milton jumbled in my head with my own missing family. I could not shake the sense that this mystery revolved around the letters from Francis Lovelace, and that Peter Fowles knew a great deal more than he had admitted, and yet it seemed that I was stymied and must wait for Warbeck, or else for Moseley's lad to come and find me.

I needed to get away, to feel the wind on my face again. It struck me that if Francis Lovelace was the key to this then perhaps I should learn a little more about him, and so I saddled my mare once more and set off through the early afternoon to the north and the east until I had left London entirely behind me. I stopped as I came through the village of Romford and its market, and spent a few pennies of Warbeck's money on a little bread and cheese, and on some carrots freshly dug from the earth. Much of the market was given over to leather, and the air stank from the tanneries nearby. I asked directions to Rivenhall, the village where Lovelace had once made his home, and was directed to follow the old Roman road towards Colchester. I would find it, I was told, on the way.

I stopped for the night in Mountnessing. An old man who spent his every evening propped in a corner by the fire gave me better directions, and by the middle of the following day I had found my destination. Rivenhall seemed an affluent enough village, comfortably placed beside the Blackwater River and untouched – as much of this quarter of the country had been – by the ravages of the war. There was a medieval hall that had become a chimera of meeting place and market and tavern. They had no stables as such, but I was promised that my horse would not stray and would be watched, and that I could sleep soundly on the floor in some straw if I wished to pass the night. From there I received directions to the farm of Francis Lovelace and his widow.

'Poor woman,' said the carter who told me the way. 'He was gone for years but she only knew a few months back that he was dead. What with that and her cousin in Chelmsford drowning on account of that witch-finder—'

'Witch-finder?'

'Master Hopkins.' I had heard the name before; but as best the carter knew, the witch-finder had moved north and was far away. I couldn't tell whether he thought this was for the best or a trouble, and that witches would now spout in every village around him. 'Quite a thing how many witches there are about. Makes my bones shiver,' he said, with a shudder and a shake of his head as we went our separate ways.

The Lovelace farm, when I found it, was on rich land, and with gardens that remained cared for. I knocked on the door and received no answer, but the sounds of children led me to a small orchard where a woman and two young boys were rooting in the dirt with the aid of a young pig. They stopped at once as they saw me, all of them frozen except the pig, who seemed entirely unconcerned.

'I beg forgiveness for my intrusion,' I began. 'I am searching for the widow of Francis Lovelace.'

It took a moment, I think, for the woman to decide I was not some wandering vagabond or thief come to rob her. As she rose she nodded to the boys to carry on digging for whatever treasure they were searching, and led me back to the house. I introduced myself. Her own name, she told me, was Beth.

'Francis was your husband?' I asked her. She nodded. 'And those are your boys?'

She nodded again, a tautness in her face now. 'Edward and John.'

I paused, struck by the coincidence of their names. Each one common enough in its own right, but strange that they were the same as Anne Agar's sons.

'Francis died years back in the fighting.' She spoke with bitterness. 'Are you here because he owed you money like the other one? Because if you are then you'd best know there's nothing to be had. There's no money here and there never was.'

'Francis never owed me anything,' I told her. 'I never met him.'

This seemed to confuse her. 'Then why are you here?'

'Tell me about this man who came claiming Francis owed him money.' I sat on a stool by the window and offered a little of my bread and cheese, what I had left of it. Beth Lovelace eyed it with some suspicion at first. When I pushed it towards her, she snatched at it.

'Came a few months back. Early spring. Was him that told me my Francis was dead.' She let out a heavy breath. 'Not that I hadn't supposed it might be so. But he might as easily have run off with some trollop that turned his head while he was off a-fighting. Every soldier has their whore, that's what they say. Were you a soldier, Master Falkland? Did you have a whore?'

'I was and no, I did not. I had a wife who was waiting for me to come home.'

'And is she waiting still?'

The question caught me unawares. I wasn't ready for it, and it cut me deeper than I would have thought. I turned away for a moment, swallowing the sudden lump in my throat.

'I have not yet found her,' I said quietly. 'We are both still waiting.'

A silence hung between us.

'So what do you want?' she asked.

'You were telling me of this other man,' I reminded her.

'He came and told me that Francis was dead. Killed when his company was staying in a house they'd taken from some King's general or other after some battle. Gayton? Gaysbird?'

'Gainsborough?'

'That one. He told me it happened three years ago.' She wrinkled her nose. 'Said he was a soldier too, that they were in the same company, that a band of the enemy came on them one night. They were driven off, but poor Francis took a musket ball in the chest and died. Then he started on about how Francis owed him money and had he ever sent any? I laughed in his face at that. Francis Lovelace, send money when he could spend it on whores and trollops? My husband? And this fellow said they'd soldiered together. Didn't he know the man?'

I was beginning to get a picture of this Francis Lovelace, I thought. 'Did he ever mention a lady called Anne? Anne Agar, or perhaps Anne Milton?'

'No. But then he never mentioned any of his trollops. I found out about them the other way, didn't I?' She spat.

'What did you come here for, Master Falkland?'

'Did Francis write letters?'

'Plenty, for what that was worth, when he knew perfectly well I can barely read. Why? The other one asked the same thing. What's it to you?'

'What happened in Gainsborough?' I asked.

'My Francis died, that's what.' A flash of bitter anger sparked in her eyes. She turned away and started busying herself about her cottage. 'You can leave now, Master Falkland.'

'I would like to see the letters he sent. May I?'

'No. I don't have them any more.'

'This man who came to see you. He said your husband owed him money?'

'And I told him there was none to be had.'

'What did he do then?'

'I told him about how Francis had sent letters and made no mention of any money. Got very excited about that, he did. He asked to see them, same as you. Then he left.'

'Did he ever return?'

'No.'

I described Peter Fowles as best I could. 'Was that him?'

'Sounds about right.' She turned on me, brandishing a pan as though it was a weapon. 'What do you want?'

I saw little point in pretence. 'I am charged by Parliament with investigating the disappearance of a woman. Your husband wrote letters to her. They have been stolen. I believe the man who came to your house took them. I am trying to determine why.'

'Then you've wasted your time coming here, Master Falkland. Those letters are gone. Your man took them when he left. Said maybe they'd be a way for Francis to pay his debt, and that he'd leave me be.'

'You didn't try to stop him?'

Elizabeth Lovelace spat into the fireplace. 'Do you suppose that he asked when he took them? Besides, they were no use to me. My reading isn't good, and my Francis was lost to me years ago, long before he ever went to war. Now get out of my house. I don't want nothing of him no more.'

I returned to the old hall of Rivenhall and found a boy who promised to look after my horse for a penny. I asked him if he'd known Francis Lovelace, but he only shook his head.

'Do you know anyone else who knew him well?' I fished another penny from Warbeck's purse. The boy eyed it with greed.

'There's Beth Lovelace's ma,' he suggested. 'She lives not far.'

'Can you show me?'

He pointed along a track. 'A mile or thereabouts. Look for the white tree.' He cocked his head. 'Are you a soldier?'

'I was,' I said.

'Is that what happened to your head?'

I smiled and thanked him, gave him a penny and promised I would return in an hour or so. There would be another, I said, if he found some clean, dry straw and made up a place in the hall for me to sleep. I took the track he had shown me, and after some minutes I saw ahead a magnificent silver birch standing on the edge of a wood of oak and ash amid holly and hawthorn. A tiny cottage sat by the track a little way beyond it. As I approached, an old man rose from where he'd been tending a cabbage patch. I hallooed him and dismounted. He watched me while I walked my horse the last few yards as though I was some manner of creature he'd never seen.

'Good afternoon to you, sir,' I said. His expression didn't change. I looked down at his cabbages. They seemed fat and ready. 'You must be proud of those, I hope.'

'It's the caterpillars,' he said, and held out his hand and opened his fist. In it were about a dozen of the crawling things. 'Keep coming back, don't they? I have to come out every day.'

'Do you know Beth Lovelace?' I asked.

'Know her?' He laughed. 'She's my daughter.' He looked me up and down. 'You a soldier?'

'I was.' I held out my hand. 'William Falkland.'

He looked at my hand as though it was something odd, and didn't take it. 'Don't see many soldiers.'

'Beth was married to one, wasn't she?'

Now he snorted. 'He wasn't no soldier when she married him. I told her she was a fool, but he quite turned her head. Him and his big words and always off gallivanting. Spent more time off in London than he did here – or so that's where he *said* he was. It don't matter, I kept telling her, as long as he comes back with money. Smart fellow like that with a horse and those clothes, he has to have money. That's what I said, but it seemed like he never did. Hardly put a hand into keeping that farm of his. Left it to poor Beth. At least she's got the boys to keep her going now.'

'I hear he died.'

'So my Beth tells me. Good riddance, that's what I say. All those fancy words and knowing his letters, but he didn't know nothing about cabbages.' The old man took careful aim and hurled his handful of caterpillars across the track and into the grass.

'Did you know him well?' I asked.

'Francis Lovelace?' He spat into the dirt at his feet. 'Better than I wanted, I can tell you. I knew he was wrong from the start. Man like that rides through, man with his own horse and all those clever words, and takes a shine to our Beth. Oh, she was pretty right enough. Had half the lads in the village wooing after her, but then this Lovelace comes and she wouldn't have eyes for anyone else. Turned her head good and proper, he did. They were married quick and he soon put a son inside her, but it weren't long before he got bored. I knew it would happen. Used to go to London every month on that horse of his for a few days, even at the start. Didn't say what it was for. Then it got more and more. Then he didn't come back at all.'

'He went to fight in the war?'

'So Beth said. Couldn't see it myself, not a man like him. Gone off with some other woman, I told her. Gone and abandoned his wife. But seems like I was wrong and war it was. I suppose he had it in him. Right temper. Meek and kind as anything when you first see him, but tell him he was wrong about something and he'd kill you soon as look at you. Couldn't keep his eyes still, neither, nor his hands. Anything pretty and he'd be off. There's a bastard or two of his hereabout, I shouldn't wonder.' He frowned and looked at me hard. 'Why you asking about my Beth?'

'A man came through not long ago. The one who told her that Francis was dead. Did you see him?'

The old man shook his head. 'Few months past, that was.

Round when the weather turned and snow was a-melting. Didn't see him. He didn't stay. Poor lass.'

'Francis wrote her letters. Did Beth ever show them to you?'

He shrugged as if it was the most pointless thing he'd ever heard. 'Couldn't read them. Even poor Beth only managed a few words here and there. Don't know why he bothered. I think he was tormenting her. Always did like to remind her how she was stupid and how he was so much more cleverer.'

We spoke a little more, but he had nothing further to say about Lovelace save to mutter about his unsavoury temperament and the injuries he'd laid upon his poor wife. I returned to the village hall, and I must have tossed and turned in my sleep that night, for I awoke in the small hours with my head a burning agony, the torn flesh of my ear throbbing to a beat as hard and steady as a drummer's march. Try as I might I could not find a way to lie so as to ease the pain.

I dozed fitfully, and left for London again early with the dawn, pushing on until I could take no more and stopped at a small tavern in Epping. As I sat before an empty hearth, nursing a cup of beer and a bowl of pottage purchased with close to the last of Warbeck's money, I tried to piece together everything I had learned into some sort of picture. Lovelace had died in Gainsborough. Fowles had said so, and the document that Miss Cain had retrieved from Sir Willoughby of Parham on the standing of his company stated the same. He was, if I were to believe Beth Lovelace's father, a man of passion and poor temper. He had written letters to his wife, though she could barely read, and to Anne, and Peter

Fowles, I believed, had taken them all. There was something in those letters, then, but what? What could matter so much after so long a time? Lovelace had carried some secret to his grave, perhaps, and Fowles was looking for it, but even then, what did that have to do with Anne? I was quite sure in my mind that I must confront Fowles himself to find the answer, but I could not see how it might be done. Were he simply to deny everything, what evidence did I have with which to trap him? I could not believe the letters were not somehow connected, but at the same time I could not see the wherefore of it. It was as if I had two sets of pieces for two entirely different puzzles.

Perhaps, after everything the old man had said, there were other letters, written to other women. If there were, I could not see how I might learn of them.

I did not drink much in that tavern in Epping; but I found, by the time I left, that my aching head had eased. Perhaps the still and quiet of simply sitting with my thoughts had been succour. Certainly I found the pain grew worse again as the day drew on and I approached London, a dull and steady throb without the searing fire of the morning, but wearing nonetheless. It had been a long day by the time I turned into Covent Garden. I was disposed to head early for my bed, and so it was with something close to despair that I greeted the sight of Waterhouse waiting for me in the Bucket of Blood. He must have seen me as I rode around to the stables, for I had barely dismounted when he accosted me, and none too kindly.

'Where in Heaven's name have you been, Falkland? I've been looking for you since yesterday.'

'I had another enquiry I wished to pursue.' I made as if to

loosen the saddle on my horse, but Waterhouse laid a hand over mine.

'Do you not remember, Falkland? Warbeck invited us to dine with him tonight. And then it's the Whalebone. There is some meeting of the Levellers. Your man will likely be there, and then we can put an end to his mischief.' He slapped my shoulder, a gesture meant as one of brotherhood, though it rattled my bones and set my poor ear burning once more.

He grinned at me then. 'We'll have him good. An ear for an ear, eh, Master Falkland?'

CHAPTER 13

I was, it seemed, already late for my rendezvous. Warbeck was waiting for us beneath the gates of Gray's Inn. He gripped my arm.

'Falkland, where exactly have you been?'

I muttered an apology to my mare as I dismounted and loosened her girth. 'I went to Essex to see the wife of Francis Lovelace.'

'Lovelace?' The name exploded out of him like a ball from a musket, and with every bit as much violence.

'Francis Lovelace wrote letters to Anne. The letters were stolen when she disappeared. When I told Peter Fowles that I had one in my possession, I was attacked for it that very night. I now know that Lovelace wrote letters to his wife, even though she could not read them, and that Fowles went to see her some months ago. He took those letters too. They are at the heart of this, I am sure of it.'

Warbeck's fingers were so tight on my arm that they hurt even through my coat.

'Get Fowles out of your head, Falkland. Our concern tonight is the Whalebone.' He walked the three of us into the great hall and bade us wait; and when he returned he came with a dusky bottle and three cups. He poured us each a draft of the strongest, headiest wine I had tasted since I had once been invited to the King's court while we wintered in York. When Waterhouse took his first taste, his eyes fair bulged from his face. I dare say he had never before tasted a wine so rich.

'The spoils of war,' hissed Warbeck. 'Do you remember Basing House, Falkland?'

I remembered the story of it, how it had held out against the New Model, how it had finally fallen to Cromwell himself, how it had burned – some would say at dear Oliver's command – and how Cromwell had ordered the remains demolished, stone by stone, until every last one was removed. When I did not answer, Warbeck raised his cup to me nevertheless.

'Your health, Falkland. So one of us must return to John Milton and tell him that everything he thought is founded on a lie and we have, in fact, no notion at all of who has taken his sister Anne or why. Which of us shall it be, Falkland?'

I dare say Warbeck did not relish the notion. 'He will not countenance it from me, I think,' I said. 'Indeed, I am not certain he will even open his door. But it is not true that we have no notion. We have Anne's letters. We have Peter Fowles. It is surely no coincidence.' I would say nothing, I thought, of Anne's mysterious visits to Fleet Street until I understood their nature.

Warbeck shook his head. 'You would have us return to Milton's house and compound our failure with accusations against his guest? His friend? No, Falkland. Even if you are right, best to wait until we can offer something more. The Levellers are meeting in the Whalebone tonight. If we find your man there, we will find Anne.'

I confessed to my ignorance. 'Who are these men, these Levellers?' I asked. I had not given it much thought during my ride through Essex, occupied as I was with my injury, and these gangs and associations of men were wont to come and go. They had flourished even under the King, and Parliament's London was rife with them. I had not supposed them significant, but Warbeck, it seemed, thought otherwise.

'They are a loose association of men who would . . . who would take things further than most of Parliament will consider.' I knew at once from the way he said it that, whatever the views of these Levellers, Warbeck had his sympathies for them. 'There are those, Falkland, who would see the King restored to his crown under terms to be agreed. The Levellers would not. I have heard it whispered they plot to assassinate dear Charles if ever he returns to London. I do not think this is true, but they would surely prefer it if he would take away on a ship to Holland or the Rhine, or France, or wherever takes his fancy, and did not return.'

'And you would not disagree.' I could not resist. I caught a flash in his eye that told me I was right, although his words were more careful.

'The requirement of serving Parliament, Falkland, is that one must serve it in both those things of which one approves, and those of which one does not.'

I met his eye and smiled nastily. 'Might one not say the same of serving a king?' And now I had struck with that particular knife, I could not refuse the twist it offered me. 'And a man who turns against one master on the urging of his conscience – if conscience it can be called – might as surely turn on the next, might he not?'

Warbeck cocked his head. 'Are you speaking for yourself now, Falkland? Be that as it may, the Levellers are certainly no friend to any royalist or supporter of the King. John Milton may not count himself among their number, but his views lean towards theirs. They see him as an ally. They would court him, not seek to offend him by abducting his sister.' He leaned towards me in this fervour of words, and it was all I could do not to turn my head away from the stink of his breath. 'They would not have done this, Falkland! Something else is afoot. It is a King's man who has infiltrated their number. Or wears the green to misdirect us from the truth. We will see that they fail!'

I nodded my acquiescence, although I wondered at the strength of Warbeck's vehemence. There was an affront to it that went far beyond an enthusiasm to unravel Anne Agar's fate.

'You know these men,' I said at length. I could see it in him, the anger and the conflict. These Levellers were the sort of men who kindled in Warbeck a sympathy, and so he wished for them to have no hand in something so base as the kidnap of an innocent woman. I am ashamed at how I revelled in that, for I had felt the same when the accused had been the King's supporters. It should have given me a measure of understanding, perhaps; indeed, I would say that it did, but I revelled in his discomfort nonetheless.

'They gather tonight in the Whalebone close to Newgate. We should go after dark to find them at their most numerous. If your man is there, we will take him quietly aside and get to the truth of it.'

Outside was twilight, the sun hanging low over Westminster. Warbeck summoned food, a leg of roast mutton dripping in its own grease. Waterhouse and I both boggled at this, drooling with greedy eyes at fare far beyond our usual means. It came with some manner of bean broth chunked full with cabbage and carrot. I found myself ravenous, and did not hold back.

Soldiers will tell their stories when they come together over a hearty meal. I have rarely seen it otherwise, and believe it to have been that way since one man first took up a spear against another. Yet though Warbeck, Waterhouse and I had all seen our share of battles, we ate without words. Our tales were too different. There was no camaraderie to be had in them. One man's defeats and setbacks became the other's victories and advances. Divided thus, we found nothing of which to speak; and as I mused on our silence a part of me feared that this was how it would be across the whole of England now the war was done. No shared purpose, no common cause, just kingdoms and counties divided as they had been when they took up arms; cities and towns and villages and even families. It was an old fear, one long harboured; yet as our bellies filled I began to feel a sense of hope instead. Oddly it was Milton himself who confounded me. Milton who espoused views so empty of compromise, so absolute in their finality, yet who treated his sister's likely-dead husband as a brother, no matter that he had supported the King in this struggle. A man who tore with ruthless vitriol into any opinion set against his own, yet wrote poems of ethereal beauty.

I glanced more and more at Waterhouse. We had devoured as much as seemed civilised, both of us, and licked our fingers, and I caught him staring at the plates after we were done, no doubt thinking the same as I – that in less refined company we might have licked those clean too. I found that I did feel a brotherhood with him after all, unlike anything I felt for Warbeck. At heart we were both simple men, soldiers on different sides, yes, but our lives had much in common. I tipped my cup to him when I caught his eye, and took back my plate and licked it clean, to Warbeck's great disgust. Waterhouse did not follow my example, but I caught a glimmer of a wry smile courting the edges of his lips.

Perhaps the work Miss Cain was doing in Lincoln's Inn would go some way to heal these wounds. And for all the grief and death it had caused, the war had been fought decently enough. Towns and villages had not – for the most part – been sacked and put to the torch. Prisoners on the whole were not hanged or murdered, my own case notwithstanding. I had heard a little of the horrors of the German wars that had preceded ours, the bloodbaths and the atrocities of slaughter and pillage. For whatever reason, we had not slid into that wholesale murderous state, but I had sensed, towards the end, a change, a desperation. Cromwell and Fairfax had found a way to end it with the New Model before we fell upon one another as animals, and I was glad of that.

It was a delicate thing, this hope I felt, but it lived.

'Why should we care?' I asked Waterhouse.

'There was a lad in the Bucket of Blood looking for you yesterday, Falkland,' he said. 'Didn't get his name, but he said he was from a printer or some such.' Waterhouse smiled as he picked up his plate at last and licked it.

I would, if I had been afforded the opportunity, have rushed away at once to Saint Paul's and its bookshops, but it was already dark as we left Gray's Inn and headed back along Fleet Street and into the city, and so Moseley's lad would have to wait for the morrow. Candles burned in the windows of the presses, still hard at work. We passed under the portcullis and arch of the Lud Gate, and there Warbeck turned north away from the river, across Cheapside, and continued among a maze of narrow streets and alleys until I saw ahead of us a tavern lit up by a great many lanterns. Two men pushed past us in an eager hurry as we approached. They were almost running. As they turned inside I saw they had ribbons in their hats, though I could not be sure of their colour in the gloom.

I pressed my pace, then slowed as I felt Warbeck's hand on my shoulder.

'Careful, Falkland. You can't just walk into the Whalebone, find your man and walk out with him. Try that and it will go badly for all of us.'

'What do you suggest?'

'That we go and sit quietly in a corner. You cast your eyes about the place and tell me if any of the men who came at you that night are present. Then we wait for them to come out and we follow them. We confront them when they are away from their confederates and do not have a dozen friends eager to leap to their defence. Start anything in the Whalebone and you'll have a score of Levellers on your back.'

There was sense to Warbeck's plan.

'Let me go in first,' he said. 'Keep your face down and hidden behind Waterhouse in case there are eyes who might know you.'

In this way we entered. The Whalebone was a lively tavern, every bit as vibrant with the buzz of conversation as the Bucket of Blood, but without the smell of iron and piss that tinged the air of Covent Garden. I kept my head down as Warbeck had advised, but I couldn't stop my eyes from roaming, peering out from under the brim of my hat. Many of the men here wore green ribbons, I saw, although not all. A good few paused from their talk as we entered, glancing our way. I quickly came to understand that Warbeck was no stranger here. The nods he received gave him away.

He led us to a dark corner and drew up stools for each of us. The men who had attacked me were not here.

'Well?'

'I don't see them,' I said.

This seemed to please him.

'You're known here,' I remarked.

Warbeck shot me a hostile glance. 'I am known in many places, Falkland. It is my position to be known.'

'Then perhaps you will know the men who struck me down.'

While Waterhouse removed himself to find us each a cup of ale, I described the men who had come at me in the middle of Fleet Street. The last of them, the one with the unkempt beard, was the most memorable of the four, but I knew I would recognise the others. There was a stocky fellow with a large, bulbous nose and three missing teeth and the mashed face of a fist-fighter. A young man with scars all over as though he had survived the pox. The last had a pointed face and arms and legs that seemed too long for the rest of him. I enumerated these various features, but none seemed familiar to Warbeck.

Waterhouse returned. We sat in silence, each casting our eyes about the tavern.

'Were the others also Levellers?' Warbeck asked.

'They did not pause from their beating of me to proclaim their affiliations,' I replied.

'But did they wear ribbons in their hats?'

'I do not remember seeing such, but I did not pay their hats much heed. My attention was considerably occupied with their fists and their clubs and their boots. Ask me of their boots and I will tell you everything.' Soldiers' boots, all of them. Nevertheless, Warbeck's question had its merit. I ran through what I remembered of that night, what I had seen of each of them. 'I do not think so,' I said at last. 'But I cannot be sure.'

It did not matter. We had been there for perhaps half the evening when two of the four strutted through the door of the Whalebone. I saw them and knew at once that I was not mistaken. The one with the bulbous nose and the pox-faced lad. Quietly, I prodded Warbeck.

'Those two.'

He turned his eyes to them long enough to study their faces.

'Do you know them?'

He shook his head, but I thought more in despair and dejection than in denial. 'You're certain of those men?'

'Entirely.'

'Then in a moment we go. Outside, we watch and we wait.'

We delayed long enough for the new arrivals to settle themselves and become engrossed in their own business, hoping, I suppose, that they would not pay us any attention as we left. I could not help myself, however. As we reached the door I looked back again, perhaps to be sure I had the right men, and found one staring at me by return. Our eyes locked. I knew I was right, and I knew too that he had seen me and remembered me as well. I made as if to hurry away, and pushed past Waterhouse and Warbeck.

'What are you doing?' Warbeck hissed as I bundled him out of the way.

'They saw me.' I glanced back once more. Both men were rising. I pushed Warbeck hard, knocking him to the ground; outside I began to run, south towards Cheapside. As I looked over my shoulder I saw Warbeck waving his fist – he had the wit, as I thought he might, to play to the scheme that now sprang to my mind – and then out came the two men from the Whalebone, racing after me. I do not know why they gave chase this way, nor why men do this. It is an animal thing, I think. They chased after me because I ran.

I turned into an alley and slowed, looking for a dead end where they might trap me. As soon as I saw one, I took it, ran to the end and pounded on a door. My pursuers, seeing they had me cornered, slowed.

'One beating not enough for you, eh, Falkland?'

'You know my name? How is that?'

'You're known more than you might wish it, King's man.' The last was spat out into the night as though some kind of poison. Neither man wore the green ribbon, but their sympathies were clear enough.

I braced myself and raised my fists as if for a fight. The pox-faced lad had a narrow club that he now took from his belt. Bulbous Nose had no weapon, but this lack did not seem to trouble him. They advanced slowly, wary I would make a run for it. Bulbous Nose, I remembered, had been the most vicious of all of them with his boot. I think he would have killed me that night had he not been pulled away.

'Two makes for a more even fight than four,' I hissed, although in truth I was far from prepared to fight even one man alone. My ear throbbed from the exertion of running, while the bandage around my head marked my weakness. I pointed to the pox-faced lad. 'Where's your friend? The one who struck me from behind? Or what about your master? The one with the beard? Does he know of this? And what do you know of me, aside from my name?'

'That you're one of the King's curs,' hissed the man with the bulbous nose. 'A kidnapper of women. Thought you'd steal our spoils of war, did you? You'll pay for that now!'

Curious words indeed. I would have asked for their meaning, but a cry came from the darkness behind them before I could speak.

'Stop!' They froze and turned as, out of the shadows, came Warbeck and Waterhouse. Waterhouse carried a bludgeon. Warbeck had a pistol in each hand, raised and ready.

'Henry Warbeck,' snarled the man with the bulbous nose. He did not seem unduly concerned to find a pistol levelled at his chest.

'Nathaniel Blackwater. It comes as little surprise.'

'You run with the King's dogs now?'

'I am, as I ever was, a servant of Parliament.'

'This villain is a King's man, Warbeck. Leave him to us and be on your way.'

'This man is in my employ, Nathaniel.'

The look on Blackwater's face was one of pure hatred. He drew a knife from under his coat and tossed it into the air, spinning it and catching it by its haft. Warbeck aimed his pistols a little straighter, both of them now pointing at Nathaniel Blackwater.

'Stand down in the name of Parliament.'

'Not in the name of the King, Warbeck? Are you sure?'

'Quite certain.'

'But I find I am not.' Blackwater jumped sideways and threw the knife at Warbeck. There was a flash and deafening roar as Warbeck fired one of his pistols. The man with the bulbous nose lurched and stumbled against the alley wall. He stopped and looked down at himself. Warbeck hadn't moved, save to lower the pistol he had fired. The other remained resolutely pointed at Blackwater.

'You have killed me!' Blackwater leaned more heavily against the wall. He turned his back to it and sank to his haunches, a hand pressed to his chest. His skin was dark when he drew it away again. He stared at himself. The night washed out all colour, but I had no doubt that his fingers were covered in his own blood.

'An abductor of women, Nathaniel? I wonder, do you speak of Anne Agar, John Milton's sister? Who told you such nonsense? What are these spoils of war of which you speak?'

'You're a traitor to us, Warbeck.' Blackwater coughed, and dark blood dribbled from his mouth. 'You'll be fawning at the King's feet come the end of summer, you and the rest. At least you killed me quick so I don't have to see it. The devil take you.' He looked at the pox-faced boy. 'Tell these dogs nothing, lad.'

'This man is William Falkland. He acts under orders from Cromwell himself to find Milton's sister. He did not *take* her, you fool.'

'Cromwell, who would make peace with the King when we have just rid ourselves of such! What was it all for, Warbeck, if we would see that papist idolater back on his throne?'

Warbeck growled. 'It is the will of Parliament to choose the outcome, not of you or I by force of murder. Like it as little as we may.'

'So say you, Henry Warbeck, but what do you call this if not murder?'

'Clear your conscience before you die, Nathaniel. Where is Anne?'

'Wherever you villains have taken her.' Blackwater spat blood and moaned. He slumped a little, and then his head fell forward. He tipped sideways and lay still against the stone.

Warbeck's pistol shifted to the other lad. 'Take him, Waterhouse.'

The lad backed away in terror for his life, but he had nowhere to go. I clasped a hand on his shoulder as he stepped away from Waterhouse. Now that I saw him closer, the boy couldn't have been more than fourteen or fifteen years old.

'There were four of you who came at me that night on Fleet Street,' I said. 'Who were the others? Who told you I had abducted Anne?'

'I don't . . .' He pulled away from me, but Waterhouse was on him now. He tried to run. Waterhouse grabbed his arm and pulled him back, and threw him against the alley wall with such force that I swear the very bricks shivered. In a flash Warbeck was on him, one hand clenched around the lad's throat, the other holding the pistol so the end of its barrel was but a few inches from the boy's face. The boy wailed. 'I swear it! I don't know anything about it!'

'Warbeck . . .' I began.

'Keep your silence, Falkland, if you know what's good for you.' The rage in his voice was a weapon in itself, a terrible thing. He shifted, pressed the lad harder against the wall. If Warbeck had not been the shorter of the two, I swear he would have lifted the boy clear off the ground by his neck. 'Boy, who were the others?'

'The one with the long arms,' I said. 'And the one with the beard.'

'I swear I . . .' The boy's words ended with a strangled gasp. With one violent heave, Warbeck threw him to the alley floor. He stood over the boy, pointing the pistol at his face.

'The next words you speak will either be a name, boy, or they will be your last.'

I felt the boy's terror as my own. I had no doubt that Warbeck would shoot him, wouldn't even hesitate. I was minded to throw myself upon him to stop him, but Waterhouse stood in my way.

'Fletcher,' wailed the boy. 'Ned Fletcher.'

'Which one was he?'

'He has the beard, sir! Please don't shoot me!'

'And the other?'

The boy was weeping now. 'I don't know him, I swear. He came with Fletcher. Fletcher and the other one knew Nathaniel from the fighting, sir. I swear, that's all I know! They said this man had taken a good woman from her home and now held her hostage at the King's bidding, that he carried a letter to prove it. Please . . .'

'Where will I find Ned Fletcher?'

'I don't know, sir! I saw him now and then in the Whalebone in the days before, but not since. I swear! Please, have mercy. I am a godly man, I promise.'

Warbeck stepped away, though he didn't lower the pistol. As he did I crept closer. I crouched beside the boy and offered him my hand. It felt a strange thing. The last I had seen of this face it had been twisted with hate and fury as he swung a club into my ribs. He and Nathaniel Blackwater would have killed me that night had the other men not stopped it. Yet now I felt a pity for him.

'What did this Ned Fletcher tell you, boy?'

'It's known all over London. John Milton's sister. Fletcher said you took her. He said you carried on your person that night evidence of your masters.'

'The letter.' I began to see. 'You came to the Bucket of Blood to look for me.' He nodded. 'You didn't find me. You searched my rooms. Shall I hazard a guess that Fletcher did the searching while the rest of you kept watch for my return?'

'Him and his friend. Nathaniel and I kept lookout.'

'And when he didn't find what he was looking for?'

The boy declined my hand but rose, shaking, to his feet. His eyes flitted nervously back and forth between Warbeck and me. Warbeck's pistol never wavered.

'He said he knew where you might be. He said you would have the papers with you to prove your guilt and that of your masters, and that we'd have to make an ambush.'

'And so you did.' I touched my ear, gently because even the slightest movement seared at my face. 'Which one of you knocked me down?' If I remembered aright, it had been the one with the long arms, but I could not be sure. I had barely seen much of any of them before I grappled with Fletcher himself.

'The other man. He never said his name.'

I balled my fist and punched the lad in the gut, hard and fast. I did not imagine, until I did so, any desire to do such a thing. I stepped back as he doubled over and retched, as surprised as he. I turned to Warbeck.

'We have a name. We find this Ned Fletcher, we find the men who took Anne.'

Warbeck nodded. His face remained a rictus of rage. 'Go home, Falkland. Waterhouse, take this boy around the corner and wait.'

Waterhouse did as he was bid at once. I hesitated, staring at Warbeck, trying to understand his rage. The lad and Blackwater had been duped. They were not the first, nor would they be the last.

'Go, Falkland,' he snarled again. 'I'll take the boy to Newgate. We'll get it out of him what he knows, one way or the other.'

The look on his face told me that Warbeck much desired to shoot me, and he still carried a loaded pistol. I backed away and turned the corner. Waterhouse stood there with the pox-faced lad. For all the murder the lad had meant me, it pained me to see that boy. He was barely older than my son John had been when I last saw him, younger than John would be now. I wondered if he, too, had a father somewhere, desperately searching. I put a hand on Waterhouse's arm.

'Go gentle on the lad unless he gives you no choice. He's been played for a fool and now he's seen a man he called a friend killed because of it.'

Waterhouse grunted, as if he did not care much for such sentimentality.

Before I turned away for my bed, I crept back to the corner of the alley. Warbeck was crouched beside the body of Nathaniel Blackwater. It seemed to me that he was shaking. At first I thought he was weeping, but surely that was wrong, for Henry Warbeck was not a man to weep. Yet still, I understood that the pox-faced lad had not been the only one to lose a friend here tonight.

Perhaps Warbeck sensed me, for he spun suddenly about, and with such a look of murder on his face that I shrank away. He strode from the alley, passed me as though I wasn't there, and marched upon the Whalebone, an army of one and with such forceful intensity that I wondered if any company ever mustered might have dared stand against him. I followed, curious to see where this would end. Warbeck slammed the tavern door open and stood inside the threshold. When that alone did not silence the hubbub of conversation, he raised his remaining pistol and fired it into the tavern roof.

'Fletcher,' he roared. 'Ned Fletcher. Where is he?'

He received at first no answer save a room full of hostile glares. Undeterred, Warbeck strode across the commons. He lowered his second pistol and aimed it straight at the chest of a man with a green ribbon in his hat. It was the same pistol as had killed Nathaniel Blackwater, and Warbeck had had no opportunity to reload it, yet such was the ferocity of his countenance that I do not think a single man who saw him in that moment could have dared imagine his intent to be anything but deadly.

'A leveller is dead tonight because of Ned Fletcher.

Another is bound for Newgate, and a godly woman is taken from her family. Where is he?'

The man at the end of Warbeck's pistol stared Warbeck down, daring him, I think, to fire; but then another man close by spat out the name of a place, a street, and then followed with a string of curses upon the name of Henry Warbeck. Warbeck turned on his heel and left, and across a dozen battlefields I have never seen a face so lethal in its expression. If looks had carried edges then every man in Warbeck's path would have bled tonight.

'With me, Falkland.' He tossed me one of his pistols, and then powder and shot to lead it, and did not look back.

I did not know whether the place we sought was near or far, nor did Warbeck trouble to tell me, but we had not walked for long before he stopped at a door in a tight row of old houses squeezed together like fish in a barrel. He paused a moment, cocked his ear to the latch, and then quietly tested the handle; but the door was neither locked nor barred, and the house beyond lay empty. The hearth was cold, the embers there long forgotten. A thin film of dust covered the table.

'Fletcher!' Warbeck bellowed his name, though I think he must have known we had been falsely directed. At first I did not think that anyone had lived here for some weeks, but when I went up the narrow stairs to the tiny room in the eaves I found a mattress that seemed more recently used, and a chamber pot hurriedly emptied. This room, at least, had been occupied within the last few days.

Warbeck stormed outside, a whirlwind roar of fury and frustration. As he did I caught a glance of a face peering from behind the upstairs drapes of the house across the way. It stared at me over the narrow divide of the street, warped by leaded glass. An old man, grey haired and weathered. I moved the chamber pot aside and opened the window. The old man stared at me. I beckoned to him; and then at last he opened his own window as well so that we might speak.

'I am sorry if my friend has roused you from sleep,' I said. 'The man who lives here, do you know his name?'

The old man shook his head, but I saw a spark of recognition as I began to describe Fletcher's beard and his mad eyes.

'When was he last here?'

Another shake of the head. 'Comes and goes. Always late at night, always gone in the morning.'

'Does he come alone?'

A nod this time. Then a deep frown. 'Except one time a few weeks back. Had a woman with him. Some whore, I suppose, though she didn't look like one. Dressed as a gentlewoman, but on her own with him here?' The old man let it be clear how he disapproved.

I thanked him and let him back to his sleep, and returned to Warbeck's side.

'Anne was here,' I said. 'I am sure of it. And I am every bit as sure that she came of her own free will.'

Warbeck walked away and did not look back. I do not think, then, that he wished to hear.

CHAPTER 14

I did not sleep well that night. The tear in my ear had slowly begun its healing, but it was swollen and angry. I could not lie on that side without quick and searing pain; yet whenever I closed my eyes, I tossed and turned. In Miss Cain's list of names of Sir Willoughby of Parham's militia of 1643, I had seen more than one Fletcher. I had seen a Blackwater there, too, but with only an initial that might have been an N or an M. I had not scanned the list fully. In the darkness I found myself wondering if I would find the name of Henry Warbeck.

My dreams, when sleep finally came, were tumultuous. I found myself again in that alley, over and over. Sometimes I was crouching over the pox-faced lad and he was my son John. Other times I was Warbeck and I had shot a man, and now I was on my haunches beside him, and knew I had done a terrible thing, though I could never see the dead man's face. Later I dreamed of running to a house. I knew it to be a grand manor, and yet when I opened the door I found myself in Beth Lovelace's cottage. A woman stood there with her back to me, and I had come because I had found, at last, my Caro – or so I thought – but when the woman turned she was a stranger and, though I had never seen her face, I knew with the certainty of dreams that I had found Anne Agar instead; and there was no joy in finding her, for I knew I had made a choice not long before, and had chosen this path instead of some beckoning other that would have led me to my Caro. I ran from that house and searched back for the fork in the road I had taken, but it was not there, only an endless graveyard.

I awoke sweat-stained and fevered with no sense of having rested. It was not hard to understand that my dreams were telling me what I told myself almost every day – that I should never have accepted Cromwell's command, that I should have left the gatehouse of Woodstock and turned my back on all of them and walked to Oxford itself to look there, siege be damned. I cursed myself again for not having gone directly from Bristol. I had been afraid, that was all, afraid that I would find myself once again drawn against my will into the King's armies. I do not think the King and his commanders would have taken a refusal well. Or perhaps, now that I had acted as Cromwell's intelligencer, they would have hanged me as a traitor.

I sat in the Bucket of Blood, staring into nothing, telling myself I was waiting for Warbeck to return from a fruitful night in Newgate Prison with that lad from the alley. It pained me that I hadn't even learned the boy's name; but I knew, as the morning wore on, that I fooled myself, and the knowledge was like the stone of Sisyphus around my neck as I idled my time contemplating my failing, alternating between fits of shivers and sweat. My ear burned and throbbed. I should have seen that I was not well and scorned these visions and fits of despair for the derangement of fever, but that very fever had drawn a veil across my eyes so I could not see my own condition.

This, then, was how Moseley's lad found me. He sidled into the tavern cautious and wary, and I did not spot him until he came and stood over me, feet shuffling with nerves.

'Sir?'

I did not even recognise him at first. My thoughts felt dull as if with drink.

'Sir? We met in Raworth's printers, sir. Miss Anne said you asked after me?'

Miss Anne? For one startled moment I thought he meant Anne Agar, but then I remembered. Anne. The bookseller Moseley's daughter.

'Yes.' I laboured to my feet. 'Harry, is it?'

The lad nodded. I couldn't help but think of my son John as I looked him over. John had been about this age when I had last seen him, that gangly age when boys shoot up, when their arms and legs grow long faster than they grow wide.

'I am looking for John Milton's sister,' I said. 'You know John Milton?'

He nodded.

'Did you know his sister Anne?' For a moment I laboured to keep my eyes focussed. I forced myself to take a long, deep breath, and endeavoured to steady my mind.

'Never spoke to her, sir, but I seen her, yes. She came by the shop now and then on business for Master Milton.'

'But you know something else.' I had seen it in his eyes. That leer in the printer's doorway, though there was no sign of it now, only an awkwardness. 'You've seen her on Fleet Street,' I said, as gently as I could muster.

The lad shuffled his feet and would not meet my eye; but at last he nodded.

'Yes, sir. I seen her in Fleet Street. There's a printer there she used to go and visit. But . . . well, sir, there was never any printing done, if you catch my meaning.'

I caught well enough where his own imagination had led him, at least. 'Who was this printer?'

'Master Wallis, sir.'

'Could you take me to him?'

I followed Moseley's lad out of the Bucket of Blood and quickly to the hubbub of Fleet Street. There I had to lean against a wall to retrieve my breath. I felt nauseous. My head was spinning.

Moseley's lad frowned at me. 'Sir?' He pointed me to a printer's outside which a small wagon was parked. 'That there's Master Wallis, sir.' Men were unloading what looked like a new press shipped in from Holland. I gave the lad my last sixpence, pulled myself upright and forced my way through the crowd to where a tall, bony man with a prominent nose stood shouting at three workmen unloading their wagon. Inside the shop I saw two other men who had already begun the assembly of the device. The rest of the shop struck me as strangely bare.

'Master Wallis?' I asked.

The bony fellow shot me an unwelcoming glance. 'Good day, sir. How may I help you?' His attention remained on the unloading of his press. As I opened my mouth to reply, one of the men uttered a string of gibberish, and Wallis immediately retorted with more of the same. It took me a moment to realise that they were speaking Dutch.

'John Milton's sister, Anne Agar, made a habit of visiting your press,' I said.

I had, I saw, his sudden and full attention. He hurried me

into his shop, past the half-assembled press and into a small back room that was a chaos of stacked papers. I had barely stepped inside when he rounded on me, his voice sharp and far from friendly.

'Who are you?' he asked.

'My name is William Falkland.' I would have offered my hand, but his demeanour suggested that he wouldn't take it. 'You knew Anne Agar?'

'In passing. What of it?'

'You are aware that she has disappeared?' A chill shiver shuddered me, though the air in the room was stifling warm.

He hesitated. 'No,' he said at last. 'Disappeared?' Though he remained wary, his hostility ebbed.

'She has not been seen for close on a month.' I watched his face and saw a flash of surprise and shock. And, I thought, of something else. Guilt.

'I did not know that,' he said.

'I have been tasked by Parliament to find her if I can. She made several visits to your shop, did she not?'

Wallis pushed past me. He closed the door behind us and slumped onto a stool, then waved at me to do the same. 'Sit if you wish, William Falkland. Tasked by Parliament, you say? Then yes, Anne Agar came to my shop, but it wasn't to see me. She came for my brother, John Wallis. They would meet here, out of sight of prying eyes. Do you know of him? My brother John?'

A wave of faintness sucked at me. I sat, heavy as though my legs were done, and then realised with sudden shock that I did indeed know the name of John Wallis. Not that we had ever met, but I had heard of him. 'Parliament's master intelligencer?' I gasped. It was said among the King's commanders that there was no cipher he could not break. 'But why . . . ?'

'She had letters. She thought there was a message hidden in them beyond the plain words. Something to do with her husband Thomas. I don't know much more of it.'

'Letters? Do you have any of them?' Letters again. The key was here, I was sure. I could feel how close I was to the heart of it.

'She gave a few to John. On her last visit she took them back. John never found a cipher. I did not listen to their conversations, but I know enough to know that he was intrigued; but of course, if you're Parliament's man, you will take the trouble of asking him yourself.'

I would indeed. I rose, intent on seeking out John Wallis at once, but my legs seemed struck by a sudden weakness. I leaned against the door to stop myself from falling. A thought struck me. 'When did you last see Anne?'

'A month ago. That was when she took back her letters. She came with another man, one I had not seen before, and I will say I did not like the look of him. They did not stay for long.'

'This other man . . .' I thought I already knew. Fowles.

'Oh, I don't know his name, but there would be no mistaking him again if I saw him. Foul-mouthed and brutish, with a great bush of a beard.'

Fletcher?

I stumbled through the door of the printer's shop and pushed away from the crowd, desperate for air. My wounded ear throbbed and burned. These sweats and shivers and waves of weakness did not bode well. The veil at last lifted and I saw that I was feverish. My wound. I would need someone to peer beneath these bandages, though I feared I would not like the answer. Anne. Letters. Ciphers, now? My head spun. I needed . . . To rest. To lie down.

In my feverish state I could think of nowhere else to go but to Miss Cain. I walked from Fleet Street southward among the yards of the printers and binders, struggling, it seemed, for every breath of air. Away from the noise and bustle I sat beside the River Thames and rested among the little piers and quays of White Friars. I sat with my head in my hands, my thoughts scrambled as though hit by a ball from a musket; but in time the feeling passed. I remained weak, but I was able again to walk without fear of the strength simply vanishing without warning from my legs.

I reached Lincoln's Inn to find Miss Cain at work in her rooms. She turned to look as I stumbled upon her, saw it was I, and resumed as if it were perfectly natural that I should come and sit beside her. Indeed, that was how it felt to me, also.

'You look pale, Falkland. Have you seen a ghost?'

'I would see the list of names of Sir Willoughby's militia again,' I said, perhaps more curtly than I had intended. I found myself annoyed at Miss Cain herself, for she had seen my parlous state and yet worked on as if it were nothing. Exasperation at my own selfish wants followed. I shuffled restlessly on my stool. I think perhaps I may have muttered under my breath.

With a sigh, Miss Cain put down her papers.

'I am of a troubled mind,' I said. 'Pay me no thought.'

'Easier said than done, Master Falkland. You're as wriggly as an eel today.'

Was I? I had not noticed. I sprang to my feet, struck by a

sudden surge of vigour. 'Why must everything revolve around Milton? Could it not be something else, something that had nothing to do with him at all?' I knew I wished it would be so, and I found that that vexed me too; perhaps Warbeck was as right about my prejudices as I was about his, and simply mistook the cause. 'It is all to do with these letters, yet Anne was not *taken* as Milton would have it. Ned Fletcher may be a villain, but Anne went with him willingly, and she was already looking for something in those letters herself when she did.'

Miss Cain regarded me carefully, her expression changing from one of annoyance to concern. 'You look pale and waxy, Master Falkland. Are you not well?'

'My ear burns.' I tapped at the side of my head, gingerly so as not to provoke a fresh eruption of agony.

'Here. Your list of names.' Miss Cain handed it to me, then rose and plucked at the cloth wrapped around my head. Her closeness fuddled my thoughts. I shivered, and then flinched as I felt her touch my bloodied ear.

'Edward Fletcher. Nathaniel Blackwater.' I looked over the paper and there they were, both on the list of Sir Willoughby's company. I suspected the other man would be there too, Fletcher's friend, but I had close on two hundred names to choose from. There was no Henry Warbeck, at least.

'Keep still now, Master Falkland.' She had the knot untied and was unwrapping the cloth. Each time she unravelled another layer from over my ear, I flinched a little more. I drilled my eyes into the page, determined to think of nothing else. Fletcher came from Lincolnshire. A place somewhere in the north of the county, I thought, but the name wasn't familiar.

'Doesn't smell so good, Falkland.'

'Rot smells far worse. Believe me, Miss Cain, you would have known gangrene from the moment I entered your room.'

'Hold this.' She dropped the partly unwrapped cloth into my hands and walked around the writing desk. One end of the bandage yet dangled from my ear. I cringed at the weight of it. I thought to ask how my wound appeared, but was too afraid of the answer I might receive.

'Were you happy, Kate?' I asked instead.

She frowned as she reached behind the desk for a thin-bladed knife, and regarded me with an expression of bewilderment. 'I beg your pardon?'

'Before the war came to Crediton. Were you happy there?'

'I had no complaints, Master Falkland.' She came to stand behind me. 'I apologise. This may hurt. I'm no surgeon.'

'Did you have a sweetheart?'

'As it happens I had several. Not that it's a concern of yours.' I gasped as I felt a sharp tug at the side of my head, a pain as though she had driven the knife into my flesh. 'The skin is starting to knit. It's oozing and bloody, though, and swollen up like an egg. Best we wrap you up again. You'll not be wearing a hat for a while, I think.'

'Can you wash it first? As clean as you can.' I wished now that I could see it. I had seen plenty enough wounds over all those years of fighting. I would have a shrewd idea, I thought, of how it would go. Perhaps there was a mirror? 'If it oozes aught but fresh blood, clean the pus away if you will.'

Miss Cain left me a moment. She returned with a bowl

of water and a cloth, and began to dab at the side of my head; I winced with every touch.

'What became of them?' I asked. 'Those sweethearts?'

'One chose another. I hated him for a month or two and then forgot all about him. The others . . . the war took them, one way or another.'

'Did that not trouble you?'

She made a bemused sort of noise. 'Of course it did, Master Falkland. What other answer could you expect? But that was years ago. When you came to my house, I had long resigned myself to spinsterhood until this war was done.' She dabbed at the wound itself now. I fear I let out a yelp, yet that was but the start. I did not see what she did next, but though I had not seen a red-hot needle in her armoury, that is certainly how it felt.

'Steady, William.'

I let out a noise I can only imagine more suited to the anguished torments of Lucifer's domain. Miss Cain sighed and put her bowl and cloth upon the table.

'I've done what I can.' She began wrapping a new bandage around my head. The pain was reluctant to recede. I risked a glance and saw the blade of Miss Cain's knife stained with blood-streaked pus. I did not, I decided at once, wish to see more.

'Do you miss them?' I asked.

'I did for a time. I have grown used to my own company now. When the war came I had more immediate perils with which to concern myself than any aching heart. I had no mother and so became wife, in many ways, to my own father. By which I mean I kept his house, and saw to it that the pantry was full . . . or at least never quite empty. It was survival, Master Falkland, that was all. I did not have much time for anything else.'

That much I could understand. In the end, that was what the war had become for most of us.

She tied the bandage tight. I felt a steady throbbing pain, but a relief too. She had drained the poison.

A silence lingered between us.

'Milton will write to Cromwell if he hasn't already,' I said at last. I was thinking of the promises he had made, and that Kate had made too. 'He asks that I be discharged from my obligations to him.'

'I hear Cromwell is back in London,' she said. The news shook me. I could not imagine for a moment that he had come back on my account, but it added an immediacy to my fate. Seeing Miss Cain return to her work, I rose and wandered to the room next door where all those papers were stored. They seemed to mock me, so many floor-to-ceiling piles against all the walls. My light-headedness returned. Perhaps, somewhere among those pages, lay a clue as to my family and their fate. More likely not, but they seemed to capture my plight. Somewhere in England I would find them, or what had become of them. Somewhere, and yet how could one man alone look in every town and village, in every farm and mill?

I did not hear Miss Cain come up beside me until she took my arm. She leaned her head to rest against my shoulder.

'I wish I could tell you where they were, Falkland.'

'I did not stop thinking of them.' My words were choked. 'In all the years I followed the King's armies, not a day went by where I didn't feel them, marching beside me.'

'They march beside you still.'

I shook my head. 'I don't feel them any more, Kate. They gave me strength for a time. But now I can't think of anything but what terrible ill must have befallen them. It is crippling to me.'

'If anyone can find them, Falkland, it will be you.' She gently turned me away from the torture of that room. 'But you'll not find them there, William. You will find them by riding your horse from town to town. You will find them because you won't give up.'

I wished I could share her faith. To me it felt as though I had given up already. That pigsty in Uxbridge where Warbeck had found me, that was the hell of my despair. He had done me a service, perhaps. I would have sunk lower still, as low as I could find to go.

'What was your wife's name before you were married?'

'Tregaskes. She said it meant something about a farm.' I laughed. 'She once told me that was why she married me. She was a farm and I was a farmer, and so clearly we were meant for each other.' I shrugged. 'Though there were plenty of other farmers she might have chosen.'

'Come.' Kate led me back to the room where she worked. She sat me down on a stool beside her and drew me close; as we pressed up against one another she stroked my hair, mothering me as though I was a child. I did not resist it. I could not deny the comfort. If I am honest I lost myself for a while there, as the room around us vanished into memories of happier times, of sitting close to my Caro, of her arms around me and mine about her in return. I wept a little, I think. To a part of me it seemed so very wrong that I should take comfort from any other as I thought of my beloved. I imagined at first that I was long past caring enough for that to stop me, but that part grew and widened and swelled until I drew away, though I did not much want to, though a great part of me wished to draw much closer still.

'I am sorry, Miss Cain.' I rose. 'I should go. I should not have come.' At the door I stopped and turned to her. I saw nothing in her face but a pain and a sadness that were my own, reflected back at me. 'I should not have brought this here to you. I know I will not find her in your room of letters.'

'Nor will you find her in me, Master Falkland.'

I took that at first as a rebuke, and perhaps richly deserved, but the glisten of her eyes told me it was not meant that way. Or if it was, at least only in part. She looked away then, and said nothing more, and I understood that I was dismissed. I left, my thoughts in such a disarray that their tangle remained impenetrable even as I returned across the threshold to the Bucket of Blood.

Waterhouse was waiting for me. I saw him at once and groaned, and thought of running away, for it seemed that I could barely set foot in this forsaken tavern without him or Warbeck accosting me. But run to where?

'You're to come with me.' He nodded and smiled as he said it, but there was something in the way he stood that made it clear that I should not suppose I had a choice.

'Where to?'

'To Master Oliver Cromwell himself.'

I did not much like that as an answer. Waterhouse had a tension to him, as if he half expected that I would run, and that he would be obliged to give chase. In truth I gave it a thought, but I was in no state for any running today.

'Am I to come in irons, or is it to be with a sack over my head?' I asked. This, at least, seemed to bemuse him.

'Neither, Master Falkland. Why would you ask that?'

I thought it best if I said nothing more. If we were headed to Newgate or Clink then I would know it soon enough, and then we would find whose legs were faster. I had a fair chance, I decided, if the weakness of my fever did not betray me. We were both big men. Waterhouse was younger, but I dare say I had had a great deal more practice in running away over the years. Desperation will breed things in a man, I have found.

CHAPTER 15

We walked side by side out of Covent Garden, past Saint Martin's church and the Charing Cross, then turned west, following the bank of the Thames. I relaxed then, thinking I knew where we were going. The pain from my ear had shifted into a strange fiery tingling. I still felt the sweat of a fever, but it had receded from the swimming fog of the morning.

'Parliament, is it?' I felt both exhausted and light-headed. A little of that came, I think, from a sense of relief.

'Aye. Does that trouble you?'

'No,' I said. 'I have been expecting this.' I had, I found, a new spring in my step. I would tell what I knew of Anne and the letters and Ned Fletcher, and that would be the end, and I would begin my own search anew. Milton had all but spat in my face when last we parted, but Cromwell would not send me back to Newgate, no matter how I had offended the man he had meant for me to help. It was neither kindness nor loyalty, but more a ruthless practicality. Perhaps he overrated my value, but if the King was about to come to terms, I didn't doubt that he would see a use for me in the peace that was to follow. My opinions as to whether I wished to have such a use would perhaps be an entirely other matter; but then Cromwell, I had found, had a knack for getting his way.

Waterhouse led me alongside the stink of the Thames towards St Stephen's Chapel, where the common members of Parliament held their debate. We passed the sprawling palace of Whitehall where the King had once had his throne, to the older palace of Westminster, where other kings once ruled. I will admit it sent a shiver through me to enter the gates into the palace yard and see the looming spires of the chapel before me, which would become, short of some miraculous reversal of fortune, the centre of power in the new England that was to be. I had set foot inside this place once before, the ground white with snow, yet today, under the summer sun, the chapel towers struck me as darker and taller than before, as if the very building itself had somehow grown with Parliament's imminent victory.

We did not enter. Waterhouse kept a steady pace onward; but as we passed the grand oak doors of the chapel several soldiers emerged. They wore the coats of Parliament's cavalrymen.

'Falkland!'

There was no mistaking the voice. I had heard it too many times before. Cromwell. I faltered in my stride and stopped.

'About time, Falkland! Come with me!'

Cromwell led the way across the old palace yard towards the corner facing the Thames, and a smaller hall in the shape of an octagon. Several soldiers of the New Model stood nearby. I supposed they were assigned as guards, but from the way they slouched and leaned against their pikes, I imagined their purpose less as guardians and more as a sullen threat of reprisal. At least the two Ironsides by the great oaken doors stood smart and stiff. Waterhouse lingered behind. He was, I fancied, a little awed. Cromwell stopped before the doors. 'Do you know where you are, Falkland?'

I looked around, uncertain. Parliament, yes, but . . .

'This is the Star Chamber.' The look Cromwell gave me was that of a man sorely vexed, as if repeating a lesson to a forgetful child. 'Where kings mete the justice that suits them.'

The Ironsides opened the doors as we reached them. Cromwell led the way through and into a gloomy hall. A thick smell of smoke and musk entwined about, old leather and old scented furs, tobacco and a lacing of frankincense. I will admit it made me pause. Caro's father had brought me once to a gentlemen's club on our passage through London, he a country gentleman and I aspiring to be the same, though neither one of us had truly belonged. I forget the name, and the name of the man who took us as his guests too, but I remember the smell. It was the same.

'Harry the seventh invested this chamber,' continued Cromwell. A second pair of black oak doors barred the way ahead. Care and expense had gone into their design, and they were carved with the royal arms. 'To ensure fair enforcement of the laws of the land against those so powerful that the ordinary courts could never convict them for their crimes, and, too, as a court of equity to impose punishments for deeds that did not, in the strictest sense, violate any law, but were deemed reprehensible nevertheless. It was intended as an instrument of justice.' He paused here and looked about him as though lost in thought a moment. A familiar voice echoed from beyond. John Milton in full flow. 'The intentions of men are never how they are remembered, Falkland,' Cromwell continued. 'The kings and queens who followed warped this court to other purposes, and none worse than our king now. The council who made their judgements in this chamber sentenced victims of the King's wrath to the pillory, to whipping and to the cutting off of ears. With each embarrassment to arbitrary power they became emboldened to undertake further usurpation. They summoned juries before them and imprisoned them for disagreeable verdicts. They imposed ruinous fines. They spread terror, Falkland, and this very chamber became the chief defence of our King Charles against any and all rightful assaults upon his usurpations of law and justice, until Parliament abolished it and put an end to arbitrary imprisonments, impeachments and executions . . .'

I half listened to Cromwell's words as I strained to hear what Milton was saying on the other side of those doors, and so intent was I on this that I did not see Warbeck already present, quiet and still and wrapped in black in one of the many shadowed corners, until he moved and sidled beside me. He bared his teeth in a vicious leer, perhaps barely able to contain his glee at my imminent dismissal. The stink of his breath brushed over me, wreaking brutal murder upon the delicate scent of the hall.

Cromwell leaned in to me, his expression unusually fierce. 'The punishments of that court are to a very great degree why we fight, Falkland.' He opened the doors and brought me into a chamber with eight sides, with benches along each of them. On one side sat two men I did not recognise. In the open space between them, John Milton stared and pointed an accusing finger. His words faltered as he saw Cromwell beside me. Fowles sat quietly on another bench, alert and, I thought, a little tense. Milton's voice had somehow conspired, as we entered, to fill the chamber; yet as it faltered even the man himself seemed to diminish. This was a hall made for many men to sit together in debate, that much was clear at once, and its space seemed somehow to resent our paltry presence, as if we were too few to be worthy of its occupation.

As Cromwell marched to a vacant bench on yet another side and took his seat, I stood and looked about me, a little bewildered as to where I should sit, or whether I should simply stand until they were done with me. I had come here eager to be finished with this business, yet in this place I was less certain. I felt the weight of my surroundings press upon me. Cromwell thought me ignorant, perhaps, but even among the King's army the Star Chamber carried a heavy notoriety. For most of us our safety had always been that we were lowly men, I and those who served around me, common folk from common homes with no great land or title. Our misdemeanours, if such occurred, were addressed by common courts, not by kings and ministers.

I looked up. There were indeed stars painted into the ceiling.

The three cavalrymen who were Cromwell's escort sat beside him. Cromwell himself cocked his head and looked upon me as though in continuance of our conversation. 'There is an association of men whom some have recently taken to calling Levellers. I believe you are acquainted with at least one of their number. The man they follow was summoned to that court. He refused to take their oath.'

I nodded dumbly. I did not know to what point Cromwell was leading, nor if there was even such an end to be had, or if this was simply another polemic against the injustices of our sovereign. In truth his words washed over me. I did not feel entirely myself. I wished they would simply be done with it.

'John Lilburne.' Milton broke in abruptly, apparently unable to constrain himself to silence any longer. 'They took him for his writings. Him and John Bastwick, for their polemics against episcopacy. For printing materials not approved by that vicious clench upon the freedom of intellect that was the Worshipful Company of Stationers and Newspaper Makers, all of them dogs running at the hand of the King. When Lilburne would not take that court's oath, they had him dragged by his hands behind a cart from Fleet Prison to the Westminster pillory and flogged him as he went. In the pillory he railed against his censors until they gagged him, yet his "unlicensed" literature spread among the populace all the same. Sing his name, I say, for even kings cannot silence ideas, though men will ever try.'

His finger pointed accusation towards me, yet I sensed that his last words were directed in part at Cromwell himself.

'Lilburne fought at Edgehill too,' said Cromwell. He turned back to Milton, answering his veiled charge. 'There will be no taking of oaths here today. We are but men seeking the truth. This is not a trial and we are not a court. This Star Chamber is, by act of Parliament, naught now but a simple hall in whose occupation we shall not inconvenience the continuance of government.' Cromwell leaned a little further. 'So. Oxford is on the brink of surrender. The King's capitulation will shortly follow. Yet, amid this momentous upheaval, here we are. Master Milton, in answer to a plea made by you and with an eye to the peace that must follow the King's defeat, and notwithstanding the strenuous nature of the times, I sent this man to your aid, William Falkland. Before I bow to sending you another, I would hear the information he has—'

'Information?' Again Milton could not restrain himself. 'If only this man had invested a tenth of the effort to winkle out the vile conspirators who plot against us as he has directed at the besmirchment of my sister's character!'

'I beg you, sir, do repose yourself.' Cromwell sounded bored and irritable, as though he had far better places to be and things to do. I supposed the surrender of Oxford and the submission of the King to terms agreeable to Parliament, and the end of what had become six years now of fighting, might indeed have seemed such. I would have agreed, had I been asked. Yet here Cromwell was, reminding us with some force by his mere presence that he considered the abduction of Milton's sister a threat to the very peace he now sought.

Warbeck prodded me out into the centre of the chamber. Cromwell nodded. 'Speak then, Falkland. I require no oath of any man here, but you will oblige me with the truth as you have found it. Do the King's supporters conspire?'

Cromwell had said this was no trial, but that did not change how I felt, surrounded by these men. A trial for whom, though, I could not entirely be sure. If this was a court no longer, still I felt its menace.

Cromwell grew impatient. 'Speak, if you please, Master Falkland, and let us be done with this.'

I turned my back on Fowles and Milton, ignoring their

glares, and took a long breath. Walking here with
Waterhouse, I had imagined a very different end. A brief
dismissal, not an inquisition.

'Sir,' I began. 'A witness claimed to see Anne Agar
abducted by two or three men while walking towards Clink
Prison. The witness identified one of these to me as a man
she had seen in the company of the prisoner John Ogle.
Although she did not mention Ogle by name when
previously questioned, it has been deduced by others that
Anne was taken by men acting in support of the King with
the aim of blackmail, of forcing John Milton to silence
when the King offers terms . . .'

Cromwell gestured for me to proceed with haste to the
point of the matter.

'Sir, when I questioned this witness a second time, in
the presence of Henry Warbeck and the soldier Daniel
Waterhouse, I determined that these claims were false. She
had indeed seen Anne Agar enter a carriage with two men,
but there was no struggle, no evidence of violence, and nor
could she identify them. The witness confessed to her false
statements and claimed they had been made under threat. I
believe she truthfully reported what she saw at first, but was
coerced later to embellishment.'

As I said this, I turned to look upon the faces of John
Milton and Peter Fowles. On both I saw an expression of
shock. Milton's was mingled with outrage and ire. Fowles, it
seemed to me, had turned a little pale.

'I put it to you, sir, that had Anne been abducted by the
King's supporters, they would not have threatened the only
witness so as to incriminate themselves further.' I kept my
eyes on Milton and Fowles, waiting to see which of them

would be unable to keep silent. But it was Cromwell who spoke next.

'Your story, Master Falkland, would be greatly improved if you had the man who threatened your witness and a confession from him that he had done so. *Do* you have him?'

'I do not.' I had his name, but I was not willing to reveal it, not here and now in front of everyone. I would give Fowles that little piece of rope to see if he might yet do me the kindness of hanging himself. Cromwell would have the name from Warbeck easily enough.

'A pity, Master Falkland.' A thin smile flicked around Cromwell's bloodless lips. 'Shall we move on, then, to the matter of the letter you stole from Master Milton's house?' He chose his words most carefully, I thought, to incriminate me as best he could, yet he must have known of my suspicions from Warbeck, else why summon Fowles to this sham of a court?

I told them all, then, of the letter I had found and the circumstances of it, truthfully and sparing nothing save Miss Cain's part in the theft. At my mention of the militia company of Sir Willoughby of Parham I saw Cromwell's expression change. I had his interest. 'I dare say I might have given these letters and poor dead Francis Lovelace little more thought had I not been ambushed that night by four men who robbed me of that stolen letter. I do not know their relevance to Anne's disappearance, but I am certain they are intimate to its cause.'

Cromwell had asked me to be truthful and so I had obliged him, but he had not demanded that I also be thorough and speak without omission. I took him to be an intelligent and thoughtful man who would understand my intent, but I could not let Fowles know that I knew Ned Fletcher's name, that I knew that Fletcher had been the one to rob me, to threaten Jane Hardwick, and that he, too, had been in the same militia company in '43. Together those tied Fowles to Anne hard enough for any man, I thought, but my goal was to free her, if she still lived, not to send another man to Newgate, and I hoped that Fowles might yet lead me to her. I prayed that Warbeck, who knew all these truths, would keep his silence. I thought he would. He was more a man for silence than for speech. He was certainly a man who understood how a trap might be laid.

'I have a further curiosity,' I said, watching each of them closely, yet taking care that Fowles would not see himself singled out for scrutiny. 'Although I do not know who he is, Miss Hardwick was able to describe the man who threatened her. I have discovered that Anne took letters to a printer in Fleet Street where she met with John Wallis.' I fixed Cromwell with a look then, for John Wallis himself was surely not far from where we stood, and might yet be summoned if Cromwell had the inclination. 'She hid that she was doing this and did not tell her brother. She was looking for a hidden message. A cipher, if you will. On the last occasion she met Master Wallis, she was accompanied by the same man who threatened Miss Hardwick. I believe that to be the day after her "disappearance". Wherever Anne Agar went, I do not think she went unwillingly. At least, not at first.

'There is one other thing,' I said, when no one spoke. 'I visited Francis Lovelace's widow. He wrote letters to her also, a curious thing since she can barely read. She told me that a man came to visit her some months back. He came to tell her that Francis was dead, and then he asked about some money. When this man learned that Francis had written her letters, he took them away with him.' I turned to Fowles. 'That was you, was it not?'

After a long pause Fowles nodded. 'It was.'

'When you came to see me in the Bucket of Blood, to admit to me that you knew Francis Lovelace, you'd already confessed to Milton about Anne's letters, I think. Is that so?' Milton, I saw, had kept his silence while I spoke, but his face had turned the colour of well-stewed rhubarb. Had Cromwell given him licence to do so, I think he would have tried to rip me apart with his bare hands. I had drawn a picture of his sister, I think, that he did not wish to see.

'Peter told me everything as soon as you left,' he snapped.

'But you didn't know about them before? You're quite sure of that?'

'As I told you!' Milton's voice grew shrill. The colour in his face deepened further. At any moment I thought he would fall into a fit.

I turned back to Fowles.

'When you came to see me, I told you I would return the letter I had found—'

'Stolen!' snapped Milton.

'—and return it to John Milton. You seemed to me mightily disturbed by such a prospect.' A stray thought struck me as I spoke – that I had no notion of how long Fowles and Milton had been acquainted, nor the circumstances and nature of it. I had not thought to ask.

Fowles considered my accusation. 'You are mistaken,' he said.

'Why did you visit Francis's widow?'

'To give her the news of poor Francis being dead, of course!' He frowned, as if bewildered I should ask such a question.

'You are aware that Master Cromwell here writes letters to the families of his dead soldiers?'

'Not in 'forty-three, Falkland,' said Cromwell. 'Even now, it is for the men who ride with me. The Ironsides and a few others.'

I ignored him and pressed on with Fowles. 'Why go to her in person?'

'Because Francis was dead!' Fowles jumped to his feet. 'Master Cromwell, I will speak everything there is to know about Anne and Francis Lovelace if you wish.' His outrage seemed to me the excessive indignation of the accused who knows they have much to hide. His puzzlement about Beth Lovelace, though, I took to be the truth. He really had gone there to tell her that Francis was dead. What, then, were these accursed letters?

He astonished me even more as, a moment later, he slumped where he sat and held his head in his hands, and I would swear that behind his fingers he wept.

'It is all my fault,' he said as he shook. 'I put the idea to her.'

'What idea?' I asked.

'Did you take letters from Anne Agar's room, Master Fowles?' asked Cromwell. 'Pray answer me that, before you begin.'

Fowles, speared by his own folly, did not lift his head. 'Yes. That I did.'

Cromwell rose to face him from across the chamber. 'Then you had best speak, Master Fowles. Falkland, you're done.'

I took Cromwell's words as instruction to leave the chamber and return, perhaps, to the pigsty from which I had come; but as I made to leave Warbeck shook his head and gestured to the bench beside him, patting it gently with those delicate fingers of his. I sat and closed my eyes a moment as Fowles continued. I found my head spinning, still touched by my morning fever.

'Francis never told me all of it,' said Fowles. He sounded downcast, and I could not tell if his reluctance was simply for show or if he truly wished not to speak. 'He said he was looking for a man called Thomas Agar, that he hoped to find him, and that in doing so would meet with the approval of a lady in London. What gratitude he sought I cannot tell you. Francis was a man of strong passions. It is a thing he would have done. He saw himself, if I may be excused the notion, as a dashing knight crusader. There was much of the preening cavalier to him. In time I learned that this lady was sister to the notorious John Milton. I think Francis was the sort to revel in such sensationalism. He was a man of much imagination. I didn't know that he wrote letters until I went to see his wife to tell her that Francis was dead. When she spoke of them, I asked if I could see them. I took them . . .' with this he shot me a foul glance '. . . because she claimed she had not read them, since she could not, and because I would have spared her the anguish of what perhaps they contained.'

'And what was that?' asked Cromwell.

'His infidelities. Sir, Francis was my friend, but he was not kind when he spoke of his wife. That she was beautiful he would freely admit. But he remarked often on how crude and stupid she was, and how dull in her . . . bed ways. He would tell me he considered it his duty to educate and improve her in all regards. The whores who followed our company about were most grateful, I would say, for Francis Lovelace, and much mourned his passing. When I found out he had written letters to his wife, I knew he might also have written letters to Anne.' He turned briefly to Milton. 'I did not want to besmirch the name of a man who was my friend. Sir, I did steal Anne's letters. I took them to bury a past that died with Francis. I did not read them, but simply burned them. All except the one Falkland took.' He hung his head. 'But there was a time, I will admit, when I thought they might contain more, and I said as much to Anne. When Francis died he was looking for Thomas Agar. I believe he had found something. I do not know what it was. None of us ever did, but I wondered if he had hidden something in his letters. It was a foolishness, for Francis knew nothing of such things, but I fear Anne took my foolishness and multiplied it. She became obsessed with the notion of a cipher. She asked me if I knew of such things. I did not. But I did not know that she had taken it further.'

I had been slowly putting something together in my mind. 'Did you try to steal the letters once before?' I asked. 'After you first learned of them? I understand there was an intruder into the Milton house not long after you came to know them.' I had a picture of it now. Fowles had learned of the letters from Beth Lovelace. He had come to London and inveigled his way into friendship with John Milton. Knowing when the house would be empty, he had tried to steal the letters but had been unable to find them. Then followed a charade as he tempted Anne with the thought they might contain hidden news of her husband's fate – I did not believe

Fowles had a whit of care one way or the other for this – as he tried to winkle them out of her. Her secret visits to Fleet Street to meet with John Wallis were thus explained. These had not yielded him what he wanted, so he had acted directly. Yet for there to be any sense to this, Fowles himself must believe the letters to contain a clue to something. But what?

Nathaniel Blackwater's words came back to me as he thought he had me cornered in an alley. *Thought you'd steal our spoils of war, did you?* What spoils did he mean?

'No.' Fowles fixed me with a level glare. 'I did not.' I met his eye. I did not believe much of what I had heard, I will admit. I hoped Cromwell would share my view.

'The letters that survive – where are they now?' asked Cromwell.

'That I know of? Falkland had the last. He says he was attacked and that men stole it from him. If that is true then I must suppose the letter to be in their possession. I cannot say, sir, for I had no part in it.'

Cromwell frowned at this. 'Then who did?'

'I do not know and cannot begin to guess.'

'I can,' said Warbeck softly. I gripped my knees, fearful that Warbeck would now reveal all I had not disclosed. He addressed himself to Cromwell. 'Nathaniel Blackwater. A man well known to me and now sadly dead. Matthew Wainwright, whom I have in Newgate. Ned Fletcher and one other. Those two remain at large.'

I realised at that moment that Warbeck likely did not know that Ned Fletcher and Nathaniel Blackwater had once been a part of the same company as Fowles and Lovelace, for I had only this very morning confirmed it. If I were to mention, now, that Fletcher was the same man as had threatened Jane Hardwick then Fowles would know his ship was run aground. Yet he would deny everything, and what evidence did I have that was against him and not this Ned Fletcher?

It was Cromwell himself who saved us, though I suppose he did not mean to, nor indeed knew anything of it.

'How did this Lovelace die?' he asked, aiming his question directly at Fowles.

'Near Gainsborough, sir. He was shot.'

'Yes, men often are in war. I asked you how, sir, not where nor when. I was at Gainsborough myself.'

'After Sir Willoughby took the town, a handful of us were billeted in villages nearby. We were to keep watch, sir, as you will understand. There were eight of us. We had taken a small manor house occupied previously by supporters of the King who had defended the town. We were Sir Willoughby's Forlorn Hope, the first band of men to lead the charge, and this house was our reward. The men were gone, prisoners perhaps, or else killed when our company took the town. We knew the King's armies would come down on us soon enough, and we knew that we would soon have reinforcements of our own. Our duties, sir, were to look out for both. We were close to the village of Lea, sir, which you will know if you fought there. We had billeted at the house for about ten days when a force of royalists stumbled upon us. We saw them off, but Francis was killed.'

'What was the date?' asked Cromwell brusquely.

'They came upon us on the twenty-seventh of June, sir.'

'We joined battle on the twenty-eighth.'

'I know, sir. We all heard how the King's army had the

advantage, but you nevertheless drove their horse from the field and fell upon their reserve, driving them into the marshes beside the river and cutting them down, and their commander too.'

What I had heard differed considerably: that, after a small skirmish, Lord Newcastle had sent Parliament's reinforcements scurrying back to Lincoln without a fight, and had retaken Gainsborough after an easy three-day siege. One hears such very differently coloured sides of the same stories in war. To this day I imagine both Parliament and the King claimed Edgehill as a victory.

'What was the name of this house where you stayed?'

'I do not know, sir.' Fowles shook his head.

'The name of the family then.' Cromwell glared at Fowles with such a fierce intensity it seemed to paralyse him.

'Well-Pope, or some such. Sir Malcolm, I think. He fought in Gainsborough's defence. I don't know what became of him, sir.'

'Walhope. I know that name. Sir Malcolm Walhope was indeed one of the town defenders. He was killed in the fighting along with his two sons.' There was a long pause before Cromwell continued. 'John Meldrum and I were forced to withdraw our companies on the very day we arrived. Newcastle's force was overwhelming. I heard a rumour, some months later, that a band of thugs had ransacked Walhope's home, murdered his wife and daughter and hanged his servants. I thought little of it at the time. I put it down to Newcastle's men.' Cromwell leaned forward from his bench, fixing Fowles to the spot with a fearsome scowl. Every hair on my skin prickled. Here it was, the terrible secret for which Fowles had been looking in those letters.

Fowles closed his eyes. For a long time he said nothing at all. No one else made a sound.

'Understand, sir,' he said softly, 'that Francis Lovelace was a friend, and that he was dead. I did not want to see his name ruined. Not, perhaps, for his sake, but for his family. His wife.'

The truth. At last we were getting to it.

'Does this in any way concern my sister?' said Milton irritably, though even his irascible wit, it seemed, was dulled by this revelation. 'Because if it does not, of what matter is it now?'

'It is of matter to me,' said Cromwell quietly.

Peter Fowles bowed his head. 'We billeted at the house, eight of us, advance scouts for Sir Willoughby. The lady of the house and the daughter remained, along with a maid and two old men who tended to its grounds and its horses. Francis was our commander. He declared the women under his protection and refused to allow us any pillage. He declared us gentlemanly folk who would act in gentlemanly ways. I will tell you, sirs, this did not go well among some of the men. There was no New Model then. We were not paid soldiers but took our rewards in the spoils of victory. We had taken to being Sir Willoughby's Forlorn Hope to earn our share of the best of whatever was to be had. Yet here we were, and while others of our company filled their pockets from the King's servants in Gainsborough, there was to be none for us. Francis was my friend. I tried to make him see that he must allow a little indulgence to his men, but he wouldn't have it, even when I had to stifle mutiny. It was the woman, sirs. The lady of the house. She saw him for what he was, a fool won by a smile. She was wanton in front of him, a temptress in the vein of all lady cavaliers. She turned his head, sirs, but she did not turn the rest of us. It was plain how she played him. She took him to her bed like some common whore and made him up to be the new master of the house, and for the rest of us there would be nothing.' The bitterness in Fowles came through his words, clear as the sun. I could see it through his eyes. A handful of men fresh from battle, men who have seen others killed and maimed and yet come through it, flush with victory and filled with thoughts of rape and plunder. Yes, I had known many such men.

'He held us back, sirs. That is much to his credit. But the royalist whore was false with him from the start. She knew the King would not stand to see the town fall without retribution. She found a way to slip word to a band of marauding dragoons to ambush our company. As fortune had it they were seen in their approach by a vigilant sentry. They entered the house in the dead of night, expecting to find us amid dreams and snores, but we were ready for them, muskets primed and loaded. Their ambush became ours. In the hallway we waited in the shadows for them. All of us, Francis too. We did not give them warning before we fired and then we fell upon them. We overwhelmed them, and not one escaped, and not one of our men was much hurt, at least not by bullet or blade. But after it was over . . .' Fowles took a long, deep breath and let it out slowly. He was shaking.

'Francis discovered his lady's betrayal. He was incensed. There was no reasoning with him. He ordered the entire household executed right then and there. I tried to intervene, but he wouldn't have it. I am shamed, sir, by what we did. I do not know by whose hand the lady and her daughter met their end. There were more shots, three, perhaps four. The maid two of us managed to let loose to make her own way off into the dark. Newcastle's wounded soldiers and the two men who served the house were hanged. We did it in the night, cheering. The house was ransacked. We would have burned it to the ground, too, but it was our only shelter. On the next day Francis came to his senses. At the same time word came that the King's armies were approaching, and that the relief force had withdrawn for Lincoln. We were abandoned. We could not stay, and so we left, sirs, and in some haste, but Francis did not come with us. When I looked for him I found him beside the body of his treacherous lady. He had taken his own pistol and shot himself.'

Fowles took another moment to gather his thoughts. 'There was nothing to be done, sirs. If the truth came out then we feared we might hang for it, though it was surely Francis himself who had murdered the lady. He had sent a report to our commander every day, describing our disposition, and he had written one that morning before he shot himself. Nathaniel had taken it with him and gone ahead as we set to break our camp. I did not know, then, that he had written other letters, but when I learned he had written to Beth I feared it would come back. I feared he had written a confession. He was the sort, sir, to have talked about his infatuations, and I saw no good in it coming out. That was why I took the letters. In the end it was for nothing. He wrote none of them from Gainsborough. Sirs, I did not try to steal them, nor was I the intruder into Master Milton's house. Master Milton knows this, for we were in one another's company as it happened, and returned together to find the evidence before us.' He hung his head. 'But I confess to giving Anne the notion of finding something in Francis's letters. I thought she might then bring them to me, and we would read them together. But she took another course. I curse myself for it now, but there is the truth of it, all I know. I cannot say how this bears on poor dear Anne's vanishing.'

Fowles' horror struck me as real, that here, at last, was an honest story. Yet I still could not understand why Anne would vanish in secret and for so long. I had been certain, that morning, that Peter Fowles was at the very heart of this conspiracy, if not the architect of her disappearance. Now I found myself wondering. Fletcher and Blackwater had been in Gainsborough too. They would know the same story. Had Fowles let slip some word? Had the others taken matters into their own hands? But *why*?

'I will need,' said Cromwell slowly, 'the names of the other men who were there who can corroborate this story. Our fight was ever meant to be a godly one, not some terror sweeping upon the ordinary people of the land.'

'Of course.' Fowles sat down.

'Where was this house?' I asked abruptly. I did not know quite why, but something about Fowles and his story didn't sit right with me. Perhaps Ned Fletcher was the one I wanted and Fowles knew nothing of the abduction at all. Perhaps, but perhaps not.

'Near the village of Lea, a little south of Gainsborough.'

'Where did the hangings take place?'

'From a tree beside the—'

'Enough, Falkland.' Cromwell looked immeasurably tired. 'Enough.'

Milton came slowly to his feet now. 'Oliver, as sad as I am to hear this sorry tale, I do not see how any design might spring forth from it to climax in a whirlwind sweeping my sister from the street. It seems to me that these letters are another matter entirely. Sir, I would ask that you have your tame King's man explain what elemental shred of evidence he has to connect one to the other. If he cannot, then by all means let us applaud him for tearing open some old wound. Let us sing his praises through the streets, if that pleases you, sir, for ripping at the souls of decent men who have fought for right and reason against this tyrant who would be our king; but be not in doubt that, if this is so, some other inquisition will soon arise to unearth the misdeeds of those who fought against us, and then another and another, until all is vitriol and hate.' Milton again pointed an accusing finger across the chamber at me. 'Perhaps we will find what *this* man has done in all his years of war. Was it all so noble? Upon whose grave shall we next tread? I beg you, sir, send to me an intelligencer who can find within himself a whit of concern simply for my dear sister, who has surely offended no one, whether a King's man, a Leveller or for Parliament, who will content himself with the crime to which he is tasked and launch no slurs and insults at my family and my friends for his own seditious purposes!'

At this, Cromwell nodded. 'Warbeck, you will attend once more to the matter of Anne Agar's disappearance. Falkland, it is no longer your concern. Fowles, Milton, you may go. Milton, we will talk again tomorrow before I return to Oxford. Falkland, stay a moment. I'm not done with you.'

As Warbeck rose I tugged him down. 'See that Waterhouse follows Fowles. See where he goes. I have a notion it will be to Fletcher. Leave word at Newgate.'

Warbeck glared but gave a little nod as he followed Milton and Fowles out of the Star Chamber. The doors closed behind them, and in their hollow clang I found again that sense of unease that had filled me as I first entered. Whatever purpose had been intended for this place when it had been built, the burden of its past hung in the air, weighting the very dust that filtered through stray shafts of sunlight. Perhaps Parliament would see fit to cleanse themselves of the building itself as they had of its purpose, and then it would be gone and quickly forgotten. I wondered if the weight of this war might be banished so simply from all those who had suffered by it. I did not think so.

'There is no plot among the King's supporters, then?' Cromwell rose from his seat and walked slowly down to the centre of the chamber. He moved stiffly, as if carrying some injury that had not yet healed. Or else perhaps it was simply the long ride from Woodstock to London.

'I cannot tell you for certain that there is not, but were I a King's man who had abducted the sister of a vocal Parliamentarian then I would not coerce the witness to my deed so as to incriminate my own cause.'

'Yes. As you said already. I cannot allow you to continue, Falkland. Warbeck will search on for Milton's sister, though it will not please either of them. I thank you for your time. You may leave with my gratitude. If there is any word of your family then I will see it comes to you.'

'May I have your leave at least to confirm Fowles' story?'

Cromwell shook his head. 'You are a free man, Falkland. Do with your time as you wish. But would it not be better spent on the present than in the past?'

'Sir, I did not reveal everything in front of Fowles. I told him of the letter; hours later Fletcher's men attacked me. Jane Hardwick told him what she'd seen in Clink Street; the man who later threatened her was Fletcher, and then a second time shortly after Warbeck first introduced me to Milton's household. Fletcher and Fowles were both a part of Sir Willoughby of Parham's company in the summer of 'forty-three. It is a pretty tale he has spun for us, and perhaps much of it is true, but I do not believe it to be complete, sir, nor a matter now mired entirely in the past. Fowles is up to his neck in this. He will lead me to Anne.'

Cromwell digested this for a few seconds.

'Then go and find her, Falkland,' he said; and for a moment I thought perhaps he almost smiled.

CHAPTER 16

I came out alone from the Star Chamber with every intent to hurry at once to Newgate and stalk Peter Fowles across London; but I had barely taken a step when John Milton placed himself squarely in my path and accosted me with a finger to my chest. While Warbeck, Fowles and Waterhouse had all been quick to set off about their business, Milton had waited.

'Cromwell has let you off the hook, I dare say,' he sneered. 'He might have greater things on his mind, but I will not so easily be moved aside. You are a clown, Falkland, a thief and a liar. Do you—'

I gripped him with both of my hands about his jacket, tight about his neck. The guards standing stiff by the doors to the Star Chamber remained at their posts. I do not know what disposed him to confront me in such a way, alone and with no ally close to hand, nor did I care. I was the bigger, stronger man, and I would take no more of this.

'Clown if you must. Thief I acknowledge, though in defensible cause, but liar? Show me once where this is true else have your slur back at you and still your tongue. From the very start you have seen nothing but yourself, ignorant and arrogant like a man who stares into a glass, admiring his own features and without one whit of thought to the world about him. Your sister is taken, yet you see nothing but how John Milton is threatened, how John Milton is hurt, how the world might now perceive John Milton. You do not see the pain of your sister's sons, only your own. You do not see Peter Fowles' lies but only his flattery. I understand quite well, sir, why it is that I offend you: it is because I do not give one whit of my care to John Milton. My thoughts are for Anne, wife and mother, and for her alone.' I pushed him away. It was no wonder to me at all that his wife, Mary, had run back to her parents after they were wed. It was more a wonder that she had ever returned.

Milton bared his teeth. He backed away and kept his distance, but such was his fury that flecks of spittle flew as he spoke.

'You think that big ham fists and slashing swords are all it takes to put fear into a man and bring him down, Falkland? Words. Words will cut and rend far sharper than any such crude bludgeon. William Falkland. Thief and traitor. King's sycophant, and now Parliament's too; a man who will lick any boot for the most paltry scrap of food, him and his whore too.'

He was meaning Miss Cain; and for a moment, had I carried a sword, I might have struck him down for that. But I carried no such weapon, and after the moment passed I calmed. I nodded to him.

'So be it, John Milton. Write your bile and print your pamphlets. Spread them far and wide. Place one on the door of every house in England. I will thank you for it. You want your sister found and returned, but is that yearning born of compassion for her fear and for her suffering, for her children, for love of her and for them? Or is it born merely out of love for yourself? Is it simply that someone has slighted John Milton and must pay for their insolence?' I pushed past him. 'How long since she was taken from you – a month now? Four years since I have seen my Caro and my son and my daughter. So yes, spread your pamphlets far and wide and tell them that I still live. I will search for Anne, for her, not for you.'

I walked briskly away, not wanting any more part of this man, his arrogance, his narcissistic self-obsession; but Milton ran after me.

'Stop!'

He placed himself in front of me yet again. His face was twisted with emotion. Anger and fury, yes, and yet I could see that my words had cut him deep. There was pain there too and . . .

'I am afraid, Falkland,' he said.

I stopped. In that moment I could not be sure whether he meant to strike at me or to embrace me and weep upon my shoulder.

'I am afraid,' he said again. 'I'm afraid she might be dead.' And I knew that fear, for I had carried it with me these last six months. It was a black and heavy stone that festered deep within me and would not be shifted.

Westminster lay at my back. Ahead of me, Parliament Street ran northward to the Charing Cross. On one side, to the west, lay the fields of St James's Park and the fashionable promenade where the rich and ennobled once played pall mall before this war came upon us all. On the other lay vast and sprawling Whitehall. Caro's father, when we had come to London, had shown it to me. It had, he told me, once belonged to a great cardinal and had dwarfed even the King's palace of Westminster; and so King Harry had taken it for his own. I wondered who, if anyone, lived there now. It seemed a crime to keep such a vast palace empty.

I was thinking of my Caro again. I had almost forgotten Milton standing before me.

'I am afraid of that too,' I said softly. 'But Anne has been gone only a few weeks. The men who took her did so with some purpose. I do not rightly know, even, whether she is held against her will, though I suppose after so long it must be so. But if you are right and they mean to hold her against you, they must keep her alive . . .'

And there, in those words, came an epiphany. I saw and understood with sudden clarity the true reason for Milton's unwavering assertion that supporters of the King had taken her to use against him. I understood at last why he vilified me so for bringing that assertion into question. For yes, if that way lay the truth then his sister must, by necessary logic, live; but if the truth lay elsewhere then all was uncertainty and doubt. It was not all-consuming arrogance that had made Milton as he was towards me. It was a deep and dreadful fear.

'I did not speak of everything I knew in that room before Cromwell,' I said at last. 'Ned Fletcher was among the same company of men at Gainsborough as Fowles and Lovelace. I have seen a record to show it. He is the one who coerced the woman Jane Hardwick to embellish what she had seen. I did not say this while Fowles was present. Yet each time when words are spoken to Peter Fowles, Fletcher is not long to follow. Perhaps Fowles is as innocent as he claims, but one way or another he will lead us to Fletcher, and Fletcher will lead us to Anne.'

Milton did not answer, but I saw it in his face. The doubt. I had made him question everything he wished to believe true.

'Jane Hardwick from Clink Street who changed her story – who knew that there was a story to change?' I asked. 'Who but Fowles and Anne's son John? And who was it who came upon the idea of speaking to her a second time and pressing her for more? Was it John or was it Peter Fowles? Did your nephew press her to lie and invent some royalist conspiracy? I do not think so. I would ask you, sir, one more question: for how long has Peter Fowles been a friend to your family? Did either you or Anne know him before Francis Lovelace died?'

Milton seemed smaller now than when he had confronted me. The anger was gone. Though I did not doubt it would soon return, I saw now only despair.

'He came to us three months ago.' Milton's voice was hoarse. Gone was the pomp and power of the orator. 'Anne said she had met him once before, in London early last year. He was well known among . . . men with whom I have sympathies.' In this I took him to mean the green-ribboned Levellers of the Whalebone. 'I took to him, Falkland. I let him into my house. He talked about Francis Lovelace. I didn't know that Anne had asked the man to look for poor Thomas. She was . . .' He slumped a little more. 'She missed him so very much. She had let him go, grieved for him years ago, but Fowles brought it all back. I told her that she was a fool, that Thomas was long dead, that it was hopeless. I suppose that's why she said nothing more to me of her letters.'

For all the words spoken between us, I could not despise

him now. I saw his agony and felt it as my own. I clapped him on the shoulder.

'Then let him now lead us to Anne,' I said.

We traversed the city at speed. Outside Newgate Waterhouse waited for us. It did not surprise me to learn that Fowles had gone directly to the Whalebone, nor that Warbeck himself had gone to set watch. We reached the tavern to find the commons largely empty. Fowles sat alone and tapped his fingers on the table as if fearful or impatient, perhaps both. I did not see where Warbeck kept his watch at first, but Milton would have marched in directly if I had not caught him before he could enter, dragging him away.

'Get off me!' he hissed.

'Wait!'

'I will have the truth from him one way or another! If he has a part of this, he will tell me. I will see to it!'

I drew Milton steadily back. 'See how he sits and waits? He is here to meet with someone. I will wager what little I have that he attends on Ned Fletcher. We will watch them and see what they do. When they part ways, Waterhouse will take Fowles to Newgate and Warbeck will have the truth out of him.' I paused, not wishing to dwell upon my memories of the cells in that prison of the damned. 'I will follow Fletcher. Either he will lead us to Anne or I will take him to Newgate too. You will have truth from both of them before we're done, but remember we are here for Anne, not for pride or vengeance.'

Warbeck must have spotted us, for he sidled beside us from whatever shadow he'd found. We did not have to wait long. Perhaps half an hour passed before a man in black with a green ribbon in his hat came hurrying along the street. I recognised Ned Fletcher at once; and I will admit, at the sight of him, that I understood Milton's impulse, for Fletcher and his gang had beaten me to the ground and left me in the street, battered and bloodied, and I wanted nothing more than to return that favour. I must have flinched towards them, for Milton seized my arm.

'Your own words, Falkland.'

'Aye.'

I stilled myself to watch. Fletcher entered the Whalebone. He moved swiftly, as though driven by some urgency. Warbeck hissed at Waterhouse:

'Go inside. Watch over them. If either leaves by any way save the front, come to us at once!'

Waterhouse nodded. He followed Fletcher in, while I clasped and unclasped my fingers, nervous as a boy before some great test. My face was known to Fowles and Fletcher both, and Fowles would recognise either Milton or Warbeck at once, so Waterhouse it had to be, yet the lad was no intelligencer, and was so large that he could hardly pass unnoticed. Had Fowles seen him before? Waiting outside the Star Chamber, perhaps? If he saw a face he knew, he would spook, and all would be lost.

The minutes passed. Milton paced the street. I tried to reassure myself that if Waterhouse had given himself away then Fowles and Fletcher would have made haste to depart, but I was in no mood, I found, for uncertainty. What if they had done more than recognise him – what if they had overpowered him? Were there other men already inside and a part of this conspiracy? Eight men had gone to that house in '43. Lovelace was dead, and Blackwater too. Six remained. Fletcher, Fowles, the long-armed man for whom I had no name. And three others of whom I knew nothing.

Such were my musings as Fowles abruptly exited the Whalebone. He looked up and down the street as if in great alarm, but did not spy us lurking in our shadows. He walked south towards Cheapside. He was barely out of sight when Waterhouse came charging out.

'Master Warbeck! Master Falkland!'

'Were you seen?' I seized his shoulders in my anxiety.

'No, sir, but the other man, Fletcher, he heads out back for the stables. I think he has a waiting horse, sir.'

My heart jumped. I had not considered this. A horse and he would be away from us! Warbeck and I exchanged a glance. 'Fowles went for Cheapside!' I said. 'Catch him and bring him down! Take him to Newgate as he deserves. Run, man!'

Warbeck hesitated. 'You will take Fletcher?'

'I will take him with pleasure.'

We had our reasons, each of us. Fletcher had kicked me to the street. Fowles had played Warbeck for a fool. There were scores to settle; thus Warbeck nodded and bared his teeth, and he and Waterhouse ran in Fowles' wake, while I turned away from the door and started for the stables, hoping to catch Fletcher before he could depart. Milton again caught my arm.

'Falkland! What are you doing?'

I pulled away. 'Better that he lead us to his fellow conspirators. Better yet that he lead us to Anne herself, but we cannot at any cost let him escape lest we never set eyes on him again.' Fletcher, I felt, was not like Fowles. If he knew of our pursuit then he would vanish into the country. I feared that was his intent even now.

'Wait!' Milton grasped me more tightly. 'Go and watch, then, but do not confront him unless you must.'

'If he leaves on horseback we cannot catch him!'

'Unless we have horses of our own! Just wait, Falkland!' He let me go and hurried into the Whalebone while I ran to the stable at the back. I crouched in the street outside, peering through the cracks in the planking walls. A man moved among the horses. I could not see his face, but I remembered those boots. Curled on the stones of Fleet Street, I had seen them all too well. Ned Fletcher, saddling a horse. He was crooning to the animal, talking to her as a cavalryman might, or perhaps a dragoon. He did not seem in any hurry; yet he was almost done when two other men rushed in. Milton's voice was unmistakeable.

'. . . is returned to London. Oxford has surrendered! I am overwrought with gratitude that you find it in your heart to assist me with this.' Milton and the other man moved among the horses. 'I will write such searing verse against the dreaming vanity of this Prince Rupert. Let us at last be rid of him and his preening ilk. Back to Germany with them. Back with them all. You, sir, might I ask you for a moment?' He was addressing Fletcher! My heart almost stopped. 'I must ride directly to Oxford with all speed to be there before nightfall. Do you hear the news? The glorious word of it?' As he spoke he continued saddling his horse. The second man, who until now had said nothing, worked on another. I could not see their faces.

'News?' Was that voice Fletcher? It must have been so.

'Oxford has come to terms, man! Cromwell has returned to London, bringing them to Parliament. The war is done! The war is done!'

'And the King? Does *he* come to terms?'

'It will be soon, my friend. I see the ribbon you wear, and it gladdens my heart. Whatever terms the King shall propose, let Parliament denounce them. Let his pomp and vanity be eviscerated upon the will of the common folk, I say. All men shall vote, commoner and lord alike, all equal, and a king shall be no better than a tenant farmer!'

'I pray you take from them as much as you can, sir,' grunted Fletcher, 'and I pray to God that Parliament shall not betray us. Better, say I, to have no king at all. Good day to you.'

I scurried across the alley to another, narrower still and shadowed into darkness by the buildings that grew overhead like a roof. I crouched as small as I could. Fletcher's horse walked from the stables a moment later. I watched him to the end of the alley and saw him turn north into Whalebone Street. As soon as he was out of sight, I ran and peered after him. He continued northward for Cripplegate. In the stables Milton had almost finished.

'Falkland!'

'Milton.'

'About time! My own horse is lame, but this good man understands our cause. He will loan us his horses for the ride to Oxford. We must have a care not to drive *them* lame also.' He spoke with such an arch look to him that I feared he might even wink in his encouragement that I play along with his charade.

'We need to leave. Now.' I finished the second mare, tightened her girth until I was satisfied and jumped into the saddle. The stirrups were too short, and nothing was set quite as I would have wanted it, but such things would have to wait. I urged the mare out into the alley and thence to the street, clucking to her as I followed Fletcher's path. When I could not see him, I urged her to a trot, searching each road as we passed for any sign lest he had chosen to double back; but I need not have been so anxious. I caught sight of him as we reached the Cripplegate itself. Fletcher rode out beneath it, while I slowed and hung back, keeping as much distance between us as I dared.

'Is it true?' I asked, as Milton came alongside me. 'Oxford has surrendered?' If it was so then I would be free to enter. It was the one place left I could think to search for my Caro.

'It is not. A sleight of the tongue, Falkland, forked and deceitful. I know these men of the Whalebone, these Levellers, and they know me. We consider ourselves friends enough that I might borrow a horse now and then, which is no mean friendship at all, but only with a compelling cause. Thus was I obliged to concoct one.' His eyes fixed on Fletcher, far ahead of us. The road, I was glad to note, was busy enough that two riders in the distance behind were not likely to cause him any alarm. It would become more difficult later, as we travelled out of London.

Milton shook his head. 'These men and I, we have common cause. My own views are not quite as theirs, but we would none of us shed a tear to see the King's head on a pike. Why would they do this to me? To Anne? What is the reason, Falkland?'

'No cause of King or Parliament, of that I am certain. What is the reason ever?' I had no answer. Francis Lovelace had carried with him to his grave some secret, which Fowles and Fletcher and others now sought within the letters he had written; but whether they searched for it in fear or hope,

I could not decide. After I had visited Beth Lovelace, I had thought of Fowles' claim that Lovelace owed him monies, and had wondered if there was perhaps some treasure whose hiding place Lovelace had known but had never revealed. Nathaniel Blackwater's words came again to haunt me. *Our spoils of war . . .*

'Greed and fear,' spoke Milton, as if plucking my thoughts and reducing them to their most simple essence, 'are what move all men.'

We were soon among fields, although the road remained busy with traffic moving in and out of London. Everywhere I looked, a church spire poked from among the trees and between the hedgerows. I had, I supposed, imagined Fletcher would head for some nearby house where he and his fellows laid their heads and, I hoped, had imprisoned Anne. Yet he pressed steadily north, leaving London ever further behind, then veered to the west along the St Albans road.

The afternoon wore on. Travellers grew few, while Fletcher continued at a pressing pace. He was, I thought, a seasoned soldier, one used to scouting ahead and with a wary eye for any first sign of the enemy. He would soon notice he was followed – two horsemen keeping a steady distance to his rear would be obvious to a man like that. I tried all manner of schemes I had learned as a dragoon, when we might be put upon to shadow some detachment of the enemy with intent that we remain unseen and then report their disposition: when the road traversed open country, I would ride up to the nearest rise and spy out the land ahead, and then drop back and we would remain out of sight for as long as we dared; other times I would have Milton hang back a mile behind me, or else the other way around, so that

Fletcher would see only one horseman should he turn to look; in villages, now and then, we would wait outside, or else rush on in front. Twice I managed to get us ahead of Fletcher so that he was following us instead of us him; and then we would pull away and wait and then resume our pursuit. I did not convince myself that he was fooled – he was as much a veteran of these wars as I and doubtless knew the same intrigues – but if he noted our presence, he made no effort to throw us off. As the evening approached he rode into St Albans, once the Roman city of Verulamium. I spied on him as he stabled his horse at the Round House tavern. St Albans, I knew, had sided with Parliament through the fighting, all except some foolish High Sheriff who had proclaimed for the King outside the clock tower at the same time as Cromwell himself had marched in. I had not heard what happened to that sheriff, but doubtless no good had come of it.

I watched Fletcher settle to his supper. My stomach rumbled its discontent, reminding me I had not eaten today since first light; and I found in that discomfort a disgust for myself. I had marched on an empty stomach many a time. I had starved for days fighting for the King. Yet now I was a soldier no longer, my stomach cramped at a single missed meal?

I turned away from the Round House to rejoin Milton, imagining the early start we must make to ensure we were not foxed by Fletcher leaving before us. As I hurried on my way, I chanced upon several pots of limewash placed up against the side of the street and as yet barely used, while the cottage wall above them was half whitened and half bare wattle and daub. On impulse I took one pot in each hand. I returned to the stables where Fletcher had left his horse and, unobserved, threw the contents of the pots willy-nilly about the place as if in the fit of some derangement, careful to ensure a goodly quantity found its way onto the rump of Fletcher's mare as well as several of the others. The animals, I will say, did not take well to this treatment, and caused a commotion such that I was obliged to flee lest I be caught. The whitening would brush out, if Fletcher cared to spend the time before he left, but I thought perhaps he would not.

Milton, when I explained to him what I had done, did not think this a clever ruse at all.

'You fool! He'll know something is wrong, Falkland!'

I shrugged, for I still thought he must already have seen that he was followed. 'There is a good chance he knows we track him. This will show us. He must either delay to make his horse clean or else it will be distinct enough that we will have no need to keep him in sight. Every person he passes will remember a horse half painted white.'

We ate well, Milton as generous with his purse as he had once been with his scorn, and retired early and rose before the dawn. Fletcher, I quickly learned, was already away as I had feared, but when I looked around the stables in the light of sunrise, I saw no white powder scattered all across the floor. I wondered if, in the night, he had not even seen what had been done.

'Fletcher's gone,' I told Milton on my return. 'He is alert to us.'

'Could he not simply have risen early, Falkland?'

I could not explain precisely. It was the instinct of a soldier; and Fletcher had been a soldier too, and no matter that we had fought in armies that had once stood against one another, we were both a part of the same damaged brotherhood. I knew without any doubt that he had seen us, and so had raced away with the first light of dawn to throw us from his tracks. I knew because I would have done the same.

He had left London for the north, and so we left St Albans that way too, questioning every sentry and watchman and early-rising farmer we passed, until at last we found one who had seen a horse half painted white. In this way we resumed our pursuit. Fletcher had taken the Huntingdon road and was moving at a speed that made us struggle to gain on him. I urged Milton on, heedless of his difficulty in keeping to such a pace, anxious we should catch sight of Fletcher before nightfall, for when next he stopped he would surely brush his horse clean.

Perhaps, then, the intensity of my haste was why I did not see the ambush he had made for us.

CHAPTER 17

I should have thought of it. I might have done the same myself. He came at us out of a copse beside the road. Before I knew it he was almost upon us, a brace of pistols across his chest and one in his hand. The first I glimpsed was a rush of movement from the corner of my eye. As I turned I saw the pistol raised, aimed at my chest. I knew his face at once, that great beard. He was barely twenty yards short and closing at a canter.

'Falkland!'

Instinct saved me. I was looking straight at him as he fired. I saw the flash of powder, and yet I was already hurling myself forward flat against the neck of my mare. The shot missed, but the thunder of its retort spooked the mare and she lurched into a terrified gallop. I heard Milton cry out behind me but stayed as I was, flat down, urging the mare to flee as fast as she cared to gallop, for I had no pistol of my own nor even a sabre to bring Fletcher down.

'Falkland! I should have killed you back in London!'

Perhaps, but I was grateful that he had not. Nor did I have breath to waste on trading insults. The mare's panic began to ebb, but she kept her speed at my urging. When I heard a second shot, more distant, I turned from the road and aimed for a stand of trees. Perhaps my horse would outlast Fletcher's or perhaps not, but I did not care to find out when the man still carried loaded pistols. I preferred, if it must come to it, that we stalk one another among the trees. I rode my mare to the edge of the copse and then cast a glance behind me, but Fletcher had abandoned his pursuit. He had chased me far enough that I could no longer see Milton; but even as I debated my course, I heard a third shot. I led my mare into the copse and dismounted to hide. A minute passed, and then I saw a single rider gallop away along the road. Fletcher on his half-painted horse. I watched him go, and knew there was nothing I could do to stop him.

Milton, when I returned to him, was not dead. I had supposed that Fletcher had returned to finish him, but it was not so. Instead I found the polemicist sitting in the road, rubbing at his head in pauses between cradling his left arm.

'Are you hurt?' I asked, my eyes looking him over in a fevered search for blood. I could not believe there was none. I had thought that Fletcher's first shot, though meant for me, had struck Milton.

'A fair crack on the shoulder and another to the head and a great deal of injury to my pride. Nothing more.'

'He didn't shoot you?' I dismounted and helped Milton to his feet. Then I looked about for his horse. I could not immediately see it.

'He didn't. Oh, I felt the first one skim my nose like the breath of Satan himself, and then that cursed horse threw me and bolted.'

'But when he came back . . .'

'When he came back he pointed a pistol at me and told me he had a mind to shoot me. So I told him that if he returned my Anne then he might hang with some hope of redemption, but that if he didn't then he would hang anyway, and also burn for eternity in the fires of hell, scoured by those terrible winds beside Achilles and Tristan and flayed by the seven-pronged whips of Lucifer's favoured generals.'

'You said this to a man holding a pistol on you?' This did indeed sound like the Milton I had come to know; yet now it made me laugh. I felt around at his shoulder, searching in case there were bones broken. 'I heard more shots,' I said.

Milton pointed. I had not seen his horse because I had been looking for a beast upright. Fletcher had not shot the man, but the animal.

'He told me I was a godly man, as if I needed to be told from such a verminous creature, and that he did not murder godly men. Then he shot my horse. I do not know if my horse was an ungodly horse, but I must suppose that to Fletcher it seemed that it was. The last shot was his mercy, putting the poor beast from its agony. He is away, Falkland. We will not catch him.'

I nodded. That much was true. 'But that does not mean we cannot follow. His horse is still marked.'

'He will wash it clean at the next stream. It will slow him, but not enough for us to catch him riding double.'

'No, but he will put some distance between us first. Then he will ride off the road and find somewhere safe to do it. Perhaps then he will think himself free of us.'

'And so he will be.'

I shrugged. 'Perhaps, perhaps not. A lot depends on whether he thinks to cut that great beard of his. It will be harder, but do not say it cannot be done. I would try, at least.' I offered Milton my hand. 'Can you still ride?'

'If you will bear my cursing.' He mounted behind me.

Perhaps Fletcher supposed that his killing of Milton's horse would be sufficient to dissuade us. Had he known Milton better then doubtless he would have considered otherwise; but I was grateful to him for his misconception. By means of asking after his horse we were able to follow almost to Huntingdon, although by then he was far ahead. We passed through the town, asking after a man with a chestnut horse and a great bushy beard, but to no avail. We pressed on nevertheless, I suppose hoping for some luck, riding the long, straight roads north between a flatness of fields and low hedgerows that stretched to both horizons. In Peterborough we found several men who had sighted a man who might have been Fletcher. He had ridden through in the middle of the afternoon, while we had come upon the town in the evening, tired.

The mare troubled me. I did not think she would last another day carrying us both. In truth we were none of us greatly invigorated. Milton's shoulder caused him a deal of discomfort which he tried to hide from me, and my own injury throbbed. My head had settled, by now, into a constant dull ache. The fever, at least, had diminished.

'I should follow alone,' I said to Milton once we had settled into a coaching inn a few miles outside Peterborough. Milton bought us each a bowl of thick, greasy stew. Lumps of delicious pork fat floated in a gravy enriched with blood. It was fine fare, and all the more delicious for our weariness and aching limbs. 'That mare will not take us both for another day at such a pace, and we cannot let him get much farther ahead of us. People will forget even a beard such as his readily enough.'

Milton pondered this and then left, instructing me to wait. When he returned an hour later, it was to inform me that he had purchased a second horse from a stables but five minutes from here, and that we might yet proceed together. Then he placed three pistols on the table between us, together with a pouch of bullets and two small horns of powder.

'I am not a soldier,' he said. 'And you are not armed. This will not do.' He pushed two of the pistols to me and took the last for himself.

'I would prefer a good sabre,' I said, but I took the pistols nonetheless. Later I would load and arm them. I would not be caught so easily by any future ambuscade.

'Would it hurt you, Falkland, to congratulate me on resolving not one problem but two in the space of your supper?'

For a moment he seemed to be the Milton I had first met a week ago, full of his own importance and as arrogant as any king. A brief flash of anger passed through me. This time I let it go. 'I meant no offence,' I said, as mildly as I could muster. 'Our pursuit will indeed be sounder with two instead of one.'

'I never marched with any company, Falkland. You must instruct me.'

'With a pistol?' I laughed. 'There is little to learn. Do you know how to lead it?'

He did not. We went to the stables, away from our fellow travellers, and I showed him how we dragoons had learned to carry them, loaded and ready to fire. I showed him how it might be held in such a way that the barrel did not hang down and there was no risk of the wadding shaking loose from hours of riding and losing both powder and ball. I showed how a dab of molten wax applied to the wad might seal the ball and powder in place, and also keep out water should it rain. I showed him how to check his flints were good and sharp, and that his firing pan was properly primed.

'It is not a weapon to be relied upon,' I told him. 'Beyond twenty paces they are prone to miss, and they often do not fire at all, particularly if there is damp in the air. I have seen many a skilled armsman betrayed by a misfire.' I watched a while and made him practise his aim. 'A patient and steady hand is the key unless some monster with a pike is charging upon you.'

My headache was growing stronger, demanding I rest. Yet as we returned to the commons, Milton stopped me.

'You are not a vain man, Falkland. Nor superstitious, nor in any sense foolish. I see now why Cromwell chose you. Why did you fight for the King?'

'Why does any man?' I asked in return. I will admit I was taken unawares by his words, for Milton – and of this I was beyond certain – was no flatterer.

'Because he is coerced. For a cause. For justice. For God. For what is right. Which was it for you?'

I could not contain my smile. 'You have not marched with any army that I would recognise.'

'I have not marched with any army at all. But I have known many of our soldiers and asked them what lies in their hearts. These are their answers.'

'Then they are the answers of soldiers who have returned to London to write pamphlets and run presses and speak in Parliament. I have met their sort.' I shook my head. 'They are not the answers of men who left their land and farms and families. Most do not care one whit for cause or justice or what is right. Some, on your end, have in their heads that they fight for God . . .' I paused a moment there. I did not know the strength of Milton's beliefs. It's a strange thing, that which we call faith. Friends may become the most terrible enemies simply over a difference in that little word. Milton, I fancied, would put it into poetry, but I could not. I had abandoned God long ago, as He had abandoned me. 'I marched to London in 'thirty-nine in the company of my father-in-law's militia. I marched because it pleased him and thus it pleased my wife, for whom I would have done anything. I do not know why the King went to fight the Scots, those very same with whom he now takes shelter. I do not know what had roused their ire that they would take up arms against their own monarch. Nor, to be blunt, the rest of you. After that, when it grew into something that consumed us all, I fought because . . . because he was the King, and because I knew nothing else. Because I could not get away from it.'

'Do you rue it, Falkland?'

How could I not? Yet Milton's question was barbed. He implied I had chosen the wrong side, and implied in this that the other side was right. I would have disagreed and told him that each side was as wrong as the other, but I was tired, my head ached, I could barely keep my eyes open, and I already stared with loathing into the barrel of an early start to continue our pursuit.

'I rue that there was a war at all,' I replied. 'Why did you *not* fight?'

'I fight with words, not bullets.'

'Then sharpen your words well, John Milton, for Fletcher will most definitely prefer bullets.'

That night I slept the same troubled sleep as had afflicted me since I had found my home abandoned, filled with dreams of fire. I saw my Caro and my children staring back at me through the flames, unable to reach them, and unsure as to which of us was burning.

Through virtue of Fletcher's distinctive beard we were able to follow his progress as far as Lincoln. He had stopped there, it seemed, in the early afternoon ahead of us, but remained now half a day ahead. I scoured the town to look for any sight of him and which way he had gone, but by the time darkness was setting in I had not found his trail. I feared we would lose him, and that would be the end of our chase, but among the morning markets, as Milton and I questioned everyone we found, a man pointed us to the Gainsborough road. Fletcher had stayed in the town for some hours, it seemed, and left late the previous afternoon. It was slow work to follow his trail now, and I knew he must be gaining on us once again, but I thought too that I now knew where he was going. We tracked him steadily to the village of Lea, a quiet, leafy place of lazy summer willows, long, flat fields, birdsong and the gentle rippling of water. Fletcher, I was surprised to learn, was well known here and had often been seen about until two months past. The villagers could not tell me where he had gone or where he lived, but they knew the path to the old Walhope manor. I was certain, now, that this had been our destination all along.

We came upon the manor itself early in the afternoon. The track was part overgrown, as though rarely used. The earth was dry and hard from days of hot summer sun. I stopped as we drew near and dismounted to peer more closely at the grass. I found bent and broken blades, freshly done. When I dropped my head close to the ground to peer along it, I could see a shining line where the wheel of some carriage had passed not long ago. I told Milton, and then guided his eye so he might see it for himself.

'A carriage came through,' I told him.

'Can you say when?'

'Yesterday, I think.' I could not be sure, but it was no older.

The house seemed at first glance intact, not a burned out roofless ruin. Fowles had told us they had been forced to leave in haste by the arrival of Newcastle's army before they could fire the place. Yet as we drew closer, I saw much damage had been done. The front doors hung ajar. Windows and shutters were broken. Shreds of ivy had taken root in the walls, and one of the chimneys was part tumbled. I paused a while to listen and smell the air, but there was no scent of smoke. The only sounds were of the birds and the rustle of the wind. I thought the place abandoned, though I could not be sure that no ambush awaited us.

'His horse isn't here,' observed Milton.

'I think our goose has flown,' I said, 'but I will go inside to be sure.' I dismounted and tied my mare loosely to a tree. 'Wait for me here and keep your pistol close to hand. If you hear shots, do not wait to see who emerges but ride at once for Gainsborough and for a magistrate.'

I crept towards the door, pistol in hand. As soon as I entered, shrouded in gloom, I knew the house had not been long abandoned. The air carried a sweet tang of woodsmoke, and the more bitter scent of men cramped together. Beneath lay smells of the earth, of old wood and a little rot. I entered the hall and went to the window beside the door. It was thick with grime. I ran my finger across it and smelled the residue. Soot. I flung the doors wide then, letting in the sun. I was in a hall the full height of the house and, I thought, most of its depth. A stair rose along the left side to the upper floor. Before it began, big oak double doors led left and right into the wings of the house. The one beside the foot of the stairs was closed, but the one opposite hung open. As I walked further in, I saw another door at the back of the hall, smaller than the rest. An entrance, I supposed, into the kitchens; and in my mind I was already laying out how the house might be, for my own home in Launcells had been of a similar design.

I paused again to listen, but heard no sound of movement, and so I returned to the entrance and inspected it more closely. In the front wall on either side of the door I found two holes drilled by musket balls that had missed their targets. I tried to imagine the scene, a small band of Newcastle's soldiers easing through in the darkness, stepping from moonlight into a much deeper gloom, thinking to surprise a rapacious band of Parliament's men in their sleep and rescue a rich lady. Even as they came through, they would be anticipating the reward that awaited them.

I moved then to the back of the hall, where the stairs loomed beside me, and crouched. Fowles and the others had waited here, he had said, invisible in the darkness. The King's men would have been in silhouette against the moonlight from the door. Who had given the order to fire – Lovelace? They would have waited until all the enemy were committed to making their entrance, but would not have dared let the soldiers spread out in the dark. Had I been here, I would have given the order to fire as they were clustered around the door. A single volley and then a roaring charge, cutting down the first of the enemy with shot, throwing fear and confusion among the rest and falling upon them at once before they might rally their thoughts. I could not think what men would not have turned and fled before such an onslaught. And then out into the night, bringing them down before they could escape into the darkness.

The open door led me into the right wing of the house where a large room greeted me. It must once have been a dining room, I thought, but was now empty except for a few hacked pieces of wood. Among them were what appeared to have been the legs of some ornate table, splintered and chipped. I thought the smell of smoke a little stronger here, and the soot in the fireplace was old but not ancient, days but not years. There had been wooden panels on the walls once, though these had long since been torn away. Under the soot I found shards of wood and embers not fully burned. They were blackened and charred, but had been something carved with delicacy once.

There was a stink of people here. I went to the windows and threw open the shutters and wiped away some of the soot, letting in as much light as the dirt would allow. A single other door led back to the kitchens and the pantry. In the corner beside it was a pile of straw, old and soiled and part rotted, and a chamber pot still half full with urine. A day old, no more. I crouched beside the straw and then pressed my face to it and sniffed. It carried the smell of whoever had slept here. On my hands and knees then, my face still close to the floor in the dim light that penetrated the windows, I fingered through the straw. I was hoping, I suppose, for some shred of fabric torn from a dress, or some ring or amulet hidden away there for safekeeping that might have told me this was where Anne had passed her captivity. I found neither, but in the middle part of the straw I saw instead a small, dark stain; and around one edge, away from the chamber pot, a few strands of hair.

I sniffed at the stains on the straw. They did not smell of excrement. I put them to my tongue and tasted blood.

'Falkland?' Milton was at the hallway door. 'Falkland, I have found something.'

I took the straw and the hairs with me. Milton led me outside and through the grounds to the side of the house and a grand sycamore. An old rope hung from one of its high branches, the end cut and frayed. I knew it at once – a hanging rope with the noose cut free – and shuddered as I saw it. I had seen its like before, on one occasion far more closely than I would have liked.

'This is where they hanged them, then.' Milton's voice was sombre. The rope was looped over the branch and then tied to something hidden in the undergrowth. I walked to see what it was and found it secured to the bole of another tree, buried among brambles. Milton, who had started after me, stopped abruptly with a cry.

'Falkland!'

I could not at first see what had stopped him short with such alarm; but as he pointed down into the tangle of thorns around us, a shape slowly resolved itself to me. A skull. I crouched and pushed the thorns aside. There was a skeleton here, its flesh long eaten away. The bones of its neck were broken, snapped as a well-made noose will do. The thorns grew too thickly around the torso to pull it free, even if I had wanted to drag it loose, but the bones had wrapped around them the rotten remains of a soldier's coat.

'They must have laid him out here after they hanged him.' I peered and prodded among the thorns and soon found another skeleton – another soldier judging by his boots. 'They must have laid them all out. They didn't loot them.' I wondered why, and replayed the story Fowles had told. In a rage, Lovelace had ordered everyone hanged. Someone had scaled the sycamore in the dark and looped over the rope. They'd killed the soldiers who were still alive and laid them out in the night, and then the two servants and Lady Walhope and her daughter – or perhaps they had killed the women first. It seemed strange that the soldiers' bodies had not been stripped, but perhaps Lovelace had chosen to wait until the morning and daylight and then been driven too quickly away by the news of Newcastle's advance. Perhaps they were already too rich with pickings from seizing Gainsborough to care for coats and boots, but I doubted that. Among soldiers, there was always money to be had for a good pair of boots.

I drew Milton away from the bones.

'This is where it happened,' said Milton. 'Everything Fowles said.'

I nodded. 'What colour was Anne's hair?'

'Dark. Almost black.'

I took out the hairs and the straw I had found inside the house, and looked at them again in sunlight. The hair was as Milton had said, dark. Black, perhaps.

'There was someone here yesterday,' I said. I passed him the hair. 'I found these beside a spread of old straw. The dining room fire has been lit within the last week.'

Milton was staring at the hairs.

'I would say that Fletcher came to the house yesterday shortly after midday. There was at least one other person here who had been sheltering for some time. There may have been others – I have not yet searched the house in its entirety. That evening or else at first light today, they left. I must suppose Fletcher took his horse, but there was a small cart or carriage also.'

We looked at one another.

'Anne,' whispered Milton.

'The hair is hers?'

'It is impossible to say. It looks the same.'

'Fletcher's gang kept her here.' I could see the sense of it. An abandoned house, a place they knew and far away from London. No one would ever come looking here.

A day. A single day. Had we somehow pressed Fletcher harder as we rode north, we might have come in time to have caught him.

'She's still alive,' whispered Milton.

'I think so.' She had been until yesterday. Would Fletcher have taken her from here only to do away with her? Where would he go? One thing to ride fast and alone, another to ride in company, with a carriage and a prisoner. They would be seen and remembered.

'The village,' said Milton suddenly. 'They had to go through the village.'

But we had gone through the village ourselves and asked after Fletcher, and heard no mention of any carriage. I shook my head. 'The other way. They do not dare to be seen.' I racked my brains. What had Fowles been looking for in those letters? What secret did they think Lovelace had known that Anne now held? It came back to this place and what had passed here in June of 1643. Fowles had told a little of the truth in front of Cromwell, but not all. There had to be more, yet I could not fathom it.

'We cannot stay,' said Milton. 'She was here but now she is gone. We must continue our pursuit!'

'Not yet.' I needed to know. Somewhere here must lie a clue, I thought. Something to unravel whatever Fowles and Fletcher were seeking. If I could find that, it would no longer serve them to hold Anne.

'Falkland! Someone must have seen them! We need to go! We need to find Anne!'

'Go then.' I walked back among the thorns where the skeletons lay. 'Scout the lanes nearby. Go to the closest farms and see whether anyone has seen anything. Come back to me here when you're done.' Fletcher had brought Anne here because it was abandoned and because it was a place he knew, but was there another reason too? What was it about this house? I could not say why, but I did not think he had gone far. Something about what they had done here tied him to it.

Between the two skeletons of soldiers I dropped to my hands and knees and pulled the briars apart, pressing ever further among them until one by one I found the other remains. Fowles had said Lady Walhope and her daughter and two servants, which made four, but I only found three, all wrapped in rotten tatters of what might once have been nightshirts. Two were tall like the soldiers. One was shorter. When I looked more closely I saw she had a bullet hole in her skull.

CHAPTER 18

Milton was already gone by the time I extricated myself from the thorns. I returned to the house, thinking to explore more thoroughly and play through the story Fowles had woven of the events that had passed here. I walked through the hall to the door at the far end; it brought me into a long passageway that ran across the back width of the house. On the far side were the kitchens and the pantry and three small rooms that must have once belonged to the maid and the two dead serving men. I peered through each, but they had been turned over long ago and were home to little but mice and spiders. There were pans and bowls in the kitchens, and some fine tableware, though much was scattered across the floor as Lovelace's soldiers had torn through the cupboards. A door led outside into what had once been a kitchen garden. My Caro had had one like it, though this one was overgrown and barely recognisable. Nevertheless I had to stop for a moment as I imagined her there, my wife, crouched on her haunches, picking herbs and lavender. A pang of despair washed through me. Whoever the lady of this house had been, she would have done the same. I found it hard, in that moment, not to imagine what fate had befallen them both, usurped from their homes by marauding soldiers.

I shook the thought away. My Caro had left of her own choice. She was alive. I had to believe that she was.

I returned to the house and explored the passage further. Another door opened to the outside at the far end, close to a handful of outbuildings that had once been stables. Yet another opened into the second large room of the house, a parlour. Like the dining room, this had been stripped. I found more pallets of straw, two of them. There were no chamber pots, but I found a small pile of tiny bones in a corner, from pigeons and perhaps a chicken or two. A part of the room was scorched as though a small fire had burned there once. This was the room where Anne's captors had slept, then, and I could only wonder at what they had done with her here, why they had brought her all this way and then held her for so long.

Fowles had told us that Lovelace's company bedded down in the hall so as not to disturb the lady and her house more than needed. I walked back around to the front door with its two musket ball holes in the wall beside it. It seemed odd to me that the King's soldiers who had meant to ambush Lovelace had come that way. Fowles claimed that the lady of the house had sent word through one of her servants, telling the King's men of her plight, yet surely it would have been simpler to call them to one of the doors at the back. To unbar the front she would have to walk through the whole of Lovelace's company, while to open the doors to the stables or the kitchen garden she would not. From the rear Newcastle's soldiers could have spread through the house and come at Lovelace from all ways at once. They would have surrounded him and made short work of his men. In calling them to the front door she had made both the wrong choice and the one that placed her most at risk.

I climbed the stairs, testing each one as I went for rot, but they felt solid – the house was not that far gone. A small passage ran along the width of the upper floor, directly over the passageway below. Doors led into three rooms over each wing. I tried the rooms over the parlour first. The closest to the stairs was a bedroom, a lady's room by the furnishings. The walls were panelled in a hard dark wood, stained almost black like the wooden door. The shutters were thrown open, the window smashed, the floor scattered with leaf litter and the droppings of birds and other small animals. A bed occupied most of one wall, an elaborate four-poster. The curtains around two of the sides had been torn down, while the third was ragged and ruined by mildew. A mattress lay across it, smeared with dirt and riddled with tiny holes gnawed by rats and mice. There was a large dark stain in the middle and there were slashes along its sides where fistfuls of straw and wool had been pulled out. The remains of a dresser stood against another wall, its drawers strewn across the floor, the rest smashed apart. A chair lay tipped over beside it. A wardrobe stood with its doors hanging open. When I looked inside, the wood was splintered as though someone had taken an axe to it. Rags of clothes lay across the floor. Everywhere had been ransacked.

A second door opened into an adjoining room. When I looked inside, I found myself in another bedroom, smaller but still richly furnished. At first glance it, too, had been ransacked, although not so badly. But my eyes were fixed on the bed. A skeleton lay here, arms and legs akimbo, rags of a nightdress draped around it. Even through the ravages of the years I could see how the cloth had been ripped open, how it had been pulled up around the skeleton's hips. A pillow lay across the skull, hiding it.

My gorge rose in my throat. I turned away as quick as I could, bent over and heaved the contents of my stomach onto the floor. When I had recovered my composure I returned and lifted the pillow. Scraps of leathery scalp still clung to the bone, with long curls of hair. This room belonged to the daughter. They had pinned her to the bed and raped her – perhaps only one or two but very likely all of them one after another – and then suffocated her. I pitied her, this girl whose name I would never know. What had she ever done to deserve such a fate? I could not stop thinking of my Charlotte. She would be the same age now as this girl had been.

I turned away, unable to face this hideous sight any longer, and returned to the room that must have belonged to the girl's mother. Fowles claimed Lovelace had shot her. I had seen the bullet hole in the skull outside, but the stain on the mattress looked to me as if it was blood. When I inspected it more closely I saw there was a hole close to its centre. That in itself meant little, for many other holes had been nibbled away over time. But when I ripped a little more of the cloth, the wool and feathers and straw beneath were stained dark as if some thick liquid had been allowed to spill into them for some time. It took a while but eventually I found the lead ball nestled deep among them. Someone had lain here, and someone else had stood over them with a pistol – I supposed not a musket simply from the length of such a weapon – and shot them in the belly; but if this was Lady Walhope who had sent word to the King's soldiers to

come for her that night, how was it that she was asleep in
bed when they burst through? I doubted that even a
seasoned soldier would sleep, knowing what was coming.
Surely a woman of any sense would have taken her daughter,
at the very least, and barricaded themselves away to await the
outcome.

Something was not right with the version of events as
Fowles had given it. The lady of the house had not sent
word to Newcastle's soldiers, I could not believe that now.

I turned to the rest of the house. The room across the
passage was a nursery, empty except for a crib, and
untouched. The rooms over on the other side were a mirror
of those I had already explored. All three were bedrooms – I
must suppose for the lord of the manor and his two sons
who had died in the defence of Gainsborough – and all three
had been ripped apart. The mattresses had been opened and
emptied upon the floor, the desks and dressers smashed. A
blade had been taken to every chair, tearing it open. Lovelace
and his men had turned the house over with a systematic
thoroughness that made me wonder if there was more to
this than looting. It struck me they had been looking for
something particular, and had been frustrated in that search.
Had it been for what Fowles now sought in Lovelace's
letters?

In the lady's room I began to search for what might have
been missed. I tapped upon walls, seeking any hollow panel
that might be levered free, but found none. Nor were any of
the boards loose. The dresser and the wardrobe had already
been attacked as if being skinned for some secret compart-
ment – such things had been fashionable in Caro's father's
time. Averting my eyes from the scene on the bed I returned

to the daughter's room and did the same. Again I found nothing. I searched until I could not stand to be in that room with its atrocity any longer, then rushed outside, gasping lungfuls of warm midday air.

Milton had not returned, and so I went to my horse and took a little cheese and bread. Fowles had said that the King's men had come through the front door and that he and Lovelace and the rest had opened fire. This, from the bullet holes, I believed. Lovelace had flown into a rage and ordered the execution of everyone in the house. Fowles had heard shots, but did not know what had become of the lady and her daughter. Yet how could Lady Walhope have remained in her bed through such a discharge of thunder and peal of arms, sleeping soundly? I could not believe it. And after the scene I had seen in the other room, I could not believe Fowles had not known what had happened there. I had not been with any company of soldiers where such a thing could pass unknown by any one of them. Such men as these formed bonds as tight as brothers, as I had done among the men of my own companies. With such thoughts I walked around the outside of the house, pacing through other arrangements of events, searching for one that better fitted what I had found.

I stopped a little way from the entrance beside the broken down doors to a wood cellar. I peered inside. At first I saw nothing but stacked piles of chopped wood half overgrown with weeds among dim shadows. I took this to show that no one had lived in the house over winter, else both this, the shattered furniture and the wooden panel walls would all have gone to the fire for warmth.

Snagged on the splintered wood of the door I found a

torn piece of cloth. Years under the sun had bleached it of any colour, but it was thick wool, the sort of cloth that came from a soldier's coat. I eased my way down into the cellar and peered about until, at the very back, curled up behind stacks of wood, I found another long-dead skeleton. This one had been untouched; though his flesh had been eaten by worms and beetles, his coat and belt and boots remained. Had I light to see by, I might even have learned the man's regiment.

I went outside and lit a fire, then took a brand back into the cellar. The coat, I thought, made him one of Newcastle's men, though I could not be sure. There was a large stain on the chest and another close to the bottom. I found a musket ball hole beside each, the upper one in the man's back. When I eased the coat away, I found the shoulder bone chipped beneath, but it was the leg, I thought, that had done for him. I could see how it had played. He had been caught in the volley of fire at the door which accounted for the wound in his leg. Perhaps he had been towards the back, but at any rate he had been able to escape. He had hurried away, but his wound had made him slow. He hadn't been fast enough. Lovelace or one of his men had burst out into the night with a loaded pistol, seen him stumbling, picked out by moonlight, and shot him in the back. They'd seen him fall, but in the darkness hadn't seen that he fell into the cellar door and crashed through it. The soldier, mortally injured now but still living, had crept into the darkest, furthest corner he could find to hide, and had quietly died. Bled to death, I supposed. In their hurry to get away from Newcastle's advancing army, Lovelace's men hadn't ever found him; or else they simply hadn't cared.

His pockets, then, might yet contain something to identify him. I rummaged through them, but found nothing save a crumpled piece of paper. In the light outside, I read it.

The fronte dor will be not garded nor with bar to night. The hour after funfet you will find them at their fleepe.

There was no name, but the writing was crude and riddled with error. It was not the hand of a lady. Someone else had called these soldiers to this house. I thought, then, that I knew what had happened; but as the understanding came over me I looked up, drawn by a snort of alarm from my horse. I saw two men already dismounted, creeping their way towards me with pistols at the ready.

One was Ned Fletcher. When he saw me he fired.

CHAPTER 19

I had told Milton that a pistol should not be trusted from more than twenty paces. I did not see where Fletcher's shot struck for I was already turning to run. I did not know the man he had with him – it was not the long-armed man I remembered from Fleet Street – but both were well armed. On the road to Huntingdon Fletcher had had three pistols strapped across his chest. I did not doubt that he had them again, and all would be wadded and primed. I bolted for the house. As I did I heard a second shot. Splinters of wood burst from the frame around the entrance. I rushed inside and slid across the hall, drawing the first of my own pistols as I did. I dropped to one knee and turned, ready lest Fletcher and his accomplice charge me. I levelled my pistol at the door, but I was to be disappointed. They were no fools to be tricked into the same mistake as the King's soldiers they had once ambushed, rushing from the light into the gloom and making a target of themselves.

I heard them pause outside and then separate. I was certain that one ran around the house, and I supposed he must head for the entrances from the stables or kitchen garden. I could not tell whether the other had gone that way too, or had quietly remained, hoping to slip in behind me.

I thought to turn and run for one of the other doors, but then wondered if that was what Fletcher had in mind, whether he hoped I would endeavour to make my escape and meant to come quietly behind me. I considered for a moment. If I were to remain on the lower storey of the house then there was no room I could defend where they might not come at me from two directions at once. If I ascended to the upper rooms then I might fare better, but I would be trapped from the outside. I did not know if they had come at me with any urgency, or whether they would be content to wait.

I crept to the stairs and began to climb, easing backwards up each step with my pistol trained on the door. I was close to the top when I saw Fletcher again. He darted across the entrance, peeking inside and then drawing quickly back. For a moment his eyes locked on mine, and then he was gone. I turned and ran then, up into the room where I thought Lady Walhope had been murdered. I bolted to the shattered window and looked out, hoping to take him from above, but he was gone. I moved back to the door then, thinking to catch him as he came after me up the stairs, but he wasn't there either.

'Falkland, is it?' The voice came from the hall, somewhere out of sight. I moved to the corner of the stair, pressed up against the wall.

'Fletcher?' I saw him peer from the dining room. I lifted my pistol, but he withdrew too quickly for me to fire. I must, I knew, be sure with each shot. I had two pistols and two men come here to kill me. I did not know how many weapons each had brought, but more than one. I had no sword or knife.

'It is you, is it? William Falkland?'

'That it is.'

'Then I am he. Ned Fletcher. At your service.'

'And your friend?'

'Jacob Westlock.' His voice lifted. 'Jacob! To the dining room. I have him cornered from here at the top of the stairs!'

'Rush these steps at your peril, Fletcher. I have more than the one pistol.'

'As do we, Falkland.'

I heard a movement down below, boots running quickly through the passage along the back of the house.

'Where is Anne Agar, Fletcher?'

I received no answer. For the next minute all was silent. I thought I heard a rustle of movement from the dining room, and then whispers. I supposed Fletcher and this Westlock to be conferring, concocting some plan to flush me out and be done with me. I took the chance to return to the windows of Lady Walhope's room. I had hoped, perhaps, to take advantage of their conference to make my escape, but the drop from the window was too great to jump without risk, and I saw no easy way to climb.

'Falkland!'

I returned to my post at the corner at the top of the stairs. I could not risk allowing either man to rush me.

'Where's John Milton, Falkland?'

'You took his horse, Fletcher, and he was sore hurt when he fell. He returned to London to visit your friend Peter Fowles in his new accommodations in Newgate Prison. I have a proposal for you, Fletcher. Turn yourself over. Both of you. If Anne still lives it may count for you and spare you the gallows.'

'I doubt that, Falkland. I have a counter. Surrender yourself and we will not kill you.'

'I find that I, too, have my doubts.'

'I did not shoot John Milton, Falkland, only his horse.'

'I do not think you will extend such courtesy to me.'

Fletcher laughed. 'You may be right there, King's man.'

'Here is another choice for you then. Tell me where to find Anne. Then leave. Run. I will take Anne back to London and return her to her family. That is all I am commissioned to do. You will have plenty of time to make good your escape. Other men may hunt you, but I have no interest in your capture.'

I heard a croak of laughter. 'Ah, but you are not John Milton. He is like a terrier.'

'Still, your chances are better. Much of the country is occupied in other matters. Even Milton will struggle to catch the ear of Parliament in these times.'

'Perhaps you would have me run to Newcastle and hide among the Scots, act the sordid coward like your king? I think I like my chances better as they are.'

I had expected nothing less. But if he believed me about Milton then perhaps he would reconsider his choice once there were two of us. It would be an easy thing for a man of Fletcher's beliefs to put an end to some lapdog for the King – for that, it was clear, was how he saw me – but he had already hesitated to murder John Milton.

'Fowles told me a story about a lady who lured a band of the King's men to this house to kill you all in your sleep and deliver her from your hands. That story is not true. Which one of you murdered her, Fletcher? Was it you?'

'I put the last ball through her skull, Falkland. Call it

murder if you wish. I do not weep nor judge. The whore had it coming.'

'And the daughter? Did she also? How many of you took her before you murdered her, too?'

'She squealed like a wounded pig. She was a pretty one.'

Would that I could have shot him. I aimed my pistol at the door and almost pulled the trigger before I stopped myself. He was goading me, trying to make me waste my shot. But to my surprise, a moment later he burst from the dining room door and raised a pistol of his own. He stood still, unafraid, aimed and fired. The moment of his aiming gave me warning enough to duck behind the wall. The bullet struck on the far side of the landing. I whipped back around, ready to shoot him down, but he had a second pistol already raised. I sprang out of the way barely in time as a bullet chipped the corner of the wall where I stood. When I looked again, I caught only a glimpse of his coat as he disappeared into the parlour room directly at the foot of the stairs. I peeked to watch and see if he would emerge once more.

'I have a story of my own, Fletcher,' I called. 'Would you hear it?'

'I am not much of one for stories, Falkland. But I have two pistols to reload and so a little time to listen before we have at it again. Speak, if you wish. It's of no matter to me.'

Did he seek to lure me down, thinking he was, for a moment, unarmed? But I had seen him on the road and he carried three pistols, not two, and I had no doubt that the last had been loaded again while he lurked in the dining room.

'Who among your company of men that billeted here

could read and write, Fletcher? Fowles and Lovelace both knew their letters. I've not met so many soldiers who did, so I'll wager they were alone. Am I right?'

'I neither know nor care, Falkland.'

'It was not the lady of this house that called those soldiers here. They were lured to the front door, into a perfect place for ambush. I do not think Lovelace one to do such a thing so I shall suppose it was Fowles. He drew them here, and your company was ready for them. When your sentry saw their approach and gave his warning, seven of you took your positions in that hall to riddle them with holes as they entered. But one of you came up the stairs to this room here. Lady Walhope was not killed after it was done as Peter Fowles would have it. She was murdered in her bed while she slept. Fowles himself, was it? Was it because if she had been alive to speak then she would have denied all, and Lovelace might have believed her?'

'A pretty story, Falkland.'

'He must have been standing over her, pistol at the ready, waiting for the first volley of shots from below to mask his own. He could not fire before for fear of giving alarm to either Lovelace or the King's men outside. So he waited. He stood over her as she slept, minute after minute with pistol poised, and when the time came, he shot her in the belly. A slow, lingering agony of a death. What sort of a man murders a woman in her sleep in such a grotesque way?'

'The royalist whore had it coming to her, Falkland.'

Was it Fletcher himself who had done it?

'A bullet to the head would have been kinder,' I called. 'Or stifle her with a pillow as you stifled her daughter after you and your men raped her. And then, in the confusion of the fight and its aftermath, Fowles finds Francis Lovelace, this man he calls his friend, and shoots him in the head. An unfortunate casualty of yet another skirmish against the King. Tell me, Fletcher, was every man in your company a part of this conspiracy?'

I heard him laugh. 'You have it wrong, Falkland. Fowles did not kill Lovelace.'

'But Lovelace did not kill Lady Walhope.'

'That you may have right. Much good it may do you.' Fletcher's head popped around the corner of the door for a moment, too quick for me to fire. He shot at me once. As I ducked back I saw another movement. Further along the passage, across the top of the hall, the door opened from the bedroom over the dining room where Sir Walhope had once laid his head. The second man, Jacob Westlock, burst through it, a pistol raised in each hand. I do not know how he had climbed to the upper rooms, nor did I have time to consider it. I dropped to my haunches, having no other place to go. I saw the flash of his first pistol and heard its roar. I raised my own and took aim. The moment seemed to stretch between us. His first shot had gone high. I believed I could see the barrel of his second pistol lowering to point directly for my face. I aimed for his chest and pulled the trigger. The flash from the pan dazzled me and the cloud of smoke hid him for an instant, and I could not see what effect I had made, but I saw him lurch. I heard footsteps then, running up the stairs. I rolled towards the door to Lady Walhope's room, dropping the pistol I had fired and reaching for my second. As I dived through the door, Westlock staggered back, one hand pressed to his chest. He fired at me again but missed. I scrambled through the ruined bedroom and on into the next, still unable to rest my eyes on the skeleton sprawled across the bed.

'Falkland!' Fletcher was at the top of the stairs, enraged. I had hit this Westlock, if that was his name, but I did not know how badly he was hurt. Fletcher, I thought, would come straight after me now, ploughing my wake as fast as he could before I had a chance to recover, perhaps hoping that I too was injured. I whirled about, taking a stand with my pistol aimed at the door through which I had come, waiting for Fletcher to burst from Lady Walhope's bedroom; but he did not . . .

I knew, an instant too late, what he had done instead. The other door, the one from the long passage, burst open. I twisted hard and jumped away. Fletcher fired his first pistol and missed. I crashed into the opposite wall and raised my own at him as he stood in the doorway. His second pistol was raised now. The distance between us was closer to ten paces than twenty. For a moment each of us looked down the barrel of his pistol at the other.

'What was it all for, Fletcher? Because Lovelace would not let his men ravish the women here under his protection and pillage their home?'

'Because he kept it all to himself, Falkland. The whore took him to her bed. She bought him with her flesh, as Eve did to Adam. Beguiled fool wouldn't let us touch her or the girl either. He raved at us as though we were animals. But we were godly men, all of us. It wasn't *them* we wanted.'

He took his eyes from me and made a small step back into the passage, giving himself a little cover from the wall. I moved, as sudden and fast as I could. I threw myself to the floor beside the bed where the skeleton lay, and fired. I knew at once that I had missed, and cursed myself for my stupidity. Fletcher aimed and fired back as I fell. The ball tugged my coat but did not touch my flesh, but Fletcher had another pistol and I did not. I jumped to my feet and grabbed at the wardrobe beside the bed and pulled at it, meaning to tear it down and throw it between us, perhaps confusing him enough that I might make my escape into the other room and thence to the stairs and out and away.

As I pulled and the wardrobe came down, I heard another shot.

CHAPTER 20

I had misjudged. The wardrobe beside the bed was heavier than I had imagined. I did not throw it between us as much as heave it and cause it to topple towards me. I pushed away, hurling myself across the room as the wardrobe fell, knowing full well that I was caught in the open, an easy target for Fletcher but a few paces away. At any moment he would fire. He could hardly miss at such a distance; and yet from the corner of my eye I saw him turn and stare back along the passageway. His head sank to his chest. He crumpled.

The wardrobe smashed to the floor. I stood gasping, staring at Fletcher as he collapsed. All I could think of was that his accomplice, Westlock, had shot him, but I could not begin to fathom why. It made no sense at all.

'Westlock? Jacob Westlock?' I scrabbled to my feet and rammed powder into my pistol as fast as I dared.

'Falkland?'

'Milton?' I could not believe he had returned and Fletcher had not seen him.

'Are you shot, Falkland?'

'I am not. Have a care behind you. There is a second.' I dropped a new ball into my pistol and pushed in a little wadding.

'I am wary of him. But I think you have injured him.'

A little powder in the pan and I was ready and armed again. I ran to the door where Fletcher lay gasping out his last. Milton stood in the middle of the passage with his back to us, pistol pointed away. He had left Fletcher to die with a loaded weapon in his hand. And dying he was, and quickly, but not so quickly that he didn't try to raise the pistol and take Milton with him. I stamped Fletcher's hand to the ground.

'I have your back,' I said to Milton. To Fletcher: 'If not them then what *was* it that you wanted?'

'What does any man want, Falkland?'

The answer to that question, I had found, was not so simple as other men would have me believe; but Henry Warbeck had taught me well where I should start. 'Money? You did this for their money?' I could make no sense of it. That they had ravaged this house three years past and looted and pillaged it, yes, I had seen such excesses from those who called themselves soldiers more often than I cared to accept; yet if they had taken their loot back then, why come again three years later . . . 'Something in Lovelace's letters! You missed something!'

'You know who we were, Falkland? Do you?' Fletcher spat at my face, a fine spray of frothy blood. 'God's red right hand, William Falkland, that's who we were. I'll be waiting for you.' He coughed up more blood, and then his eyes rolled back and his jaw fell slack. I watched a while longer as he lay there, drawing fast, shallow breaths. He would not be long. Milton's bullet had gone through the right side of his chest, square through the lung. Men shot this way would drown in their own blood in a few minutes, more often than not. I took his pistol and left him there.

'Your other one is in the room ahead, Falkland,' Milton said. He had not moved nor lowered his pistol. I saw he was shaking. It would not take much for Westlock to poke an eye and the barrel of a pistol around the corner and take Fletcher's revenge. I sprinted along the passage past the door into the bedroom where Westlock was hiding, and called out to him from the other side.

'Jacob Westlock? My name is William Falkland. The man with me is John Milton. The lady you hold hostage is his sister. I would rather talk with you than shoot you a second time. I know you are wounded. If it is mortal then make your peace with God and guide my friend to Anne.' *My friend.* It did not feel awry. I had formed a different view of Milton these last few days. As he had, I think, of me.

There was no answer. I began to back away towards the further rooms, fearing Westlock might circle to take me from behind.

'You have shot me, William Falkland,' called a voice at last.

'I will do so again if you do not toss your pistols away from you and allow us to approach in safety.'

Another pause and then came a thud from the bedroom. A pistol slid from the doorway and skittered to a stop. I crept to the door and peered around. Jacob Westlock sat on the floor against the wall beneath a shattered window, his legs straight out in front of him, his right side from the shoulder down covered in blood.

'I think you have killed me, William Falkland,' he croaked as I entered. I crouched beside him and prodded at his coat, looking for the hole I had shot in him. I found it high up, near the top of his shoulder.

'It is not mortal. A surgeon would say that the ball must

come out and the wound be washed in aqua vitae, then
wrapped and bandaged. If God is willing then all will be
well.' I tapped the side of my own head where Miss Cain's
bandage still wrapped my ear. 'I cannot vouch that it is
pleasant. I have this courtesy of one of your company.' I had
not paid my own injury much heed these last few hours,
immersed as I was in the past of this house. Given a moment
of attention again, my head took the opportunity to remind
me of its ache.

Milton came in behind me.

'There were eight of you,' I said. 'Lovelace died here.
Fowles is in a prison cell in Newgate. Fletcher is dead and so
is Nathaniel Blackwater. You are here and I believe there is
another still in London. That leaves two. They have Anne,
don't they, Westlock? And you must hold her somewhere
nearby. Fletcher came last night and said she was to be
moved, did he not? This morning you and he came back.
Did you mean to ambush me in case I had not given up the
chase?'

Westlock coughed. 'Fletcher was sure you'd still be
following. He meant for you to come and find us laid up in
wait. We'd have taken you like we did those other royalist
curs back in 'forty-three.'

'Where is she, Westlock?'

'The Devil have you, William Falkland. A cavalier, Ned
said. Is that what you were?'

'I fought for the King, yes. But I was born a farmer's boy,
just like you and Ned Fletcher. That is how this war is
fought, Westlock, farmers' sons fighting farmers' sons over
ideas none of them can begin to understand.'

'It is about tyranny,' spat Westlock.

I had more questions to ask, but before I could speak them Milton barged me aside. He rammed the barrel of his pistol into the hollow of Westlock's throat hard and deep. Westlock thrashed as though he was choking.

'I will hear nothing from a man like you about tyranny!' Milton raged. 'A Tyrant was a man chosen by the people of Rome to lead and protect them when danger threatened that glorious republic. By such meaning, it is Cromwell who will become our Tyrant in glorious submission to the will of Parliament, as the Tyrants of Rome were bound to the will of the senate. You speak of tyranny without understanding its meaning. You refer to the oppression of will, the taking of the freedoms of one man by another, to subjugation, servitude, slavery, you, who have taken the will and freedom from my sister; yet you speak without trace of irony. Take it to your grave!'

I stared agape as Milton pulled the trigger on his pistol, already reeling away from the noise and burning sparks and spray of blood that would follow. Yet all that came was the flash of flint against the frizzen. Westlock whimpered in terror.

'I did not load another ball,' said Milton. 'I did not have the opportunity.' And I could not tell, in that moment, whether he had remembered before he pulled the trigger, or not. He withdrew and glowered from across the room.

'Where is she, Westlock?' I asked.

'I . . .' He was staring past me at Milton, who was now loading his pistol with a very deliberate lassitude. I waited. Milton rammed the ball inside and wadded it down as I had shown him. As he opened the flash pan and sprinkled a little powder there, Westlock hung his head.

'There is a farmhouse. Three miles south of Lea.'

I had him tell me precisely how we might find the place. 'Who awaits us?'

'I will tell you no—' He choked as Milton's pistol again crushed his throat. When I pried Milton loose, Westlock told us in broken words of the two men who remained. The last of Lovelace's company, I supposed. Soldiers both.

'Is there some phrase by which a friend might announce themselves?' I asked. He shook his head.

'We are as brothers. We would know one another by sight before a word was spoken, even before we might see one another's faces.'

'I have questions about what transpired here,' I began. 'It was not the lady of this house who sent word to Newcastle's men of her predicament. Who wrote the letter? Fowles?'

Westlock nodded.

'So Fowles lured them here into an ambush. Why?'

'To break the hold that whore had over our sergeant.'

'Lovelace. And as you killed the soldiers you lured here, Fowles murdered the lady. That I understand. The rest, that I understand also, though the gallows await you for what you did to the poor girl.'

Westlock gave me a bitter look. 'I had no part in that. Pillaging the house for a little loot put no weight on my conscience. But the murdering. There was no need of it. The women and the servants.' He shook his head again. 'No need of it at all. But Fowles and Fletcher would not stand to see otherwise.'

I found I believed him, though it would not save him in the end.

'And the haul from the house? Was it worth it?'

'We did well enough.'

'But Fowles was not satisfied?'

'Nor Fletcher. Fowles swore there was something else, something much more than a little silver. But Newcastle's men were on the town and coming for us all and we had no time to search harder.'

'The letters.'

'Letters?'

Milton was tapping his foot. 'Come, Falkland, Peter Fowles holds the key to this. We will get it out of him in Newgate and then he will hang. They all of them will hang.' He spat. 'And he masqueraded as a friend. I will not forgive that. Nor will I forgive any of these men for what they have done to Anne.' He leaned close to Westlock. 'If any of you have so much as touched her, I will make it the work of my life to bring you such pain and suffering that you will wish Hell itself would swallow you.'

'What was it they were looking for?' I asked. Fowles might have the answers, but Fowles was in Newgate, and Westlock was the man I had before me, and with a bullet in his shoulder.

'They didn't say. I do not think they knew exactly. Something Lovelace had found. After it was done Nathaniel went scouting in the morning. We were all on edge after what had happened in the night. The soldiers were one thing. The hangings, though, and the murders . . .' Westlock shivered. 'Lovelace and Fletcher were right to murder one another the moment Fowles wasn't standing between them. Then Nathaniel came back with word of a large company of Newcastle's men headed our way. Lovelace wrote his dispatches to Gainsborough to report what had happened and that we were forced to withdraw. He sent Nathaniel to take them. After that . . .' he coughed and for a moment struggled for breath. 'There was another dispute. Fowles and Fletcher and Lovelace again, while the rest of us hastened to make ready to leave. None of us saw it, but it ended with a pistol shot and Lovelace dead. We ransacked the house quick as we could and then hurried away. The war went on. We stayed together until the coming of the New Model embraced us all. I don't know, after that. Fletcher found us again. Was a little after Easter.'

'What did he want?'

Westlock's head sank towards his chest. I rose to shake him from his torpor, for I had not yet reached quite to the bottom of this and it vexed me. But before I could find the question that would at last unravel it, Milton had my arm. He tugged at me, pulling me away.

'Leave him, Falkland. Let him bleed out. Let the wound turn bad and let him die in slow agony. It's no more than he deserves.'

Perhaps I would have thought differently if it had not been for the skeleton lying in the bed a few doors away with her last scraps of golden hair clinging to her skull.

'You may choose, Westlock. Remain here and we will return for you. I will treat that wound or not, depending on the state in which we find Anne. Or run and take the slow death that the ball inside you will bring.'

I would have left him there as Milton suggested. I did not know which way it would go for him and nor, I found, did I much care; but as I reached my horse outside, Milton stopped me again.

'I have a better idea,' he said.

CHAPTER 21

The farmhouse lay as Westlock had told us, dark and seemingly abandoned at the top of a low hill. The fields around had grown wild for some years, perhaps since the battles of '43, but they were not so overgrown as to deny the house a fine view over the track towards it. We were three riders returning where two had ridden away, and I did not doubt that Westlock had the right of it: the men inside would know us for strangers long before we reached the door. Such is the way among soldiers who eat and live and march and fight beside one another, month after month. They had chosen their shelter well, too, with good sight over all approaches. I could only suppose they were much on their guard, with two of their number already dispatched to intercept me.

The only way a man might get close unobserved would be to crawl inch by inch on his belly through the long grass. These soldiers would have muskets, I had no doubt, and would load and reload fast enough to take two or three shots even at a horse galloping from the closest cover towards them. Nor would any exchange of fire bode well for Anne, if she was inside. If she still lived.

Milton pushed Westlock forward. Westlock was on his

own horse, his hands tied behind his back and his mount tethered to mine. Together this way the three of us approached the farmhouse. I kept Westlock ahead of me, shielding me at least in part from any musket fire that might come our way. Milton stayed a dozen paces behind. I would have preferred if he had remained in shelter, but he would not have it.

'Their names,' I hissed to Westlock. 'How might I address your friends?'

'They are brothers. Benjamin and Edward Allhurst.'

'The oldest?' Fifty yards from the farm I drew us to a stop.

'Ben.'

I pressed the pistol into Westlock's side. 'Even with a musket they will more likely miss than hit from this range. I mean to bargain your life for Anne Agar, but I will bargain theirs if I must. You understand your role in this?'

Westlock spat. 'I understand it, King's man.'

'Raise the flag.' I turned to see that Milton had already done so. A fallen branch sufficed for a pole, a stained rag from the house passed for a flag. It was hardly white, but its purpose was, I thought, clear: we had come to parley.

'Benjamin Allhurst!' I cried. 'I am William Falkland. I am sent here by Oliver Cromwell. The man beside me is your brother in arms, Jacob Westlock. You three are the last. Ned Fletcher lies dead. Nathaniel Blackwater also. Peter Fowles rots in Newgate.' For a moment I lifted my pistol away from Westlock and held it high. 'I am armed but will keep my distance. Show yourselves if you wish to parley. Both of you. There is but one way you may keep your lives and that is to accept my terms.'

I waited then, certain that the next I would see would be either the opening of the door or the flash of a firing pan. I was glad when the door creaked slowly ajar. A man stepped half out with his musket at the ready. He levelled it at me.

'Falkland, is it? What regiment?'

I hesitated. I could not tell them I had fought for the King, for then they would not believe I spoke for Cromwell or, indeed, for anyone save the Devil himself. I could not say I was no soldier at all for fear they would not treat with me.

'I ride with Cromwell himself,' I declared at last. It was a lie with at least a vestige of truth to it.

'Cavalryman, is it?' I heard a twang of disdain.

'It is, though I began by carrying a pike and have been a dragoon also. Let your brother come out so I might see you both and know he's not creeping around in the grass to take me from the side. I have but pistols and would do well to hit the house around you from this distance. You may lower your musket if you wish. I believe it pains your friend to see it levelled at him so.'

The soldier did lower his musket, although he did not put it down. He stepped back to the door and called inside, while his eyes stayed on me. A few moments later a second man came out. He, too, carried a musket. He rested it on a barrel close to the door and crouched behind it, pointing the weapon at us.

'Are there more of you?'

'State your terms, William Falkland.'

I poked Westlock with my pistol. 'Are there more or is this the sum of your company?' I asked him. 'Know that if any shots are fired, my first will be into your side.'

'This is all,' growled Westlock. I don't doubt he would

have lied had he seen some merit to it, but I was inclined to believe him. I had accounted for all of Lovelace's company now save the man with the long arms, and him I believed to be still in London.

'Well,' called the first of the brothers. 'What terms do you offer?'

'You hold a woman captive. Bring her out so I may see she is alive and unharmed. If she is not then there are no terms to be had and the gallows await all three of you. Understand this: my sole interest is Anne Agar and her safety. Release her to me and I will be gone. Others may come after you. I cannot promise you otherwise.'

The brothers exchanged words I could not hear. The first left his musket against the barrel and returned into the house. He was gone some minutes, and I began to fear he had slipped out the back to make good his escape, or else meant to ambush us; but in time he returned, pushing before him a woman in a black dress. I could not make out her face well, but we were close enough that Milton would surely . . .

'Anne!'

She was alive. I felt a weight lift from my chest.

The woman lifted her head. 'John?'

'My terms are this,' I called. 'I mean to withdraw a little way, past where you may think of hitting us with your muskets. You will let the lady go. You will let her walk towards us. You will hold your position as we will hold ours. When she is halfway, I will let Westlock go. When we have Anne, we will withdraw and attend to her. When you have Westlock, you may do as you wish. He has been shot, and I would suggest you take him in short order to someone who might remove the ball from his shoulder. I will not pursue you further. For the magistrates of Gainsborough, of Lincolnshire, I can make no such promises. You would do well not to linger.'

The brothers conferred.

'Westlock?' shouted the one behind the barrel. 'Is it true what he says about Ned?'

I poked Westlock again.

'Aye. Dead back at the house.' It pained him even to raise his voice. I wondered if walking the yards to the house would be too much for him, but found, again, that I did not much care.

Another pause, then: 'We would have your guarantee of safe passage, William Falkland.'

'I cannot.' I shook my head. 'I can make no bargain with you in the name of any other. Cromwell will pursue you or not as the whim takes him. In this I can speak only for myself. Return your hostage and I will return mine and be gone. You will be wanted men, and hunted perhaps, but I fancy you resourceful enough. It is better than the gallows or a shot from a pistol.'

'You fancy your chances to take us, Falkland?'

'Alone? No. But I am here for the lady, not for blood.'

For a time the two brothers conferred again.

'William Falkland! We agree to your terms. Be warned that if you play us false, we are well armed, and the first bullet will be for you.'

The older of the two pushed Anne away from the house. Her steps were uncertain at first. She looked over her shoulder back at the brothers more than once. When she had taken a few paces, though, she began to hurry. She did not, from the way she moved, seem too ill-treated, nor had they bound her hands.

'Withdraw, Milton,' I warned. The brothers had not waited for us to back away. Were I to let Westlock go here, their muskets would be uncomfortably close. I backed my horse, pulling Westlock with me. Milton didn't move. He was staring at Anne as she came towards him.

'This is not the place,' I began. 'We are too close!'

He was transfixed, clear and open to their fire if they chose to raise their muskets. I dismounted so that at least the body of my horse might afford me some protection. I pulled Westlock down so that he must walk instead of ride – this, I thought, would earn us both a little more time and a mount for Anne. I waited as I had promised, until Anne was halfway to us, before I let him go. Milton had dismounted also. As Anne came close he abandoned his reins and ran towards her. Westlock ran too, as best he could with wrists bound and a bullet in his shoulder. For a moment the two of them were side by side. I held my breath. I had not prayed to God for years, not truly, but I almost reached out to Him then, begging that the two brothers in the farmhouse would not fire.

'Anne!' Milton swept her up and wrapped his arms around her. 'Anne! Praise the Lord. John and Edward are at the end of their wits!' He pulled at her at last, urging her away from the farmhouse. Westlock hurried on. He reached the farm some seconds later. The brothers took him at once into cover and continued their watch on us. Anne looked to be in a daze. She was pale and thin, her cheeks hollow, a sallow sheen to her skin. She did not look well, yet her wits, at least, were not addled. She stared for a moment at her brother and then leaned against him and took his arm. They passed me, and I walked my horse behind them as they hurried away down the track, sheltering them from the muskets in the farm. The minute it took to reach the bottom of the hill and the cover of the first hedgerow felt an age, and with every step I felt my skin a-tingle; but there were no shots, no peals of bottled thunder. We reached shelter and were away. The brothers had kept their bargain.

We rode to Gainsborough at a slow and gentle pace. Anne did not speak much, yet I found that I kept looking at her and then looking away, only to find my eyes drawn back once more. I knew that I saw in her some vestige of my Caro, and had done almost from the very first. My hope for her. My heart soared and dived like an addled swallow: joy at a life saved, a family made whole again; despair that it was another's and not mine.

In Gainsborough, John Milton took a room and sat in private with his sister, and I was left alone to ponder what would follow. I could not blame him for that. My part was played and done. I was nothing but the burden of unwanted obligation now; yet as the evening drew upon us they emerged from their retirement and came and sat with me for supper, and I saw her properly then, a little frail perhaps, gaunt and worn at the edges, but with the same mix of compassion and tempered steel in her eye as John Milton found in his words.

'I thank you, William Falkland,' she said. 'John tells me you were the architect of my rescue.'

I thanked her in return, and watched as she picked at the food Milton brought to our table. Her appearance marked her as starving, yet she did not eat like a ravenous man brought at last to sustenance. She poked at her food, while I could not help but stare. Here was this woman, at the centre of a storm not of her own making. She struck me as so very plain and ordinary, yet she held herself with a fortitude I could only admire.

'You were not taken against your will,' I said at last. 'Not at first.' They were foolish words to say to her so soon, and I regretted them almost at once.

Milton gave me a sharp look. 'You don't give up, do you, Falkland?' he said, but there was no ire in his words this time, no rebuke.

'The man Fletcher told me he had word of Thomas,' Anne said simply. 'At first he said there was a man in Clink Prison who knew what had become of my husband. We arranged that we would meet there, but when he came, he was in a carriage. He told me that the prisoner had not known Thomas after all, but that he had had letters that mentioned me. He showed one to me, and I recognised the hand of Francis Lovelace. The letter was torn and I could not see to whom it was written, but I saw my name there. "Go to Anne Agar in London and show her this, and it will lead you to something to your great advantage." Those were the words.'

A heavy sadness settled across her face, of old wounds torn open and a dull pain made sharp again.

'John speaks highly of you, Master Falkland. It all must seem absurd to you, I suppose, but there is more. You see, a man had broken into our house some months before,' she said. 'Perhaps John has told you? We thought it was the work of some rival, come to spy on what words John was writing for his latest polemic. But I saw that my room had been searched.'

'Fletcher,' I said, for I could think of none other.

'I must now suppose it was. I must seem such a fool.' She shrugged. It was a small gesture, wreathed in a despair I knew all too well. 'But as it was, Peter asked me if I had any letters. I thought nothing of it, although I see now that he was guiding me to them. I showed them to him, let him see there was nothing of any consequence to them, but he would not have it. He started talking of codes and ciphers. He seemed so certain that Francis had hidden some secret there, but if he had then neither he nor I could find it. I thought it a foolishness at first, yet the last letter Francis wrote me was so strange. So different. Short, but as though he knew there would not be another. His words were strange and distorted, his language odd, as if pieces were missing from it. In parts I could not make sense of it.'

'So you took them to John Wallis. Cromwell's cipher-master.'

'I did. You see, amid these unconnected thoughts he wrote that Thomas had survived Edgehill. It had been such wonderful news, but then a year passed and I heard nothing more, and so I knew he must be mistaken otherwise Thomas would have written. And yet now I could not let go that perhaps there was more.' She glanced at Milton. 'John told me I was foolish. He has since told me of your own circumstances, Master Falkland. So I know you will understand how hope can be the most vicious injury of all.'

I looked away. Yes, indeed, I understood that all too well. 'Master Wallis found nothing, I suppose,' I said.

'Oh no!' She almost laughed, and shook her head.

'Master Wallis found that there was a cipher indeed. But I had only half the message, the words were divided in two, you see, and without the rest we could go no further. So perhaps you can understand how it was when Ned Fletcher showed me what he did and told me that Francis had found something before he died, and that we would find the answers here in Gainsborough.' There was, I think, a tear in her eye as she spoke. 'I said I could not, that I must be with my family. But by then I was in his power, and he brought me here anyway. I quickly understood it was not any news of Thomas he was looking for, but something else.'

She rose then and begged her leave of us with a tiny nod, and left without another word. Milton followed her away and was gone a while. His face betrayed his anxieties when at last he returned.

'She is not well,' I observed.

'She is sleeping now.' Milton closed his eyes and shook his head. 'When we are back in London, I will have a physician attend her.'

'They did not hurt her, it seems,' I said. 'That, at least, was a mercy.'

'If by hurt you mean cuts and wounds of blade and ball then no, they did not. But hurt is measured in many ways, William Falkland. You, I think, know this well.'

I did.

We did not say much more to one another, but stared at the windows and the candles on the walls and the lanterns, each lost in our own thoughts. Milton's, I must suppose, were of Anne and the reunion that awaited her, her sons and daughter. My own strayed constantly to Oxford, to my Caro and the resumption of my search for her; but also with rigid equality to Miss Cain and her library and her little room in Lincoln's Inn.

'Anne will need a carriage to take her to London. I will ride with her,' said Milton as he rose for his bed. 'I will not keep you from your return. I will pray to God that your search may end as mine has done, and that He will guide you as you have guided me. Will you do me the service of returning these horses to the Whalebone?' He offered me his hand as I nodded. 'Thank you, William Falkland. You will always be a welcome guest at my house and table.'

I rose too. I was being dismissed, and found I was content with that. I would perhaps have enjoyed watching Anne return to her family, seeing her speak and smile. In an absurd way I wanted to thank her for allowing me to be a part in this. I would revel in the joy of their reunion even as it tore pieces from my heart. But it was better this way. That moment was for her and her children and for them alone, and I did not belong with it.

'I would speak to your sister one last time if I may,' I said, my words faltering and stumbling hesitant from my mouth.

'She sleeps, Falkland.' Milton smiled and shook his head. 'Besides, she has nothing more to say that will surprise you.'

He mistook my desire for that of an intelligencer, wishing to unravel the last of a mystery. It was not.

'She tells me they asked her on and on about Francis Lovelace's last letter and the strangeness of it. At first they did not believe she knew nothing. Then, in time, it seems that they did; and with that they no longer knew what to do with her. Fletcher would have put an end to her, but the others would not have it. They kept searching the house.' He shrugged. 'Whatever they sought, clearly they did not find it. And Anne never told them what John Wallis had said, how the two letters contained a cipher between them, and now both are lost, and good riddance to them, I say. I think, by the end, those two vagabonds who held her were glad to be done with it all.' Milton looked to his hand, still reaching towards me. 'I was not a gracious host to you when first we met, Falkland. I beg your pardon for my hasty words that were uncouth and out of place.'

I took his hand and shook it.

'Your words distinguish you,' I said. 'Men will remember you for them, I think.'

At that, Milton laughed. 'They already do, Falkland, and not always to my benefit.'

CHAPTER 22

I did not delay for further farewells, but rode south early with the next dawn. My own matters pressed me now. I had done as Cromwell desired and, while I had little hope that he would by some sorcery produce my family, there was indeed a favour he might grant me in return for my services. I would enter Oxford with the first soldiers of Parliament when that city at last gave its surrender. I would question the commanders of the garrison there, and I would learn whether my Caro had indeed found shelter within its walls. Alone with nothing else to distract me, I thought of little but my wife and my children, picturing them in my mind as I last remembered them. I cursed myself for having once more found a hope that I would some day see them again, but hope I had. In those bleak, dark days in Uxbridge where I had lost their trail, though I had not realised it at the time, I had given up. I had begun, at last, to grieve for them.

I thought of Miss Cain, labouring in her little room beside the library of Lincoln's Inn. She struck me as content in a way I had not seen her before. I was glad. I thought of Milton too, of the look I had seen on his face when the brothers Allhurst had brought Anne out through the door of that farmhouse, when he had known at last that she lived. All these things conflated in my head. Anne became my

Caro, or sometimes Miss Cain. This hope, this sense of future, it had infected me.

Yet among this joy – a joy I was reluctant to embrace but nonetheless stood helpless before it – I could not quite shake a dissatisfaction. Perhaps no one cared what had happened in that house three years ago in the midst of a war, but I had not, I thought, quite reached to the bottom of it. A conspiracy among Francis Lovelace's company? An attraction of the heart turned to a sour and tragic end? I did not know, nor did I know what treasure Fowles and Fletcher imagined hidden there.

I stopped at the house again on my return, wary of the brothers from the farmhouse, but I need not have feared. No one had come. Fletcher lay where I had left him. I took his pistols and searched his coat and his pockets, but the letters were not there. Whatever clue Fowles had hoped to find in them, whatever cipher Francis Lovelace had crafted, it was lost, and his secrets with it.

I rode south, overnighted in Huntingdon and pressed onward, as fast and hard as I dared push my borrowed mare. As I passed through the village of Hampstead and approached London itself, I was minded to go directly to Newgate and ask Fowles for the truth. Sometimes, I have found, men who know they are condemned are wont to tell their story, all of it, even the wickedness. Perhaps I would call it confession, though I would not let such a word pass my lips before Warbeck and Milton and their ilk.

But I did not travel to Newgate. My return to London brought me, it seemed, direct to Lincoln's Inn. It seemed odd that I had come here except that I had been guided by unconscious purpose, a notion I found much unsettled me. I forced myself to ride on past and return my horse to the Whalebone. The tap-keeper there regarded me unkindly. When I led him to the stables and told enough of what had transpired to explain the loss of one of his horses, I thought he might strike me.

'John Milton sends word he will compensate you as best he can,' I said. 'He thanks you for your kindness and the return of his sister.'

The name of Milton furrowed his brow in a murderous way I did not expect. Previously it had seemed that Milton was well regarded among the Levellers of the Whalebone. A hand crept to my pistol as I withdrew.

'He will return in person,' I told the man. 'I do not doubt it. He is, I believe, a man of his word.'

The man eyed me and took note that I was armed. He spat at my feet. 'You may tell Master Milton he need not trouble himself. Keep watch in the shadows, he should. He'll find no welcome for him here, not any more.'

I backed to the stable door. 'Ned Fletcher. Peter Fowles. Nathaniel Blackwater. You knew these men?'

'Aye. Good men all.'

'They are murderers all. Fletcher took Milton's sister from her family. Is that what good men do?'

'Murderers, you say, and you a King's man. You have no hold over that word after what your royal master has brought upon this land.'

I reached the alley. 'I fought for the King, yes, yet I was never once called upon to murder women in their sleep, nor those alongside whom I fought.'

The tap-keeper – I did not know his name, nor did I wish to – sneered his disgust. 'War makes murderers of all honest men, does it not? Be away, King's man. Stay gone if you value your skin.'

I walked quickly away to the comforting crowds of Cheapside and from thence westward. I had learned enough of the city's geography by now to understand that Warbeck, on our first visit to Milton's house, had taken me past Newgate quite needlessly, and so doubtless with deliberate intent to remind me of my previous incarceration. I crossed the open square around the church of St Paul's, scarred as many churches were by the depredations of Parliament's men. I paused there a while and looked. The stained glass church windows were broken by musket fire, the stone around them peppered with the tiny craters of lead shot. The great oak doors bore the marks of some forced entry. I have no great fervour for icons and the worship of images, but I have never understood this devil that besets men to smash and shatter that which brings comfort to others and a closeness to God; though perhaps I felt no understanding because I felt no such closeness either. Yet I looked on, lost for a time in contemplation. The great church rose above me, battered and weathered by years, aged by the turning seasons and scarred by the fickle nature of men, yet it seemed to me that it stood unperturbed. Perhaps, in this, the church mirrored our land, this England, now that the war was all but done. We would bear our scars, but at the end we remained standing. Cromwell and his ilk had set out to change the world, but perhaps the world did not wish to be changed. Perhaps they would find it more stubborn than they hoped.

I turned my back to the church and looked around me. Saint Paul's was home to a dozen booksellers and more, Humphrey Moseley's among them. I knew Parliament

disapproved of bawdy theatre, yet every shop was piled high
with pamphlets and poems, books and palimpsests. A busy
trade plied their doors, whatever Parliament had to say of it,
and what then, if even men like John Milton would write
poems and elegies, and sell them to a bookseller who
unashamedly spoke out for the King?

I was wrong, I thought, about the world. It was not
stubborn and static and resistant to change. Quite the
contrary. It would change in its own way, without any care
for parliaments and kings. It already was. I cannot say why,
but for some reason the thought pleased me immensely.

It was a quick and easy walk from the square of St Paul's
through the Ludgate and across the Fleet, north onto
Chancery Lane and thence to Lincoln's Inn. I found Miss
Cain at her work in the dingy rooms beside the library,
poring over some list of dispositions with such intensity that
she did not at first notice my presence.

'Kate . . .'

She started and looked around with alarm. When she saw
it was me, she slumped on her stool and rolled her eyes.

'Falkland. Do you not announce your presence as others
do, with a quiet tap on the door?'

I apologised; and then to my surprise she rose from her
stool and came at me, and embraced me with unexpected
affection.

'Where have you been? I haven't seen you for days. Even
Master Warbeck cannot hide his concerns, though naturally
he pours scorn and supposes you must have fled and
abandoned your task.'

'I went with Milton in pursuit of Ned Fletcher. We
found Anne.'

For a moment Miss Cain hesitated. 'She is . . .'

'She is whole in body and soul. Her abductors did not harm her; though I fear she is unwell. The circumstances of her recent lodgings have done nought but ill in that regard. Milton returns with her in a coach. She will be with her family soon.' There was, I think, a catch in my voice as I spoke those last words. Miss Cain regarded me strangely for a moment, then quickly looked away and took up a paper from the table.

'I have found a list of men. Eight soldiers missing from Sir Willoughby of Parham's company following his withdrawal from Gainsborough, dead or deserted is not known.'

I looked at the names. Lovelace, Fowles, Fletcher and the rest, all of them familiar except the last. Charles Wainright. He would be the man with the long arms that I remembered, another name for Warbeck to hunt and haul to Newgate. I fancied that a quick search of the Whalebone might reveal his presence, if he had not already fled the city.

I had business elsewhere, lodgings to return to, questions for Fowles still in Newgate and demands to be made of Warbeck and Cromwell; nevertheless I found an odd reluctance to take my leave, and so I sat on the stool beside Miss Cain, aware of the comfort of her presence. I told her the story of our adventure north, of Fletcher's ambushes and of Anne's return to freedom. I spared her the gruesome skeleton in the house, but shared all else; then began on what I thought had occurred there three years past, the love of an ordinary soldier of Parliament for a royalist lady placed under his watch, and the tragedy it had inspired. She listened with rapt attention, eyes wide, and it seemed that, without conscious thought, we drifted a little closer with every moment, until by the time I reached the meat of my tale she had rested her head on my shoulders, and my arm was around her.

'Falkland!'

I started, as startled as Miss Cain had been upon my entrance. Warbeck stood at the door.

'Another one who never knocks,' grumbled Miss Cain.

'It's a fine thing that you grace our presence once more, Falkland,' Warbeck growled, 'and I'm sure we're all duly grateful and uplifted and so forth, but might I remind you that your duties are to me and to Parliament? I do hope you will find a moment, with some urgency if you will, to enlighten me as I perceive you have already enlightened Miss Cain as to your whereabouts these last days? I would ask you oblige me and be both swift and terse.'

'Fletcher is dead,' I told him bluntly. 'Anne is free. Milton is bringing her home.' Swift and terse. I could not conceal a smile of satisfaction at how this disarmed him.

'Then you are with me, Falkland. To Newgate. Let us be done with Fowles and this whole sorry affair.' He frowned. 'And Master Milton himself? I trust you did not lead our polemicist to harm?'

'A little bruised, but nothing broken that will not mend. He is a steady shot with a pistol for a man who has not fought in any battles.'

Warbeck shuddered. 'I advise you omit mentioning this to Cromwell if he questions you.' As he began to shoo me towards the door, I turned once more to Kate.

'I will return as I can to finish my tale, if you will have it, Miss Cain.'

'I will listen to you a little more, Master Falkland, if I must.' She smiled with a warmth I had once thought never to receive again. Warbeck let out a grunt of disgust; he took,

I thought, some pleasure in hurrying me away, and some pleasure more in riding his horse while I was forced to walk breathless beside him. We crossed the Fleet at Holborn Bridge and on to Newgate. Warbeck rode through the gate and dismounted. He appeared, for reasons he had yet to share, to be in some hurry.

'Did Fowles confess while I was away?'

'He confesses .to the theft of the letters. With regard to Anne Agar, he maintains his innocence.'

'He is very far from that.'

Warbeck grimaced. 'Nor do I believe it either, but I cannot hang a man simply because you tell me to, Falkland.' We passed through a gloomy arch into a high-walled yard, a place I remembered all too clearly. It had been a year ago, almost to the day, but the weather then had been thunderous and filled with rain, the air awash with the stink of damp filth and sewage. Today the sun shone bright as it had throughout most of June, and the stink was the sweet rot of offal and death. I had expected to pass through three or four turnkeys and descend to the deep cells where the most hopeless resided, where I myself had once been kept; but Warbeck passed us through one locked gate and into a room that bore more semblance to a comfortable scholar's room, not unlike Warbeck's own in Gray's Inn. There was no bed, and the décor was a little spartan even for a Puritan, but it had a fine desk and several chairs. Fowles sat on one of them, his wrists and ankles in manacles.

'You treat him well,' I said.

As if to show me wrong, Warbeck launched a thunderous kick at Fowles' chair, tipping it over and sprawling him across the bare floor.

'Do I? He has a visitor coming, this one. But you may have him first.'

I looked about me. On the desk was a quill, and ink and a roll of paper. I grabbed Fowles by the shoulders and hauled him back to his seat.

'I had you all wrong,' I said. 'I had thought you some murderous abductor of women, that it was all about some notion of money, but that wasn't your intent with Anne at all, was it? Francis Lovelace didn't write those letters. You did.'

'What?' Warbeck seemed as startled by this as Fowles, but I fancied that he was a man who saw a ruse when it was played, for my claim was clearly preposterous.

'I wrote no letters!' Fowles slurred.

'I say you did, sir. I say you lay in sin with Anne Agar. I say that you wished her for your own, and when she rebuffed your advances you took her against her will in some deluded passion, imagining that if you were to demonstrate your desire with sufficient force she might accede to you again as she did before.'

Fowles looked at me in bewilderment. 'You are deluded.' He shook his head. 'Francis wrote those letters. Not me.'

'No. You simply put his name to them. It was a ruse to hide you from discovery.' I did not wait for an answer but turned at once to Warbeck. 'It is easily proved. Help me!'

Warbeck appeared bewildered, but he did not refuse. I went to gather up Fowles, chair and all, and together we carried him to the desk. I placed a piece of paper before him and a quill in his hand.

'Write your name and we shall have it. No! Better! Write the words as I have found them written in one of those letters you failed to steal. Write the words: '*meet me in the hour after sunset when the others are at their sleep.*'

'You're quite mad, Falkland,' Fowles hissed.

'Prove me so.'

I watched him write the words as I had asked. When he was done he took the paper and waved it at my face. 'There. Or shall I write it again and again until it says what you wish it to, in whatever hand you have decided?'

A glance at Warbeck's face told me they had already tried to force a confession. They had not, I surmised, succeeded. I made a show of inspecting the paper and then handed it to Warbeck.

'You're quite right,' I said with a shrug. 'Your writing is nothing like Francis Lovelace. He must have written those letters himself after all, and I must indeed be mad . . .' I lingered for a moment, letting Fowles have a moment to savour his imagined triumph, and then a moment more to understand that he had been somehow tricked. I drew another piece of paper from my pocket and passed it to Warbeck without comment. 'You have, though, written a letter or two in your time, I think.'

'I have. What of it?'

'It's done, Fowles.' I leaned over him, as menacing now as I could be. 'After Cromwell summoned us, Milton and I followed you to the Whalebone. You knew you were done for. You sent Ned Fletcher to kill Anne before we found her so that her word could not incriminate you.'

'I did not!'

I banged the table in front of him. 'You lie! I saw you speak with Fletcher. I had good cause, after all, to remember his face!'

Fowles fixed his eyes on me. His look was of contempt and loathing. 'It is true that Ned Fletcher was once my friend, and that he had taken it upon himself to help Anne search for her husband, as Francis had done before him. True, too, that I told him you had thieved one of Anne's letters after you admitted as much, and that I told him of our inquisition from Cromwell. What of it? Is it a crime, now, to speak of such? The King might hang a man for speaking an unwanted truth, but I had thought Parliament better, else what did we fight for? As for Fletcher taking Anne, I know nothing of it.'

I withdrew and turned a glance to Warbeck. He still held the two pieces of paper I had given him, Fowles' words and the other. His look was one of deep perplexity.

'You admit Fletcher was a friend, at least,' I said, speaking as if to some invisible audience. 'A friend because you were soldiers together under Sir Willoughby of Parham at the battle of Gainsborough.'

'I have told you as much.' Disdain continued to drip from every word Fowles spoke.

'Willoughby's Forlorn Hope, sent in the first wave to breach the defences, and licensed in return to plunder as you saw fit.' I paced behind Fowles. 'But Fletcher had another name for your company. You were God's red right hand, a blaze of righteous vengeance. You told us how, after you had survived the assault of Gainsborough, you occupied a house close to the village of Lea. You said the lady of that house sent messages in secret to Lord Newcastle's soldiers, begging for relief. You told us that a party of them came to the house in the night, that an alert sentry spotted their approach and thus allowed you to prepare an ambush and fight them off.

You told us that Francis Lovelace flew into a rage and had the members of that house killed, every one of them. Do you deny you said these things?'

Fowles shook his head sharply. 'I do not.'

'You and Fletcher and the rest of those men, you tried to hide those killings.'

'We were forced to leave the following morning.' Fowles twisted to look at me. 'We fought as soldiers. Perhaps Francis was wrong in what he did. Do you mean to hang me for the crimes of a dead man?'

I returned to the desk and leaned over him again. 'I have been to that house, Fowles. Fletcher led us there, though I dare say he didn't mean to. It is where you were keeping Anne Agar prisoner.'

'*I?*' Fowles all but screamed. '*I* have been in London! *I* had no part in this!'

'I will tell you what happened in that house, Fowles. Yes, men from Newcastle's companies were lured there. You and Fletcher and the rest were ready for them, that much I believe. Yet I have to wonder how your sentry gave you such warning that you were assembled in the hall with muskets primed and ready. I have seen marks around the entrance left by your musket balls. You fought those men and killed them as good soldiers should, all but one of you, but Lovelace did not kill the lady of that house after the enemy soldiers were routed. Someone murdered her in her bed. I found the stains in the mattress from her blood, and the pistol ball in the wool beneath. The man who killed her could not have done so before Newcastle's men came for fear of alerting them. Nor could he have done so after the fighting was done, for the lady would surely have fled her bed. No. One of you stood over her as she slept, pistol in hand, waiting for the attack that you already knew would come. He stood, patient and planning murder. Who was it, Fowles? Who waited there? Who, when the moment came amid the raucous commotion of shouts and gunfire, shot her in the belly and condemned her to slow but fatal lingering agony? Was that you?'

Fowles stared at me. His eyes gleamed with hate and, I thought, a glimmering of remorse. He shook his head, but with little force.

'Or,' I asked, 'was it Ned Fletcher?'

'Fletcher,' he said after a moment. 'Fletcher killed her.'

I think I almost believed him, though I didn't doubt that at that moment he would have clung to any lie he thought might save him. He didn't understand, not yet, that it was all too late.

'But not after the soldiers came, Fowles, not *after*,' I said. I did not notice how my voice rose with every word, but I felt the anger, a tide of it flowing out of me. I thought of the poor lady of that house, and of Anne, taken by Fletcher and his gang, and I could not stop myself from seeing my Caro's face in their place. It left me aquiver with cold fury. 'You knew those men were coming. Someone did indeed send word to Newcastle's companies, begging for relief, but it was not the lady of the house. It was you.'

'No.' He shook his head. 'That is not true!'

'Then who, Fowles? Who wrote to them? Who among you could write such a letter? Lovelace? Why would he?'

Warbeck came to stand beside me, facing Fowles down. He placed the two papers I had given him on the desk, the paper on which Fowles had written a few moments ago, and the letter I had found in that dead soldier's coat back in the wood-cellar near Gainsborough. The writing was the same. Warbeck gripped Fowles by the hair and forced his head to turn, forced him to look at the papers before him.

'You, Peter Fowles,' I said. 'The words are yours. You lured them there. It was your plan. All of it.'

For a long time Fowles said nothing. He tried to look away, but Warbeck would not let him.

'Yes,' he whispered at last. With a twist of vicious force he pulled himself free of Warbeck's grip and glared up at us. 'What of it? I lured a party of the King's soldiers into a trap and then we killed them. Such is war. Such things are done! It was no crime.'

'Then why did you lie, Fowles?' hissed Warbeck.

'Because he would steer us always away from Anne and what he and Fletcher were looking for,' I told him. 'So here is the truth of the tale.' I turned back to Fowles and loomed into his face as he sat helpless at the table, tied to his chair. 'You billeted yourselves in that house, but Lovelace would not turn the lady and her daughter from their rooms, nor let you ransack their properties. You railed against it. You and Fletcher and Blackwater and the rest, all of you . . .'

'There was almost mutiny!' howled Fowles. 'Lovelace was a besotted fool! That royalist whore took him to her bed! She turned him against us!'

'Ah, but there is more, Fowles. You came upon the notion that there were riches hidden away, and that Lovelace knew of them. Perhaps he would take a share, his price for keeping his dogs at bay. You were envious.'

'I tried to reason with him!'

'To reason with him? Was what happened that night reason?'

Fowles bowed his head. 'It was Fletcher. He put it to me blunt. Francis was my friend. I was to turn his head back to us, to right and proper thoughts, or he would murder them both. He had the rest behind him. I told him I would not stand for murder of one of our own, and he said that Francis no longer was one such. So I found another way.'

'The letter.' As I crouched beside him, Fowles nodded.

'I drew a company of the King's men to the house. I meant to make it seem as though that royalist whore had been in secret communication with them all along.' His voice rose again. 'So Francis would see her for what she was, a conniving, treacherous harlot who blinded him with her quim!' He closed his eyes a moment. His words dropped to a whisper. 'When Newcastle's men were done for, we'd ransack the house as Francis should have permitted us in the first place, and we'd find the treasure Francis was trying to keep for himself.'

'But then you changed your mind. You murdered her.'

'No!' Fowles slammed his shackles against the desk. '*I* did not. Fletcher, he . . .' He gasped for breath. His voice dropped to a snarl. 'I do not say she didn't have it coming. Nor do I say she deserved her fate. But it was not I who killed her. It was dark. We knew Newcastle's men must come that night or not at all. We waited, dressed for the battlefield, muskets ready. Francis would not believe it, but he had no cause to deny us. Edward and Ben kept watch. The rest of us were inside. When Edward saw Newcastle's men approach he gave the signal to his brother and stayed outside with a brace of pistols. Ben came in the back to warn us to be ready. Fletcher took a position at the top of the stairs. I did not see what he did next until after it was done. Newcastle's men came a-creeping in the door. We burned them in our ambush, but there were several who got out. We raced after them. Edward took care of two. There was a third we never found. Nathaniel swore he saw the man take a ball, but in the night we lost him. I went back inside. There was screaming and shouting up the stairs. The screaming was the woman and her girl, both of them. The shouting was Fletcher and Francis. I ran to stop it before one killed the other. There was the whore, stretched out in the bed, wailing and writhing with blood all over her.'

Fowles' voice broke to a croak. 'Fletcher had shot her, and he had Francis held tight, making him watch her scream. Making him watch her die. I told him to stop, but he wouldn't have it. He had Edward and Ben pick her up and carry her outside for the wild animals, because that was what she was. He told them that if they did that then they would be the first to have their way with the girl when they were done.' He held his head in his hands. 'I went with them, as if to help. Francis screamed at me, called me traitor and all manner of words. They carried her down the stairs and threw her to the ground and left her there, eager for sweeter things. Men do not live from wounds like that, Falkland. You were a soldier, and so you know this. Hours of agony awaited her before she would stand before Saint Paul to answer for her sins. I stayed with her a minute, until we were alone, and then I put my pistol to her head. Call that murder if you wish.'

The very same words I had heard from Fletcher. 'So you would have it that while the rest of them took their turns with the girl and turned the house upside down looking for hidden treasure, you had no part in it?' I was hearing something close to the truth, I thought, but not quite there yet. Fowles was broken now. He was almost sobbing.

'No,' he breathed.

Warbeck slapped him. 'Speak up, man!'

'No!' Fowles glowered. 'No, I had no part in it.'

'And Lovelace?' I asked.

'We knew they were hiding something, him and his whore. Certain of it, but Fletcher could not find it, and Francis would not tell them. Fletcher was contrite at first, full of condolences at the treachery of the King's whore, but Francis wouldn't have it. He would have killed Fletcher and nothing would ever change that. While they searched the house and found trinkets and a little silver, Nathaniel, whom Fletcher had sent to watch the roads, reported that a company of Newcastle's men were coming, too many for us to resist. Lovelace remained furious. He wrote a message for Nathaniel to take to Gainsborough, warning them of Newcastle. Fletcher wouldn't let it go until I read it lest Lovelace said something of what we'd done, but there was nothing, simply a warning that the King's soldiers approached. But he must have fooled us somehow. After Nathaniel was gone we had a little time. Fletcher's anger got the better of him. He beat Francis to a bloody pulp, trying to get that treasure out of him, but Francis never said a word. He waited until we had no chance to go after Nathaniel and catch up to him before he reached Gainsborough, and then said he had sent letters to say what we had done, and that they would reveal the hiding place of this treasure to anyone who was clever enough to read them right, but that Fletcher would never have it, not one piece of it. That was when Fletcher shot him.' He looked away. 'I think Francis knew it would end that way.'

'And the others?'

'I don't know how they killed the girl. I did not look or ask . . .'

'They smothered her once they were done with her,' I said.

'We had hanged the rest at first light. Except the maid-servant, who had the good sense to run from the house in the night when she heard the shots and never came back. Maybe she saw some of what passed, maybe not. It never came back on us. We went our separate ways, not long after. Fletcher and some of the others stayed together. I took my place in a different company.'

I came close to him, eye to eye, so little space between us that I could smell his rancid breath. 'And then the war comes towards its close. Francis was your friend. You go to his wife to tell her that he is dead. Did you think his ghost had found some way to spirit this treasure to her?'

Fowles laughed, bitterly. 'Francis was a fine enough friend before Gainsborough, but he was a poor husband. Like as not he might never have gone back had he lived. She deserved to know he was gone, truly gone, not run away with some other pretty face.'

'But then you found he had written letters to her, though she didn't even read. You wondered why he had written them at all, and then you remembered what he had said. So you took them. You didn't find anything to tell you where this treasure might have been, but they led you to Anne. Lovelace had told you about her. You befriended her family. You tried to find these other letters but you couldn't. So you found your old friend Fletcher again and together you hatched a plot. You waited until the house was empty and then signalled him to break in and search. When Fletcher didn't find them, you concocted a story about Thomas surviving Edgehill. You coaxed Anne to reveal Francis's letters, and still you found nothing. But now Anne had an interest of her own. Was it her or was it you who first got it into their head that perhaps there was a secret cipher in that last letter Francis wrote? She took the letters to John Wallis. You and Fletcher both hoped she was right, and that your imagined treasure would at last be revealed. But you feared it too, for what if Francis's last letters revealed what you had done? So you devised another story. Fletcher approached Anne himself. He told her that some prisoner in Clink had news of Thomas. He met her there. He must have concocted some other story then, enough to persuade Anne to reclaim the letters from John Wallis. But when she demanded to return home, he took her north instead and made her his prisoner.'

Fowles spat. 'I don't know what you're talking about, Falkland. I had nothing to do with Anne's taking.'

I continued, unperturbed, certain now in my understanding. 'He was supposed to let her go once you had all the letters and had found Lovelace's secret. But still you could find no cipher, and now you were at an impasse. *You* had had the letters, and Fletcher didn't trust you. He wasn't holding Anne hostage against John Milton. He was holding her hostage against *you*.'

Though Fowles did not answer, I saw his face tighten and knew I had the truth of it.

'And then? Then I think you simply didn't know what to do. You had no use for Anne. The letters told you nothing. It must have been clear quickly enough that she had not unravelled their secret before you. How long did it take? A day? Two? A week? Yet now you could not let her go. She knew too much. So you kept her hidden, a prisoner, until the noose began to close and you had to decide. You knew the game was up when Cromwell summoned us to the Star Chamber. Afterwards, to save your own skin, you met with Fletcher. I do not believe your tale. I believe it was you who waited in the dark with a pistol in that house in Gainsborough. Fletcher did not shoot Lady Walhope in her bed.' I thought of his words while we had exchanged shots. He had had no reason to lie. I thought, too, of how he had spared Milton. 'That was you, Fowles. It was Fletcher who went outside and put an end to her misery. You remained within, and in what happened to her daughter, you are as guilty as any of the rest. Lovelace too, I dare say. You are a cold murderer, and so you sent Fletcher back to that house to kill Anne.'

'No.' Fowles spoke as a rasp now. 'You are wrong. I did not send him to kill her. I told him to let her go.'

His words hung between the three of us a moment. What he had said. A confession, at last, of his part in the conspiracy.

'There *was* a cipher,' I said, as the silence lingered. 'And Anne knew it, and what it was. But she never told you, and the letters are now lost.'

Warbeck grinned, showing off his rotten teeth, as I paused a moment to let that last revelation sink in.

'You conspired to abduct Anne,' I said. 'And you are a murderer and a rapist.'

'You cannot show that to be true.' Fowles' voice was a broken whisper. Warbeck let out a snort.

'Nor will we try,' he said, 'for you hang either way.'

CHAPTER 23

'Bravo, Falkland. Bravo.'

The door lay behind us. I had not heard it open nor any man enter, such had been the intensity of Fowles and his confession. Nor had Fowles himself seen, for Warbeck and I between us obscured his view. Yet now we moved away and all turned to see. Warbeck had said that Fowles was awaiting a visitor, and from the circumstances in which he was kept I had supposed one of some importance. I had not imagined Cromwell himself.

'I came here expecting a quite unpleasant conversation, but I see I might now have a more civilised one. Is the matter resolved, Falkland?'

I bowed. Habit, grown from serving among kings and lords and earls. 'It is.'

'Milton's sister?'

'Her name is Anne, sir. Anne Agar,' I answered. 'When I left her she was with Milton himself. They were travelling by coach from Lincoln. She is as well as can be expected.'

'And the conspirators among the King's supporters intending to silence the strident voice of Master Milton himself?'

'I must suppose they conspire as much as they ever did.

But for this you are forced to look among your own.'

Cromwell called a pair of brutish guards to haul Fowles back to his cell. We sat then, the three of us, and for an hour or more I told the story as I had unravelled it. I could not say for sure who had been the architect of the conspiracy, whether Fletcher had been its mastermind, as Fowles would have it, or whether it had been Fowles as I believed, and Fletcher was but his lieutenant. Cromwell did not think it of much import. Fletcher, Lovelace and Blackwater were dead, Fowles would hang, and I did not think we would see Westlock and the two brothers Allhurst again. Perhaps the last man, this Wainwright with the long arms, might tell a different tale if Warbeck caught him. Now that Anne was safe I no longer cared.

Cromwell invited Warbeck to dine with him with Henry Ireton and others among his generals – there was news, it seemed, of Oxford, and some proposal as to the terms of its surrender – and thus I returned from Newgate alone. I went to Lincoln's Inn to look for Miss Cain, but I could not find her and so left a note among her work in the room beside the library, telling her I would most likely ride for Oxford in the morning, and inviting her to join me for supper.

I received no reply, and ate alone. When Warbeck found me the next morning, I had already saddled my horse. His horse, I suppose. Parliament's horse.

'Leaving us already, Falkland?'

'I have another reunion to attend to.' I had set my mind to it. I would find my Caro in Oxford. If she had left Cornwall to find me, that is where she must have gone; as far as the King was concerned, that was all that was left.

'Not yet, Falkland.'

'I have done as Cromwell asked. What more is there?'

'The Walhope family of Gainsborough is a distant relation to Sir Thomas Glemham, who happens just now to be the governor of Oxford. Dear Oliver would have us hire a coffin-maker, recover the bones of those poor ladies in Lea and return them so Sir Thomas might give them over to what remains of their family for proper burial. He wishes to show that we will, in our victory, treat our enemies with, if not kindness, at least an honourable respect.'

I shrugged. Such gestures were of no concern to me. 'If you are in need of directions, Warbeck, I believe Fowles may assist you.'

'The gates of Oxford will not open before the end of the month, Falkland, so you may as well do something useful while you wait. Besides, as I recall, you have neither money nor –' and he looked pointedly now at my horse '– mount.'

'I will manage. The walk will do me good.'

Warbeck rolled his eyes. 'You may keep the horse as payment for your service to Parliament. But what do you mean to do, Falkland? Scale the walls in the midst of a siege?'

'I mean to find my family, Warbeck.'

'Then come with me and do this one last thing. Cromwell will give you papers.' He waved something at me then. A baton, I thought at first, then amended my impression to the sort of leather tube that I had seen used as an officer's map case. This one was, by such standards, unusually ornate.

I stared at it, puzzled.

'These are documents to say that you may pass freely in Oxford,' Warbeck said. 'You will need them once the siege is finished. Without them you will like as not be arrested by the first patrol who come upon you. A sorry end to your mission that would be, and I would find it tedious beyond measure to be sent to recover you from yet another jail.'

It is not easy to move freely amid a hostile occupying army when a siege has lifted. I had seen it so more than once; and thus it was that I found myself riding north again and back in Lincoln two days later. We talked little save for the details of what I had found in the house – pointless talk, I thought, as Warbeck would soon see it all for himself. In Lincoln he found a coffin-maker and a cart and a pair of grave-diggers willing to carry the pieces of a skeleton to their last repose. We left them to find their way to the village of Lea and from there to the house, and rode ahead, in part from my own impatience to be done, and in part to be sure that no unpleasant turns awaited us. With an unspoken agreement, both Warbeck and I had loaded our pistols before we left.

We approached the house with caution, but none of Fowles' confederates had returned. I showed Warbeck the skeletons outside, still wrapped in rags of what had once been clothes, where they had been all but lost under the briars. I showed him the skull of she who had once been the lady of this house, with the hole of a pistol ball shattered through it. I took him inside and, when we had convinced ourselves to our satisfaction that we were indeed alone, to the place where they had kept Anne. I pointed him to the pits in the wall beside the entrance door where the musket balls had struck. Last of all I directed him upstairs to see the rooms for himself where the worst of it had happened; but I did not accompany him, for I had seen more than my fill.

Instead I returned outside and tried to imagine, sat there in the warm summer afternoon, baking gently in the sun, how this place might have been in happier times.

'Falkland!'

I looked up. Warbeck had been gone some time; now he was calling from the window of what had once been Lady Walhope's bedroom.

'Bring a hatchet from my horse.' His head disappeared back inside.

With some reluctance I took a hatchet from Warbeck's saddle and made my way to the corner room where Fletcher had trapped me. I tried to avert my eyes from the skeleton on the bed but could not; yet every time I found myself looking I cringed from its indecency. If I had put the story together aright, she had been fifteen years old. Men had ravished and murdered her, and for his part in that Fowles, I was certain, would burn in Hell.

'Here.' Warbeck beckoned me closer. He was crouched over the fallen wardrobe. 'Look.'

I peered closely. The wardrobe was, as I had found when I had almost toppled it upon myself, a sturdy construction of thick wood, and it weighed as much as a man and a half; yet the fall, I saw, had jarred it. A fine crack ran from side to side along the back of it, a foot from its carved parapet.

'Help me lift it.'

With some effort, Warbeck and I rendered the wardrobe upright once more.

'Turn it.'

We turned the wardrobe sideways. Warbeck complained and gave orders about its position until we had it standing a good foot away from any wall. Then he walked a slow circle around it, inspecting the crack he had found. I could not help myself from doing likewise, and found that the crack ran around all four sides; and when I ran my fingers over it, I found that the top portion of the wardrobe seemed to have come very slightly loose.

'Go round the other side, Falkland. Brace your shoulder against it.' Warbeck weighted the hatchet in his hand. I did as he asked, and Warbeck struck near the top of the wardrobe with the hatchet's haft. The uppermost part moved and separated a little from the rest. He struck again and it shifted a second time, and then the two of us lifted down what appeared to be a shallow chest on four very short feet, built into the top of the wardrobe. I looked for any means by which the lid might open, or for any sense that there was, indeed, a lid at all, but the craftsmanship defeated me.

'The catch will be underneath.' Warbeck ran his hand around the bottom of the chest and then stopped. He gave a little grin of triumph. I head the click of a latch and the top of the chest hinged slowly open. We stared at what was inside. Gold. Coins and cups. And jewels. Bracelets and necklaces. Diamond and emeralds. A sheaf of papers tied in a sapphire blue ribbon, and a few more lying loose.

'So there really was a treasure,' I murmured. 'It looks enough to ransom a king.'

Warbeck cocked his head. 'Kicking yourself you didn't find it when you were here alone, Falkland?'

'I had Milton with me. I do not think he would have made a comfortable partner in any thievery.' I took out the loose papers and looked at them. It was the first that caught my eye.

My dear Anne. I write this not knowing if I will live
or die . . .

I did not read on, but skipped then to the end, to the name
there. Thomas Agar; and the date. October 27th, 1642. Four
days after Edgehill.

'Look.' I handed the letter to Warbeck. For a long time he
stared at it, a strange play of emotion on his face. I had not, I
thought, seen him moved by anything at all save for that
night when he had killed Nathaniel Blackwater; yet here I
swear I saw a glistening in his eye.

He pocketed the letter. 'We make a list,' he said at last, as
he stared at the contents of the chest. 'You and I. One for
each of us. Thus we keep ourselves honest.' And I might
have been insulted by such a suggestion, but I sensed it was
not I whose honesty most troubled him.

Despite Warbeck's assurances, we returned to find London
in a state of jubilation. Oxford and Prince Rupert had
surrendered two days before, and the news had arrived that
same morning. Though the King himself had yet to come to
terms, the war was all but over. Cromwell had returned
again to London in triumph, and we were summoned at
once. As Warbeck supervised the transfer of the two coffins
to a carriage more suited to their standing, Cromwell took
me aside. In his hand he held the leather case that Warbeck
had carried with him, his promise of free passage through
Oxford.

'Warbeck did not tell the whole truth of what I mean to
offer you,' he said. 'Anne Agar is returned to her family
home. John Milton speaks of you highly. Those are no mean

words from a man such as him for a soldier who fought for the King.'

'I am sore pressed to find aught but common cause with any man deprived of his family,' I said. 'I have not forgotten your promise.'

For a moment Cromwell gave no answer. He offered me his papers. 'I cannot tell you where you should go nor where to look. But these documents say you may pass freely through any place by order of Parliament, that you are about the business of Parliament and that you may request the assistance, subject to such assistance being neither onerous nor of any impediment to their duties, of any other officer of Parliament or appointed official of the land, and of any soldier or officer of the army.' He waved them at me again. 'Well, Falkland? Will you take them?'

I stared at this leather case as though it was a snake, fangs bared to bite me. If such was true then Cromwell offered to ease my search a hundredfold. I did not believe it. This was too generous. 'Such papers are the papers of an intelligencer,' I said.

'Yes. They are.'

I did not much like the way he smiled. 'What do you want from me?'

'What I want from every man,' he answered. 'Your conscience and your endeavour.' He pressed the papers into my hand. 'I give these to you knowing that you will use them to perhaps more than one good end. May God hear your prayers, Falkland. I hope you find them. If I have need, perhaps we will meet again.'

He walked away and I sensed that I was, at last, free. I looked about for Warbeck, wondering how to go about

making my farewells to such a man as he, but as luck would
have it he had absented himself and I could not find him.
Perhaps that was for the best. It would have been an
awkward thing for us both, I think, to shake one another's
hand. I returned instead, then, to the Bucket of Blood, to
gather what few belongings I claimed as my own. I had
planned to pay a visit to Miss Cain once more before I rode,
but waiting for me in my room I found a note. The writing
was delicate and careful, yet somehow artless and clumsy.

> The war is all but done, Master Falkland, and soon all
> soldiers may at last go home. My eyes and my ears
> have done work on your behalf. I have heard of a
> Lady whose name is Caroline and a daughter,
> displaced persons from the west of the country. They
> shelter in a house in the village of Riverhead in the
> hills of northern Kent. It is all I have. I have thought
> of you. Indeed, I think of you often, and of families
> driven apart and come once more together. I have
> decided I shall return, for a time, to my own. I wish
> with all the strength of my heart that you find your
> happiness, and for the Lord to show His favour upon
> you.
>
> With all my warmth,
> Kate

I did not know how long this message had waited for me
and nor, it seemed, did the boys who kept the rooms of the
Bucket of Blood. I rushed at once to Lincoln's Inn, hoping
to find Miss Cain before she was gone, thinking I must
thank her for such intelligence and . . . and something more,

though I did not know quite what that more might be. But she had gone, two days hence.

I turned my back then to London and rode, not to Oxford as I had thought I must, but southward into Kent until I was in among the downs. I stayed a night in a tiny coaching inn that serviced the road south to the coast and the old ports and forts of the Channel. I received directions to the village of Riverhead, and in the morning I set out. Before the sun reached its zenith I had found the place, nestled in a valley. I halted my horse at the track that led to the house I sought, and drew long, deep breaths as I stared. The manor was small but comfortable, not unlike our own in Launcells. It spoke of a steady prosperity without any great riches. I looked it over for what seemed an age. The country was awash with families displaced from their homes, with wives and mothers bereft of their sons and husbands. And Caroline was not such an uncommon name. It would likely not be my Caro who had landed here.

And yet I could not give up the desire that burned my heart. With Cromwell's papers, I would continue my search, and if this was not my Caro then I would try the next, and the next, and the next.

With hope, then, I walked up the track and approached the door.

Acknowledgements

With thanks to my editors Ali Hope and Flora Rees. To Sarah Bance and Darcy Nicholson for the copy-editing and to the proofreaders and production team, whose names I've rarely known. A special thanks to my agent Robert Dinsdale and again to Sam Childs, without whom William Falkland would not exist.

William Falkland is a work of fiction, as are Peter Fowles and the rest of the Gainsborough militiamen. John Milton himself and most of the rest of the characters around him are as real as my research could make them, although after my early investigations into Anne Agar suggested she survived the Civil War, deeper reading was rather irritatingly contrary. It seems that no one knows for sure, so here she is. The real Thomas Agar survived the war and lived on for some time. He *was* a royalist and Milton got on well with him nonetheless. What he did during the war itself is unclear, though it seems unlikely that he actually fought.

If you liked this book and would like to read more of William Falkland, please say so. Loudly and to lots of people.